ABOUT THE AUTHOR

Assaf Gavron is the author of seven books, and his fiction has been translated into ten languages. He has won the Israeli Prime Minister's Creative Award for Authors, the Buch für die Stadt award in Germany, and the Prix Courrier International award in France. The son of English immigrants, he grew up in a small village near Jerusalem, and currently lives in Tel Aviv.

Praise for *The Hilltop*

'A brilliant book.'   *New York Times Book Review*

'A book that further cements his place as one of today's truly committed, political Israeli novelists.'   Nathan Englander, author of
What We Talk About When We Talk About Anne Frank

'Expansive, humorous … Gavron's satiric touches can be coruscating.'
The New Yorker

'It is no exaggeration to say that Assaf Gavron is the most exciting, inventive, and thought-provoking Israeli novelist of our generation. I loved this book.'   Reza Aslan, author of *No god but God*

'Gavron treads delicately and lets readers draw their own conclusions.'
Metro

'Gavron's story is infused with gentle, everyday humour and flickers of kindness.'   *Financial Times*

'Assaf Gavron's clear and honest writing blasts right through the clichés and the politically correct surface to touch the chaotic, ambiguous core of the Israeli identity. His perspective is a must-read for every seriously curious reader.'   Etgar Keret, author of *The Nimrod Flipout*

'One of the most agile and necess━━━━━━━━━━━━━━━━━━━━━
literature.'   Colum McCan

'Brilliantly attuned to the madhouse complexities of the current settlement crisis ... The superbly orchestrated chaos that results makes this an indispensable novel of, as one character dubs it, the Wild West Bank.'

Wall Street Journal

'Memorable ... marked by its great depth of feeling.' *Publishers Weekly*

'The Great Israeli Novel ... Assaf Gavron stakes his claim to be Israel's Jonathan Franzen ... Like Franzen, Gavron writes realistic fiction with a comic edge that aims to take the temperature of his whole society, to tell us how Israelis live now ... a cutting satire.' Adam Kirsch, *Tablet*

'Ambitious ... uses fiction to explore the human reality of the settlers' lives ... echoes the wry, ironic tone of Amos Oz ... reads more like an American novel than fiction in translation.' *Times Literary Supplement*

'This many-storied, funny, shrewd and tender satire dives into the heart of Israel, a land of trauma and zeal, fierce opinions and endless deliberation ... Gavron's spirited desert saga embraces the absurd and the profound and advocates for compassion and forgiveness, even joy.' *Booklist*

'A middle vision between the ridiculous and the sublime ... Highlights the way nothing (or no one) is isolated anymore. Investment bankers may become Israeli settlers; Palestinian villagers have lawyers in the family ... The pleasure of *The Hilltop* is that it doesn't offer easy outcomes.'

David Ulin, *Los Angeles Times*

'Crisp insight and dry humour ... Gavron's story gains a foothold in our hearts and minds and stubbornly refuses to leave.' *Kirkus*

'Gavron expertly works with a large cast of characters to create a resonant portrayal of life at the centre of one of the world's main trouble spots ... This novel, an award winner in Israel, is very funny and entertaining.'

Library Journal

'Deals with Israel's overarching conflicts – Jew versus Jew, Jew versus Palestinian – and presents them with a nuanced complexity that feels very real. It's a funny and ultimately melancholy read.'

NPR, 'Great Reads of 2014'

THE HILLTOP

ASSAF GAVRON

Translated from the Hebrew
by Steven Cohen

ONEWORLD

A Oneworld Book

First published in the United Kingdom and Australia
by Oneworld Publications, 2014
This paperback edition published in 2015

ISBN 978-1-78074-719-4
ISBN 978-1-78074-558-9 (eBook)

Printed and bound in Great Britain by Clays Ltd, St Ives plc

Oneworld Publications
10 Bloomsbury Street
London WC1B 3SR
England

For Hila, Gali, and Maya

CONTENTS

Hot Days 115

Feeding on Carrion 269

Back to Basics 355

CAST OF CHARACTERS

Othniel Assis Veteran settler and founder of Ma'aleh Hermesh C. On his farm he grows vegetables and makes cheese. Husband of Rachel and father of Gitit, Yakir, Dvora, Hananiya, Emunah, and Shuv-el.

Gavriel Nehushtan (Gabi Kupper) Grew up on a kibbutz with his brother, Roni. After a religious awakening he moves to Ma'aleh Hermesh C.

Roni Kupper Gabi's elder brother. After years of living in the United States, he arrives at Ma'aleh Hermesh C. penniless.

Hilik Yisraeli One of the first settlers of Ma'aleh Hermesh C., and Othniel's right-hand man. Husband of Nehama and father of Boaz, Shneor, and Yemima-Me'ara.

Captain Omer Levkovich The IDF section commander with oversight of Ma'aleh Hermesh C.

Neta Hirschson Feisty right-wing patriot and cosmetician. Married to Jean-Marc and hoping to expand the family.

Nir Rivlin Studying to become a chef. Husband of Shaulit and father of Amalia, Tchelet, and Zvuli.

Yoni A young IDF soldier permanently stationed in Ma'aleh Hermesh C.

Shaulit Rivlin Teacher and wife (and childhood sweetheart) of Nir.

Rachel Assis Wife of Othniel and the first lady of the settlement. Head of the local nursery/kindergarten.

Gitit Assis Teenage daughter of Rachel and Othniel.

Yakir Assis Othniel's eldest son. Manages the online orders of vegetables and cheese for his father. Second Life enthusiast.

Jenia Freud Russian-born math teacher. Wife of Elazar and mother of Nefesh.

Jeff McKinley *Washington Post* correspondent in Jerusalem.

Jehu Ma'aleh Hermesh C.'s young loner. Mostly seen on his horse, Killer.

Musa Ibrahim Resident of neighboring Arab village, Kharmish. Roni approaches him about a business venture. Father of Nimer.

Uzi Shimoni Veteran settler who founded Ma'aleh Hermesh C. with Othniel, but left after a falling-out.

Josh Levin Brooklyn-born settler. Shares a trailer with Jehu. The settlement's de facto English translator.

The Gotliebs Nachum, Raya, Tehila (Tili), and Shimshon (Shimi): a new family who moved from an established settlement to this new and remote settlement.

Anna Gabi's classmate from a neighboring kibbutz, who reappears later to claim a major role in his life.

Dad Yossi and **Mom Gila** Gabi and Roni's adoptive parents on the kibbutz.

Uncle Yaron Roni and Gabi's uncle, a war veteran who lives in a kibbutz in the Golan Heights.

Eyal A kid in the kibbutz, three years younger than Gabi, with whom he has a violent encounter.

Yotam and **Ofir** Gabi's friends from the kibbutz.

Ariel A friend of Roni's from his Tel Aviv days. He always has a new business idea.

Giora IDF's head of Central Command and the most senior commander in the West Bank. An old friend of Othniel's.

Meshulam Avneri Gabi's boss in Florida at the Jewish National Fund.

Idan Lowenhof A former IDF commando who becomes Roni's Wall Street mentor in New York.

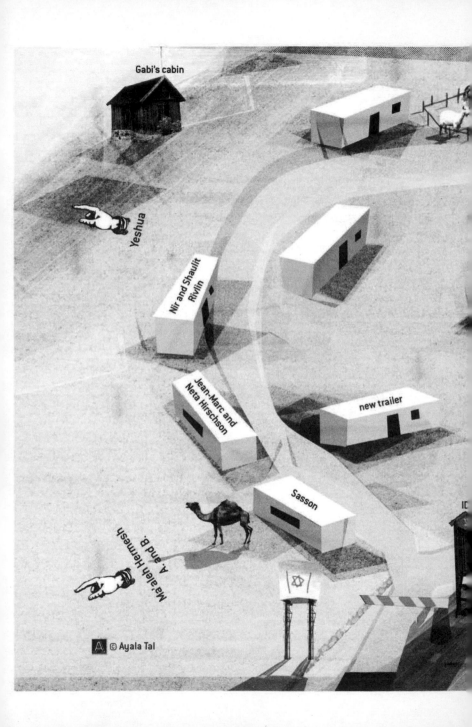

Gabi's cabin

Yeshua

Nir and Shaulit Rivlin

Jean-Marc and Neta Hirschson

new trailer

Sasson

Ma'aleh Hermesh A. and B.

ID

A © Ayala Tal

Othniel and Rachel Assis

Hilik and Nehama Yisraeli

desert

Josh and Jehu

olive grove

synagogue

Gabi and Roni

Kharmish

Elazar and Jenia Freud

soldiers

fields

MA'ALEH HERMESH C.

PROLOGUE

THE FIELDS

I n the beginning were the fields.

Back then, Othniel Assis was living in Ma'aleh Hermesh, merrily raising a goat and growing arugula and cherry tomatoes in his backyard. The goat was for his kids, the arugula and tomatoes for his wife Rachel's salads. And Othniel saw that it was good, and he tired of his job as a bookkeeper, and he found himself a small plot of land within the bounds of the settlement, on which to expand his crops. As fate would have it, however, the field bordered the vineyards of another settler whose grapes produced boutique wines that were sold to Tel Aviv's Golden Apple restaurant and other fine-dining establishments, including, the vintner claimed, several in the Dordogne region of France, and in Paris, too. And the vintner turned up his nose, declaring that he had received a permit from the regional council to plant additional vineyards on the very plot of land that had caught Othniel's fancy. The soil, he insisted, along with the cold winters and temperate summer nights, had imbued his grapes with an outstanding quality, a unique *terroir*, which produced a full-bodied wine with a nutty aroma.

And so it came to pass that Othniel deferred to the vintner and went out hiking through the surrounding land, for he deeply loved his country, and deeply loved solitude, and deeply loved to pray, and deeply loved to walk. Having left his job, he allowed his beard and hair to grow long, and wore only blue work clothes. He hiked through riverbeds and ravines, and across neighboring hilltops, until he came upon a wide-open plain, which wasn't particularly rocky, and wasn't already occupied by the olive trees of the neighboring Arab village of Kharmish. "Here," he said, "I will stake out my fields."

Othniel experimented—cucumbers and tomatoes, parsley and cilantro, zucchini and eggplant, radishes, and even lettuce. The crops wilted under the hot summer sun and froze stiff in the winter's chill, and also fell victim to mice and desert tortoises. But Othniel persevered, and finally decided on asparagus in the field and mushrooms in a greenhouse—and, of course, the arugula and cherry tomatoes, which Rachel, his wife, and Gitit and Dvora, his daughters, snacked on like they were peanuts.

He duly requested council approval for his farming enterprise, and asked permission to bring a shipping container to the site to serve as both office and warehouse. Because the local military administration required governmental approval for all such plans, barring those that fell under British Mandate–era legislation, Othniel Assis asserted, "Sure, they're Mandate Era; whatever you say, my Jewish brethren," and promptly received his permits, with the political echelon none the wiser.

Othniel relocated his lone goat to the field, and took out a small loan to purchase five more, which he turned to milking, collecting their fine produce in small pitchers and taking it home to conduct various experiments in churning and cheese-making with Rachel's help. And Othniel dared to dream, and he said to himself, There'll come a day when I will establish a small modern dairy here, and I'll plant vineyards, too, and the winery I set up will surpass that of my former neighbor, and I'll show him what's what, him and his Dordogne!

The World Zionist Organization's Settlement Division required Othniel's signature for a twenty-kilowatt power generator, and he then requested a permit for a guard hut, following an incident with the neighboring Ishmaelites, who had plundered the fruits of his labor. Armed with his Desert Eagle Mark VII pistol, Othniel stood guard now and then, but for the most part the hut remained empty. After all, his harvest had been raided just that one time, after which he rounded up some guys from the settlement, drove into the center of Kharmish, fired some shots in the air, and issued a stern warning to any villager who dared to do the same again.

One member of the posse was Uzi Shimoni, an imposing Jew with a beard to match, and a deep-seated devotion to the Land of Israel. Years earlier, he had studied with Othniel at the same yeshiva high school in Jerusalem, before Othniel left his religious studies in favor of full and active military service in an elite combat unit. Shimoni appealed to Othniel's heart, and urged him to establish a formal settlement on his land. Othniel, however, was reluctant, because his permit pertained only to a farming enterprise and a guard hut.

"Don't you worry," said Shimoni.

"But where will you get the money for homes and construction and transport?" Othniel asked.

"I've organized a donation from a good Miami Jew," replied Shimoni.

At the time, Othniel was planning to build a permanent home in Ma'aleh Hermesh but had run into a seemingly endless web of red tape with the council engineer, a troublesome neighbor, and a corrupt real estate attorney.

"Screw them all," he finally said to Rachel. He'd had his fill of the exhausting bureaucracy, the sleepy, complacent bourgeoisie of Ma'aleh Hermesh, and the daily walk to and from his plot of land, a mile in each direction.

He loved the hilltop, the winds, the ancient landscape; and he longed for the pioneering spirit of his youth—the sorties into Hebron and Kiryat Arba, the visits down south to Yamit before the Sinai town's dramatic evacuation, the Sabbaths spent in settlements reeling from the barrage of Arab terror during the first intifada, the stormy protests against the Oslo Accords, when he and his fellow demonstrators faced off against club-wielding riot police and water cannons.

Othniel gave in to the urgings of Uzi Shimoni, who had somehow gotten his hands on a pair of twenty-two-square-meter trailers, one of which Othniel, with the help of an expert welder, connected to the office-warehouse container and the guard hut and turned into a home for his family. The Shimonis settled in the second trailer. The two men went off together to the Registrar of Non-Profit Organizations in Jerusalem to set up an NPO, naming it the Hermesh Cooperative Farming Association.

Next came the clearing of an access road to the hilltop. Giora, the brigade commander of the sector, and a friend of Othniel from his military days, claimed to have been unaware of the newly cleared route, which ran, invisible from the main road, from Ma'aleh Hermesh B., down through the deep, dry riverbed, and up the hill. Soon afterward, however, following a call to a friend in the National Infrastructures Ministry, the Public Works Department erected safety guardrails along the dangerously steep makeshift road.

The brigade commander told later of receiving a call on his two-way radio one cold winter night with a report of five new twenty-two-square-meter prefab trailers that had been set up on the land adjacent to the Assis farm. He arrived on the scene to find several trucks and trailers at the site. The settlers, he said, blocked his command car from approaching. The head of the regional council turned up, things got heated, and the brigade commander, who came under a barrage of abuse, called the Civil Administration for advice on how to proceed. The new trailers, he was told, were there without a permit. However, their removal, too, required authorization, which they didn't have. And thus the soldiers loaded the settlers onto the military vehicles and drove them away—with the records of the army and Defense Ministry duly noting that the outpost had been evacuated. The settlers returned the very next day, and the brigade commander turned his attention to more pressing matters.

Thus the outpost took hold.

The five trailers were leased from the state-owned Amidar housing company, with the Housing Ministry's approval forthcoming, thanks to the regional council head's ties with the deputy minister. Despite the biting cold, mosquitoes abounded, and the prefab structures themselves were somewhat dilapidated. But the settlers fitted nets to the windows, attached wooden doors to the makeshift homes, used a digger to carve out access roads, and paved pathways. One of the structures was set aside as a synagogue (a recently refurnished Jerusalem synagogue had donated its old items, including an ark in good condition, and one of the men turned up with a Torah scroll, without saying where it had come from). At night, after working long, hard days, they stood guard, because the Arabs from the neighboring village were keeping a watchful eye on them. The water and electricity supply remained erratic, but the residents made do with a rusty, leaking water tanker and oil lamps. A mountain hyena occasionally plundered food and items of clothes, and rock rabbits and rats liked to visit, too.

Two of the families left within the first few weeks, but the Assises and Shimonis stuck it out, while the third survivor was Hilik Yisraeli, a political science student in his late twenties whose scraggy face was adorned with thin-framed glasses and a mustache. Seeking to satisfy his pioneering spirit and belief in the redemption of the Land of Israel, Hilik, who grew up in Ma'aleh Hermesh but had tired of its gentrification, moved into one of the prefab trailers with his wife and two toddler sons.

But where there are two Jews, there are three opinions, and where there are three Jews, well, God help us. Hilik questioned Shimoni about the promised donation from the wealthy Miami Jew, as Shimoni appeared to be pumping sums of money into construction and infrastructure, but precisely how much, and who got what and why, remained unclear. Uzi Shimoni, in turn, went straight to Othniel to complain about "that cheeky kid I invited here and who now has the balls to ask me questions." Othniel nodded in agreement, but after returning home and discussing the matter with Rachel, he realized that the young man had a point, and he went back to Shimoni to get some answers. How much money did they have? Could they get a more powerful generator? What about erecting a security fence and setting up lighting for nighttime? "Everything is under control" and "Stop worrying," Shimoni grumbled in response. Othniel promptly began to worry.

And then, speaking to them through his car window one day, Shimoni informed Othniel and Hilik that two new families would be moving into the vacated trailers within the next few days.

"What families?" a surprised Hilik responded. "And who decided to take them in, based on what criteria?"

"Listen up, kid," Shimoni said, glaring at the young man and stroking his thick beard. "Any more of those questions and you'll find yourself out on your ass."

From that moment on, Othniel and Hilik formed a united front. When they tried to delve deeper into the money-from-Miami story, the evidence provoked their strong suspicion that Shimoni was dipping his fingers into the NPO's coffers. Othniel was livid. He had run into a fair amount of corruption in his lifetime, but stealing from the settlement enterprise took the cake. Was nothing sacred these days? He didn't confront Shimoni directly, choosing instead to pull some strings of his own. Shimoni was well connected, but Othniel also was acquainted with council officials, and he had close ties with its head and with the secretary of Ma'aleh Hermesh. Little by little, Shimoni found himself excluded from the circles of influence.

One morning, Othniel was making his way up to the outpost in his Renault Express. Shimoni's dog was lying in the middle of the road, scratching himself behind the ear.

"What the hell! Why him? What did he do wrong?" Shimoni yelled as he and the rest of his family came rushing out their home at the sound of the animal's anguished cries.

"He jumped in front of the car. I couldn't brake in time," Othniel responded, still stunned by what he had done.

"Don't lie! You ran him down intentionally. He's never done anything to you!"

Uzi's girls were sobbing. He looked at them in pain and then turned to glare furiously at Othniel. "I never thought you'd go this far, Othniel," he growled. "Will you guys stop at nothing?"

Under the barrage of Shimoni's continued accusations, Othniel's shock soon transformed into a growing rage. "What about the NPO, Uzi?" he asked, glaring at Shimoni. "What's with the finances?"

Shimoni didn't respond. He drew his pistol, loaded it, and put an end to the dog's suffering with a single shot. "Come," he said to his family and turned back toward their home. The following morning, he packed everyone up and left for a hilltop in Samaria, branding Hilik and Othniel "worse than Korah," the biblical villain who led a revolt against Moses.

Left behind were two families, united in their love for the land and in a singular viewpoint as to the nature of the outpost and its management, yet penniless. Slowly but surely, however, their luck changed. Because an Israeli anywhere in the Land of Israel is afforded protection in the form of a security perimeter to keep Arabs out, Israel Defense Forces troops were dispatched to the area to keep watch over the Assis and Yisraeli families and the three empty trailers, bringing with them a guard post, a water tower, and a generator that was ten times more powerful than the small one provided by the Jewish Agency. Othniel called in a favor from his friend Giora, the brigade commander in the sector, and asked to be allowed to draw electricity from the military generator and water from the tower for the trailers. "Sure. Why not?" Giora responded with a wink.

The WZO's Settlement Division took to the idea of the farm. After all, who could say no to fresh asparagus and mushrooms, and fine goat-milk cheese, too, not to mention the true pioneering spirit of old? Settlement Division officials thus retroactively approved the expansion of Ma'aleh Hermesh B. and even included the farm in the Outposts Agreement—in which it was recorded under the name of "the South Hermesh Goat Farm"—in return for the removal from the site of one of the trailers. A new family moved in, however, and the trailer, in fact, was never removed—despite that family's departure a few weeks later.

The Amidar housing company was then free to move additional trailers to the site.

And the Postal Authority had a green light to set up a mail-distribution post.

And the National Infrastructures Ministry could instruct the Public Works Department to make good use of days when Civil Administration officials weren't patrolling the area, to lay down some asphalt.

And the Agriculture Ministry was able to approve Othniel's status as a farmer and his eligibility for water quotas at a reduced cost.

And the deputy accountant general at the Finance Ministry could instruct Bank Tefahot to offer mortgages for housing units at the site—a move that brought automatic Housing Ministry authorization for infrastructure work and widened the Arab-free radius in one fell swoop.

And Amana, the settlement division of the right-wing Gush Emunim organization, got in on the act, proposing initiatives and determining criteria for working the land.

A combine harvester even turned up one day, courtesy of a German Christian organization sympathetic to the concept of a Greater Israel.

An aerial photography exercise perpetrated by some left-wingers resulted in calls from the Defense Ministry, the Interior Ministry, the Housing Ministry, and the prime minister's office: Whose decision was it to establish a new settlement in Israel? Who owned the land and/or the rights to the land? Was it state land, state-designated land, survey land, or perhaps private land appropriated for security reasons, or maybe private land purchased from Palestinians, or even Palestinian-owned land that wasn't purchased? And if the land was privately owned by Palestinians, was it being used for agricultural purposes or not? Was the land on record anywhere, registered anywhere? Was it Mandate-era land? Who gave the go-ahead? Were any formal planning procedures carried out? Had architects submitted master plans to the relevant planning committees? And if such plans had been submitted, were they approved? What was the jurisdiction of the new settlement? What did the state budget director have to say about it? Was there any word from the custodian general? Had they discussed the matter with the coordinator of the government's activities in the West Bank? And the brigade officers, what did they think? And had they spoken to anyone at the office of the IDF commander of the area?

Endless questions!

All the callers were politely informed that the so-called new settlement was nothing more than an agricultural enterprise within—at least for the most part—the judicial boundaries of Ma'aleh Hermesh, merely an expansion of the existing settlement that was not subject to government approval, as the establishment of a new settlement would be, and there was nothing to be concerned about. What was the big deal? All Othniel Assis had sought was to grow the very mushrooms, asparagus, and arugula that these bleeding-heart left-wingers themselves cut into their salads and served steamed alongside a slice of salmon at their Tel Aviv dinners. So, please, give me a break, okay? The outpost nevertheless made it into Peace Now's Outpost Monitoring Report, and even found its way onto the interactive map on the *Haaretz* daily's news website. Civil Administration officials then showed up with orders to cease all work related to the family residences.

The move served only to prompt a flood of callers requesting to join the outpost.

Followed closely by approval from the defense minister's deputy on settlement affairs for the transportation to the site of two additional Amidar trailers.

Then came assistance from the Housing Ministry's Rural Construction Administration.

Along with a budgetary allocation from the regional council.

More families arrived, and young couples, and singles, too—some were lovers of the Land of Israel; others were lovers of serenity and nature; still others, lovers of low costs. Everything was out in the open—the minutes of the meetings dealing with the division of the land were posted on the synagogue notice board for all to see!—but no declarations were handed down. From time to time, threats of evacuation were voiced and scolding fingers were raised. But more babies were born on the hilltop, and thus, modern-day pioneering flourished, and Ma'aleh Hermesh C. grew and expanded.

THREE CAME AT NOON

FOUR YEARS LATER . . .

The Convoy

A hilltop. The earth light and still, almost barren: a brownish yellow, dotted with rocks and lonely olive trees, and, here and there, soft patches of green brought on by the rain. Cutting through the center of the hilltop ran a narrow and bumpy single-lane road. A trailer—a mobile home—attached to the back of a large truck slowly climbed and descended its winding path. A yellow Palestinian cab bearing a green license plate crawled along impatiently behind. And after the cab chugged an old and dusty white Renault Express, its rear window bearing stickers declaring MY GOLANI DOESN'T EXPEL JEWS; HEBRON—NOW AND FOREVER; and BRING THE OSLO CRIMINALS TO JUSTICE. Behind the wheel of the Renault sat Othniel Assis—bearded, wearing a large skullcap, just as dusty as his vehicle. Weeping miserably in a car seat in the back sat his youngest, three-year-old Shuv-el. He had dropped his packet of Bamba as they rounded one of the sharp bends, and neither he nor his father could pick it up off the floor of the car. Yellow crumbs from the peanut butter–flavored snack had stuck to one of the child's sidelocks. The fourth vehicle in the impromptu convoy that day on the rough road through the Judean hills was a military jeep, a David, carrying the section commander, Captain Omer Levkovich, along with his crew.

The road rose sharply. The truck shifted down a gear; its engine screamed and carried the vehicle up the incline, the same slow pace of the herd of goats that ambled indifferently along the side of the road. The cabdriver mumbled something in Arabic, blew his horn, and pulled off a dangerous passing maneuver. Seconds later, one of the cab's tires blew—a dull thud, the sound of rubber being dragged across the tarmac, the car bouncing along the road, the driver's curses. The cab came to a halt, blocking the road. Out stepped Jeff McKinley, the *Washington Post*'s Jerusalem correspondent, on his way to interview a high-ranking Israeli government minister who lived in a settlement some six kilometers from where they had stopped. McKinley looked at his watch and wiped a bead of sweat from his wide brow. The evening before, his father had told him about the snow that was falling in Virginia; here he was in February, already perspiring. He had ten minutes to get to the meeting at the minister's home. He couldn't wait for the flat to be fixed. McKinley handed the cabdriver a fifty-shekel note and walked off in the direction of the hitchhiking station he spotted a few dozen meters away.

But, as if the perspiring, the time crunch, and his heavy breathing—a sign of his lack of fitness and an urgent need to diet—weren't enough, someone had beaten him to the station and was first in line for a ride. Dressed in a finely tailored suit, the man stood there with his arms folded across his chest, a large suitcase at his feet, a broad white smile on his face, uttering words in Hebrew that McKinley didn't understand.

Before McKinley could reach the ride station, the dusty Renault signaled and pulled over.

"Shalom, fellow Jews!" Othniel Assis called out.

"Where are you headed?" the man with the suitcase asked the driver.

"Ma'aleh Hermesh C.," Othniel Assis replied, glancing at the blue suit, and then into the man's eyes, which appeared weary.

"For real? You're a star, bro," the man said, picking up his heavy suitcase from the faded tarmac.

"Do me a favor, buddy," the driver said. "Help the kid—his Bamba fell onto the floor."

Othniel then turned to the American. "What about you, dude?" he asked in Hebrew.

"Can you get me anywhere near Yeshua, where Minister Kaufman lives?" McKinley responded in English.

"What?" said Othniel.

"Settlement?" McKinley said in an effort to simplify matters, after repeating his first question to no avail.

"Settlement, settlement—yes!" Othniel smiled. "Please, please."

McKinley's limited knowledge of the area didn't include the fact that its hilltops were home not only to Ma'aleh Hermesh and its two outgrowths, B. and C., but also to Givat Esther and its offshoots, to Sdeh Gavriel, and to Yeshua, where the minister resided. He squeezed into the backseat alongside the child.

The convoy—a trailer home on a truck, a company commander and his crew in a jeep, and a dusty pickup, carrying a settler and his child and two hitchhikers, an American and an Israeli—turned onto a second road. This road was even narrower, and steeper, too, and so, once again, the two smaller vehicles were doomed to crawl along at the snail's pace dictated by the larger truck. Captain Omer's gray-green eyes remained firmly planted on the rear of the trailer, displaying a touch of apprehension at the thought of the vehicle's load detaching and crashing down on the jeep behind it. He glanced at his watch and then turned to gaze into the side mirror.

"Tell me something, don't I know you from somewhere?" Othniel asked his Hebrew-speaking passenger.

The man stared for some time at the driver's large head and at the wide skullcap that covered it.

"I don't know," he replied. "My brother lives here with you, but we don't look alike at all."

Othniel cast a quick look over his shoulder at the man with the black hair and then turned to focus on the road again.

His passenger offered some assistance. "Gabi Kupper. Do you know him?"

The driver frowned. "We don't have anyone by that name," he said. "We have a Gavriel. Gavriel Nehushtan. A great guy. A real prince. He works with me on the farm."

"Nehushtan?" Roni Kupper replied, his turn to frown.

The American journalist glanced impatiently at his watch.

The slow climb up the hill ended at the entrance into Ma'aleh Hermesh A. The three vehicles drove through the gate, turned right at the traffic circle, and made their way through the well-established settlement with its stone homes, paved streets, and small commercial area comprising a winery, a horse ranch, and a carpentry workshop. They then headed across a desolate hilltop before reaching the trailers of the sister settlement Ma'aleh Hermesh B., beyond which the tarmac ended and a dirt road plunged steeply down into the wadi, traversed the dry riverbed, and began climbing up the other side.

"All gone, Daddy!" Shuv-el announced, on finishing his Bamba.

A sickly sweet stench filled the car.

"Did you go, sweetie?" the father asked his son.

"Holy crap!" hissed Roni Kupper. "What is this place?"

Jeff McKinley did his utmost to refrain from retching.

A yellow dust rose from the wheels of the vehicles into the crisp sky above and after snaking their way along for a while, they came to a water tower bearing a crudely drawn Star of David, followed immediately by an IDF guard tower, and finally the eleven trailers that made up the outpost, spread out along a circular road. Manning the guard post stood Yoni, the soldier, a rifle at an angle across his chest, his one hand on the butt, welcoming the arrivals in his Ray-Bans with a boyish smile on his face.

An untamed landscape stretched out before them—the Judean Desert in all its splendor and beauty, with its arid hilltops and the Dead Sea tucked away at their feet, and beyond it, rising up on the horizon, the mountains of Moab and Edom. Occasional villages and settlements dotted the expanse of land, while farther in the distance stood the truncated summit of the Herodium and the homes of a large Palestinian town, some of which appeared wrapped in a giant gray concrete wall, like a gift that couldn't be opened.

A large improvised sign stood just beyond the entrance to the outpost, the handwriting almost like a child's, in Hebrew and English, reading: "Welcome to Ma'aleh Hermesh C."

The Ceremony

When Othniel Assis's Renault Express reached its destination, Jeff McKinley asked, in English, to be pointed in the direction of the home of Minister Kaufman. Othniel gestured to him to wait just a moment, called out toward the house, "Rachel! Get all the kids together and come to the ceremony," and then turned back to McKinley to say, "You come with us—we have American guy."

Jeff McKinley traipsed along with Othniel and Rachel Assis and their six children to Ma'aleh Hermesh C.'s new playground, abuzz with dignitaries and residents, where the promised American, Josh, explained to the reporter that Minister Kaufman lived in Yeshua, the settlement across the way, on the other side of the wadi. You can see his villa, the one with the tiled roof, Josh pointed out, less than a kilometer away from where they stood as the crow flies, but quite a few winding kilometers by road. McKinley looked at his watch again and then, realizing just how late he already was, pulled his cell phone out of his pocket and called the minister's aide to explain his predicament and ask for a postponement, but his request was rejected, with the aide explaining that the minister was expected in Jerusalem in an hour and intensely disliked to be kept waiting. McKinley apologized profusely, and after hanging up, he cast his eyes over the crowd around him, stopping in surprise at a tall man with an impressive paunch and thick, meticulously groomed eyebrows. "Tell me"—he turned to Josh—"isn't that Sheldon Mamelstein?"

The playground appeared to have been lowered to the ground by a giant Monty Python–like hand of god, transplanted like the organ of a stylish New Yorker into the body of a wretched Bedouin nomad. There was a rectangular patch of grass the size of a basketball court; a pair of wooden swings that swayed with a quiet, well-oiled efficiency; an expansive system of slides; and three spring-mounted rides, one in the form of a seal, another a rooster, and the third—perhaps most appropriate, given the landscape—a camel.

Laborers had worked for weeks installing the playground in the center of Ma'aleh Hermesh C.—preparing the ground, laying the strips of lawn, assembling the apparatus, and even installing trash bins and erecting signs as befitted the settlement's new hub of social activity—and it had all culminated that day in the official dedication ceremony, in the presence of the donor, Mr. Sheldon Mamelstein of New Jersey, the settlement enterprise's good friend, Member of Knesset Uriel Tsur, and various local dignitaries.

A chilly wind whistled into the microphone, through the pair of large speakers, and out into the crisp air around the playground. Most residents of the settlement and their guests were in attendance, a crowd of forty or so. The kids scampered among the swings and rides before being rounded up by their parents and placed in strollers or on the grass to listen to the speeches.

"Just a few years ago, not even five," began MK Tsur, "there was nothing here but rocks, foxes, and thorny burnet shrubs."

On the podium alongside the politician stood the donor, Sheldon Mamelstein, whose head was tilted toward Josh, formerly of Brooklyn, with his red hair and beard to match, who was serving as his simultaneous translator.

"But here we are now, in the Hebrew month of Shevat, 5769, marveling at your accomplishments, your inspiring tenacity, your good and hard work, your settlement pioneering values, and your uncompromising belief in the sanctity of this land. You, dear residents of Ma'aleh Hermesh C., have built a wonderful community . . ."

MK Tsur paused briefly. The wind whistled through the microphone and echoed off the hillside. Sheldon Mamelstein lifted his head and rubbed his neck. Pregnant women and teenagers shifted their weight from one leg to the other. The little kids asked if it was time now to go play on the slides and swings. Soon, said the parents. And Captain Omer thought, What's with the Shevat, 5769? Why not simply say February 2009?

Tsur's address was followed by a few more words of gratitude from a number of other functionaries, with Sheldon Mamelstein the last to take hold of the microphone. Josh translated his words into rudimentary and horribly accented Hebrew. His speech was met with modest applause.

Mamelstein unveiled a plaque engraved with his name and the date. He gracefully disregarded the spelling mistake in his name—an unnecessary *h* after the *s* in his surname, as per usual in Israel—and posed for a photograph with the MK, settlement residents, and a number of children. The ceremony came to a close. The kids reveled in the new playground to the sound of their parents crying, "Careful!" Women spoke to one another about pregnancies, shared recommendations for Sabbath wine, and discussed goings-on at the school in the mother settlement. Fathers chatted about Hilik's doctorate and the Knesset member's Volvo S80, and paying half price to replace a cylinder head at Farid's in Kharmish. They'd be heading off slowly in a few minutes for late-afternoon and evening prayers in the makeshift synagogue farther below, alongside the traffic circle, two trailers that had been joined together and christened with a traffic circle sign. MK Tsur struck up a conversation with Sheldon Mamelstein and tried to set up a meeting with the American. Othniel offered the dignitaries a tour of the outpost. The MK looked at his watch and said, "Oh my God," before shoving a Bluetooth earpiece into his ear, hastily exchanging handshakes, waving good-bye, and getting into his car. And after everyone was done watching the Volvo S80 drive off into the distance, they all turned their gazes in the opposite direction, toward the slopes of the ridge below them, and were surprised to see a huge truck off-loading a new trailer, accompanied by much noise, loud shouting, and carefully measured maneuvering. How did the truck get there? they wondered. And whose trailer was that? Why had it arrived today? But before they had a chance to ask him, the truck driver turned the vehicle around and headed off.

The Tour

Still in his work shirt and shoes from the morning, Othniel Assis, the outpost's longest-serving resident, led the tour, along with a spruced-up Hilik Yisraeli, wearing a checkered button-up shirt, his hair well combed, accompanied by Natan Eliav, the secretary of Ma'aleh Hermesh, the mother settlement. Red-haired Josh translated for the American millionaire and his companions. The section commander, Captain Omer, who had come to speak to Natan and Othniel about "something important," walked along with them, Othniel assured him he would make time for him immediately after the promised tour for the honored guest from America. The *Washington Post*'s Jeff McKinley tagged along too. No one paid him any attention: the residents assumed he was one of Mamelstein's entourage; Mamelstein's people assumed he was a local. A handful of bored children trailed behind.

The delegation made its way on foot through the vineyards, past the prickly pear shrubs and flower beds, the makeshift synagogue, the goat pen, and Othniel Assis's organic fields. Junk lay strewn among the yards and residences—a bicycle missing both of its wheels, a treadmill tipped over onto its side, half of a Peugeot 104 that still boasted stickers reading BEGIN FOR PRIME MINISTER and GOD ALMIGHTY, WE LOVE YOU, sofas and refrigerators and rolled-up carpets. Above all, and omnipresent— the majestic landscape, the exalted landscape, the wild landscape that appeared to be crying out, and sometimes whispering, and also playing a melody: This is the desert. This is the Bible. This is Genesis.

"What wonderful fresh air!" said Sheldon Mamelstein, filling his lungs with a deep breath. The twilight had turned the landscape into a moonscape. Standing there, they could imagine the Creation, as if thus the universe was created, and thus it had remained. "Hats off to you," Sheldon Mamelstein exhaled emotionally, and his entourage was struck silent by the splendor.

Mamelstein stopped suddenly and pointed in astonishment. "A camel!" he exclaimed.

"That's a cow," Othniel said, using the Hebrew term for a female camel, and Josh struggled a little with the translation.

"Does it belong to one of the families?"

"It's Sasson's," Othniel responded, and left it at that. "Come," he said instead, "we've reached my house. Let's go inside for coffee."

The Assis family residence consisted of the same basic mobile home that had been welded to the initial guard hut, with the subsequent addition of a shipping container and a wooden porch, the structure then partially covered in Jerusalem stone—a patchwork of assembled pieces making up some seventy square meters in area and serving as a crowded home to eight individuals: Othniel, his wife, Rachel, and their children, in descending order from the age of sixteen down to three—Gitit, the twins, Yakir and Dvora, Hananiya, Emunah, and Shuv-el, the little one. The inside of the home was dominated by the usual disarray of toys and children's books, mismatched furniture collected over the years from charities and urban streets, and a bookcase of Jewish and Torah literature that stood on the warped, peeling floor. The large windows and porch looked out over the barren desert hills and a smattering of homes on the edge of the Arab village Kharmish.

The place was bursting at the seams. Rachel served coffee and cake. The sun had set, the cold seeped in through every small opening, and the electric heater was turned up to high. Loud whistles could be heard coming from the open space under the trailer, where the wind blew among the work tools and other stored equipment. The sections of the thin, dry wall that hadn't been covered by stone offered scant acoustic protection or thermal insulation.

"Is this a legal outpost?" Mamelstein asked.

Othniel exchanged a glance with Hilik and smiled from within his beard. "All the settlements are legal," he responded. "All were established with government knowledge and approval. We are a neighborhood of Ma'aleh Hermesh, within its jurisdiction." He pointed in the general direction of the mother settlement. "Besides," the longest-serving resident of the outpost continued, "Ma'aleh Hermesh C. cannot be illegal."

The American millionaire chuckled, and his staff followed suit. Othniel was very familiar with Sheldon Mamelstein and his political views. Nonetheless, a man of his standing clearly could not afford to be involved in anything that might be construed as criminal in nature. "What do you mean, it can't be illegal?" Mamelstein asked.

"Ma'aleh Hermesh C. cannot be illegal because, according to Defense Ministry records, the outpost was evacuated years ago," Othniel replied. "The outpost, in fact, doesn't exist. But we do have an approved agricultural farm, which the military protects."

Mamelstein raised an eyebrow and turned his gaze toward the IDF officer and female soldier standing on the porch, both busy texting on their phones. His eyebrow dropped and his mouth widened in a smile. "But doesn't the army fall under the responsibility of the Defense Ministry?" one of his advisers wondered out loud.

"It does. So what? As far as the Defense Ministry is concerned, the outpost has been evacuated; and as far as the army is concerned, there are Jews here and therefore a guard post and soldiers, too," Othniel responded, glancing over at Captain Omer, who was on the phone.

"The Settlement Division of the World Zionist Organization arranged for the establishment of the agricultural farm, which doesn't require government permits. Through the Civil Administration, they also secured the generator, and the army took care of the water supply. Most of the trailers were provided by the Housing Ministry, via the Amidar public housing company. Fortunately for us, the right hand has no clue what the left one is doing."

Othniel smiled as Josh translated his words into English. Hilik smiled, too; he took a sip of coffee and cautiously placed the glass on the table again.

On leaving the house, the millionaire took a closer look at the Jerusalem-stone covering that ran along the bottom half of the walls of the trailer, nodding in astonishment. Captain Omer again tried to engage Othniel in conversation. "Five minutes and we're done here," Othniel hissed. "What do you think—that we aren't just as keen as you to be over and done with this?"

They passed by the guard and water towers and returned to the new playground. "What the hell! What's happening over there?" the American benefactor suddenly asked, pointing a finger at one of the homes. Everyone turned to see Elazar and Jenia Freud's trailer shaking like a Parkinson's patient, dancing and vibrating on the backdrop of the darkening skies.

"Ah," said Othniel Assis, "you should know that if the trailer is shaking and everything inside is moving about, it isn't an earthquake, only the washing machine!"

On hearing the translation, Mamelstein's raucous laughter was infectious, managing to put a smile even on the face of the IDF officer. "I must tell Norma about this!" the American said, slapping his thigh.

They all bade farewell with mutual expressions of appreciation, embraces, and kisses, got into their cars, and disappeared in a cloud of dust. *Washington Post* correspondent Jeff McKinley headed off on foot toward the entrance to the settlement. He had thought of asking Mamelstein's people for a ride but decided against it, preferring instead to keep his identity to himself.

Othniel turned to Captain Omer Levkovich. "Now, my friend, you can tell us what's been eating you," he said, looking at the soft-faced, fair-haired officer.

Omer opened the file he was carrying under his arm. "This," he said, handing over a document, "is a land demarcation order signed by the head of the IDF Central Command."

"A demarcation order? What are you on about?" Othniel eyed the document suspiciously. "What's this all about?" Hilik, too, peered at the piece of paper in Othniel's hand.

"A demarcation order," the section commander affirmed—and then continued, fully aware of what was going through the minds of these seasoned settlers. "Not the suspension of illegal construction. Not a Civil Administration issue. Nothing to do with the demolition of isolated structures—you know all too well that your trailers have been under demolition orders for years, and that no one has done anything about it because they know you'll just bring in others in their place. That's why they've issued a demarcation order. The structures aren't the issue, the entire area needs to be evacuated—all the residents, all the belongings.

And all the structures are to be razed. What do you think, that the right hand has no idea what the left is doing?"

Othniel read the order:

All individuals are required to vacate the area in question within eight days of publication of this declaration. Additionally, effective immediately on publication of this declaration, all construction activities in the area are banned, including entry into the area of individuals or equipment for the purpose of carrying out construction operations.

The order had been signed by the head of the Central Command and came with a map that outlined the demarcated area—Ma'aleh Hermesh C. in its entirety, all its structures and agricultural land.

Othniel stopped reading and glared at Omer. "You people are such ags," he said. "Oh well, I guess we'll have to take it up with the Military Appeals Board, and if that doesn't help, we'll petition the High Court of Justice, and if we lose there, we'll wait out the two years until the order expires, God willing. In any event, you aren't going to forcibly evict us, right?" He searched for a glimmer of a smile or supportive look on Omer's face—but found none. All he encountered was a look of curiosity and the cautious question, "What are ags?"

Othniel drew a breath and let out a deep sigh. "Aggressive little pains in the butt," he spat out as he punched the council head's number into his phone.

"Good luck and Shabbat shalom," the section commander responded before signaling his driver to start up the engine and climbing into the jeep. They pulled over at the gate alongside the soldier.

"Take these, Yoni, and tell your men to post them this evening on all the structures in the outpost," Omer said, handing over a pile of papers on which the order had been printed. He allowed the American journalist, who was hitching a ride just outside the gate, to get into the jeep, and then disappeared down the slope, into the darkening twilight and the winds. Yoni, the soldier, shifted his gaze from the departing jeep to the pages in his hands and closed the gate.

The Brothers

Roni Kupper didn't attend the ceremony. After Othniel Assis dropped him off outside the trailer belonging to "the only Gavriel in the settlement," he dragged his suitcase out of the trunk and wheeled it along the short but rough pathway that led to the property, entering through the gate and walking to the front door through the yellowish yard. ENTER BLESSED, read a perplexing sign on the door. It wasn't locked. "Gabi? Gabi?" he called out, walking through the rooms of the home. He sniffed at the air—a strange dank odor. His eyes were drawn to a dark stain in the corner. He wheeled his suitcase into the room on the right, which appeared to be the living room, and lay down on his back on the raised mattress that was serving as a sofa. He looked up at the ceiling and took a deep breath, closed his eyes, and then opened them again. He turned to look at the simple bookcase. His eyes passed over the rows of red-bound books, religious literature that Roni understood nothing about at all, taking in the titles one by one: the Zohar, the Shulchan Aruch, compilations of sermons and writings by Rabbi Nachman of Breslov, *The Guide for the Perplexed*, Rabbi Abraham Isaac Kook's *Orot*, and more. "Gabi?" he cried out once more, thinking he heard something, but no one responded.

Gavriel had attended the dedication ceremony for the new playground and had gone from there to the synagogue for late-afternoon prayers, after which he had hung around with everyone to chat for a while. Only afterward did he return home to find a large suitcase that was taking up half of the living room floor and his elder brother snoring loudly on the sofa, facing the ceiling, a look of utter serenity anointing his face. Gabi looked at his brother. At the rise and fall of his chest, at his lips trembling with every snore, at his arms folded across his chest in perfect rest, at his broad feet in their formerly white sports socks with their threadbare heels. His eyes wandered back to the large suitcase. Oh, Roni, my brother, he thought—and smiled at him, and tugged on his nose. Roni responded with a snore.

Gabi went into the kitchen to make a cup of tea. He turned on the light. He'd drink first and then make dinner for them, and then say the evening prayers. He turned on the kettle, which responded a few seconds later with an ever-loudening groan until the final bubbling noise and the automatic flip of the switch. He placed a Wissotzky tea bag into a glass cup with a thin handle and mixed in the sugar, clattering the teaspoon against the side of the glass.

"Make me one, too, whatever it is you're having," came a gravelly voice from the living room.

"Already have," Gabi responded, walking back into the living room and placing a glass, the granules of sugar still swirling on the bottom, on a small shelf beside Roni's head. "Tea," he said, and sat down on the armchair on the other side of the room. He recited the customary blessing, blew on his tea, and cautiously sipped the hot beverage. "Welcome, my brother. It's been a while."

Roni sat up, stretched, and tried to exorcise the sleep and jet lag that were clouding his mind. "Aahh!" he yawned out loud. He picked up the glass and sipped noisily. "Sweet," he said. Roni looked over at his brother, who was still smiling. "I'm going to have to stay here for a while," he said.

"I got that. The suitcase gave you away."

"Yes."

They drank in silence. What's with the big white skullcap with the pompom on top? Roni thought. The beard's still thin, but a little longer now. And those sidelocks? Aren't those only for people in the ultra-Orthodox Mea She'arim neighborhood? He admitted to himself, however, that the look suited his brother. Religious observance seemed to sit naturally on his slender build, to suit the dreamy brown of his eyes and his fair skin. Of the two, Roni had always looked like the true kibbutznik, with his dark skin and solid frame, the self-assured, sometimes arrogant, yet more lighthearted look on his face, which always appeared to be on the verge of breaking into a smile.

"How about a cookie or something?" Roni asked.

Gabi glanced toward the kitchen—but he didn't need to. There were no cookies. The silence settled in again, broken only occasionally by the sound of the two brothers sipping their tea.

"So, what's up?" Gabi finally asked, fixing his brother with a long stare. "The last time we spoke was on your fortieth birthday. You said you were busy and that you'd call back, and I haven't heard a word from you since. That was months ago. And the time before that was on your previous birthday. Aren't you supposed to be in America?"

Roni stood up from the sofa. He looked out the window. The wind whistled under the trailer. "What a view, eh? Really something else," he said, turning to face his brother. "How are things with you? The guy who gave me a ride told me you were a great guy, a prince."

Gabi laughed. "Just great, thank God. Wonderful."

"Wonderful? What's so wonderful?"

"Everything, everything's just wonderful. I'm pleased you are here."

"So I can stay for a while, then? This 'wonderful' you're talking about isn't a girl or something, is it?"

"For you, wonderful always has something to do with a girl."

"I just need to know if I can stay for a while."

"You can stay for as long as you like."

"So why the sad face? Is it too much for you to have your brother as a guest?"

"No sad face at all."

Roni walked into the kitchen. "Where's the bathroom?" he asked.

Gabi remained in the armchair, an example of simple workmanship from the 1970s, with its worn brown upholstery—his furniture was a collection of items found over the years on the streets of Jerusalem—and drank his tea. He could hear his brother's thick stream of urine splashing directly into the water in the toilet; Roni was never one to try to muffle the sound by aiming at the porcelain sides of the bowl. Gabi closed his eyes.

"Don't sit there looking upset," Roni declared on his return. He picked up his cup of tea. "I was always there for you when you needed help."

"I'm not upset," Gabi replied serenely. "But how could you have known that I needed help if you haven't been in touch for years?"

The trailer was suddenly thrown into darkness. Gabi stood up and looked out the window. "The generator's down," he said. "Thankfully, it's not from my kettle, so we have tea to drink at least until the darkness passes."

"I'm going out for a walk," Roni said, and began feeling his way to the door. Passing by his brother, however, he turned to him suddenly and spread out his arms. "Come here," he said, "give us a hug." Their embrace was a little clumsy, and brief. The darkness hid the expressions on their faces but Gabi's, presumably, was reserved, Roni's perhaps a touch forced.

"I'm pleased you came," the younger brother said after they had let go of one another. Roni didn't respond. He left, slamming the door behind him and causing the entire structure to shake. Gabi decided to say his evening prayers at home.

The Night

The trailers cast in darkness. The entire hilltop blacked out. The profound silence, the all-encompassing blackness, the sounds from the Arab village—so different from his own life in recent years, yet still capable of summoning a vague familiar feeling, from his childhood on the kibbutz, perhaps. Roni felt exhausted from the long journey and jet lag.

The strumming of a guitar could be heard coming from the far end of the outpost. A sad, slow song, somewhat solemn. Roni imagined himself heading toward the notes. He passed by a number of people and spotted the man who had given him the ride, standing outside his home alongside a young boy wearing a skullcap, a tranquil expression on his spotty face.

"Good evening," Roni said.

Othniel Assis smiled. "Well," he said, "did you find your brother, the saint? Was it him?"

"Yes, yes, thanks."

"We're going over to see what's up with the old generator. Wanna tag along? We may need a helping hand."

Roni Kupper followed Othniel and his son Yakir to the entrance to the outpost. Yoni was already there, shining a flashlight, and one of the other soldiers was restarting the generator with a sharp tug on a cord.

"How many more years will we have to wait before we're connected to the electricity grid?" Othniel growled as lights flickered on in the nearby homes. "There are women and children here; they shake in fear every time the generator goes down."

Roni continued to tag along behind the group, which headed back from the gate toward the center of the settlement. "Did you know anything about a new trailer?" Othniel asked Yoni as they passed by the latest arrival.

"No," the soldier responded.

"Did Omer not say anything about it?"

"Omer didn't say a word aside from telling me to post the new orders. He was with you all the time."

"True," Othniel said, rubbing his beard thoughtfully. "Interesting." He took the flashlight from Yoni and directed the beam at the silent structure. "Very interesting," he mumbled, and then walked around the trailer. "He simply off-loaded it here without a word to anyone. There's no infrastructure here, no preparations for water or power or sewage. Hello there?" Othniel called out. "Anyone home?" He approached the door and knocked. There was no door handle.

Roni bade farewell to the group and continued walking. Minutes later, he noticed that he had left the confines of the outpost and that the darkness now weighed heavier around him, and he was overcome with a sense that civilization was a step too far away. He turned and walked back. The sound of the guitar grew louder, the same slow, sad melody. Roni thought for a moment that he recognized the song, but the playing suddenly ceased.

"Halt!" came a sudden instruction from the darkness. Roni turned to see a thin young man standing some ten meters away from him. It took him a second or two to recognize the glint of a weapon, pointed directly at him, and another few seconds to see the guitar beneath it. "Or I'll shoot," the young man added, trying to disguise the tremble in his voice.

"No need for shooting," Roni responded, raising his arms. He was tired and unfocused, and couldn't decide whether to be amused by the fact that a young man with a guitar was now pointing a gun at him, or to panic. Despite the cold, he could feel sweat oozing from the pores on various places over his body. He replied confidently nevertheless. "I'm just walking around, having a look," he said.

"Why would you want to be walking around here? What's there to look at, especially in the dark?" The young man approached him, still hesitantly.

"Perhaps you should get that thing out of my face."

The young man's hand remained motionless. "First you need to tell me who you are," he said. "The generator goes down and a suspicious stranger suddenly appears. I have to follow procedures."

"I'm simply visiting my brother here for a short while."

"Who's your brother?"

"Gabi. Gabi Kupper."

"Gabi Kupper? There's no one here by that name." The barrel of the pistol moved a few centimeters closer to Roni's forehead.

"Ah, yes, he changed his name. Gavriel . . . Umm, Gavriel . . . Shit, I don't—"

"Gavriel Nehushtan? So why didn't you just say so? Yes, I can see a resemblance," the young man said, lowering the weapon. "It is subtle, but it's there. Would you like a cookie?"

The cookies, the young man went on, were baked by Jenia Freud, a math teacher who lived in the trailer adjacent to the gate at the entrance to the outpost with her husband, Elazar, a lieutenant in the reserves who worked in computers and had grown up in a settlement on the other side of Jerusalem. Jenia, he continued, was in the habit of making cookies for the soldiers and leaving them out on a tray at the guard tower.

"Not that I'm a soldier," said Nir Rivlin, armed with a guitar and pistol, as Roni enjoyed the coconut-chocolate cookies. Rivlin gave him the lay of the land. There were usually four to six soldiers stationed at the outpost; one of them, Yoni, was there permanently, while the others came and went. The soldiers did most of the guarding, but the residents helped out on occasion at night. Guard duty was divided equally among all the men, although there were some who paid others to take their shifts—men with families would usually pay the young single men, who had more time on their hands, to replace them. "Not that I'm single," Rivlin stressed. He had a family but was happy to guard; besides, he didn't have the money to pay someone to take his shift. He was studying to be a chef at the Kosher Culinary Arts School in Jerusalem, and he was being tested that week on his knife work, advanced dicing and slicing. The week before, there was a seminar on basic pastry making—quiches, crumble, yeast dough . . . Nir Rivlin rambled on until finally the exhausted Roni suggested, "Why don't you play something?" Nir picked up the guitar and asked, "What would you like to hear?" Following a brief discussion, they agreed on Lou Reed's "Perfect Day."

They sat on a tattered sofa that someone had discarded and gazed up at the stars twinkling above the dark desert. The generator hummed monotonously.

"Do the other guards pray and play music during their watch, too?" Roni asked.

"To each his own," Nir responded. "You can spend two hours walking around and pondering, and sometimes studying and praying. I play the guitar. Some watch DVDs on the laptop, or merely sit here with a cigarette and coffee. Sometimes you get a chance to chat with someone walking or driving by."

"And my brother?"

"Gavriel? He's a true saint. He always asks for the midnight shift and then recites the Tikkun Chatzot prayer. Do you know what that is? Have you heard 'To declare your loving kindness in the morning, and your faithfulness every night'? You're a nonbeliever through and through, right? Nighttime is the principal time for solitude, when the world rests from its troubles; the time to muster up the good from within the evil. Sometimes he stands in the guard tower and memorizes the teachings of Rabbi Nachman of Breslov. And sometimes you can see him walking to the edge of the hilltop, with not another soul around, only him and the stars and the desert. Speaks to the Almighty's desert. 'In solitude, turn sadness into joy.' Want a hit?"

Nir reached into the inside pocket of his coat and pulled out a joint he had rolled before beginning his shift. He puffed on it noisily, exhaled a thin plume of smoke skyward, and passed it to Roni. "Grass. 'How wonderful it would be if one could only be worthy of hearing the song of the grass. Each blade of grass sings out to God without any ulterior motive, and without expecting any reward. It is most wonderful to hear its song and worship God in its midst.' Pretty good stuff, no?"

The darkness lay thick and heavy, as it is wont to do far from big, illuminated cities. The outpost had no streetlights. They could hear frogs croaking, grasshoppers gnawing, crickets chirping, the occasional whinny from a horse in its stable ("That's Killer, Jehu's horse"), dogs barking in their yard ("Othniel's dogs, Beilin and Condoleezza"), the wind rustling, the wailing cry of a baby ("Nefesh, perhaps, or Shuv-el"). At night, at the height of winter, Nir told Roni, the rain came down with deafening force, and the wind threatened to carry the trailers off into the heavens. The summer nights, meanwhile, meant weddings and parties and festivities in the neighboring village, and then the music would blast out loud, along with the beating of the darbukas, and singers would entertain the revelers of ever-higher octaves that rose up into the night sky, and on occasion there'd be a good dose of fireworks, too—primitive insofar as visual spectacles go, but impressively loud, thereby frightening Condi and Beilin and Killer and the young children into a long and loud symphony of their own design, startling the men of the outpost from their slumber and causing them to reach frantically for their weapons, their hearts pounding.

And then, too, particularly in the small, deep hours of the morning, there was the silence. When all were in their homes, after putting the children to bed, and dinner, and showers; after they had watched the news, and read, and finished off some work and housework, and had gone to sleep under thin ceilings, above which the stars shone boldly. Sleep brings a departure of the mind, its purification, and makes way for inspiration. During sleep, the soul rises to the next world, and sleep serves as the mind's pathway.

"I should get some sleep." Roni yawned. "I'm still on American time, everything's upside down."

Nir Rivlin turned to him with a look of surprise, as if he had forgotten Roni was there. He looked at his watch. "Almost midnight, the end of my shift!" he said, dipping his hand into his pocket to retrieve a piece of paper. "Let's see who's replacing me . . . Hah! Your dear brother! Thank God. Come, let's go shake him from his dreams."

Approaching the trailer, they spotted Gabi stepping out into the darkness. Weary-legged, he shuffled across the hilltop in the biting cold, the coffee in the mug in his hand cooling rapidly. Carried on the wind came the sound of distant Arabic music.

"Hey there, O righteous one," Nir said.

"Shalom, shalom," Gabi's weary voice responded. His gaze wandered back and forth between Nir Rivlin and his brother, Roni, and he stopped in his tracks for a few seconds before turning again to Nir. "How's Shaulit doing?" he asked.

"God be praised."

"When is she due?"

"God willing. She's just gone into her ninth month."

"Wow." Gabi smiled. "I wonder if it'll be a March or an April baby."

The three stood there in silence. Even Nir, who hadn't stopped talking for the past two hours, appeared too tired to find another word to say.

"Okay, off to bed, you guys. Good night."

The Morning

When Gabi returned from morning prayers, Roni was still fast asleep in the living room. He laid down his tefillin bag quietly enough, but his brother woke to the noise of the teaspoon clinking against the side of the glass cup.

"Good morning," Gabi said. "Tea?"

"Coffee," his brother's sleep-laden voice responded. "Wow! I couldn't figure out where I was for a moment. I slept like a log!"

"'Sleep is sweet and good,'" Gabi said, quoting Rabbi Nachman. "It's the silence."

Roni pulled out a cigarette from a light blue box. Gabi glanced at him cautiously. "Should I open a window?" the elder brother asked, but when Gabi stood up to open one, he continued, "Isn't it too cold for an open window?"

Gabi opened one nevertheless. "Listen, I don't have much food; I didn't know you were coming," he said. "If I get to Ma'aleh Hermesh this morning, I'll get some. But it's Friday, there's not much time." An idea came to him. "Do you have a car, perhaps? I could take a quick drive before work."

"I have nothing," Roni said.

Gabi raised an eyebrow.

"So, tell me, what's this Gavriel Nehushtan all about?" Roni asked, releasing a plume of smoke through the netting in the window frame. The gray fumes drifted through gingerly, seemingly testing its boundaries. "It's me."

"What's you? The Gavriel, I get. What's with the Nehushtan?"

"Kupper in Hebrew is *nehoshet*. Didn't you know? Our forefathers in Germany must have been coppersmiths. Copper is the strongest material in the world."

It was Roni's turn to raise his eyebrows. Gabi looked at his brother's body slumped limply in the armchair—no longer the muscular physique of old, but still manly, stubbled and thick-haired, a soft mane covering his dark-skinned chest. His brother was the broader of the two, shorter, and more hairy. A stranger might struggle to pick out any resemblance at first glance. Even though their brown eyes cut the same shape, Roni's expressed warmth and playfulness, while Gabi had been told his own reflected caution and naïveté. Gabi continued, "Someone once told me that when the Ice Age returns at some point in the future—and it'll happen for sure; after all, God spins nature in a cycle—the entire world will be covered by a layer of ice several kilometers deep. And the immense weight of this layer of ice will crush the whole world we know today into a thin layer, just a few centimeters thick. Everything will turn to dust. But if someone during that coming Ice Age were to dig deep into the heart of the earth and look at a cross section of that two-centimeter layer of what used to be humanity, they would see mostly copper. And that's because we use so much of that material and it is so strong. Everything else will turn to dust, into nothing. But the copper will survive."

"And what is that supposed to say about our family? That we're strong?" Roni laughed his small laugh. Gabi shrugged. "Did you change your name officially, at the Population Registry?"

"No."

They drank in silence for several minutes. Then Gabi asked, "What do you mean by 'I have nothing'? What's happened?"

"It's a long story."

"I'm listening."

Roni opened the screen and threw out his cigarette butt. "Not now," he said. "We'll find the time. Aren't you off to work now?"

"Yes, but I'd also like to know what has happened to my brother. And it'd be nice to know how long you intend to stay. Are you in some kind of trouble?"

"No, no, everything's great, nothing's happened. I simply need to air myself out a little. Who's that? That's quite a look he has there," Roni said, pointing at a picture the size of a large postcard that stood on one of the bookshelves, a black-and-white photograph of a bearded man wearing a furry hat.

Gabi looked at the picture. "That's Rabbi Kook, *Ha-ra'aya*," he said, using the common Hebrew acronym for the revered Torah scholar.

"*Ha-ra'aya*? What's that supposed to mean?"

"Such zeal, right?" Gabi responded, turning to face his brother again. "But why are you changing the subject? Is it 'nothing' or is it 'a long story'?"

Failing to elicit a response from his brother, Gabi went back into his bedroom, returned shortly afterward dressed in blue work clothes over his tzitzit, and sat down to lace up his heavy work shoes. He then smiled and stood up. "Okay, we'll talk later. I really do need to get going."

"Don't worry," Roni said, "I won't be a burden for long. I just need to chill, get back on my feet, and then move on. In any event," he continued, getting up to put his head out the window and look around, "I haven't got what it takes to live in a place like this for too long."

Gabi smiled. "Okay, I'm outta here. Have a good day."

"Have a good day, Gavriel Nehushtan!" Roni exclaimed, breaking into a loud laugh, but when the door shut behind Gabi, the smile on his face instantly disappeared.

"What an insane morning," Gabi heard Shaulit Rivlin say to Nehama Yisraeli as he passed by the two expecting mothers and nodded in acknowledgment without looking at them directly. The morning sun felt good on the back of his neck. He walked by the new trailer and then the new playground just beyond it. God must be so righteous, he thought. If He had sent his brother to him on a day filled with new and joyous beginnings for the settlement, surely that must be a blessing. Something caught his eye. A small shoe. He picked it up off the playground grass. A Nimrod sandal, size 23. He took it over to the toddlers' day-care center before continuing on to Othniel's farm. Othniel was there already, standing outside with one hand shielding his eyes from the sun and the other holding a telephone to his ear. "Let's get moving, Nehushtan!" he said, hastening Gabi along. "We need to prepare the crates for Moran. Just a minute, I'm on the phone."

Fridays were short workdays, and getting hold of anyone at a government ministry was no easy feat, but, thank God, Othniel Assis had the mobile telephone numbers of several influential individuals, the first being MK Uriel Tsur, who had spoken yesterday at the dedication ceremony for the playground.

"Good morning, Uriel, Othniel here . . . Yes . . . Thank you . . . Tell me, do you know anything about this demarcation order we received yesterday? . . . Demarcation, demarcation . . . Captain Omer . . . Berkowitz, no, Levkovich . . . Yes, after the ceremony . . . Okay, thank you, thank you . . . But before Sabbath, right? Thank you, sir."

Othniel spent a fair deal of time on his phone that morning. Gavriel, meanwhile, worked alongside him, preparing the crates of vegetables and dairy products for Moran, their distributor. Regarding the new trailer, explained Natan Eliav, the secretary of Ma'aleh Hermesh A., who had personally made calls to Dov, to the council head, to the IDF Central Command, and to various other officials, apparently there had been a mistake. The new home was intended for a different outpost, Givat Yeshua, an extension of the Yeshua settlement on the other side of the wadi. After losing his way and failing to reach anyone on the phone, the truck driver simply off-loaded the trailer at the first seemingly vacant spot and departed.

As it turned out, the removal of the trailer from the settlement would probably take some time. Yesterday, Natan Eliav continued, there was a transportation permit for the mobile structure, but there was no construction permit or approval for its connection to any infrastructure, which would have allowed for the home to be off-loaded and placed on the ground. Since then, apparently, a construction permit had come through with the help of their guys at the Housing and Construction Ministry, but the defense minister himself had intervened and was no longer willing to issue a second transportation permit. Someone must have gotten word to him, leaked something to him.

"Who knows, perhaps you've got a Shin Bet security service informer among you," Natan Eliav muttered, which got Othniel thinking, Perhaps we do—it wouldn't have surprised him. But who? Maybe that new guy, Gavriel's brother? He glanced over at Gavriel, who was working beside him, and wondered if he should say anything. You never know. In any event, Natan continued, the defense minister won't allow it to be moved. In fact, he added, the defense minister's antisettlement intervention means that the new abode will be staying in the settlement for quite some time, so perhaps it would be a good idea to go through the waiting list and invite a new family to set up home there.

Othniel knew precisely in which drawer at home the waiting list could be found. Rachel, his wife, headed the settlement's Absorption Committee, together with Hilik Yisraeli. He decided to wait a few days, and if the defense minister remained adamant about withholding a transportation permit, they'd move a family in. He went outside to help Gavriel with the crates.

MK Tsur eventually got back to him. "The order has something to do with the separation fence," he told Othniel.

"What!" Othniel replied. Surveyors and architects and military officers and various other officials related to the fence had indeed been wandering around the area. But they had been doing so for years, and no one paid them any attention. "I thought they weren't building the fence in this area."

"I don't know if they really are going to build it, but apparently they've decided to do something about it there," the MK said. "And based on what I was told, it is supposed to run through the olive groves of your neighbors from Kharmish."

"So what's that got to do with us?" Othniel questioned.

"Well, the area that falls under the seizure order issued by the IDF for the purpose of building the fence and for the security zone on either side of it includes a portion of your land."

"But how is that possible?" Othniel cried out. "Since when have they been building the fence through Israeli settlements? Haven't they heard of democracy and basic human rights over there in Jerusalem?"

"You're right," the parliamentarian replied, "it is unusual. The land they are appropriating this time is again private Palestinian land, but it seems you have settled on part of it. There's another problem, too. Your settlement doesn't appear on any map."

"What are you talking about?" Othniel responded, knowing all too well, like Tsur, that this was indeed the case, and thankfully so. It would be better if the maps weren't updated and for the air force to refrain from any aerial photography. It spared everyone headaches. Years of experience in the settlement enterprise had taught them this.

"Besides," Tsur continued, "the lefties are making noise with the Defense Ministry. They want to know why the fence is being built through an olive grove belonging to Arabs when right next to it sits an illegal settlement that has continued to expand, with a playground, new trailers, and the like. The defense minister wants to look good, so he's telling them that the outpost, too, will be evacuated, and he's sent you the demarcation order. Are you with me?"

Othniel's one hand held the phone up against his ear. His other hand rested on his forehead. He tried to think. Who had told them about the playground? And what new trailers? Only one had arrived, and mistakenly, at that.

"Anyway, Shabbat shalom, my friend. I wouldn't worry too much if I were you. We'll take care of it next week. Hang in there. Give my regards to the lefties," Tsur said, and laughed.

"What lefties?"

"Haven't you heard? The lefties are staging a demonstration this afternoon in your Arab village."

Othniel closed his eyes and rubbed them. As if he didn't have enough to deal with before the Sabbath, he thought. "But . . . What are they demonstrating about?" he asked. "They got what they wanted, didn't they? The order's been issued."

"God only knows! Against the fence. Against the outpost. In support of the Arabs' olives. There's no shortage of things for the lefties to demonstrate about in Judea and Samaria on a Friday afternoon, is there? Trust them to find something. Okay, my friend, today's a short one. Shabbat shalom."

The Demonstration

The tip, the point, the bulge. What was it about them that excited him so much? His eyes were always drawn to them. He knew it was impolite, but he wasn't the one who made the decision, his eyes did, and they always went there, before anywhere else. And the best days were those last days of the winter, when the caress of the morning sun created a sweet illusion that suggested dressing in short, thin clothing, before the sun remembered that the spring had yet to arrive and disappeared behind the clouds, and a sudden chill set in.

What he liked most was that there was no barrier, nothing in the way, and that they were right there, just beneath the thin cotton. That was a far more beautiful image than bare breasts, which left nothing to the imagination; they could be too thin, too big, too small, asymmetrical, saggy, eggplant-shaped. Bare breasts could look exactly like the things they are— fatty milk glands, and fatty milk glands did nothing for him. Titties, too. *Titties* was a word for teenagers. But breasts—*breasts* was a man's word.

And when they were right there, hidden minimally under a thin layer of worn silk or cotton, that was what really got his blood pumping.

And that's what Roni could see, freely bouncing up and down under a shirt bearing the slogan THE OCCUPATION WEAKENS US—large and juicy, and at their center, poking against the fabric, erect, fleshy nipples of volume and experience, the nipples of someone who knows they are there and how to leverage them.

When he left San Francisco two days earlier, with no intention of ever going back, thin, revealing clothes were a distant memory. And after arriving in Israel, and heading east from Ben Gurion Airport, he figured that such sights, which, with the coming of the spring, would sprout up and flourish in Tel Aviv, would be lacking at the settlement where he was headed. Less than twenty-four hours later, however, he was standing, arms folded across his chest, in the large olive grove of an Arab village adjacent to his brother's outpost, facing dozens of demonstrators brandishing signs that read DOWN WITH THE SEPARATION FENCE and SETTLERS GO HOME—OUTPOST OUTLAWS, with his deviant eyes unable to budge from that one protestor's magnificent chest, until he forced them to do so and his gaze drifted up to her pleasant, somewhat porcine face, and to the placards, and then across to a group of residents from the village. And he couldn't help but notice the eyes of one of them fixed precisely at the right height, their lines of sight intersected—Up with promiscuity! Down with the separation bra! End the occupation of the breasts!—and, like sharers of a secret, their mouths curled upward into smiles of mutual appreciation. There are some things that transcend politics and justice.

Roni's gaze wandered on, aiming higher and farther afield, and then stopped suddenly in its tracks in surprise: Herodium! And he became aware of the perfect roundness of the hilltop in the distance, how it surged forth sensually from the body of the flat desert, light in color and so inviting—a breast! A breast in the middle of the desert! I've come to the right place, Roni thought, and looked around at the hilltops, at their soft curves, their gentle contours, and their feathery, after-the-rain covering. A few days from now, Nir would tell him that Yosef Ben Matityahu or Titus Flavius Josephus himself had written of the Herodium that it looked just like the breast of a woman.

The leader of the demonstration, a thin, spectacled young man with a prominent, square jaw, bellowed slogans into a megaphone: "Cease construction of the fence! End the theft of Palestinian land! Stop the government-supported expansion of the outposts! No more settlers!" He was standing at the forefront of a small group of youths wearing T-shirts emblazoned with the logo of the left-wing Meretz party, a handful of anarchists, a number of silver-haired individuals from the old generation of the Peace Now movement, and the attractive protestor. Across from them were a number of folks Roni recognized, among them Gabi. Roni approached him and rested a hand on his shoulder. "Great action, brother!"

"I'm pleased you're enjoying yourself," Gabi said, and smiled, and then went on to explain why so few of the outpost's residents had bothered to show up. It's Friday, the women are baking cakes for the Sabbath and are cooking meals for the coming twenty-four hours; the boys and girls are helping in the kitchen or looking after their younger siblings; and the men are returning from errands in Jerusalem.

"Who's that orange one?" Roni asked, gesturing with his eyebrows in the direction of one of the woman settlers, who was wearing an orange head scarf.

"Ah, yes, that's Neta Hirschson, she wouldn't miss this for the world," Gabi responded.

The woman marched purposefully toward the demonstrators, fixed them with a stare, and began shouting: "You should be ashamed of yourselves! Enemies of Israel! It's all over; your rule has ended! You had your chance and you failed! You had Peres, you had Rabin, you had Oslo. And you're still shooting your mouths off? What chutzpah! After the things you did to this country, you should be ashamed to show your faces here!"

Someone answered her, "Land thieves! Criminals! You're stealing the budgets of the development towns and the poor! You're wasting the soldiers' time! You're shaming us around the world, the country is sick of you!"

And Neta responded, "Lunatics! No one gives a shit about you! So much self-hatred! Look at you, groveling at the feet of the Arab enemy! You have no God, you have no future! Get out of here, you won't achieve a damn thing!"

And the other one, "You're contemptible. Here you are, living at our expense, on our taxes and our blood, with our children in the army to protect you, and yet you're still complaining? Take a look at yourself, teaching your kids to be bullies and to hate! What happened to 'All Jews bear responsibility for one another'? What happened to 'Love thy neighbor as thyself'? Enough with the hatred! Down with the fence!"

And it was on that precise point that Neta refrained from differing with the protestor. She had already heard from Othniel and Hilik that the planned fence would encroach on the settlement's land. Besides, the entire idea of the fence, which created a border and, for all intents and purposes, created a Palestinian state in the Land of Israel, was contemptible to the core.

"Yes, down with the fence," Neta yelled.

"Stop the barrier from running through here," the left-wing demonstrator shouted back.

"Stop the barrier from running through here," the settler cried out. And for one brief moment, the two united, like two ends meeting to form a circle, but the harmony was soon shattered when a soldier approached the demonstrator and was greeted loudly with "What's your name, you piece of shit? Don't you dare touch me!"

Neta watched the protestor walk away, still mumbling "You'll stop at nothing" and "Go back to where you came from" in a lowered voice, perhaps to herself. She then glanced at her watch and quickly headed toward home; she had a booking with a client from Ma'aleh Hermesh A. who needed an urgent pre-Sabbath manicure and pedicure.

Aside from the incident involving Neta and her rival, the demonstration passed quietly. The soldiers who had been deployed from the outpost remained idle. And when it was over, Roni kept track of the attractive demonstrator. He saw her approach the Palestinian who had been eyeing her earlier. Son of a bitch. The two exchanged words. Roni moved closer. The woman handed over some money to the Palestinian and received a large metal container in return. Someone else, also in an End the Occupation shirt, produced some cash in exchange for another container. Roni edged nearer. The braless woman looked at him and he responded in kind.

"You should be ashamed of yourselves," she blurted out, and walked off. The Palestinian's eyes followed her for a few seconds, and then he turned to Roni and winked.

"What's all this?" Roni asked, gesturing toward the Arab's wares.

"Olive oil, dirt cheap," the Palestinian said.

"How much is dirt cheap?"

"Eighteen liters, three hundreds of shekels."

Roni did the math in his head—a little over fifteen shekels a liter, less than four dollars. Cheap indeed. "Two-fifty and it's a deal?"

The Palestinian smiled. "No, three hundreds of shekels. Dirt cheap," he said.

The two men looked at each other. Roni fixed his stare, hoping the Arab would break. He recalled a business school lecture from his time in New York. The professor had said that all commercial negotiations—whether they be haggling in a marketplace or merger talks between two giant conglomerates—were a duel in which body language played a decisive role. The Arab stared back at him, refusing to back down.

"What's your name?" Roni asked, wrinkling an eyebrow in the direction of the olive farmer.

"Musa Ibrahim," replied Musa Ibrahim, a well-built man with a white mustache and white hair that started far back on his scalp, in stark contrast to his tanned skin.

"Pleased to meet you. Roni Kupper," said Roni Kupper, extending a hand. Musa shook it. "So, you say there's a chance I can get you down to two-fifty?" Roni inquired.

"Did I say there was?" Musa smiled.

Roni took out his wallet, which he had found one day in the snow in New York, and opened it. "Well, look at that, bro, I'm spending my very last shekel on your oil," he said, counting out a total of exactly 292 shekels in notes and coins, shrugging apologetically. Musa snatched angrily at the handful, and Roni hoisted the tin container onto his shoulder and turned around.

The Sabbath

The Sabbath settled on the hilltop like a shawl on hair, pleasing and soft.

The soldiers went off to rest. The left-wingers were gone. And the distributor Moran's pickup truck was already on its way westward carrying crates of asparagus, mushrooms, cherry tomatoes, and arugula, as well as cartons of yogurt and goat-milk cheese—all bearing the label Gitit Farms, named after the Assis family's firstborn daughter, and Moran's address in the Sharon region of the country.

Gabi, with the help of the slightly built Yakir Assis, gathered up a large piece of canvas that read STOP THE EXPANSION OF OUTPOSTS UNDER GOVERNMENT PROTECTION—they'd use it to help fence off Othniel's fields, which were already demarcated by stretches of canvas bearing the slogans END THE OCCUPATION AND TWO STATES FOR TWO NATIONS, in response to a long length of canvas glorifying Rabbi Nachman of Breslov that the Arabs of Kharmish used during olive-harvesting time.

The Sabbath settled on the hilltop like a veil on the shoulders of a bride, quiet and airy.

Roni made his way to his brother's home, the eighteen-liter jerry can of olive oil digging deep into his shoulder. The air filled with the smell of meals being prepared. He could hear the rustling of pages of weekend newspapers being turned. A young girl slept soundly in a hammock in one of the yards. The dogs, Condoleezza and Beilin, gnawed on bones. A dusty sedan, laden with bags and children, unloaded a visiting family that had arrived from God knows where to spend the Sabbath on the hilltop.

Final pre-Sabbath preparations were under way in Gabi's home: his cell phone was switched off, the Sabbath hotplate was switched on, light switches were flipped up or down, toilet paper was torn into measured lengths, for the twenty-four hours ahead. The Sabbath dropped down like a generator that had crashed. The outpost's generator crashed, and came back to life just minutes before the deadline. A siren heralding the Sabbath was barely heard coming from distant urban neighborhoods. The Sabbath came down like a setting sun, to the accompaniment of soft gusts of wind.

"What's that?"

"Olive oil, man. Eighteen liters for two-ninety shekels, a great deal," Roni responded. "It's on me, my brother, use as much as you need. There's enough here for months."

"I thought you were broke. And suddenly now you're spending three hundred on oil?"

Roni plucked a cigarette from the sky-blue box. "I had just the right amount," he said.

Gabi looked at him, astonished. "Are you telling me you spent your last three hundred on olive oil? What are you going to do now?"

Roni bent over to reach into his sock and retrieved a purple banknote. "They weren't my last," he said. "Look, I have another fifty. And some dollars, too. I'm going to need a little help in the meantime."

"I don't get you. Do you expect me to fork over money? All I earn, I spend on my home and food. And why buy from the Arabs? We have excellent olive oil here, made by Jewish hands. I have some in the kitchen."

Roni went into the kitchen. He opened several cupboards before he found the bottle, which still bore its price tag. He did the math in his head again, and his eyes widened. "Dude! It's almost twice the price!"

"And right before Sabbath, no less," Gabi continued. "You appear out of nowhere, without forewarning, you won't tell me what has happened, and say you'll be staying. I said you were welcome, but now all of a sudden, you're asking for money . . . Didn't you make millions in America? Where did that go?"

Roni smoked in silence and looked out toward the olive groves of Kharmish. His brain kept doing math.

"And I'd rather you didn't smoke inside. Certainly not on the Sabbath." Gabi went to his bedroom to take his white Sabbath clothes out of the closet.

Roni stubbed out his cigarette and called after him, "There we go, it's out."

"Why have you come here?"

"Do you want me to leave?"

Gabi returned to the living room, buttoning his shirt. "No, I'm pleased you're here. But what happened?"

The brothers exchanged a long stare. Neither backed down. Roni's face finally broke into a smile. "Nothing, I've already told you," he said. "I simply need some space, that's all." But the smile had faded, and the stare went on.

"What kind of trouble have you gotten yourself into, Roni?" Gabi asked, the doubt in his eyes deepening. "Will anyone come looking for you?"

"No, no, what are you worrying about? You've always been one, a worrier. Take it easy."

Gabi backed down. "I'm not worried. An eye that sees and an ear that hears, and all your deeds are written in a book," he said. "Are you coming to prayers? At the very least, come help make up a minyan if we are short."

Roni smiled. "Sure, I'll be there. Go, go, I know where the synagogue is. I'm just going to change my shirt and I'll come. Start without me."

After the door closed behind Gabi, Roni rose from his seat, went over to the window by the door, pulled back the curtain, and watched his brother walking off down the path. An eye that sees, an ear that hears, what's all that crap? He chuckled. He returned to the living room, heading straight over to the shelf on which his brother had left his cell phone. Roni switched it on. He sat on the sofa, the phone in his hand, and forced his eyes shut. He struggled to remember a number he hadn't used in a long time. Finally, he dialed.

"Hello."

"Ariel? It's Roni."

The line went quiet for three or four seconds. "Roni! Really? Where are you? I can't believe it. Holy crap! What's up? Have you popped over for a visit?"

"Yes. No . . . Never mind. I'll explain another time, I'm a little rushed now. All okay with you?

"Never a dull moment with you, is there? Fucking hell."

"Are you still married? Still at the office? Still looking for business opportunities?" Roni asked, knowing all too well that the answers to all would be yes. Ariel was one of the most stable people he knew. Aside from losing his hair, and perhaps having children, he would never change. And that's why Roni had called him. He was a drab accountant, not one of the Tel Aviv bunch, whom Roni wanted to avoid. Ariel lived in Herzliya.

"Do you know of a business opportunity?" Ariel asked.

Roni smiled to himself. "Three hundred shekels for eighteen liters of olive oil, is that a good deal?"

"I'll check it out. Is it good olive oil?"

"Good isn't the half of it. It's the crème de la crème of olive oils. Straight from the tree and into the bottle."

"Organic? Organic's the rage now."

"Of course it is. Originally organic," Roni said, glancing over at the unlabeled tin container.

"Which press does it come from?"

"Which press? Roni and Musa Limited. Who cares which press?" Roni said.

"Musa? Where are you? Okay, give me two minutes, I'll get back to you. You've caught me on a Friday afternoon, but I know who to call."

Roni used the time to rummage through his suitcase and find a nice shirt. He then went into the bathroom to roll on deodorant under his arms, apply a spray of cologne, and put the shirt on.

Ariel called back. "That's rock-bottom," he said. "Good olive oil sells in the stores in Tel Aviv for at least forty a liter, and olive oil boutique stores have begun sprouting up in the city. Have you seen them? It's madness. I have a friend who's a partner in one, the Olive Boutique, on Rothschild Boulevard. Do you know it?"

"I haven't been to Tel Aviv in years, Ariel. That's why I'm calling you."

"Anyway, he said you should bring him ten pieces, to sniff out the market. Roni and Musa, you said? Where are they located?"

"Listen, I don't know if I'll be able to organize ten pieces so quickly. Let me have a word with the people here. I'll see what I can do."

"But is it really good? Organic? Baladi olives? All that extra-virgin, cold-pressed shit?" Ariel asked.

"I'll be in touch, Ariel. Got to go."

The Sabbath fell on the hilltop like rain, bounteous and fresh.

There was no one outside as Roni hurried off, but the sound of the prayer song drew him to the large structure at the center of the outpost, two trailers that had been joined together. Elsewhere, absolute silence reigned, with the occasional gust of wind disturbing a sheet of plastic somewhere.

The two halves of the synagogue teemed with life and prayer. The men, complete with their long beards, swinging tzitzit, and skullcaps as broad as their self-assured smiles, prayed rhythmically. Roni spotted Gabi at the front, close to the Torah scroll, immersed in his God, swaying fervently. It wasn't prayer; it was a dialogue, a scream, an intense cry, ecstatic applause. An individual swept away to the point of utter detachment, crying one moment and laughing the next, his face displaying anguish, then pleasure. Roni watched his brother with a mixture of wonder and pride from a bench at the back of the synagogue. Wonder sparked by the fact that the kid was a champion, the outpost's champion of wild prayer, whose fervid movements threatened to tip over the entire structure; pride sparked by the fact that the kid was whole, a believer. He appeared content, and to have found his place. Or so his elder brother hoped.

Roni lost interest after a few minutes. He wasn't able to follow the service. He sneaked out, suppressed the urge to light a cigarette, and stood around watching the children at play. One boy came up to him and asked who he was.

"Roni. And you?"

"Hananiya Assis," the boy responded, looking curiously at Roni's non-white clothes and the stubble on his face. "How old are you?" he asked.

"Forty and a half. And you?" Roni said.

"Forty and a half? Whose grandfather are you?"

Roni laughed.

When he went inside to the back benches, two bearded men were talking there in soft voices about Mamelstein and the Civil Administration. Roni flipped through the Sabbath leaflets that lay scattered on the tables. The two bearded men suddenly stood and broke into song along with everyone else. Roni followed their lead, standing when they did and sitting accordingly. It wasn't long, though, before he gave up trying to keep up with the flock, realizing that no one really cared anyway. He enjoyed the synagogue, browsed the leaflets, watched the worshippers with interest, and was fascinated by the combination of the sheeplike communal spirit (singing together, genuflecting in unison, everyone dressed in white) and the individualism (their skullcaps and prayer movements, the way they covered their eyes during the Shema prayer).

Some fifty hours had passed since he had fled the United States. He smiled wearily and allowed the noise that had been buzzing in his thoughts in recent months to subside. He'd stay here for a while. He'd take it easy out in nature, and rest. Perhaps he'd look into the possibility of doing something with that Musa guy and his olive oil. Or maybe he'd move into the new trailer that had arrived at the outpost. He closed his eyes, and all around him, the men sang to their God with increasing intensity. Yes, he thought, that's what he'd do. He'd leave the mess behind him. He wouldn't hurry to move on elsewhere. He'd get his life back in order.

A joyous melody started up, a Hasidic song. Initially, Roni didn't even open his eyes, the song gelled with the prayers, but then he felt it. First, the change in the mood, the stunned stares of the worshippers, and then, the vibration in his pocket. What was the phone doing there? And who calls on the Sabbath eve? He cast a fearful look over the synagogue. Did they know it was him? Did they recognize the acoustic tune as Gabi's ringtone? Yes, they know for sure. He lowered his head, stood up, and headed hastily for the door. The tune—which he would later discover to be "There's a Fire in Breslov" by Israel Dagan—played on and grew louder; the glares burned into the back of his neck.

Outside again, he answered the call. It was Ariel. He had been thinking more about the idea, and it sounded fantastic. When could he come by to see and taste the oil? he asked.

BRAIN SHORT-CIRCUIT

The Beetles

E very summer, the kibbutz was overrun by the black beetles. Industrious little things, with eight or six spindly legs—he could never remember how many for spiders and how many for beetles—walking along the gray concrete paths, which they appeared for some reason to prefer to the lawns, just like the people. They gave off an awful, pungent stench, which may have been a secretion or may have simply come from the rotting bodies of the unlucky ones that lay crushed by the boots of the kibbutzniks, or met their demise by other means. In retrospect, his memory offered up the disgusting stench along with the bizarre spectacle of hundreds and thousands of small black bodies on the backdrop of the smooth, bare concrete that ran between the beautiful lawns tended by Dad Yossi and his landscaping team and the small homes that were known as "rooms."

Of his father and mother, on the other hand, he had no image, odor, or sound to hold on to, but he did have biological facts: names, ages, causes of death, height, hair color. Where did the beetle invasion come from? From the mountain, said Mom Gila. And why did they come to the kibbutz? To look for food, to look for shade, said Dad Yossi. Mom Gila, Dad Yossi—as opposed to his real mother and father. It was never a secret. It wasn't a story that had remained hidden until one day in his teens, the father-who-he-had-thought-was-his-father had taken him for a drive and told him that he wasn't his father, and shock had turned into tears: But why didn't you tell me? It wasn't a tale about children whispering and giggling behind his back until one day, one of them had said, with a touch of curiosity, and cruelty, too, perhaps, You know, my father made me swear not to tell you, but he says that your father and mother are not your real father and mother, followed by him bursting into tears and asking, What do you mean by a father and mother not being real? There's no such thing; and then going home and asking them, and them giving each other a look that said It had to come at some point, we could never have kept it a secret forever, and then his father taking his hand and saying to him with sadness, Listen, Gabi . . .

No, it wasn't that kind of a story. Mom Gila and Dad Yossi were, from the very beginning, Mom Gila and Dad Yossi, never Mom and Dad, and Roni's and Gabi's family name was always Kupper—until Gabi Hebraized it years later. As for the story about their real parents, well, Roni and Gabi heard that more or less at the same time they heard their very first words.

He could remember his brother, Roni, shouting, "Mom Gila! Mom Gila!" after finding him on the other side of the perimeter road, nearby the kibbutz fence, beyond which lay the plum orchards, with two black beetles in his mouth, alive but no longer whole. "Mom Gila! Mom Gila! Gabi's eating beetles!"

"What?" came the cry from the house.

To her credit, you'd have to say, she reacted quickly, initially with the cry and then by running outside in her nightdress to scoop him up in her arms. She wasn't mad at him, didn't spank his tush, didn't scold the older brother for failing to look after the little one. Instead, she hastily washed out his mouth and gave him some juice and a candy to get the taste out. And then she looked at him, and he smiled back at her, seemingly somewhat indifferently, perhaps a little inquisitively, and she burst into astonished laughter.

When Dad Yossi returned home, he took the infant in his arms, bronzed by the summer's labors, and said, "What's this I hear about you, you little cannibal?" And little Gabi, who wasn't talking just yet but certainly knew how to laugh, did exactly that, and from time to time thereafter, Dad Yossi would call him Cannibal, more frequently when he began devouring the bloody steaks that Dad Yossi would prepare on the barbecue on Independence Day and the other springtime holidays, and even after he became a vegetarian several years later, following the incident in which a few more black beetles, of the same kind he had eaten that day, ended up in his mouth again. Dad Yossi returned from work, picked up little Gabi, and called him a cannibal, and all four members of the family laughed out loud—a warm and fuzzy family picture from the 1970s.

His first memory was of a mouthful of beetles, and the memories to follow were also associated with his mouth. He always had something in his mouth. Like that pink device that pushed against his upper lip so that his teeth could grow. It was a special device that no one else, including the grammar teacher, had ever come across.

"Gabi Kupper, do you have gum in your mouth?"

"No, miss."

"So what do you have in there?"

"It isn't gum, miss."

"Come here and show me."

He walked over from his chair toward the teacher and pulled back his lip to show her the pink plastic device, trying at the same time to again say, "Ib ibn't gub, mish," and not to hear the other children giggling.

And the plates, and braces, the various kinds of straightening devices, the retainers, those for use only at night, those with the apparatus that went around the head—he had one of those, with its framework covered in denim fabric, so he could look cool. Yes, cool Gabi, at the age of seven, with the plate in his mouth joined to a brace apparatus covered in denim fabric so that instead of resembling a torture device, it looked more like a lampshade that at any moment would connect to the ceiling, where the lighting element known as Gabi Kupper would dangle and thus illuminate the room with his teeth—crooked, yet glowing bright. Images etched into his mind for various reasons: the rides with Mom Gila, to see the orthodontist who came once a week to the neighboring kibbutz, or to Kiryat Shmona, or even to Haifa, when the treatment progressed further; the walks with Roni along the kibbutz pathways, to the pool, to the dining hall; Shimshon Cohen, who had returned to the kibbutz after serving ten years in jail for killing someone in a fight in the army, stopping the two of them, looking at Gabi, and saying with a smile, "What is that, a bird?"

Shimshon Cohen was the talk of the kibbutz ahead of his release from prison. Most of the children didn't remember him at all, most weren't even born or were very young when he was sent down, but everyone knew the story, and in the days leading up to his release, the anxiety level among the kibbutz children—and, to be fair, among the adults—rose to unprecedented heights. All went well, and everyone spoke of how peaceful and nice he appeared, and how good he looked, and everyone talked, too, about the VCR that someone had brought him from Lebanon and how no one on the kibbutz dared to say a word to him about it, despite the fact that some thought he should bring the device to the communal TV room. And what was this nonsense about him watching alone in his room, not to mention the sounds emanating from the device, Roni and his friend Tsiki had heard them, they dared to go listen outside the window at night, and they weren't the only ones to do so.

And here before them stood Shimshon Cohen, curly-haired, wearing a white undershirt, his shoulder tattooed decades before every kid on the block boasted one, his cheeks unshaved. His appearance clearly suited the mythology, the most terrifying fantasies, to a T. The man who, with his bare hands, had killed another for pissing him off. So what then do you say to such a man, a week after his release from prison, when you are eleven years old and he asks if your seven-year-old brother is a bird?

"Yes," Roni said to him.

Shimshon laughed. "Who are you?" he asked. And Roni, his voice trembling, answered him, and Shimshon Cohen thought for a moment and then said, "Ah, yes, the kids who . . . yes." And Roni nodded, his eyes welling up with tears, and eventually Shimshon Cohen ruffled his hair and said, "Look after the bird, okay?" And Roni nodded again.

From then on, every time the released convict saw Gabi, he'd break into a broad smile and affectionately pinch the boy's cheeks, and whereas Roni's heart would begin thumping again every time he heard the gruff voice or saw the large tattoo, Gabi would respond to him just like he did to the other grown-ups, one of the nice ones.

Beetles, and the pungent smell, and burning heat on the soles of bare feet, and the pool in the summer. Muddy boots and driving rain and radiators in the children's dormitory in the winter. Devices on teeth and the regional school and trips to the Golan Heights, and Mom Gila and Dad Yossi, and their room, and Shimshon Cohen. And Ofir's Yemenite father on bedtime duty, reading to the children from Russian history books in the belief that his voice had lullaby-like qualities, but it always frightened Gabi, and he'd run from his dormitory to Roni's in the middle of the night, and Roni, half asleep, would always let him in, and they'd fall asleep in each other's arms. And getting up once whoever is on bedtime duty leaves, certain that everyone is asleep, and making coffee, and frying popcorn in a pan on the gas burner until all the seeds danced about in the utensil and exploded into tiny, crunchy cauliflowers. Getting locked in the dining hall's cold-storage room and riding at night on tractors to the plum orchards and stealing tampons from the girls and putting them in glasses of water. Who could say they didn't have a happy childhood?

The Diving Board

R oni Kupper spent the long summer holiday between eighth and ninth grades working with the cattle—the kibbutz's elite unit. He secured the job, for which he had volunteered, of course, thanks to his well-tanned and developing muscles and his serious attitude, and also his basketball talents, which had led the kibbutz team to the top of the Upper Galilee youth league and turned him into a small, local star, and had particularly impressed Baruch Shani, the cattle unit's manager and a passionate hoops fan. It was the summer in which Orit, Roni's classmate and the prettiest girl he knew, lost her virginity, thanks kindly to the very same Baruch, who had completed his military service in an elite commando unit two years earlier. It happened at the kibbutz's summer camp, on the shores of Lake Kinneret, near the banana plantations. Roni Kupper was among only a handful of others who knew about the budding romance between the twenty-three-year-old man and the fourteen-year-old girl, because he had seen her slipping quietly into his sleeping bag in the dead of night.

Roni, for his part, remained a virgin throughout the summer. The girls were usually a step or two ahead of the boys when it came to that sort of thing, but working with the cattle, under Baruch's command, made a young man out of him nevertheless. His younger brother would listen in awe to the heroic stories he brought home—of mending fences, watering down the herd under the blistering sun, fertilizing and seeding, moving one of the cows that got stuck in the middle of the winding road that climbed north from Tiberias to the Galilee. He was up every day by 4:30 a.m., when he'd get a ride in one of the cattle unit's vehicles down to the kibbutz's grazing fields. At 7 a.m. everyone would go back up for breakfast in the dining hall, and then it would be out to the pastures again. Noon meant lunch back up in the dining hall; and at 3 p.m., Roni would go to sleep, except for the days on which he played basketball, when Baruch would release him early. The schoolkids, of course, worked in the various units of the kibbutz during the holidays, but sometimes, in very busy periods, like before slaughtering or when new calves would come in, Roni managed to convince Baruch to call for him during school time, too.

Gabi still had braces on his teeth that summer. He was in the final two years of his long-term orthodontic project, and the tough part was already behind him. Toward the end of the long holiday, with the summer camps over, adult supervision was at its most lax. The adults were hot, and they were busy, and all they wanted to do was to remain indoors with their new, recently installed air conditioners—how they had survived without them, none of them knew. The children swarmed outside without a care, taking full advantage of their final days of freedom, hanging out. Merciless months of accumulated heat had left teenage brains fried almost beyond repair. The tarred roads were scaldingly hot, and walking barefoot along the gray concrete pathways was out of the question, too. With large towels draped over their shoulders and blue-and-white-striped flip-flops on their feet, Gabi and his friends Yotam and Ofir headed for the pool, their slight, browned bodies in swimming trunks only. The heat stuck to their skin. Yotam focused his gaze on the path, trying to stamp on as many beetles as he possibly could. The beetles, too, were at the end of their summer, sluggish, spaced out, their intolerable stench already beyond the point of troubling anyone, let alone being noticed at all, except by random visitors to the kibbutz. Yotam counted . . . eleven, twelve since they left the dining hall . . . thirteen.

"You should have given that jerk a piece of your mind," Ofir said, and Gabi felt his face redden, the anger rising again.

"He'll get what's coming to him, don't you worry" was his only response.

"For sure," Ofir said, "he was asking for it."

"Fourteen and fifteen in one step," Yotam said.

"You should have smeared the cottage cheese all over his face," said Ofir.

Gabi thought, Why didn't you smear the cottage cheese in his face? But he didn't say a word. The large diving board, three meters of concrete, came into view, and there in the distance, someone was doing a back somersault off its edge.

"Who was that?" Gabi asked.

"I think it's that volunteer, what's-his-name," Ofir replied.

"Orit's boyfriend," said Yotam.

"He's not her boyfriend," Ofir responded.

"How do you know?"

"Wanna bet?"

"Fifteen," Yotam announced as they approached the pool.

"You've already said fifteen," Ofir noted.

"Really? So sixteen, then."

That boy, Eyal, was standing in front of the giant bowl of cottage cheese. What's up with him? Gabi wondered. Why isn't he moving along? Was he trying to decide how much to put on his plate or simply daydreaming? Whatever—he shouldn't be holding everyone up. What grade is he in?

Gabi was waiting for Eyal to move on from the cottage cheese, and then Ofir poked Gabi on his shoulder, a painful poke.

"What do you want from me?" Gabi barked, turning to Ofir.

"What's going on? Why aren't we moving? What's with the cottage cheese?"

Their faux wooden plastic trays were lined up one behind the other on the steel rails that ran alongside the food stations. The identical trays bore light blue plates containing scrambled eggs, which by then had cooled and hardened and acquired a bluish tint around the edges, one tomato and one cucumber, and a set of cutlery. All that remained to complete the perfect breakfast was the cottage cheese. "Get moving," Ofir urged. Gabi nudged his shoulder into the kid, Eyal, the second-grader.

"Hey, what's your problem, Jaws?" Eyal said, looking Gabi squarely in the eyes. When all was said and done, Ofir acted the big hero, and wondered why Gabi hadn't smeared the cottage cheese in the kid's face, but truthfully, when it happened, Ofir and Yotam had chuckled at first, and waited to see how Gabi would react. As if they weren't his friends, as if the cheeky little kid hadn't shot his mouth off at all three of them, three years his senior. They chuckled, and Gabi said, "What did you say?" The kid replied, "Jaws," without shifting his gaze, fearless. Gabi shoved him with his shoulder again, but not hard enough, because the kid managed to stand firm and say, "Hey, okay, just a moment, Jaws, I'm just taking some cottage cheese, show a little patience." And Ofir and Yotam laughed again, and Gabi, more taken aback than anything else, waited, his face reddening. Eyal, his confidence boosted by the laughter, added, "Anyway, the cottage cheese will just get stuck in your braces. You don't need that, do you?" And then he added another "Jaws," for good measure, and one or two of his friends nearby tried to stifle their laughter.

Eyal loaded his plate with cottage cheese, and Gabi followed suit, alongside the scrambled eggs, and went to sit down. Ofir and Yotam did the same and sat down next to him.

"Did you see that cheeky little shit?" Ofir said as he sat down, like he didn't know the answer, like he didn't know that everyone had seen, and heard, too, that cheeky little shit, like he and Yotam hadn't played a part in Gabi's humiliation.

"What grade is he in?" Gabi asked.

"He's going into second grade, he's with my sister."

"These kids, they don't have an ounce of respect," Yotam said, and Ofir responded, "You shouldn't have let it slide," and Yotam said, "Jaws," and giggled, and Ofir joined in, and Gabi, too, in the end, as if he had a choice. When the giggle died down, Yotam peeled off the wrapping from a wedge of cheese, took a bite, threw the silver foil into the wastebasket, and added, "I haven't heard that before." He upped a gear from a giggle to full-on laughter, and Ofir went along with him, and Gabi shifted down to a smile, which turned bitter at the edges. It wasn't, of course, the first time he had heard it. He had heard every name imaginable: Brace Face, Metal Mouth, Train Tracks, Magnet Mouth, Cheese Grater, Zipper Mouth, Tinsel Teeth, Tin Grin, and, yes, Jaws was certainly one of the popular ones. That said, he wasn't accustomed to hearing such impertinence from a second-grader. What had the world come to?

"Jeez, that jerk, how did he not get a good beating?" Ofir repeated.

Gabi's ears still burned red.

We reached the pool, entered through the black gate, and walked onto the lawn, passing by the lifeguard's shaded bench where Orit sat with her volunteer and Zahavi, the lifeguard, and with another volunteer who wore an earring in his right ear, which, Roni told me, meant he was a homo, but then they said he was the boyfriend of Dana the eleventh-grader, so I didn't get it. And we walked on, behind the diving boards—the small, springy one-meter board that the small children were jumping from, and the big three-meter concrete one that no one was on at the time—and rounded another corner of the pool until we came to our usual place, under one of the awnings on the lawn, and threw down our towels, and shed our flip-flops, and headed straight for the large diving board. From up there, you could see the back of the sports hall and hear the bouncing of the basketballs, boom-boom-boom, and the screeches of sports shoes changing direction on the PVC flooring, eek-eek-eek, perhaps it's Roni, no, Roni is with the cattle, someone else is doing the bouncing, the boom-boom is thumping in my head and I'm hot, the sun is beating down, I'm thirsty but haven't drunk, and there he is, there he is with all his friends—Eyal, who'll be going into second grade next week. I'm on the big diving board behind Yotam and Ofir (Yotam closed his tally at seventeen dead black beetles), I'm standing on the edge and looking at Eyal, his friends are looking at me and smiling, but I am looking directly at him, and he is no longer smiling. I don't look down at the green water but straight ahead, whoosh, an arc, an easy and simple dive into the water, and emerge from the

water with my hair dripping, Yotam and Ofir are lying down on their stom-
achs on the speckled tiles in the sunshine, but I want another go and head
straight back to the steps of the diving board, reach the top, and walk slowly
to the edge. He and his friends are now jumping off the small board nearby, I
pretend not to look, but check out the scene out of the corner of my eye, and see
him say something and look at me and laugh, and his friends laugh, too, he
probably said "Jaws" or something else ingenious, I wait, watching from the
corner of my eye, waiting for him to jump into the water, if you jump from
the big board to the left, you can land in the area of the small one, there's the
boom-boom-boom of the basketballs and the eek-eek-eek of the screeches, and
I take a few steps back to gain some momentum, and, again out of the corner
of my eye, I see Eyal take his jump, and while he is still in the air, I make my
dash and jump down on top of him, right on him, take that, brave man. I
hear nothing while I'm in the air, no boom and no eek. I hear only the air in
my ears and feel only the sun on my back, and the water that is still dripping
from my previous dive. I'm in the air, my body folded over, my legs stretched
forward, and I land on his head. I'll show you what Jaws is all about, ha-ha,
big hero, very funny. Jaws? Take that, take a bite from Jaws, here I come, you
worthless prick, enjoy second grade.

The Falcon

Gabi took to walking more and more on his own to the mountain that lay beyond the perimeter road, beyond the fence, beyond the plum orchards. That was many years before his nighttime hours of solitude on distant hilltops, before he knew that solitude was a supreme virtue, and the greatest of them all. Back then, there were other reasons. Roni had finally reached the age at which the four-year gap between them could no longer be bridged. Gone were the years in which Roni was the big brother who watched out for his smaller self, who took him into his bed, who drew strength from his all-powerful abilities in rela-tion to him—all-powerful in speech, all-powerful in comprehension, all-powerful in the strength of his muscles that allowed him to impose his will unchallenged. And thus Gabi remained a boy, with Roni, in his own eyes at least, already a small man, slowly but surely falling hopelessly and deeply in love for the first time. Yifat, from a neighboring kibbutz, was in the same year at the regional school, and he'd known her since first grade, but in tenth grade, they suddenly hooked up and stayed that way. Yifat's roommate on the kibbutz spent most her time with her soldier boyfriend in Haifa, so Roni and Yifat would go back to her room after school, and after dinner they'd go to the pub and drink beer and play darts with the volunteers, and they went to a Tislam concert in kibbutz Ayelet Hashahar, and to a HaGashash HaHiver show at Kfar Blum, and a Shlomo Artzi concert at Tzemach, and one by the Bootleg Beatles at the kibbutz pub, and to the home games of the Galil Elyon basketball team with its deadly sharpshooter, Brad Leaf (Roni, meanwhile, was no longer an active player, much to the dismay of Baruch Shani and his other fans on the kibbutz). Yifat visited their kibbutz two or three times, but Roni didn't introduce her to his little brother, or to Mom Gila and Dad Yossi.

They, too, were another reason for his frequent hikes to the mountain. Mom Gila and Dad Yossi's room wasn't a home. They still lived there, shared a bed, went together to the dining hall, but Gabi knew they hardly spoke to one another; and when they did speak, they usually yelled; and when they were done with the yelling, Dad Yossi would go out on his rounds, which, based on Gila's screams, included visits to the rooms of volunteers and other female members of his groundskeeping team; and Mom Gila would stay at home and drink and smoke.

In all likelihood, even if their parents' room had been awash with harmony and love, Roni would still have spent most of his time on the neighboring kibbutz, and Gabi would have made his treks to the mountain; because at the age at which Gabi and Roni were now, the phrase *adoptive parents* took on a different meaning. Following a childhood in which those terms, *real* versus *adoptive*, are meaningless because Mom is Mom and Dad is Dad—they're simply there—the time had come when the thing that cut and hurt the deepest, that screamed out loud and clear, was: You are not my parents! At those ages, even birth children alienate and distance themselves and are left astounded when confronted with the slimmest chance of there being a link between themselves and the pair of adults who purport to exercise authority over them, so it's easy for the adopted ones to justify to themselves their need to disengage—to the room of a neighboring kibbutznik, to a distant mountain, to wherever it may be.

Gabi, too, had had a girlfriend, Noga. He, too, had tasted his first kiss, behind the tractor at the Lag Ba-Omer bonfire, near the storehouse. A month later, however, Yotam asked if he minded becoming her boyfriend. He said okay, and never spoke to her again, which was a little weird because Yotam was his roommate, so he'd see her from time to time. Once, Yotam was showering while she waited for him on his bed and Gabi lay reading a book on his. The radio was tuned to Menachem Perry's *Hot Chocolate* show, which was playing a song by the Thompson Twins. Gabi knew she liked the song, yet still not a peep. Gabi didn't get all the fuss that was made out of girls, or how Roni could be so caught up and distant and alienated because of a girl. So Yotam was with Noga, and Ofir hung out with other friends, and the real truth of it was that Gabi liked being alone. To seclude himself. To slowly ascend the mountain. To see his shadow cast on the earth in the light of the sun or the moon or the streetlights. To think. To converse with himself. To discover and find things.

The mountain was where he found the falcon. The bird's leg was injured, bitten by a snake, perhaps? Or maybe a larger animal had hurt it in a fight? Gabi spotted the falcon lying on the ground, moving its head, lightly flapping its wings. He approached and stared at it, and stared at it some more, and didn't know what to do, so he sat down on a rock and watched. When he saw that the falcon could do him no harm, he moved a little closer, kneeled down alongside it, and reached out to touch its head with his finger. The falcon flinched at his initial touches but was incapable of really moving. Gabi could see its leg was broken, and after a few attempts, he stroked the falcon's head and carefully lifted it. The bird flapped its wings in panic and tried to resist, but Gabi reassured the animal—"Shhhhh . . . Shhhhh"—and made his way back down to the kibbutz.

Gabi installed the falcon in an unused room, a small storeroom, in the children's house, and then went with Yotam to the dining hall. When he told him about the bird, Yotam got excited and asked to see it. Gabi said he'd show him after they had eaten and asked Yotam how they could find out what to feed it. Yotam said there was an encyclopedia of birds in his parents' room, and if that didn't help them, he would ask his father.

"Okay," Gabi said. "Maybe you should get the encyclopedia so we can see exactly what a falcon looks like. I think it's a falcon, but how would I know? We always see them from afar, in the sky."

While descending the mountain with the falcon, Gabi thought at first that he wouldn't tell anyone about it, that it would be his secret, and that he'd send the falcon out on spying missions and use the bird to convey notes and messages to his allies. That evening, however, he felt fortunate to have told Yotam in particular. Not only was his father a bird enthusiast who owned an encyclopedia that confirmed the bird was indeed a falcon and offered other crucial information, Yotam also vaguely remembered his parents' storeroom containing a large cage that once served as home to two parrots, Pinches and Simches, which his father had raised when Yotam was a young child. Yotam located it, somewhat rusted and dirty, and not very big after all, but a perfectly suitable starter home, and brought it over to their room.

Apparently, they needed to find pigeons, the flesh of which, Yotam's father said while engrossed in Maccabi Tel Aviv's basketball game against Squib Cantù on TV, falcons loved to feed on. The encyclopedia offered other alternatives—millipedes, scorpions, lizards, snakes, frogs, bats, grasshoppers—but Yotam and Gabi believed pigeons to be tastier and easier to lay their hands on, and there were pigeons at the kibbutz, on the roofs and electricity poles. And thus, the two boys retrieved their biggest slingshots, of the many they had patiently fashioned from the electrical cable covered in colored plastic that was dumped on the kibbutz by workers from the electric or phone company, and went to the field adjacent to the children's dormitories. The pigeons perched at ease on the high-tension wires. The boys took up position, peeled a clementine, and began firing folded pieces of the rind—a fast-moving, accurate, and readily available projectile.

They kept missing. "This isn't working," Yotam said, putting a segment of the fruit in his mouth. Gabi agreed, and helped himself to two segments. They ate in silence, and the pigeons cooed above.

"What else does a falcon like to eat?" Yotam asked.

"Nothing as simple as pigeons."

"Let's try stones," Yotam suggested, and picked one up.

The stones missed, too. Dejected, they returned to the dormitory.

At dinner that evening, Gabi spotted Roni, who was on his own, and went over to sit down next to his brother.

"What's happening?" Roni asked.

"Everything's okay," Gabi responded bleakly.

"What do you mean, okay?"

Gabi told him about the pigeon-catching efforts.

"What do you need pigeons for?" Roni asked.

"We just need them," Gabi said.

Roni smelled of cigarettes, and his hair was overgrown. He thought for a moment and then said, "Okay." And then, after thinking a little more, he added, "I'll come by in the morning and we'll go find some pigeons."

Roni showed up with an air rifle that his classmate Tsiki liked to use for shooting at birds—and cats, if the rumors were true. Gabi and Yotam followed him off the kibbutz to an abandoned Muslim inn where dozens of pigeons were perched on the roof, flying off from time to time, returning, landing on the electricity wires. Roni approached as close as he could without attracting their attention, took his position with the butt of the rifle pressed into his shoulder, closed one eye, placed a finger on the trigger, and began firing. By the time the pigeons realized they were caught in a battle zone and flew off, two unlucky ones had fallen to the ground.

The two boys were unaware that serving the body of the pigeon as is to the falcon wasn't the way to go. The falcon looked at the fat corpse and then at them. Had it been blessed with shoulders, it surely would have shrugged them—and if with lips, an incredulous smile would surely have followed. The boys revisited Yotam's father, who explained that the meat itself was the answer. They looked at each other. That makes sense. Who wants to eat feathers? On the other hand, isn't it the falcon's job to get to the meat? After all, it doesn't have cooks to prepare its food in the wild. When they returned an hour or so later, the pigeon's status was unchanged. The falcon hadn't gone near it. Gabi picked up the pigeon, went into the field outside the children's dormitories, and, with the aid of the large penknife Roni received for his bar mitzvah and passed down to him, first cut off the dead bird's head, and then its legs, and finally the wings. He tried not to inhale through his nose, and also not to see what he was doing while cutting into the bird. Yotam stayed back. Gabi then sliced down the length of the pigeon's stomach, removed the internal organs, and did his best to cut away the breast meat and separate it from the small bones. "Bring a plate," he said, continuing to hack at it. He heard footsteps leaving and returning, and a plate landed by his side. He transferred the pieces of butchered flesh to it, rose from his crouch, lifted the plate high in front of him with bloody hands, entered the building, and headed to the small storeroom. He placed the plate in the cage and went to wash his hands. The plate was clean when he returned. If the falcon used his tongue the way a human would, he thought, the pinkish puddle of blood on the plate would be gone, too.

Roni was a rare sight at the kibbutz; and when Gabi caught up with him one day during recess, in the smokers' den behind the high school building, Roni said he wouldn't be coming to the kibbutz anytime soon, and that he wouldn't be able to bring the air rifle again, or ask for it for Gabi, who was too young to shoot it. So, after the falcon had polished off the meat of the first two doves, Yotam and Gabi were forced to upgrade their hunting tactics.

They first lured the pigeons to the window of the small storeroom in the children's dormitory with the help of seeds and various pigeon delicacies they'd read about in the encyclopedia of birds, and after a sufficient number had gathered there, they frightened them inside and shut the window. It was pretty crafty, but pretty simple, too; pigeons, they discovered, are really dumb. They left the birds in the dark room for several days to blind them. Then Gabi went into the room and caught one— easy enough, given that the room was small and the bird was blind—and carried it out to the yellowish thorny field alongside the children's dormitories. He gripped the head of the bird between the forefinger and middle finger of his right hand, lifted his arm high above his head, and with four or five lassolike twirls of his wrist to gain speed and momentum, he threw his hand forward, leaving the bird's head between his fingers, while the body, disengaged from the head, flew five or six meters forward from the impact and landed on the ground, the wings still fluttering.

Gabi looked down at the head still in his hand, kissed it lightly above the beak, and tossed it aside; then he walked over to the warm, shaking body and, using the penknife again, sliced it open and cut away the best pieces of flesh and served them to the falcon on a plate. All told, the entire process lasted mere minutes once he had mustered sufficient experience, cool-headedness, and skill. Yotam helped with laying the traps and chasing the pigeons into the room. The rest of the work was left to Gabi—the carrying, the swinging, the decapitating throw, the discarding of the head, handling the meat.

And thus things continued until the grade's head teacher got wind of the rumors spread by some of the girls who were grossed out by it all and turned up to confirm them. She told Yotam and Gabi that they weren't allowed to keep a falcon in their room. It was to be released into the wild right away, and they'd been wrong not to go to see the vet. Who knows what diseases it might be carrying, and where it actually came from, and the whole business of killing the pigeons had to end.

Following their scolding, Yotam told Gabi he was sick and tired of the falcon anyway. Gabi agreed; the head teacher's timing was good. They thought about releasing it on the mountain, but there was still a problem with the bird's leg, they thought, so they handed it over to someone at the kibbutz's livestock department. Then they returned to the small storeroom and issued pardons to the two blind pigeons that remained imprisoned there.

The Jaw

Not long after the falcon incident, Gabi was abducted while walking alone through the plum orchards toward the mountain. He didn't know who abducted him—a man, an adult, large-bodied, with hairy arms and big hands—that's what he had felt. Over the days that followed, he paid close attention to the arms of the kibbutz men. The abductor covered Gabi's eyes and mouth with his hands and embraced him powerfully for several minutes with a force that far outweighed Gabi's ability to resist—until Gabi got used to the idea and realized he'd be better off simply accepting his fate. The abductor then released his one hand and immediately tied a bandanna in its place—first over the mouth and then the eyes. He pulled Gabi's arms back and tied them behind his back—Gabi could hear the flexing and clicking of the plastic—with a zip tie.

His abductor pushed him forward, into a walk. Because he had hiked through the area during nights of total darkness on many an occasion, he knew he was being led between the plum trees to the far end of the orchard, where there was a gravel road. Then he was loaded onto an open vehicle of sorts, a pickup truck or a jeep (over the days that followed, he paid close attention not only to hairy arms but also to the kibbutz's fleet of vehicles, in an effort to find clues), and driven south, to the edge of the orchards and the cattle fields beyond.

Not a word was spoken throughout the ordeal, nor was he beaten. All the abductor did was fill his mouth with black beetles and, perhaps, various other bits of flesh, insects, dirt, stones, fluids that smelled like the urine of certain animals, soft solids whose sharp and concentrated taste indicated they were possibly animal feces of some kind—and force him to swallow. There were black beetles for certain, because at the hospital the following day, they found pieces of legs stuck between the braces that still graced Gabi's teeth; and there was probably a frog, too, because something resembling the leg of one turned up after they flushed out his stomach.

He couldn't recall how long he was there. He lost his sense of time and place at some point, between the vomiting and the refilling of his mouth. They didn't hit him, but they didn't exactly caress him, either. He didn't know how many of them there were. The large man who grabbed him must have been there, as well as a driver, because the man remained alongside him during the drive. There may have been others. He tried not to think about the things that were being stuffed into his mouth, and to block out the stench of their odor and their sour taste.

Years later he realized that the blindfold had been his savior—because, in general, being sickened by food wasn't related to its taste but rather to its appearance. Nevertheless, and despite his savior, he understood what they were doing, and he could feel ants crawling over his hands and on his tongue. He identified the beetles—a likely flashback of his tastebuds to his experience as an infant. The rest felt like things one doesn't usually put in one's mouth—too dry, too smooth, too abrasive—but he tried not to think, and ate and threw up, and ate and threw up. They left him, bound and blindfolded, outside the room of his adoptive parents.

The last time he'd been at Ziv Hospital was some two months previously, when his parents, teachers, and more or less the entire kibbutz insisted he visit Eyal. Dad Yossi went with him. They approached the bed and all Gabi could see were Eyal's eyes and the black rings around them. The remainder of his face was in a plaster cast, while the rest of his body lay hidden under a blanket in the small bed. The new school year had started a few weeks earlier, and Eyal had yet to begin second grade, but children and teachers from his class had been coming to his bedside to tutor him and fill him in on things. Eyal's eyes stared up at him, cold and dull. They looked nothing like the plucky and mischievous eyes that had looked at him alongside the cottage cheese, when he addressed Gabi as Jaws. The spectacle amused Gabi and filled him with a sense of satisfaction, but he tried not to let on. Eyal's mother and father—both named Yonah, an interesting coincidence in and of itself and the source of many a joke in the kibbutz newsletter and dining hall—were standing on the opposite side of the bed. Dad Yossi nudged his shoulder, and he looked at the parents and then at Eyal.

"I'm sorry," Gabi said, and then could no longer hold back—and cracked up laughing.

"Gabi!" Dad Yossi commanded, and Eyal turned away, and his parents shook their heads in disbelief.

After the abduction, everyone was sure it had been an act of vengeance by someone close to Eyal. There could be no other explanation for such revenge on Gabi. No one looked into it, of course; no one thought to report it to the police. God forbid! The abduction and abuse of a young boy might have been a criminal offense, but dirty laundry isn't aired in public; the kibbutz has a very efficient washing service. Gabi's cannonball onto Eyal remained an in-house matter, too. Roni would learn the identity of the abductor only many years later.

For Eyal, the pool incident had resulted in a broken jaw. He struggled to open his mouth for months afterward. Initially, he couldn't eat; his bottom teeth were bent out of shape and pushed against his molars. He spent years undergoing mouth and jaw surgery and never regained the ability to whistle or yawn. And as long as Gabi lived on the kibbutz, every time he ran into him on the concrete pathways or in the dining room or the basketball hall, Eyal's crooked face would remind him of what he had done and what he had suffered in return—the stares of the horrified kibbutz members, dozens of pairs of eyes glaring at him at every meal in the dining hall; the attitude of his friends, or those he once considered his friends. Even Yotam and Ofir gave him the silent treatment for a long time afterward, despite being the ones who had encouraged Gabi not to hold back. They fanned the flames of the humiliation. They were the ones who ignited the fire that propelled him with outstretched legs off the high concrete diving platform and into the face of the small wiseass boy.

They didn't come to see him at Ziv after the abduction. He wasn't sent any candy, and no one sat at his bedside to help him catch up on the schoolwork he missed. Aside from Mom Gila, Dad Yossi, Roni, and Roni's girlfriend, Yifat, he couldn't recall any other visitors. They gave him an enema, and his stomach was flushed twice. Blood and urine tests were done to ensure no traces remained of food poisoning, intestinal infections, or other harmful effects from the unidentifiable creatures he was fed. It turned out he had in fact contracted a disease called toxoplasmosis, but the doctor claimed it had been dormant in his body for quite a while, long before the abduction and assault. Was he in the habit of eating beetles and other creepy-crawlies before the assault? Gabi shook his head—not since the age of two. Had he been in contact with cats or had he touched their feces? No. Had he had any contact with pigeons or touched their secretions? Gabi stopped shaking his head.

He continued to vomit at frequent intervals in the days following his return from the hospital. And after his first attempt on Independence Day to enjoy a mouthful of barbecued steak, he was overcome by such

intense convulsions that he stopped eating meat—all meat, of any animal, finned, winged, or on legs, nauseated him. He could hardly bring
himself to eat salads and cheese and eggs. He wouldn't particularly enjoy
food at all for a number of years. This time, the memory of the beetles
would remain fresh in his mind for a long while. He was no longer the
two-year-old for whom sorrowful events would course through his veins
only to quickly fade from memory. He was twelve, and when the legs of
beetles get stuck in your braces, when the slimy skin of a frog is dragged
over your tongue, and when your lips feel the ooze of a deshelled snail,
you don't forget quite so fast.

Yonah, Eyal's father, had smooth arms. The arms of the fathers of
Eyal's friends were smooth, too. The volunteers' arms were smooth.
Baruch Shani had large, hairy arms; but Baruch was Roni's friend, and
Roni assured Gabi there was no way he would have done such a thing.
Baruch aside, the largest and hairiest arms on the kibbutz belonged to
Shimshon Cohen. And Shimshon Cohen, as everyone knew, had during
the course of his life done far more serious things than stuff a few beetles
into the mouth of a ten-year-old boy. Gabi, who had always considered
himself on friendly terms with Shimshon and didn't fear him like the
other kids did, tried to test his theory. He greeted him every time he saw
him, smiled at him, even tried to get up close to him to smell him, to
see if he could recognize the sweetness of an aftershave or a sour odor of
sweat. The findings were inconclusive. Shimshon remained kind toward
him, continued to smile and pinch his cheek, and never showed a hint
of hostility or anger. But Shimshon did work on the avocado team with
Yonah, Eyal's mother, so there was a possible link.

A few days after his discharge from the hospital, when Roni came to
visit him at the dormitory with Yifat, Gabi suddenly noticed just how
beautiful she was. He understood then what Roni saw in her and why he
spent every free moment of his time in her company. Her eyes, deep and
brown, smiled at him with concern. Her teeth flashed at Roni's jokes.
Her head nodded in agreement at his promises to exact revenge, to watch
Gabi's back "because no one messes with us." Semi-prone in bed, Gabi
watched as Roni's hand constantly reached out to touch hers, and how
he'd lean in from time to time to kiss her and be kissed in return.

When she wasn't at his side, Roni spoke about her. They spent almost every minute of the day together. They sat next to each other in class, and they made out during recess until they got in trouble with their teacher. They skipped classes to kiss in the hallway and played hooky to linger in their room on the kibbutz, in bed, to touch and talk for hours. She knew how to touch him better then he knew how to touch himself. She told him he was her first, and he thought either she was not telling the truth and did have experience, or she had a natural talent, because she touched him so perfectly, knew precisely the right intensity, the right softness, the right rhythm, when to speed up and when to slow down. Her endless kisses sent him to a heaven from which he never wanted to return, and the feel of her body on his, the weight, the scent, the long brown hair were intoxicating.

The first time they did it was when she turned sixteen. Some girls started younger—like the beautiful Orit with Baruch Shani on the shores of the Kinneret between eighth and ninth grades, and some of Yifat's friends from the kibbutz. But she had told him not before her sixteenth birthday, and he accepted it. He was pleased he'd be her first, and she his. Some of his friends had already been baptized by fire, but he wasn't in a hurry, he wasn't wanting for anything; and in the winter, it arrived.

Winter on the kibbutz. The rain came down hard on the roof of the Upper Galilee Regional Council's bus; the cold seeped in through the cracks between the windows and their frames. Yehiel, the driver, his gray *tembel* hat a permanent fixture on his head, whistled softly under his mustache. The large wipers on the front windshield moved from side to side with labored clumsiness, out of sync, each emitting a dull thud at the end of its respective arc—one after the other, one after the other. After passing through the hoof-and-mouth wheel disinfection dip at the entrance to the kibbutz, the bus continued onward and tried to get as close as possible to the children's dormitories, but there was still quite some distance to cover, and the children spilled through the door of the vehicle, hunched over and breaking into a fast walk, some of the girls with umbrellas, some of the boys covering their heads with their school bags, others displaying indifference, their heads held high between the drops. So intense was the grayness that it was almost dark out, and large brown puddles dotted the road and yards and open expanses, and a rich smell rose from the earth and blew in from the mountains and spiraled up from the agricultural fields that embraced the kibbutz.

Gabi and Yotam hurried to their room, and Ofir joined them. The rain brought them together—there'd be no walks to the mountain, no girlfriends, no swimming pool. Unrelenting rain has that quality, the ability to comfort and reunite. They paged through the magazines with pictures of totally naked girls that Roni had given his brother a few weeks ago, and also a small book with a torn cover by Shulamit Efroni that Roni had bought at Tel Aviv's Central Bus Station, which contained stories about totally naked girls. When he showed up with the shopping bag full of magazines and books, Roni told Gabi that it was about time he learned about such things, but Gabi knew that Roni simply wanted to clean out his room in case Yifat showed up; he didn't want to make a bad impression on her.

The three teens, each with a magazine or small book in hand, read with complete focus and in silence. The only sounds in the room came from the rain beating against the shutters, and the radiator, which emitted a metallic groan every few minutes, and the rustling of pages. Yotam lay sprawled on his bed. Gabi and Ofir shared Gabi's, each in his own corner. Yotam cleared his throat.

"What's all this wetness?" Ofir asked.

"What wetness?" Gabi responded, looking up at the ceiling. "Is there a leak?"

"No, in these stories," Ofir said, and pointed at the magazine in his hand. "When they say the woman is wet, what is she wet from?"

Yotam put down Shulamit Efroni's Central Bus Station book. "It means she is turned on, that she wants it," he said.

"Yes, okay, I got that. But what exactly is she wet from?"

Silence fell over the room, accentuating the driving rain and the heater's fatigue. The three youths scanned their literature—thinking.

"Is it sweat?" Ofir suggested—and then confirmed: "I think it's sweat."

"Sweat?" Gabi asked, and looked over at his friend, who sat cross-legged on the bed.

"No way," Yotam said. "It's blood."

"Blood?"

"Of course. It's inside the body, like you are going inside her body. There's blood inside there. And once a month, when she has her period, the blood comes out, and then she needs tampons. Surely you must know that."

"We know that, but . . ."

"And why do you think there's blood the first time you do it? Because all the blood is being held inside by the hymen, and then when it tears, the blood comes out."

Gabi and Ofir looked at Yotam, the images forming in their minds.

"Actually," Gabi said, "couldn't it be pee? I mean, because that's where the pee comes out of, right? So if you insert a finger or . . ."

"No, no way. It's not pee. The pee comes from somewhere else, and it only comes out when you need to pee. I'm telling you, it's blood," Yotam said.

Ofir wasn't convinced. "I don't know," he said. "It doesn't make sense to me. I still think it's sweat. It sounds like sweat to me."

"What makes it sound like sweat? Read it out loud, read it out loud," Yotam insisted.

Ofir retraced his place a few lines back and, somewhat uneasily, read out the part about the woman's wetness.

"To be honest," Gabi said, "it really does sound more like sweat than anything else."

"No," Yotam ruled, but now with a tinge of uncertainty in his voice.

"I'll ask Roni," said Gabi, the only one of the three who had an elder brother to ask.

They returned to their reading material.

It was Yifat's sixteenth birthday. She and Roni were in his room because she didn't want to do it in hers; she didn't want someone she knew to hear or see. He arranged for his roommate to sleep elsewhere that night, and after drinking a few beers, they were necking and laughing as usual. But they were nervous, too, and excited; tonight was the night. He took off his pants. He had on a pair of boxer shorts with a picture of an openmouthed alligator. Yifat laughed, touched the alligator, lifted her eyes to look into Roni's, and removed his underwear. Then he removed hers, and saw, and smelled, and inserted a finger—not like a lover but like a baby poking its finger into a cheesecake, and he felt the mysterious wetness and withdrew his finger, overexcited, crestfallen. He smiled embarrassedly, kissed her lips, gripped and tried to arouse himself, to no avail. So, just like that, as is, he tried to enter her, and managed to do so. The magazines from the Central Bus Station that he had cleared from his room were wrong, and so were the books by Dahn Ben-Amotz. They didn't fulfill their promises: she neither moaned nor screamed; he didn't say, "Yeah, baby"; he was still limp—not entirely, yet far from what he knew he was always able to achieve, easily, simply from reading the magazines and Dahn Ben-Amotz, simply by fantasizing, simply from looking at the female volunteers, simply from a deep kiss with Yifat. But this time, the nervousness, the beers, the pressure . . . He was in nevertheless, just so, back and forth, five or six times, for thirty seconds, perhaps, and breathing deeply, he climaxed, and giggled awkwardly again, and she smiled, somewhat confused—the first time.

The second time, a week later, was a little better. The third was already somewhat Dahn Ben-Amotz–worthy. Roni thought he was really good. A week after that, on the day they marked five months of being together, Yifat didn't show up at school but wrote him a letter to say she's confused, that she doesn't know; she's crazy about him and feels good with him, but she thinks she needs some alone time. She's going through a weird patch. The five months together were the most amazing in her life, but now she feels maybe they need to take a time-out?

Maybe? He held the lined sheet of paper on which the hurtful words were written. He didn't get it. He read again; his heart fluttered in his throat. He took the letter and went around back to the smoking den. Everyone had gone into class at the bell, and he sat there alone. He could smell the large pines and smoked cigarette butts. He read again, the drops smudged the words.

The violent pounding of his heart every time he saw her after that. Feeling sick to his stomach on being told she was seen hanging out with Ofer from the grade above them, from a different kibbutz. When he heard they were seen together in a tent at the Dead Sea. The long hours alone in his room, listening to Foreigner's "I Want to Know What Love Is" over and over again on the black cassette player, "Don't You Want Me?" by The Human League, and Matt Bianco's "More Than I Can Bear."

Tenth grade was colored with the optimistic and joyful pinks and whites of first love and arousing discovery; eleventh, with depressing and broken shades of the black and gray of intense disappointment and a heart shattered to pieces, a heart that would never fully heal, that would never let fall its barriers of suspicion and walls of defense, that would begin digging in to the bleeding wounds and asking the questions he didn't truly ask, not in earnest, despite the fact that Mom Gila and Dad Yossi didn't hide a thing. Because they, too, never really spoke of what happened back then, a little over a decade ago, when Roni was almost five and Gabi a year-old infant who still couldn't walk.

The Butterflies

Uncle Yaron moved up to the Golan Heights soon after the Six-Day War, which was indeed relatively short but nevertheless went on long enough to claim his right eye and the upper part of his right ear, from the shrapnel of an IDF grenade accidentally dropped by one of his fellow paratroopers in the battle at Burj Babil. He had just enough time to take two steps back and dive through the air like a goalkeeper facing a penalty kick—a wild guess, left or right; statistically, little chance of defense. The person or thing he landed on was hidden in the darkness. The scream came from God knows where . . . he didn't hear the bang. He woke in an improvised medical tent with a giant bandage around his head. A few months later, following his eventual discharge from the hospitals and the army, boasting a Moshe Dayan–like eye patch and feeling revitalized and ready to take on life anew, he said to his younger brother, Asher, and anyone else willing to listen: "She took my eye and ear; now it's time she gave me something in return." He was referring to the Golan Heights. During its first years on earth, the kibbutz that welcomed him with open arms was relocated: heavy Syrian shelling, another big war, all on top of the regular hardships of a young community in a young country. When Yaron invited his brother and sister-in-law and two young nephews for their first visit to his Golan Heights, Uncle Yaron and his fellow kibbutzniks were still occupying the abandoned Syrian military post where they had initially taken up residence.

In the dead of night, after finally getting Roni to sleep, Ricki expressed her concerns to Asher—with the Syrians shelling and firing and abducting, a trip now to the Golan Heights wasn't safe, and certainly not with two small children, one of them an infant. "The wars are over," Asher said. "I think by now the Syrians have lost all hope of retaking the land."

"But they're still shelling," she responded.

"Barely," her husband said. "When was the last time they got close to Yaron's kibbutz?"

"Wasn't it just a month ago?" she asked.

"Longer, I think. Anyway, in all this time, no one's been injured. It's merely a scare tactic. A barking dog doesn't bite. They have terrible weapons. They couldn't hit a thing."

"Other than that poor woman," Ricki said.

"Other than that poor woman," Asher agreed.

Gabi let out a small whimper. The parents sat up and went quiet. When they resumed their conversation, they spoke in a whisper.

"Anyway," Asher said, "I promised my brother I'd come. The guy lost half his face in the battle for that place, and has chosen to make a home for himself there. That's pretty admirable."

"I do admire him," Ricki said, although she didn't particularly admire his insistence on settling in a godforsaken place that was under continuous bombardment, and she didn't think that Asher, despite his love for his brother, admired that, either. "But can't we postpone the visit a little?"

"No," Asher said.

On arriving at Uncle Yaron's kibbutz, Ricki's arguments and concerns were forgotten. The children went crazy for the place: the open expanses, the freedom to play outdoors and run wildly in the yard or park, the air, the landscape, the animals that strolled among the houses—a donkey, a horse, a dog, several chickens, a cow. They told Uncle Yaron that he appeared to be in his natural habitat, at ease and content, and the children loved him and his eye patch when he played pirates with them (Roni played, Gabi smiled). Ricki even went so far as to tell Asher and Yaron one evening that she wouldn't be opposed to raising her kids on a kibbutz in the north. Perhaps not on the Golan Heights—which, despite remaining completely free of artillery shelling for the five days they were there, was still considered a dangerous and under-fire area, and the kibbutzim and other Jewish communities established there after the war remained isolated and remote, with very rudimentary living conditions. But maybe, Ricki said, on an older, more established kibbutz in the Galilee. Uncle Yaron would remember that line all too well in years to come.

So much fun was had that the Kuppers put off their return to Rehovot until the very last minute. Asher and Ricki had to work that Sunday. Initially, the plan was to return home from the trip on the Saturday, without rushing, perhaps with a stop along the way at Lake Kinneret, whatever—a stress-free drive. But as the last few days of freedom always seemed to have it, Saturday came around way too quickly, and the children were having such fun with their uncle the pirate on the former Syrian army base turned fledgling kibbutz. So Uncle Yaron asked, and Asher and Ricki consented, and Roni cheered. Why lose out on one more whole day of fun if work's only tomorrow? What's the rush to get into the car when it's hot and sweaty and a nuisance, and there's more traffic on the roads? Why, when they're wide awake, place the children into motionless and emotionless upright sitting positions that will require continuous creativity, numerous breaks, and endless patience? After all, stopping at Lake Kinneret, or anywhere else, for that matter, isn't really necessary. They'll leave Saturday evening. The children will sleep in the back, the drive will go by quickly, the parents will be able to talk a little. And when they arrive home in the small hours of the morning, they'll carry the children to bed, and they'll wake Sunday morning refreshed and relaxed after a wonderful vacation. That's a much better plan for sure, agreed Asher and Ricki, with the enthusiastic support of Uncle Yaron and the kids.

Things didn't work out as planned.

* * *

Roni loved the Golan Heights—close to the kibbutz, yet different and far enough from Yifat; greener and wetter and more mountainous than the Negev. Not that anyone asked his opinion, but he ended up serving most of his time in the military in the north: in the vicinity of Acre, around Safed, Eliakim. And when he got to the Golan every once in a while, he'd always remember to visit Uncle Yaron at the kibbutz, which had relocated two or three times since that family visit—itself erased from Roni's memory entirely—and was by then a long-standing and well-established community.

Every year, an IDF colonel from Roni and Gabi's kibbutz would pass on to the kibbutz's conscripts-to-be confidential information regarding their initial psychotechnic rankings and security clearance checks, along with their options in the army, so that they'd show up prepared. Baruch Shani tried to arrange for Roni to be selected for the elite Sayeret Matkal unit. He made it through the trial period and felt it had gone well, but apparently they weren't happy about something in the personal interview stage—perhaps because he was an orphan, or he had mentioned Yifat one too many times, or they had heard stories about his younger brother. He was better prepared for the Golani Brigade commando unit. Baruch Shani put in a good word for him there, too, and this time, Roni backed it up with a respectable showing, supreme motivation, and no superfluous details about his knee injuries from his basketball years or his broken heart or his brother who would sometimes run into trouble. He was accepted for two weeks of pre-basic training at Camp Peles, with the second week serving as an extremely rigorous trial period for the commando unit, just like the one for Sayeret Matkal.

All that occupied his mind throughout that week was that he just had to get through it, make it to the finish. If he made it to the end, he'd be happy, that would suffice—and the end came. After a week at Camp Shraga, he was told he had made it into the commando unit. Then came basic training in Eliakim, with the cows and the hills, and the remote geographical points, and "the orchards"—endless drills—and the constant assurances that until now, it was all child's play, with the real hard work only just beginning.

He started out as a radio operator on treks and infantry drills—

weeks in the field and learning how to prepare your own food and carry heavy loads and navigate all by yourself, or with one other comrade at best; and more exercises and orders and commanders riding your ass; and on the rare occasion, a little peace and quiet. A year and four months later, Camp Eliakim and Area 100 and the training course were behind him, and his chest bore the pin of the Flying Tiger, or, as he liked to call it, the laughing cat—sixteen months of toil, of broken sleep, of a back and legs under crippling strain, of yelling and humiliation, all for a pin.

Gabi was in the basketball hall with Yotam. He shot a ball at the basket, tried another shot, then another. Off he went to collect the ball, under the basket, or wherever it had ended up after rebounding off the court floor or the rim. He gripped the brownish-orange ball, smooth from overuse, dribbled it as he moved away from the basket, turned, aimed, bent a knee, left hand under the ball, right hand lightly keeping it balanced, whoosh. The ball left his hand in an arc, clang. It struck the outer rim of the basket. Yotam by now was a head taller than Gabi, and strong; he played for the youth team. Both boys shot at the same basket; bigger guys were playing on the other side of the court, three-on-three. Boom-boom-boom bounced the balls, and eek-eek-eek screeched the shoes. He and Yotam played in absolute silence, simply shooting baskets. Gabi had woken that morning at 4:30 and had gone out to work in the fields. He had watched as the dawn slowly broke, as the chilled air evaporated, as the darkness gradually thinned, the smell of the tomatoes enveloping him, touching him, making him itch. It was only after being assigned to that particular branch of the kibbutz's farming enterprise that he realized just how much he hated the tomatoes, particularly when the sun came up and the heat moved in, and he was bending over and picking another one and then another one, and there was no end to them in sight. They gave off a pungent odor, and some were squished, and their stems were hairy and uninviting. He wasn't particularly fond of the other kibbutz members who worked with him, either, or the volunteers, or the overseer, an immigrant from Australia who treated Gabi somewhat like a mentally retarded child.

The ball from the big boys' game on the other side bounced into Yotam and Gabi's half of the court. It happened all the time—for the most part, you'd throw the ball over to the other side and get on with your own thing, no big deal. But if you were in the middle of doing something, you'd finish what you had started and then return it, or someone from the side that lost it would go retrieve it.

The ball crossed sides, bounced, and rolled across the floor, ending up at Gabi's feet just as he was aiming to shoot. Alex from the groundskeeping department who worked with Dad Yossi came over to get it. So as not to be a distraction, however, he stood to the side as Gabi took aim and waited for him to complete his shot. Gabi sensed him there, at his back. He didn't like being watched, and he didn't like Alex. He dribbled the ball once more and took aim again. By now, the other players from the game on the other side who were waiting for their ball were all looking over to see what was keeping Alex, and watched as Gabi was getting ready to shoot. Gabi looked back to see the five of them, sweating and panting, looking at him and waiting for him to shoot. He bounced the ball one more time and again took aim, feeling all the sets of eyes piercing his back and shoulders. Yotam, too, had stopped his bouncing. The hall had fallen quiet, everyone waiting for Gabi to take his shot. He bounced the ball again, and then held it, left hand underneath, right hand on the side, hands, reeking of tomatoes, close to the nose, elbow bent, knee bent, one eye closed. But just as he was about to release the ball, Alex let out a small and pressing "Well . . ." that threw off his shot completely, and the ball left his hands in a pathetic arc, a muffed shot, too weak, too close. The ball rose and fell some distance from the ring, and Alex chuckled and ran to collect his ball. "That's what we were waiting for?" came from someone, someone else laughed, and two of them applauded. Gabi looked at Yotam, who was also smiling, and who then took his shot—swish, it dropped cleanly through the basket.

Gabi Kupper exited the gym through the back door, which overlooked the pool. He could hear two balls bouncing out of sync behind him, one Yotam's; the other, the big boys', boom-boom-boom, eek-eek-eek. He jumped the meter or so gap to the tarmac and began walking, oblivious of where he was going. The smell of the freshly cut and wet grass throbbed in his nostrils and irritated his eyes. He dug in his pocket—a crumpled Noblesse cigarette someone had given him, a few bits of gravel, a Twist candy bar wrapper, dirty grass, a box of matches, a small pocketknife key ring. He sat down on a bench and lit the Noblesse, feeling the sharp smoke swirling in his head, tearing into his chest. He dragged on the cigarette again, his body covered in sweat—playing basketball in jeans is no fun. Laying down the cigarette for a moment, he took off his shirt and wiped his brow, armpits, and smooth chest, picked up the Noblese again, another puff, then another—sharp, swirling, nauseating. The booms and eeks from the hall were now distant and weak. It was late and dark already, and he needed to take a shit. He'd take a shit on Alex, or cut the asshole's throat with a knife. He of all people had to come over to get the ball. He'd stood there and humiliated Gabi, like always, snickering and taunting at every opportunity.

Gabi stood and began walking again, sure now of his direction, with a sense of urgency, bare-chested. He passed by the swimming pool and cultural center, headed down in the direction of his and the younger children's dormitories, and reached the animal pens. The animals were quiet, asleep. But they were of no concern to him anyway. His thoughts were on the garden. Dad Yossi had spoken about it—the garden near the livestock, with its special flowers. What did he say they were? Orchids, irises, rare and beautiful flowers—

I remember now, they planted a garden there—"for the pride of the country," that's what Dad Yossi said. He called it the groundskeeping department's baby. He might have said Alex's baby, I'm not sure. Alex the asshole, all those assholes and their stares, their smiles of pity, their shaking heads and tutting tongues and condescending goading. The animals begin to stir when they hear my shoes trampling the plants, kicking them left and right. Take that, you rare and precious plants; take that, baby of the groundskeeping department; take that, Alex; my small pocketknife in hand, slicing leaves, cutting flowers, chopping branches, cutting signs; small feet, rabbits, perhaps, run to and fro; a calf stares at me with calf eyes until I threaten it with my knife, but it doesn't budge; peacocks spread their tails. But I don't care about the animals, I'm fixed on the garden. And when I'm done kicking and slicing and trampling and jumping, my stomach aches, that sweet pressure. The sickening smell of the tomatoes oozes from the pores of my skin, rises from my sweat; I hate that smell. The animals are insignificant—but there's the greenhouse and butterflies. Didn't Yossi say something about them, too? My knife, the plastic sheeting of the greenhouse, an X; there we go. I'll write "Baby!" here; maybe someone will be able to read it. I keep cutting, this pocketknife's too small, I should have brought a machete to destroy this garden. What's in here? Butterflies? Caterpillars? Plants? Dozens of species of butterflies, chrysalises, silkworms that feed on mulberry leaves. This is the place, this is the spot, I knew I'd find it, in the middle of the butterfly greenhouse, on top of the shredded plastic and broken wooden installations they built in the carpentry workshop. This is where I'll squat and drop a big steamy dump. And those avocado leaves, or whatever they are, will be great for wiping my ass, and the wet shirt, too.

A dulled sensitivity, a short-circuit in the brain; a rise in testosterone levels, a fall in serotonin levels; temporal lobe disturbances; reduced activity in the prefrontal cortex—all attempts to offer biological causes for social behavior. Do they even know what they're talking about? Needless to say, the story never left the confines of the kibbutz, God forbid. No efforts were made to seek professional assistance. What's the good in that? The father of one of the kibbutz members is a psychologist. There are libraries with books to page through. There are close friends to call and question "in general terms, about behavioral problems among youth." Yossi, for his part, read something in a book about psychopathy and ruled it apt—high level of intelligence, low self-control, an exaggerated sense of self-worth, and little expression of remorse or regret. He believed he saw all of those symptoms in Gabi—or Gabi in them—certainly insofar as little show of remorse or regret was concerned, and certainly the high level of intelligence.

Roni was called home from his army base the following day. Who else could talk with Gabi after such a direct assault on the fruits of Dad Yossi's labors, on the baby of the groundskeeping team? "He took a dump," he told Roni on the telephone. "He took a dump in the middle of the butterfly greenhouse. We opened it just this week. Roni, what kind of an animal does such a thing? And, to top it all, on the eve of our trip to Europe?"

Every day now for years, Mom Gila had puffed and puffed away at her Broadway 100s waiting for her and Yossi's first trip abroad, classical Europe, a *Let's Go*–organized tour, defined, too, as their reconciliation holiday, a last-ditch effort to save the floundering partnership. They had waited their turn patiently for several years, had worked like dogs, had ground their fingers to the bone, had raised the two musketeers until they were old enough—Hooray for Rome! Hey there, Paris! "What do we do? Cancel?" Dad Yossi asked her. And she snorted smoke and replied, "As far as I'm concerned, the entire kibbutz could go up in flames; they could torch it to the ground; tonight, I'm in Vienna."

Shortly after the parents left for the airport with another kibbutz member who was driving to Tel Aviv, Roni showed up in uniform— complete with the paratrooper wings and brown beret and laughing-cat pin of the commando unit and the shouldered weapon and the smell of oil and manly sweat. He entered the room and sat down as he was on Yotam's bed, and looked at his brother, who was lying on his back in jeans and shirtless, the very same outfit he had worn at the time of "the incident" the night before, looking up at the ceiling and throwing a plastic ball in the air—and catching, and throwing, and catching.

"Hi," Roni said.

Gabi turned his head, hugging the plastic ball to his chest. "Did you get wings?" he asked.

Roni looked down at his chest. "Yes. The unit pin. We completed the training course."

"Congratulations."

"Thanks. What happened?"

"I don't feel like talking about it."

"But why do that to Dad Yossi? What did he do to you?"

"I don't feel like talking about it. He didn't do a thing. It has nothing to do with him."

"What did they say to you?"

Gabi pulled a face. "Nothing. A short-circuit in the brain. How should I know?"

"Has anyone spoken to you about it?"

"What for? Roni, I don't feel like talking about it."

Roni stood up and unbuttoned his shirt. "Do you have a towel? I'm dying for a shower; I've been hitching rides since the morning."

"Yotam has lots in his closet. Take one from him."

When Roni emerged from the bathroom, refreshed and wearing a green T-shirt with a picture of a Heineken bottle in the center, the plastic ball lay on the bed between the crumpled sheets, but Gabi was gone. Roni's uniform, with the unit's badge and the paratrooper wings and the shiny new commando pin, was no longer there either.

The Cow

They descended on him like flies. He had barely appeared on the road, had barely stuck out his thumb, and already they were pulling over—white ones, red ones, silver ones, big ones and small ones, fancy ones and sputtering ones, military vehicles and rentals. Within two minutes of standing at the kibbutz's hitchhiking station on the main road, he was in a Renault 4 and on the way to Tiberias with a young, bearded man wearing a skullcap—and then a Simca, and then a Subaru, and then a military Peugeot, and a Tnuva dairy truck when night fell, and in the small hours of the morning, a large, comfortable, fast, quiet car that allowed him to doze off.

They all asked questions. They were all lonely and bored, stuck in their cars and journeys, eyes on the road and dying for someone to talk to. "When did you complete the course, why aren't you carrying a weapon, the MPs are going to get you for that hair, does everyone in the commando unit wear Palladium boots? What's up, have you lost your voice? Where is your unit holding the line?" Gabi didn't respond. He didn't understand half the questions. Holding a line? As hard as he tried to comprehend the question, he wasn't able to crack it. Holding a line? The question short-circuited his brain. So he chose not to answer. He said he was very tired. He tried to nap. He said he wasn't at liberty to talk about it. And they were disappointed, disgruntled. "Honestly, you're the first Golani soldier I've met who plays at being in intelligence." They wanted to talk; that's why they had given him a ride—to brighten their own journeys. Only one had said to him just as he was getting in, "You look like a kid, that uniform looks funny on you. Did you steal it from someone?" And Gabi, with one leg through the door, his back half bent, still in the process of getting in, looked at her, stopped, flashed half a smile, and didn't know what to say, and then she broke into a loud, toothy laugh and beckoned him in. "Come, come," she said. "Don't mind me. Where do you need to go?"

Another question to which he hadn't offered an answer—because he didn't have one. He'd respond with "Where are you going?" And when the answer came, he'd say, "Great, that'll suit me just fine, I'll go on from there." And then, almost always, they'd ask, "Go on to where?" or "Where do you need to eventually get to?" And he'd say, "Never mind," or "Afula is perfect," or "Atlit is on my way." And then he was in, inside their world, their scent, their things—the unsightly objects hanging from the mirrors, the piles of clothing, newspapers, bottles on the backseat. The small and bigger children, who always fixed him with the most intelligent stares, the most knowing of the truth about him—an impostor, not a soldier—but didn't say a word, being, after all, on the same team. The radio, which some insisted on singing along to. Hot air from a fan, which didn't fan anything and only added to the heat coming in through rickety windows. He went on and on, in and out, sleeping and waking, smiling and humming.

Early in the morning, behind a hitchhiking station in Kiryat Ata, he found a faucet, removed his Palladium boots and olive-green shirt and washed his feet and face and hands, humming the Kaveret song he had heard on his last ride, the one about the boy-gone-wrong who learns his lesson only after falling.

The Gam-zu-Le-tova family—a religious family whose bountiful members appeared to occupy every corner of the car, a Susita Rom Carmel, that it was impossible to tell why they had stopped for him, demanding, insisting, "Come, fellow Jew, come, we'll make room, God willing Malka, David, move over!"—took him to the first real stop on his journey.

The Susita's signal lights dangled from their wires down the side of the car. The brown plastic upholstery on the seats provided little protection from the hard springs pressing sharply into his butt. The engine thundered and rattled, and the steering wheel swung freely in the hands of the family patriarch. The hot wind shook the half-open windows and blew in dust particles. A sharp odor of urine rose from at least one diaper, filling the interior of the vehicle.

No one spoke for the first few minutes. Gabi kept an apprehensive eye on the father's hands on the wheel and the Susita's snakelike progress on the road. The children, Malka, David, and two others, of various ages, remained silent—perhaps in awe, out of fear for the individual taken for a soldier who, in such a brief instant, had stepped into their lives. The parents were surely delighting in the silence and didn't want to break it, before the mother rummaged in a packet, extracted something wrapped in aluminum foil, and offered it to Gabi. "Sandwich?" she asked. "You look hungry." And that was the signal for the resumption of the symphony— David wanted one, too, Malka asked for pretzels, the two others began shouting at each other and pulling each other's hair, and the father, who realized by then that there'd be no more delighting in the silence for him, asked, "Where do you need to go, my good man?"

The foil-wrapped sandwich didn't look inviting, but by then, Gabi wasn't very picky; all he had eaten since the night before were two wine gums offered to him by the student from Haifa. He peeled back the foil and began devouring without even asking what was in the sandwich, but he tasted challah bread, he tasted white cheese, he tasted pickles and tomatoes, it was divine—needless to say, he didn't voice that sentiment, but the word went through his mind, and after three mouthfuls to quash his hunger, he replied, "Where are you going?"

"To Ofra," the father said.

Gabi wasn't sure he had heard Mr. Gam-zu-Le-tova's response correctly over the canopy of noise of the family and the car.

"Where?" he asked again.

"To Ofra" came the answer once more.

And this time, he heard it and nodded—despite never having heard of the place.

"Great. It's on my way."

The father exchanged glances with Gabi in the rearview mirror. He wasn't familiar with all the IDF units, all its secret bases, or all the points at which it deployed its forces. But one thing he knew for sure: Ofra wasn't on the way to anywhere. He smiled at the soldier, who now appeared to be somewhat young, somewhat tired, somewhat on edge. "With pleasure, my good man," he said.

Late in the evening, packed into the Fiat 127, Asher and Ricki and Roni and Gabi Kupper began their journey south from the darkness of the Golan Heights. Uncle Yaron carried Roni to the car, and Asher bore little Gabi, both asleep, two soft-skinned and innocent infants in the backseat. Ricki embraced Uncle Yaron.

"We had a wonderful time, Yaron, thanks so much for the vacation," she whispered in his ear, and then added for even sweeter measure, "Just so you know, I was pretty nervous before coming here, I had no idea what to expect from the place, I was afraid of the shelling. But I had it all wrong. We'll come again the first chance we get." Uncle Yaron hugged her and kissed her on the cheek, her words music to his ears, and then he embraced his brother, who said, "It was really great, we'll be back soon."

Yaron laughed and said, "That's just what your wife whispered in my ear. Drive carefully!"

They did: they consumed a great quantity of coffee before setting out, remained alert, chatted. Asher told Ricki she could sleep if she wanted, but she declined. They spoke about Yaron, about his friends and neighbors they had met over the past few days, about the kibbutz, and about the children. Ricki even managed to tell Asher that she had spoken with sincerity in saying she'd be prepared to raise the boys on a kibbutz—in the Galilee, perhaps. If indeed she was serious about it, Asher said, he'd make a few calls; he had friends in various places, as did Yaron. Ricki said she was serious, and then they heard the whistling of the artillery shell, and then she said, "Oh my God." They saw something light up and flash through the sky, briefly illuminating their surroundings like in a movie, and then darkness, and then a huge explosion that lightly shook the Fiat.

"It's over, that's it," Asher said a few seconds later. Ricki turned to see her two angels unfazed, lost in their dreams.

"They didn't even notice," she said to Asher, and he, his heart pounding fast, reiterated, "That's it, it's over."

"How do you know it's over?"

She was surprisingly calm, although they both knew that her reaction came as no real surprise, that that's how things worked between them. She had been afraid of the unknown, of the danger that lurked, she had been concerned about the artillery shells before actually going to the places where they could possibly fall, as improbable as that may have been. He had been the very opposite and had waved the low-probability card, saying that if something was going to happen, it would, I'm not going to start changing my life now simply because a shell might fall somewhere. But the moment they were caught up in a real scenario, the moment the shell flew through the sky and exploded nearby, she turned matter-of-fact and practical, reacted coolly and with nerves of steel, whereas Asher turned to jelly, quivered like a coward, freaked out, and said things like "I don't know, but I believe so."

"Based on what?" Ricki asked, but he didn't respond. He looked at her, and she at him, half smiling, her lips pulled back slightly, her eyes expressing a measure of disbelief, as if to challenge him, as if to say, You're merely trying to calm yourself down, you have no idea if another shell will fall or not. She turned her eyes back to the road, perhaps sensing something, an unwanted presence, and he followed suit, perhaps noticing in that instant the glimmer of panic in her eyes, perhaps instinctively slamming his foot down onto the brake pedal before even seeing the cow—large and lost in the middle of the road, having apparently heard the shell and fled for its life, its inquisitive color-blind eyes staring down the pair of lights that approached it, rooted to the spot and unable to process the situation, the noise of the shell still echoing in its ears, the two boys still fast asleep on the backseat, the two parents, widemouthed in shock, hurtling into the large beast that stood in their way.

The cow survived the collision but was later put down, having suffered multiple fractures to its rib cage. The parents were killed on the spot when the engine crumpled in on them. And Asher was right—it was a lone shell, the only one fired that night, launched probably in error, without any precise purpose or direction, a calibration exercise, perhaps, or maybe even simply to intimidate.

* * *

The Gam-zu-Le-tova family laid it all on for Gabi. The father of the family—blue-eyed, solidly built, with a large bald spot under his skullcap—took him out for a short morning walk after he spent the night at their home, and said to him, "Listen, I don't know who you are or what you are, but the eye sees and the ear hears, and all your deeds are inscribed in the book. I don't think you're a soldier, and I don't think you know where you want to go, and I don't know who or what you are running from. But you have nothing to fear here. As we say, 'Though I walk through the valley of the shadow of death, I will fear no evil, for Thou art with me.'" Gabi didn't understand. What shadow of death? What's that eye and ear thing all about?

"We welcome any Jew with open arms," the man continued. "You can stay here as long as you like, we'll give you food and a bed. If you want to stay longer, we may be able to set you up in one of the trailers for singles. We always need help with guarding, construction, gardening work. Just tell me one thing—are you in trouble with the law or something?"

Gabi didn't like the speech he was being subjected to, but couldn't really fathom more favorable circumstances—a distant and remote location, someone who was willing to host him despite knowing he was an impostor. But something about the man bothered him. And something about the place annoyed him. Perhaps the man reminded him too much of the adults on the kibbutz—meddlesome, holier-than-thou, with that air of arrogance and absolute self-assurance of those who believe they know best and are amused by the efforts of others to question them. He shook his head. No, he wasn't in trouble with the law.

He joined the family for another dinner. He went on to spend two more nights on a mattress on the floor in the children's room, oblivious to their crying at night and the pitter-patter of their feet in the morning and their banging on the table and the crashing to the floor of their toys; he didn't even notice David's inquisitive efforts to pet his head and pry open one of his eyelids. He slept undisturbed almost until noon, when he opened his eyes to a quiet and empty home, raided the refrigerator and bread box, took a long shower, dressed again in the IDF uniform and Palladium boots, dug around in the pockets of the army pants, found a

Noblesse, crumpled and bent but not broken, smoothed it out between his fingers, pulled out a box of matches, lit the cigarette, looked around room, and thought.

Finishing off the cigarette, he threw the butt into the remains of a cup of coffee in the kitchen sink and listened to it fizzle to its death. Then he went into the parents' room, rummaged through the drawers, found 600 shekels tucked away in a prayer book, looked around, pocketed the money, placed a bag on his shoulder, and headed out in the direction of the gate to the settlement. He hated the place—but, as the saying goes, he had made the best of it.

The Orienteering

Roni was called in for a chat ahead of solo-orienteering week. They wanted to make things easier for him, they expressed understanding for his unique family situation. But they laid it out straight for him nevertheless. You have your adoptive parents, who've already returned from abroad. There's the kibbutz. An entire network has taken charge and is concerned and searching. You can't be responsible for everything. You can't wander the country high and low and expect to find one specific individual in a population of four million—particularly someone who is obviously in hiding and doesn't want to be found. What are the chances? You have commitments, they said. Be thankful you aren't in a regular unit, which wouldn't afford you these special leaves of absence. So, come on, Roni, get ahold of yourself. We have missions and duties to carry out, training and exercises. We have a week of solo orienteering. Roni nodded. Yes, yes, I know. I'm sorry for not being myself of late, it's just the whole story, you know. Yes, we know, they said, but . . .

Yes, Roni replied. He'd get his act together, he'd complete the orienteering drill in first place, he'd show everyone the real Roni Kupper. He thought about all the time wasted, all the traveling, without even getting close to a single lead. He didn't have a clue about where to go, where to try. He had thought initially about contacting the police, but in a call from abroad, Dad Yossi told him in no uncertain terms to refrain from speaking with them, so he carried on wandering around with a photograph of his brother, along with a basic description, although the Golani uniform and pin were probably discarded by then. And while he knew his chances were slim, he needed those hours on the road—to feel remorse, to cry, to think about the mistakes he had made, about the years spent distancing himself, about Yifat, the fucking bitch.

Dad Yossi and Mom Gila didn't move up their scheduled return from Europe by a single minute, despite the fact that Roni called them at their hotel on the second night (out of twelve) to tell them that Gabi had disappeared, and continued to call them almost every evening, asking them to return, begging almost, and becoming very angry. Yossi, at the hotel, asked Gila, and Gila let out a smoky chuckle and shook her head from side to side and asked, "Can you see what I'm doing? Can you see me? Do you know the meaning of this motion?" Neither Gabi nor anyone else was going to interrupt her trip. She barely showed any interest at all, while Yossi rushed every day to check for a message in the lobby, or worriedly scratched his gray head.

But the moment they returned to the kibbutz, Yossi took charge of things and set up a search command center in his and Gila's room. He didn't involve the police—it's an internal matter—but decided to release Gabi's photograph and description to the *Davar* newspaper, and it wasn't long before people began calling and offering conflicting reports. He was seen in Kiryat Ata, Eilat, Herzliya, Tiberias, and Be'er Tuvia. He was seen sporting a beard, wearing a hat, dressed in the uniform of the Israeli Air Force, wearing an elegant gray suit. Roni offered to check out all the leads himself, but Dad Yossi convinced him to return to his unit to do the week of orienteering, while he, the father, got on a bus and traveled south to Gila's brother in Kibbutz Revivim, stopping along the way at all the places mentioned in the reports, and then heading down to Eilat.

Roni decided to spend the weekend before the orienteering drill at the kibbutz, to rest and clear his head, but instead he clouded it with large quantities of Goldstar beer and a drunken and unexpected episode, the details of which he was unable to recall afterward, with the beautiful Orit from his class at school, who was serving at the time at an air force base and had a pilot boyfriend who was on duty for the weekend. He woke late on Saturday and then went over to the command center to check for an update on the situation.

Roni returned on Sunday to his base, and from there, everyone got on a bus and headed south. His unit commander sat alongside him for part of the ride, and asked how he was doing, and how the search was going, he had seen the notice in *Davar* at his kibbutz, has anyone responded? He was pleased Roni had made it, reminded him that orienteering week was important, part of a large-scale military exercise that the chief of staff would be monitoring. Their unit had a vital role to play in the drill, locating the objectives and leading the forces, and it was important to him for Roni to be involved. He knew Roni was talented, that he could do it, but he had to remain focused. It was an opportunity for Roni to put recent events behind him, he said—he understood just how tough things had been—adjust his mind-set, and reestablish himself as a part of the unit, which loved and embraced him.

The officer then stood and addressed everyone via the bus's microphone. "Until now, guys, it's all been a joke, child's play. Believe me. What have you done so far? Fitness drills? Firing range exercises? Standing battle orders? Parachuting? Courses and lessons? Forget them. They're child's play. What we're about to do today is what we live for—reconnaissance. Functioning as a commando unit. Patrolling ahead of the forces, navigating, leading the way. All through unknown territory, and at the risk of being discovered. That's why we're going down to the Negev, to an area in which we haven't worked much at all. When this personnel carrier lets out its *pssst* and you step through that door, I want you to show the world what the Golani commando unit is all about. You'll be getting the orienteering charts. Study them and memorize them until they are etched in your brains, or on your asses, for all I care. Believe me. Come on, go out there and show the world and the chief of staff what you're worth."

Roni believed him and wanted to show the world, and even the chief of staff, what he was worth. He studied the charts and navigation routes until they were etched in his brain and on his ass. He readied himself in silence, checked his weapon and ammunition and water and snacks and boots, loaded his equipment on his back, obeyed every instruction, listened to all the briefings, responded to every question, helped his brothers in arms, and headed out—tight-chested, bold-hearted, narrow-eyed, and with good intentions.

He felt good for the first few kilometers. The equipment felt light on his back; his legs carried him almost playfully; he was even enjoying himself. But then a dark shadow began working its way in, into his thoughts and into the depths of his spongy brain. Because ultimately, you're hopeless, you don't stand a chance of repelling it. When you walk through the night for hours and have to remain focused, have to stay awake, you invite them in, the thoughts, you need them to maintain your rhythm, to block out the weight and the burning that starts in your toes and on the soles of your feet, you call to them because you have the time to develop them, to organize them in your overcrowded mind. And then they came flooding back, the mistakes he had made, the years of distancing himself, Yifat the fucking bitch, the tears. He had promised to pull himself together, to finish first, but his mind was consumed and it was difficult to focus.

Roni stopped and drank some water. He must focus. He had prepared for this week. He knew he could do it, and his commander knew he could, too. Gabi would come back. It wasn't his responsibility. Others were dealing with the worrying and searching. Dad Yossi had things under control. And Roni wanted to remain a part of the unit. He retrieved a crumpled Noblesse cigarette from the pocket of his fatigues. Smoking while on orienteering exercises was forbidden, but how else was he going to clear his head? He sat down, leaned back against his equipment, pulled out a match, and lit up. Just one and he'd move on. He could picture the navigation coordinates in his mind. He was doing fine. He was heading in the right direction. The stars were helping him, the compass set him straight. He was going to finish first with ease, he'd show the chief of staff.

He continued walking. The load on his back grew heavier. The navigation coordinates etched into his brain and on his ass began to fade. He stopped to eat something small. To drink. To smoke. To shit. He'd be okay. Despite relieving it of water, food, and cigarettes, the load grew heavier still. He hadn't seen a member of his unit for quite some time, not that he was supposed to see anyone, but you usually ran into some-one, paths crossed, you'd join up and talk for a little while to stave off the boredom and then split up. But that night, not a soul. Here were the stars, here was the compass. He saw lights. What's that? Is it the kib-butz? He was drowning in sweat, he'd take the load off his back for just a moment. He rested. He drank. He wanted to smoke but was all out of cigarettes. Perhaps he should go in, only to ask for a cigarette? It was so hot. He was breathing heavily. It would get a lot hotter after daybreak.

He found himself shivering, mumbling to himself, alongside the perimeter fence of some community or other, calling for Gabi, and then he thought he saw him. Where was he? There was the kibbutz, he was at the kibbutz, there were the lawns, the gardens that Dad Yossi and his groundskeeping team planted and tended so beautifully, there was the swimming pool and dining hall, the concrete paths. He felt drawn to the lights. There was Gabi. Gabi? Gabi fixed him with an odd stare. Gabi? Do you have a cigarette? He didn't respond, but simply looked—what does he want, why does he look like that? Who the hell is that?

It wasn't Gabi. At the time, Gabi was indeed down south, in the des-ert, but hundreds of kilometers from Roni's IDF orienteering training exercises. He was in the Sinai Peninsula, in Ras Burqa, meandering over sand dunes and down to the blue water. His journey there had been a surprising, intoxicating, hitchhiking quest that took him from Ofra to Be'er Tuvia, from Be'er Tuvia to Eilat, and from Eilat to Ras Burqa. The Gam-zu-Le-tova family's 600 shekels would provide for him comfortably for several weeks, he worked out, and certainly in Ras Burqa—what was there to buy there, anyway? He befriended a group from Haifa who were collectively buying food supplies and water and ice and beer, cooking together and sharing their meals, and he paid his part and shared in the cooking, dishwashing, and trips to get ice. They even gave him a blanket and he slept on it under the stars. They didn't ask questions, that's what he liked most about them, and thus he spent his days, lazing on the sand, occasionally putting on a mask and snorkel and exploring the reef a little, submerged in the silence, with snorkel-allotted breaths of air, with colors that exploded into view and moved and dodged away. There, under the water, the embers of his mind, his spiraling rage, his scorched nerve endings found peace and cooled. On the blanket, under a star-studded desert sky, he managed to suppress his anger toward Dad Yossi and Mom Gila, his longing for Roni, his thoughts of Yotam and Ofir and the kib- butz dining hall. He managed to close his eyes and fall soundly asleep, before waking to the pre-dawn chill.

"Hey, I want a turn, too!" Nili, one of the girls, responded when he asked one day for the air mattress and diving mask and snorkel. "Come," Gabi said, and they went out together, she on the air mattress, legs on the cushion and mask in the water, he dragging the air mattress, watching the fish together. It was afternoon, the sun had disappeared behind the mountains to the west, and the visibility under the water wasn't all that great, but it was the time when the fish usually emerged from the reef, and they got the chance to observe lionfish and puffers, spotted an octo- pus and saw sea horses and butterfly fish and clownfish. Gabi pointed and Nili followed with her eyes, then looked at him, and through the foggy glass of the mask, he saw her smiling back at him. From that after- noon on, Nili sat next to him at mealtimes, washed dishes by his side, moved closer and closer to his blanket, found it a few nights later and fell asleep on it, and they woke in the morning to find themselves cuddled together, shielding themselves from the dawn chill, and she smiled at him and lightly kissed his lips, and then pulled away and went over to her sleeping bag without saying a word.

Nili wasn't the prettiest girl in the group, but she was the most enchanting. They shared their first real kiss up at the lookout point after a grueling climb in the scorching sun, totally exhausted, with the entire blue sea spread out below them, a long, deep kiss, spattered with sand and silky. Both were in their bathing suits, touching only exposed parts, not daring to cross any lines or disturb the resting places of any bands of elastic, a sweet and delicious and wet kiss. A kiss that should have marked a new and exciting stage for both of them, but remained only a promise.

The following morning, while they lay side by side on the beach, the earth trembled. He looked at her and she looked at him, and they smiled, and she placed her hand on his and squeezed.

"Did you feel the earth move?" he asked.

"Yes, an earthquake," she responded. The beach around them remained unfazed—the bodies sprawled, and the swimmers swam, and the fish were probably napping, and the tents stood firm. Nili squeezed his hand again. "It's okay," she said. "It happens here a lot. The Great Rift Valley."

Just then, a new group of guys and girls arrived in Ras Burqa. Gabi glanced over at them, and his body tensed. Among them, he recognized from afar, was Anna, a classmate from school, from a neighboring kibbutz, the same kibbutz as Roni's ex, Yifat. Anna, so named because her father was a volunteer from England or Sweden or wherever (Gabi couldn't quite recall that day in the Sinai, though in time he would become very familiar with her biography) who fell in love with her mother on the kibbutz. Gabi couldn't take his eyes off the new arrivals, who set up camp a few dozen meters from his Haifa group. All the layers he had shed during weeks of sand, sea, fish, and Nili returned to encase him.

"What's up?" Nili asked, glancing over at the new group. Gabi didn't answer, his gaze unwavering. He had recognized her in an instant, but wanted to be sure he wasn't imagining things. He wasn't. Anna, with the round face and the sad eyes and the lone dimple and the straight, dark hair, cut neck-length in a style he wasn't familiar with but liked nevertheless. Anna, with her kibbutz gait, her flip-flops and shabby jeans and gray-blue tank top with its kibbutz laundry tag clearly visible from afar. It was Anna for sure, and he needed to get the hell away from there. To go on the run again, hide. He couldn't risk her returning north and telling someone where he was; he didn't want anyone who knew him to learn where he was.

With the head of hair he had grown, he was going to have a hard time passing himself off as a soldier, and he was too young to be a reservist, but he donned the uniform again and it helped him nevertheless to land a ride just minutes after managing to slip away to the road with his bag, without a word of farewell to anyone, only a mumbled, incomprehensible explanation to the stunned Nili. Any regrets faded the moment he entered the car. The Ras Burqa chapter of his life was behind him now. It was best not to stay, not to become attached. He had to move on.

"Where do you need to get to?" the driver asked.

"Where are you going?" Gabi replied.

"Me? To Faran," the driver said.

"Great, it's on my way," Gabi responded, completely in the dark.

"To Dimona," the next driver said. "Great," said Gabi.

"Me? To Beersheba." "Ofakim." "Beit Guvrin."

"Excellent."

And the accompanying questions and remarks, too, of course: "Do they allow you to grow your hair like that in the commando unit? What's that all about, have you been on leave? Be careful the MPs don't catch you, Kastina is full of them. What? Is there a Golani base there?" Gabi didn't respond.

He got out of the car at Guvrin Junction, just as darkness fell.

"Where do you need to go?" the driver asked, apparently sensing his hesitancy. "Are you sure here is good for you?"

"Sure, sure it is, thanks," Gabi answered, not turning to look at the man.

"This area is a bit of a hole," the driver continued. "There's nothing here. Who knows when another car may pass by. Where do you need to go? I don't mind going out of my way a little."

"It's okay, thanks," Gabi said, and the man let it go and drove into his community, the sound of the car's exhaust gradually fading until only the silence remained. And he didn't have to wait long after all, a Peugeot 404 pickup truck was approaching from the opposite direction of the one he had just come from. Moments before the vehicle reached him, Gabi Kupper's mind wandered to the earthquake from that morning, the feeling of sand moving beneath him, his helplessness in the face of nature's unbridled power. What if some subterranean plate had decided to move with a little more force? He'd have been buried under the sand in a flash. Inadvertently, Gabi held out his thumb at the two circular white lights that chugged toward him.

A seasoned hitchhiker by then, Gabi sensed the difference the moment he closed the car door and the driver released his foot from the brake and stepped on the gas. It filled the air of the car like cement in a bucket, heavy and gray, solidifying gradually. Often, he had accepted a ride without exchanging a single word with the driver, not even "Where do you need to go?" or "Where are you going?" They'd come later, on the understanding that if he had held out his thumb and a car had stopped for him, they'd probably be on the road together for a while, the taker and the giver, the requestor and the facilitator. This time, however, the silence was different, steeped in tension, churning with rage. His body froze, and he felt his hair stand on end. He felt aggressive and ready, cat-like, to strike back at the first scratch. There were three men in the car. The driver, a man next to him in the passenger seat, and another behind him, alongside Gabi.

"Where are you going?" Gabi finally asked.

"Right here, nearby," answered the man next to the driver in an Arabic accent.

"You know what," Gabi said, his voice steady but his throat trembling, "I'll get out here, I left something behind, I need to go back."

"Want us to take you back?" asked the speaker.

"No, no, here is just fine," Gabi said, the earthquake, the Great Rift Valley, images from the morning flashing through his mind. And suddenly, out of nowhere, he recalled his ride with the Gam-zu-Le-tova family, too. The speaker said something to the driver in Arabic and the driver signaled, slowed down, and pulled over to the side of the road. Turning on the light inside the car, the speaker turned to look at Gabi. The driver turned to face him, too. There was no need for the man sitting next to him to turn, Gabi had been feeling his stare from the moment he got into the car. An unpleasant odor filled the car, and Gabi, his heart pounding, looked back at the speaker.

"Is something wrong, something bothering you?" the speaker asked.

"No, everything's fine. I simply need to get back to Beit Guvrin, I forgot something in my last ride."

The speaker said something to the driver. The man sitting next to Gabi added some words of his own. "You're a soldier where?" he asked, reaching out to take hold of the Golani pin. "What's this, a cat?"

Gabi didn't answer. Nor did he remove the man's hand from his shirt. Beads of sweat began trickling down his brow. I guess this is it, he thought, and through his mind flashed images of Nili and her kiss, and Anna with her newly styled and straightened hair on the backdrop of the yellow desert, and Gam-zu-Le-tova's blue eyes.

"What do you want from me?" Gabi eventually asked, looking directly at the speaker. The driver snickered.

"We want a soldier, a combat soldier," the speaker said. "Where's your rifle?"

"I don't have a rifle. I'm not a soldier. I'm at school. The uniform belongs to my brother," Gabi responded, now on the verge of tears. "I'm a kid. I'm not a soldier."

"No rifle?" the speaker said. He added something in Arabic and the man next to Gabi began frisking him, ripped a button off his shirt, felt his chest, slipped a hand into his pants, gripped his penis, and caressed his testicles.

"You're a kid? Not a soldier?"

Gabi sat there paralyzed, waiting for the slashing knife. He closed his eyes, a cold sweat told him he had made a mistake, a really big mistake. Why did he take to the road again? Why did he leave, why today, why at all? The Arabs spoke among themselves in high tones. The man sitting next to him let him be. Gabi opened his eyes and saw a car drive by from the opposite direction in a flash of blue. The Peugeot raced ahead, the Arabs continued to argue, louder and louder. Then they went silent. Gabi didn't know what was happening.

Approaching the next intersection, the driver signaled again, pulled over, turned, and glared at Gabi, and the man next to him exited the car and walked around the vehicle. He opened Gabi's door, grabbed him by the ends of his army shirt, and dragged him out. This is it, Gabi thought, it's the end for me. A whimper escaped his lips. The man threw him to the ground and kicked him several times until he rolled into the ditch at the side of the road. Long seconds passed before Gabi dared to raise his head from the ditch. His heart thumping, soaked in sweat, panting, he watched the Peugeot's taillights disappear into the distance. As his tears started to fall, confusing words danced in his mind: An eye that sees, an ear that hears, though I walk through the valley of the shadow of death, I will fear no evil.

He heard on the radio the following day about a soldier who was abducted at Eila Junction during the night. His dead body was found a few days later, not far from there, with a bullet in the head, an IDF bullet, fired from an IDF weapon, most likely the soldier's.

Gabi returned to the kibbutz that same day. He walked through the kibbutz gates in the Palladium boots and Roni's uniform, with wild hair and the soft-skinned cheeks of a young boy, and went straight to his room to crash on his bed and sleep peacefully and soundly for a few hours. When Yotam returned to their room from the basketball hall, he cautiously approached the bed to make sure he wasn't hallucinating, and then turned and raced at top speed to Yossi and Gila's room.

Roni told Gabi that he didn't care at all. The commando unit meant nothing, he'd completed the course, he'd lived through the experience. Been there, done that, and he really wasn't bothered by the fact that he was now stationed in an office job at an Intelligence Corps base in Safed. He was in charge of a storeroom, meaning in essence that he did nothing, because no one ever needed anything from that particular storeroom, so all he did all week long was remove tins of leftover paint from the storeroom and paint the side wall of his living quarters in a myriad of colors, circling and spiraling, blending and mixing, a work of art measuring 4.25 by 2.80 meters, signed in the one corner with *Roni Kupper, a vanishing soldier*, along with the year—1989.

"We only have each other, that's all," Roni said to Gabi. "So fuck the army, and fuck the commando unit. If I thought I saw you in the middle of the orienteering drill and went into that kibbutz and started talking to people—I don't recall a thing, but that's what they say I did—then it must have happened for a reason. That's what guided me. You guided me. And you are more important to me than anything else."

"I'm sorry," Gabi said to him, placing a hand on Roni's, feeling a tug on one of his heartstrings.

"You have nothing to be sorry about. The main thing is that you returned safe and sound. That's what's important."

Besides, as Roni subsequently realized, the intelligence base in Safed is great fun, way more fun than working your butt off in remote geographical locations in the Negev or Golan simply to reach some point or other that someone had marked on a map. The work was easy and quick, the evenings were free, and he came down to the kibbutz whenever he felt like it, and the girls—holy shit, the girls!

The Boot Camp

Gabi, in all likelihood, could have secured an exemption from combat duty, or even army service in general, if he had informed the military authorities of his runaway episode and the incidents of violence, or if he had undergone professional counseling. People around him, Dad Yossi included, encouraged him to do so. But he wanted to volunteer for a combat unit, and said nothing. He listed the Golani commando unit as his first preference and the regular Golani Brigade as his second, didn't list a third, and ended up in the Combat Engineering Corps. While still in boot camp, he was dispatched to Gaza and entrusted with a tear-gas grenade launcher. His unit was sent out on patrol in the Jabalya refugee camp, which the officer who briefed them defined as "not hostile" and hence suitable for a company of new recruits. And so, just halfway through boot camp training, he and his fellow soldiers found themselves heading down a long dirt road in two lines. Smoke from a burning tire drifted through the air, searing their nostrils. They moved deeper into the refugee camp, walking among children blackened with dirt, loud, self-assured, playing with rags, and women in long dresses, full-bodied, pug-faced, their eyes dull and unfriendly. Here and there, Gabi spotted a pair of pretty green eyes of a young girl or two. For the most part, however, he focused on the tracks of the soldier ahead of him.

The patrols for the first four days were slow and boring, accompanied by unpleasant odors, and they didn't get to use the tear-gas grenade launcher. But on the fifth day, they encountered a group of stone-throwing youths. The company commander stopped and crouched, and the other soldiers followed his example. He then stood tall again, took cover behind the wall of a house, and instructed his soldiers to get behind him. There wasn't enough room for them all, however, and some remained in range of the stone-throwers.

"Gas!" yelled the commander. Gabi failed to register that he was the intended recipient of the order. "Gas!" the commander bellowed again, and only after someone elbowed his arm did Gabi spring to attention and rush over. The commander instructed him to fire the grenades in an arc in the direction of the stone-throwers. Taking the launcher off his shoulder, Gabi then remembered that he hadn't yet learned how to use it. On their first patrol, he was told there wasn't sufficient time and that he'd be taught afterward. But the individual who had promised him forgot, and Gabi didn't ask, and the launcher remained hanging from his shoulder like an empty bag through the quiet, boring patrols of the previous days. Now he was being asked to fire it, and he didn't know how. Enraged, the commander ripped the launcher from Gabi's hands and showed him how to open it. "Grenades," he ordered. Grenades? Apparently, someone had filled Gabi's flak jacket with tear-gas grenades. The commander found them, showed Gabi how to load the launcher, closed it, aimed the weapon skyward, muttered, "Next time I won't do it for you, snap out of it," and pulled the trigger.

The weapon was defective. Instead of being launched into the distance and exploding on the target, the grenade detonated in the barrel itself. The commander immediately threw down the launcher, but the cloud of gray smoke rose and enveloped them nevertheless, in particular the commander and Gabi and the unfortunate soldier at whose feet the weapon had landed. The three writhed in pain, seared by the smoke that ate away at their eyes and noses and mouths and lungs, grasping blindly for water, searching blindly for cover, struggling for breath. Perplexed, the remaining soldiers, their eyes streaming with tears and coughing, stood around them, and the stone-throwers in the distance bared their teeth, laughed gleefully, and continued to throw their stones, and even plucked up the courage to move in closer. Had it not been for Dudi, a slightly built and thus far quiet soldier, who opened fire with his weapon into the air and began screaming like a man possessed, which he might have been, the incident could have resulted in consequences far more serious than three victims of smoke inhalation who were rushed to the army clinic at the Gaza command base and subsequently released toward evening.

Following the incident, the company of new recruits returned to boot camp, but by then, Gabi felt detached, no longer really there. Not only had he lost the desire to ingest gas from defective gas-grenade launchers, to force-feed others with gas from functioning launchers, to walk through alleyways with free-running sewage and through the bedrooms of families living in abject poverty, or to restrain stone-throwers; he also had no appetite for operating heavy engineering machinery or clearing explosive devices or building bridges over rivers. The enthusiasm of his fellow trainees and the words they spewed when discussing mechanization and bombs and weapons—words they had heard from friends or brothers or uncles who had served as combat engineers—meant nothing to him. In fact, he had no inclination at all to roam the country in that green uniform. He had done it once before, and it had almost cost him his life—truth be told, his life was spared only because he wasn't a genuine soldier at the time. And boot camp, with the contrived and inane hard-nosed attitude of the commanders, the middle-of-the-night scrambles, the mistreatment and shitty food, the stupid guard duty, and the assholes, oh, the assholes. He got on with a few of the guys, but as a kibbutznik, he was immediately relegated to a status that alienated him from most of the soldiers in his company. And the incident in Jabalya did nothing to boost his position.

Early one morning they were mustered, loaded onto personnel carriers, and transported to the middle of the desert. There they were divided into teams and sent out on orienteering exercises. An entire day under the desert sun, without sufficient water, with food from unattractive field rations. The day would have been bad enough had everything gone according to plan, but there were mishaps, too. Two of the teams went walkabout and failed to reach the endpoint on time. Darkness fell. Flares were fired to light up the night sky, the other teams, under the impression they had already completed the drill, were returned to the field to conduct searches, and one of the search teams went walkabout, too, and also went missing. The soldiers and commanders were tired, hungry, and on edge. After much shouting, scrambling, and punishing, they finally returned to base at around 11 p.m. The company commander and two soldiers—one of them Gabi—went to the kitchen to tell the cooks to prepare a meal. The cooks, however, weren't in the kitchen, which was locked. The commander and the two soldiers walked over to the cooks' barracks, knocked on doors, shouted, and pleaded for food. The cooks, engrossed in a game of backgammon and smoking cigarettes, laughed.

"It's too late," they said. "No one goes to the kitchen at this time of night. You didn't make it on time, tough shit."

They weren't willing even to hand over the key. Their commander, a staff sergeant major, wasn't on base, he was out on the town in Beersheba.

"Forget about it," one of them said.

"Learn not to go walkabout," said another.

"That's the way it is in boot camp," the first added, and all the others laughed and went back to their backgammon.

Impatient and hungry, the company commander confronted the head cook and tried to drag him out by the collar of his shirt. The other cooks responded by jumping the company commander and laying in to him with their fists. They threw him to the floor, kicked him in his ribs, and one even got in a boot to the head. Gabi and the other soldier remained on the sidelines, not daring to intervene. Gabi was hungry and tired. All he had eaten the entire day was a single field ration, which he had shared with another two soldiers.

Barely able to stand, the company commander assured the cooks that they'd soon be eating shit for their actions, but they didn't appear concerned. With a suspected cracked rib and bearing bad news, he and the two soldiers then returned to the company. They divided the remaining field rations among the soldiers and then released them to shower and sleep, with a promise of good food the following day.

After the shower, after the disgusting Spam, after my stomach had finished churning, my heart continued to replay the kicking the company commander had suffered, not that I was particularly fond of him, but the cooks were animals, and they were wrong, they weren't human, not human at all. The events of the whole fucking day swirled in my mind in the shower, the field rations and the sun and dumb walking around with the fucking maps and then after we were done and already in the personnel carrier, having to go out again and search for the assholes who went walkabout and wait some more and walk some more like animals. Inhuman. I couldn't sleep. It was 2 a.m. by then. I opened Mishali's footlocker and removed a number of stun grenades I knew he had kept from Gaza in order to take home, large, smooth grenades, purplish-brown, like eggplants. Mishali had more but I took just two, and returned to the cooks' living quarters. I knew where the head cook slept because I had seen it before. Inhuman. The silence around me was broken only by rhythmic snoring coming from one of the rooms. I identified the room and quietly dragged over a large, heavy wooden bench to serve as a barrier against the door. I walked around and found the window, which I managed to budge and open. I pulled the pins out of both grenades and blocked the firing mechanism with my hands. Then I reached in with both hands, released the grenades, closed the window, and fled from there to my warm bed, hearing on the way the huge booms that shook the entire precast structure. With a smile on my face, I fell soundly asleep.

This time, at least, the enemies were the ones who took the hit, not him, as in the case of the tear gas. The massive blast sprang the cooks out of bed, deafened them, and literally scared the shit and piss out of them, with one of them losing control of his bowels and the other, his bladder. Consumed by panic, they were unable to escape the room until their somewhat less alarmed neighbors moved aside the bench blocking the door.

They were sent to Soroka Medical Center's ER to be treated for shock and the ringing in their ears and, beyond their physical ailments, returned humiliated. Gabi took pride in that; he had righted a wrong. All said and done, his fellow soldiers—the investigation and subsequent naming of the guilty party lasted no more than a few hours—adopted a different view of the nerdy Ashkenazi kibbutznik who didn't know how to operate a gas-grenade launcher. And as for the company commander, although he couldn't admit it, and although to some extent the incident only deepened his own humiliation—a run-of-the-mill trainee had exacted a price and restored respect for a beating that he, the commander, had suffered—he fixed Gabi with looks of appreciation and spoke to him in a sympathetic tone while supposedly slamming him with harsh words about putting lives at risk and human and military collegiality.

After that Gabi was unable to remain in boot camp or the army. After two weeks in detention, an experience in and of itself, his military service, which had lasted a total of five months, came to an end. He saw no future for himself there, and securing a discharge wasn't difficult after he told the military psychologists about the violent incidents in his past. After returning to base from the army jail, he hurriedly packed his kit bag and left for the IDF's induction base before the foursome of cooks learned he was there.

The Future

He returned to the kibbutz, where he found a brother. They were both men by then, at peace with themselves, with each other, with the kibbutz, and with Dad Yossi and Mom Gila, too. And they had yet to cast their gazes beyond the brown Galilee mountains that surrounded the kibbutz. They were fully fledged members of the community, rank-and-file residents—workers, active participants in the farming and social life of the kibbutz, living in the simple and adequate rooms. Following his discharge from the army, Roni went back to working with the cattle, again with Baruch Shani, the overseer of the department. Gabi, meanwhile, gave up on working in the fields because he couldn't stand the sharp smell of tomatoes. The four walls and floor of the food store suited him better, and he began working there under Daliah, who was in charge of ordering the kibbutz's food supplies. But he didn't get on with her, and remained in the department for just a few months. He found her patronizing and sensed she was trying to keep him on a short leash, as if she were afraid of him—once she even mentioned the incident of the diving board and Eyal's jaw. He moved to the kibbutz factory, the country's largest producer of ready-made lawn, and a big exporter, thanks to a unique patented solution for preserving the grass for the duration of the shipment. Gabi worked in the office, and happily so, and he got on well with the factory manager, an immigrant from South Africa and a founding member of the kibbutz, a happy-go-lucky man and a joker, with a huge nose. Gabi, however, turned out to be allergic to the species of grass used for the ready-made lawns, and following incessant bouts of coughing that led to a series of rigorous medical tests, he was forced to relinquish that career, too.

Roni began playing again for the kibbutz basketball team; Gabi tried to join the choir. Roni had several brief relationships with volunteers, and one with an Israeli girl, too—a guest at the kibbutz, the Petah Tikva cousin of one of his fellow cattle department workers, who gushed and enthused and charmed and came to visit; but the moment she hinted at thoughts of moving to the kibbutz and sharing Roni's room, he panicked and stopped her in her tracks. As for Gabi, aside from a handful of fleeting experiences, his future as far as women were concerned still lay ahead of him. And thus the two brothers rediscovered each other, without the army or a girl or the pains of adolescence coming between them. They'd meet sometimes for dinner, and sometimes go on from there to the pub or a movie, or together they'd stop by the room of their adoptive parents on weekends.

One Friday night, after the festive Sabbath dinner in the dining hall, Gila felt unwell, went to sleep, and woke feeling a lot worse. Dad Yossi went over to Roni's room and asked him to drive her to the hospital in Safed. On their way to pick up a set of keys for the communal vehicle, they happened to run into Gabi, and he joined them. And thus the entire family—father, mother, and two sons, all together for the first time in ages—headed off to Ziv Hospital in Safed in the kibbutz's Subaru. Gila was admitted for tests and the three men spent the Sabbath in the hospital corridors, drinking coffee from a vending machine, smoking (only Roni), or walking around Safed's Nof Kinneret neighborhood, which offers a view not only of Lake Kinneret but also of the Galilee and Golan Heights and almost all the way to the Mediterranean Sea. The kibbutz, too, was visible from one point on the ridge, but Gila didn't get to that point; never again did she get to see the kibbutz of which she was one of the founders. The cancer in her lungs had spread, and because the hospital caught it late, she hung on for less than a month.

By the time their adoptive mother was admitted to the hospital, Roni and Gabi had already made their peace, and their bond now grew stronger. They spent hours together on the drives to and from the hospital and in its corridors, united by virtue of the need to be there and to be close, out of a sense of concern, of sorrow, and with the understanding that blood ties cannot be taken for granted. They weren't sure sometimes if they were at the oncology ward to bolster Mom Gila or to spend time together. Whatever the case, they spent that time together.

During that period, the Kupper brothers, Roni, twenty-four by then, and Gabi, twenty, became better friends than they had ever been. They used their talks to fill in the blanks of the previous years: Eyal and his smashed jaw, the abduction in the orchard, the dump Gabi took in the butterfly greenhouse, the hitchhiking quest to the Sinai, the ride at Guvrin Junction. Roni's commando training, his final orienteering drill, his burning love for Yifat, the first and second and third time they did it, and the breakup and the heartbreak. The relationships and the anger; the kibbutz members, Yossi and Gila, kibbutz work colleagues.

"And what now?" Roni asked his brother one day as they sat on a bench outside the hospital at sunset, smoke rising from the cigarette clasped between the tips of his fingers.

"Now?" Gabi asked, turning his wrist to see the face of his watch.

"I don't mean in the next hour. From here onward."

"Onward?"

Roni glanced around to see if anyone was looking and discarded the cigarette, then turned back to his brother, his beautiful brown eyes smiling. "Yes," he said. "What's next for you? Is this it? Are you going to be on this kibbutz forever?"

"Why? Do you have other ideas?"

"I asked first."

"I've got no idea. The kibbutz for now, I guess. I don't look too far ahead. It blinds me, like looking into the sun. What do I need that for?"

"Are you content?"

Gabi bit his lip and moved his head as if to say so-so. "I'm okay in general," he said.

"That's exactly what I'm talking about," Roni responded. "I feel the same. Things are pretty good for me. The air is clean, and life is simple. I work, sleep, eat, fuck. What more does a man need? Neither of us is going to be prime minister."

"So what's the problem?"

"I don't know. There's more to life, isn't there? Look at the old folk on the kibbutz. Look at that generation. They made something. They made something out of nothing. They did something for history."

"What history? They built a kibbutz. Did they have a choice? They got screwed in Europe. They got screwed with the Arabs. So they built a kibbutz and went out to fight wars."

"I, too, used to think like that," said Roni. "That we have a country, which works well, and that there's no need any longer to fulfill the Zionist dream, there's no need any longer to survive the Holocaust. So why shouldn't we simply enjoy it and that's it? Surely we don't have to go out looking for nobler ideals and greater goals only because the old-timers on the kibbutz built a country, do we? You've gotta be kidding. That's why I quit the fucking commando unit. Everyone there believed that we have to do, fight, conquer. It's enough already. Look around, everything's cool, everything's peaceful. We can enjoy life."

"Exactly," Gabi said. "So I ask again, where's the problem?"

"First of all, it's a lie. Everything can't always be cool. And second, okay, so they built a country and did great and historical things that we will never do. But that doesn't mean I cannot fulfill myself on a personal level and do something with my life."

Gabi sized him up. "What do you mean on a personal level?" he asked.

"To achieve things, I don't know. Money, success. Look at me, at fifteen I was a basketball star on the kibbutz and started working with the cattle, which is the best this kibbutz has to offer. I went into the commando unit, which is the best in the army. So, what now, is that it? Why should I remain on the kibbutz all my life and continue to do the very same? I can do more, can't I? What's with the face?"

"I'm not making a face. It's just that when you spoke about fulfilling yourself, I thought you were talking about something else. Something within you."

"Isn't that what I said?" Roni asked.

"Not exactly. You spoke about money, about succeeding, external things. I am talking about looking inward, about asking who you truly are and what you are doing here."

Roni fixed him with a look of confusion, amusement, perhaps, maybe naïveté—or perhaps all three. "You've seen too many psychologists. That's your problem. Do you know what you really need?" he asked.

"What do I need?"

"You need a good fuck, and urgently."

"I've had a fuck," Gabi said. Technically, it was true. He had had something quick and unsatisfying with Orit, from Roni's year at school. She was four years older than Gabi and still had her pilot boyfriend, who was still required to be on weekend duty on base from time to time and continued to go out drinking beer and getting too drunk and ending up in unexpected beds. "Unsatisfying" was an understatement. "Traumatic" would have been a more fitting description.

"Forget about what you've done," Roni responded. Gabi had already told him about Orit, and Roni had subsequently introduced him to someone else. That episode was slightly less surreal, because there was less alcohol involved. Nevertheless. Roni looked at the setting sun and went quiet for a moment.

"You know what?" he said. "Forget about fucking. You're right. I always thought it was the answer. For you, for everyone. But perhaps I was wrong. No, you need to fall in love."

"To fall in love?" Gabi asked apprehensively.

"Exactly, to fall in love. Then you will know who you are and what you are doing here. Yes, to fall in love. And you know what? Perhaps that's what I need, too, right now." Roni stood up and stretched. "Let's go, Gabi boy. Pick yourself up, we're going."

"Going where?" the younger brother asked.

"I don't know where. But we're going to do something with our lives."

HOT DAYS

The Order

Hilik Yisraeli headed home from Jerusalem, after hours of slogging away on his doctorate at the National Library. The working title for the thesis was "Pioneering, Land Redemption, Ideology: The Pre-State Kibbutz Movement as a Failure-in-Waiting." In his paper, Hilik sought to point out a wide range of early warning signs, arguing that the manner in which the kibbutzim were established and evolved—beginning with the appropriation of land, the decisions vis-à-vis sources of livelihood, and the receipt of state credit and benefits, including, too, the reliance on slogans and ideology, and through also to the condescension and arrogance of a closed society, alienated and on a pedestal, functioning according to its own set of rules—signaled the failure of the Kibbutz Movement some fifty years before the onset of its actual demise. Or something to that effect.

On the road back from his one day a week at the university and enjoying Gershwin's Piano Concerto in F Major, he and his car came under a barrage of rocks, one of which cracked the front windshield at the top, on the side, in front of the passenger seat, and ricocheted off the glass. Hilik stepped on the gas, his leg filled with adrenaline, his heart violently pumping blood to every inch of his body, fear shaking and numbing the tips of his fingers, the pianist playing on beautifully, and the car raced up to Ma'aleh Hermesh, and from there, home, to C.

He pulled up outside his house, got out, and conducted a comprehensive inspection of the Mitsubishi. Seeing him do this, from the window of the house, his wife, Nehama, clearly anxious, hurried outside, followed by their two toddlers.

"What happened?" she cried out.

"They cracked the windshield, the dogs."

"Sons of bitches! Where? Are you hurt?" Nehama asked, examining her husband with concern. His skullcap sat tight on his parted hair, his thin-framed glasses were in place, and his painter's-brush mustache was still neat and tidy. She didn't see any stains on his plaid button-up shirt, his dark trousers, or his Source-brand sandals. Apart from a bead of sweat across his delicate brow and the fear in his eyes, Hilik appeared unscathed and well.

One by one, the neighbors gathered round.

"Oh my," said Othniel, his hand caressing the butt of the Desert Eagle pistol stuffed into the back of his pants, "terror is again raising its ugly head."

"That head needs to be chopped off," Josh said, and he looked up at the young Jehu, who was surveying the nearby village of Kharmish from atop his horse.

"Was it the good old boys from Kharmish? We could pay them a courtesy visit," Othniel suggested.

"No, it happened at the bottom of the road, before the corner. Majdal Tur."

"Damn animals need to be wiped off the face of the earth," Othniel said.

Sporting a broad skullcap and thick, untamed sidelocks that dangled down on either side, Jehu nodded slowly in agreement.

Yoni arrived on the scene, followed by Roni and Gabi, and then Rachel Assis and her daughter Gitit in a car, returning from the grocery store in Ma'aleh Hermesh A.

"What happened?" Yoni asked.

"Terrorists. More stone-throwing," said Nehama. "Thank God for the armored glass, I don't even want to think what would have happened without it."

"Oh my God," said Rachel, her fingers stroking her throat.

"Go down to their village right now, impose a curfew, do a house-to-house search," Othniel instructed Yoni. "If not, they'll think they can get away with anything they like."

Yoni mumbled something about having a word with Omer. The crowd slowly began to disperse a few minutes later, but not before Nehama and Rachel sought to ease the anxiety by exchanging notes on a recipe for a spicy fish dish with potatoes and a tomato sauce.

Yoni called Omer to report the incident. Omer said he would dispatch a patrol to Majdal Tur as a show of force, and come up to the hilltop.

"Meanwhile," he said to Yoni, "tell Othniel and his buddies not to try anything foolish. The army's here, we'll handle it."

"Gotcha," Yoni said, and looked around to see if Othniel was still in the vicinity. Aside from him, however, only Gitit Assis remained. She had returned to the car to get the grocery bags.

"Need some help?" he asked the tall, slender, straight-haired young girl. "I have something to tell your father. Let me get those for you."

"Okay," she answered shyly.

He adjusted the strap of his weapon, picked up all the bags, and smiled at her. "Okay, shall we go?" he said.

She returned his smile, blushed, and walked lightly beside him.

The military demarcation order handed over in February by sector commander Captain Omer Levkovich to Othniel Assis may not have had a practical, or rather, immediate effect on life in the settlement, but it did spark an unusual sense of urgency in and around Ma'aleh Hermesh C. the moment it arrived. With the help of lawyers from the regional council and Natan Eliav, the secretary of Ma'aleh Hermesh A., an appeal against the order was lodged with the defense minister. As a result, implementation of the order, originally due to take effect within eight days, was suspended indefinitely, and a team of state officials was sent to the outpost with the task of determining the nature of the land rights in question. Is the land state-owned land that was allocated by an official entity for settlement purposes (or state-owned land that hadn't been allocated); is it survey land (under ownership review); is it private land purchased by Israelis (and if so, had the Israel Lands Authority authorized the purchase) or is it privately owned Palestinian land?

Othniel, Hilik, and Natan Eliav accompanied the surveyors, two women in suits and a young man, and attempted in every way possible to explain to the honorable delegation that the land on which Ma'aleh Hermesh C. was established fell within the jurisdiction of Ma'aleh Hermesh, despite its distance, as the crow flies, from the homes of the mother settlement. Over the days that followed, Natan Eliav got word from an associate who was a member of the review team that the findings were inconclusive. It emerged, as was already known, that the settlement was erected on land of mixed status. Some of it—at the entrance to the settlement—was indeed state-owned land that fell within the jurisdiction of Ma'aleh Hermesh. Some, in the playground and the center of the hilltop, where most of the trailers were located, was survey land. The southern slope, where some of Othniel's crop fields lay, was private agricultural land owned by a Palestinian living in Beirut, while the area on the edge of the cliff that dropped down into the Hermesh riverbed was in fact designated a nature reserve, meaning it was owned by the State of Israel and could not be used for settlement or construction purposes.

As expected, the appeal filed with the defense minister was rejected. The council lawyers then filed a petition with the High Court of Justice, hoping for an actual court date far enough into the future to allow for the arrival of a few more families, for Othniel to expand his farming enterprise, and for the outpost residents to cover their prefabricated mobile homes with stone. Trucks laden with rocks, sacks of sand, mortar, and gravel turned up one day and unloaded their bounty, courtesy of the regional council, and almost all the residents eagerly set about the business of stoning over their homes. ("The stone enhances the aesthetics of the structures, blends with the surroundings, serves as thermal insulation, and gives added protection against stray bullets, God forbid" read the brochure.) They erected timber piles, mixed cement in a single mixer on wheels that was moved from place to place, or manually in tin basins. Othniel's home had had stonework done long before then. And, apart from the newly arrived trailer and the trailer that served the IDF (the outpost residents did indeed offer to give it the same treatment but were turned down by Captain Omer, who argued that the stone could create the impression of a fixed structure, and that the army wouldn't want to come under fire for erecting a fixed structure in the area of Judea and Samaria without the appropriate permits, and certainly not with a High

Court decision pending), not a single trailer on the hilltop remained bare. The walls of the trailers were thus turned into a mutation of geological layers that told of the passage of time: drywall, spray foam insulation, thin aluminum, cement, Jerusalem stone.

One day, with the bright sun beating down hard from a sparsely clouded sky, two officials from the Civil Administration's inspection unit arrived on the hilltop. They looked like brothers—thin, awkward, and sharp-nosed. Resting on the head of one was a crocheted skullcap. They spent some time wandering around the outpost and focused primarily on its northeastern corner, which, following the visit and findings of the previous land inspection team, turned out to be a part of the Hermesh Stream Nature Reserve. There stood a partially built wooden structure, known on the hilltop as Gabi's Cabin, where construction had progressed at an impressive pace and which now boasted half of a sloped wooden roof. The two visitors circled the structure and cast their eyes over the basin that had been installed outside the front door and the toilet that was fixed to the cabin at the back, and then, coming to the end of a small path, they suddenly halted.

"I've been around the territories for quite a while," said awkward man number one, "but this is a first for me. What's with the bathtub here?" He approached the tub, which lay embedded in a large rock near the edge of the cliff.

"You're welcome to give it a try," said Gabi, who had rushed over the moment the two began poking around his construction site. "Never again will you have the chance to take a bath in such beautiful surroundings."

"I'm sure," chuckled the Civil Administration official.

"But what the hell is this?" asked the second inspector, motioning with his chin in the direction of the unfinished cabin.

"It's the Hermesh Stream Nature Reserve visitors' center," Othniel replied, and winked at Gabi, who smiled. The mood was a pleasant one. The rustic, pretty cabin on the edge of the cliff gleamed in the sunshine. Surprisingly, the inspectors refrained from issuing an order to suspend construction of the cabin. They said they would look into it and then went on their way.

Visitors continued to arrive from time to time, escorted for the most part by the sector's company commander, Captain Omer, but sometimes by the battalion or division commander, and once or twice by the head of the IDF Central Command himself. There were also officials from the Civil Administration, the Settlement Division, and the Defense Ministry, Knesset members from the left and the right, and, of course, officials from the Fence Administration, contractors armed with notebooks, land surveyors with their surveying instruments, levelers and their tools. A constant and somewhat slow trickle of professionals and concerned parties over a period of several weeks.

The pre-Passover High Sabbath came and went, and the High Court of Justice debate drew nearer. Leavened foodstuffs were burned, and Seder night passed by with the hilltop residents celebrating the transfer from Egypt, the wanderings, the transient nature of Jewish dwelling places through the ages, and their shared consciousness of an exiled people yearning for their homeland. The High Court hearing began, and the High Court hearing ended, and the council's petition was rejected, with the court ruling that the military demarcation order would take effect when the Defense Ministry deemed it appropriate.

"Now," said Othniel at a meeting of the outpost's Absorption Committee, "we need to cross our fingers and pray to God that the appropriate time isn't found over the next two years—be it due to the heat, the cold, snow, rain, political sensitivity, a no-confidence motion in the Knesset, the toppling of the government, the days of grace of a new government, an economic crisis—until the order expires."

The sector's company commander, Omer Levkovich, arrived to tell Othniel that he had paid a visit to Majdal Tur. The *mukhtar* had assured him that a small handful of children were responsible for the stone-throwing incident and that he would personally intervene to ensure things remained quiet.

Othniel protested. "It's always only children," he said. "And the sheikh always promises to keep the peace. And then there's another stone, and another Molotov cocktail, and it'll end one day, God forbid, with more than just a smashed windshield. And what will you have to say then?" Othniel's neighbor Hilik, the victim of the attack, who had spotted the company commander's jeep parked outside his neighbor's home and had come inside to join them, nodded and ran his fingers over his mustache.

Omer knew Othniel well. His gray-green eyes remained cool, facing the fiery stare of the settler. "It's best for everyone if the mukhtar is up to speed and assures quiet and good relations, instead of us going in and imposing a shutdown and mobilizing a battalion to maintain it," the IDF captain said. "Anyway, they'd just get pelted with rocks from the rooftops, and they'd be forced to busy themselves with bullshit."

"So hit them hard and put an end to the bullshit," Othniel responded. "We shouldn't have to tolerate cars coming under attack by stone-throwers."

"If you can't tolerate it, you don't have to. That's my decision, and it's final. We're not going to hit them hard or do anything of the sort."

"Whatever," Othniel said, his nostrils flaring. "Just don't be surprised afterward."

"Hold your threats, and I'd like to see anyone dare to take action."

"Okay, okay, let's all take it easy," Hilik said in an effort to cool the mood. "Okay, Omer, thanks for coming. Another coffee, perhaps?" Standing off to the side, Othniel was still spitting fire. "No, thanks," Omer said, and stood up to leave.

He returned just moments later. A flat tire. "Oy, my friend, you should have been more careful there in Majdal Tur," Othniel said. "It's full of ninja road stars over there." Omer wasn't amused. The clip-clop sound of Killer the horse walking nearby filtered through the air. The tire was changed and the jeep departed. Later that evening, the windshields of two vehicles in Majdal Tur were smashed, and a tire on one of the cars was set ablaze. Captain Omer's patrol was dispatched to the scene, and after surveying the damage in frustration, he relayed a report by radio to the command center.

The Cabin

When Gabi-Gavriel-Kupper-Nehushtan first turned up at Ma'aleh Hermesh C. and offered his help with anything and everything, Othniel Assis took him on as a shepherd. All Gabi had to offer was good and pure Jewish manual labor, and that's exactly what Othniel believed in and was hoping to find for his developing farming enterprise. Gabi would take the goats out into the wilderness, sit with them on top of a hill, under a tree or alongside a spring, and then return them hours later to their pen, well fed and satisfied. He enjoyed reading religious literature, the writings of Rabbi Nachman, praying and conversing with the Almighty. After a while, however, boredom set in. How much more of it could he handle, of being alone with his thoughts, even in such beautiful surroundings? A shepherd is like a monk, secluding himself, hearing nothing but the sound of the wind and the bleating of the goats and the tinkling of the bells around their necks, seeing nothing but hilltops. At some point, he came to the conclusion that he'd be better off spending his work hours in a real job, doing physical work, using his muscles, talking to people. More important, he needed to give a rest to his wounded spirit, his intense yearnings and guilt-ridden thoughts about Mickey, his young son.

With Othniel's consent, Gabi went from being a shepherd to a worker of the land, and off he went to labor in the ever-expanding fields of the Assis farming enterprise, which provided much work sowing and weeding, harvesting, loading, and packing. Because he had some experience with field crops—he had worked on the kibbutz for a short while in the tomato fields, which he detested, and then in the banana groves, which he quite liked—he had a long talk with Othniel about his career change.

"Shepherds don't let the grass grow under their feet, they're a lot more spontaneous and free-flowing," Othniel said, and Gabi agreed. A shepherd doesn't get tied down to one place, he forsakes a safe and familiar location for the nobler purpose of a devout and spiritual existence. He sees the world and broadens his horizons, whereas the farmer is fixed, enslaved to his material possessions and assets. Gabi confessed that at this stage in his life, he appeared to have the need for something solid to hold on to.

"The worker of the land has a solid base," Othniel said, clearly understanding Gabi's heart. "And he also creates something—he sows a seed and he reaps a fruit—and doesn't simply sit in the shade and allow the herd to do the work. Our people, from the very beginning, have always lived on these two opposite ends of the scale. Cain and Abel, Abraham and Isaac, even Rabbi Eliezer started out as a worker of the land, while Rabbi Akiva was a shepherd. Othniel Assis alone is both!"

"Sitting around all day while the herd grazes is pretty damn boring, for the most part," Gabi said, eliciting a toothy laugh and a slap on the shoulder from Othniel, who also promised that working with cherry tomatoes was very different from working with regular ones.

Gabi found his own special place during the long hours he spent in solitude when he first arrived on the hilltop—a stone ledge above the cliff that dropped down into the Hermesh Stream riverbed and overlooked the desert. Armed with a blanket one night, he went to sleep there under the stars, and the following day he came across a beautiful, smooth slab of rock that he pictured as a wonderful floor for a small cabin made of wood and stone. He laid out several rocks to mark the outline of the cabin's walls. If he were to add a few more every day, he thought, he'd eventually have a wall. After more than a year of lonely days and nights, the wall was completed.

At the same time, he built a number of small terraces in the area around the wall and floor and put in plants, which didn't survive Othniel's hungry goats and the dry conditions. From Othniel's fields, he borrowed several used and perforated pipes and set up a drip-irrigation system that with time allowed the plants to take hold in the soil. With the help of timber logs and beams, the original floor was turned into a beautiful wooden porch, which evolved into wooden walls and a roof.

At a certain stage in the process, Gabi realized he was building his future home, the home of his dreams. It may have been small and modest—a single multipurpose room—but "Gabi's Cabin" more than provided for all of its owner's humble requirements, and more important, it was all his, constructed with patience and love and by his own two hands. He felt fortunate, and never tired of the landscape, the translucent brown desert hills and, farther away, the mountains of Edom: a place of breathtaking beauty, close enough to the homes of the settlement to feel a part of the community, yet far enough to maintain an element of privacy, to be at one with nature, to withdraw into prayer. Gabi did his best to ensure that the cabin he'd built blended in with its spectacular surroundings, flowed with them rather than defaced them. He had never had any formal training in design, planning, or building, but he was blessed with talent and intuition.

There was room inside the cabin for a bed, a coffee table, shelves for clothes and books and CDs. Power was drawn from a utility pole some fifty meters from the cabin and a light was installed in the ceiling. The toilet facilities were outside—number ones in nature, number twos in a sawdust-filled toilet bowl. The bath, which had so impressed the Civil Administration officials, was Gabi's pride and joy. He found the youth-sized stainless steel tub discarded in Ma'aleh Hermesh, brought it to the hilltop, placed it on a concealed crag of rock, and hooked it up to a water pipe in the center of the settlement. Around two of its sides, he erected a mud wall that he reinforced with empty wine bottles and fitted with a round, cracked mirror and a small niche for toiletries. There was no roof—bathing under the open sky! He laid another pipe from the tub to a basin fitted into a wooden table outside the door. A little below the cabin, down five stone steps, some natural and some finished off either with cement or segments of rock, Gabi erected a shaded patio, and around another nook in the rock he kept a small refrigerator and a hot plate—a kitchen, a dinette, and a place to kick back all in one.

Gabi worked slowly but poured his soul into the task at hand. He carried rocks, leveled sections of earth, gathered materials from here, there, and everywhere, adding layer upon layer. He tried to devote at least an hour or two each day to the cabin—he'd wake early sometimes and head there before the farm, and sometimes he'd spend his noontime break at the cabin, and after hooking up the power cable and installing the light, he'd go there on occasion in the evenings and at night, too. He worked patiently, focusing on one task at a time, and felt a deep sense of satisfaction and gratitude after making even the smallest bit of progress. And because everyone at the settlement was fond of Gabi, they encouraged him and helped him in various ways—providing him with surplus building materials, or taking an hour off work and lending a hand, or assisting with specific tasks such as installing the power line or water pipe.

The arrangement worked well for all parties. Where else in the world would Gabi have been able to build, with his own two hands, a home of his choosing, his taste, and catering to his needs—at almost no cost at all? And from the point of view of the settlement, Gabi's pending move would free up a trailer that could then be used to house a new family. Moreover, the log cabin became a beautiful, eye-catching attraction, drawing visitors, political functionaries, and potential settlers.

Soon after Roni's arrival on the hilltop, Gabi took him for a walk and showed him the cabin, saying to him, more in earnest than in jest, "You can pay your rent while you're here by working with me here on the house."

Roni, who absolutely loved the "open-air design" of the place, was quick to respond. "Sure, sure, no question about it," he said. "I'll come to help regardless of the rent thing. Are you kidding me? Working here in this fresh air and these surroundings, it's a dream, man, it's America rediscovered. What am I talking about, America? Things like this don't exist in America, in America, things like this . . ." He took a deep breath and looked around, and his voice lost a little of its verve when he completed his sentence, "don't exist . . ."

Gabi could have counted on one hand the number of times that Roni came to help. And one spring morning, Gabi asked him to. New wooden beams and planks had arrived, and Gabi had freed up half the day and needed another pair of hands to measure the beams and nail them together. Roni glanced at his watch. "Today, of all days?" he said. "Ariel is finally coming over and we're going to have a look at Musa's oil press; it took forever to arrange." Roni looked up from the watch to see the look of disappointment in Gabi's eyes. "I'm sorry, bro, I have plans with some people. I tell you what, how about tomorrow? Let's make it for tomorrow. You really need to tell me such things in advance." Gabi, however, would be spending the following two full days hard at work on Othniel's farm. He laced and tied his shoes and left, offering only a feeble "Good-bye."

The Oil

"**A**riel!" Roni called out with a broad smile as the silver Toyota hesitantly approached along the circular road. He was sitting on an easy chair in the yard alongside the trailer and reading yesterday's newspaper that Gabi had found and brought home after guard duty during the night.

"Where's the bathroom?" Ariel, looking a little green around the gills, asked frantically as he hurried past his friend and burst through the door of the trailer. "Just don't tell me that Gabi's in there."

"Gabi's at work, feel free. I'll put the kettle on." Ariel, already out of earshot, hurriedly dropped his pants and sat on the toilet without drawing a breath. "That didn't sound good at all. Oh God, it doesn't smell all that great, either. Let's get outta here," said Roni, cups of tea in his hands, as Ariel emerged from the bathroom. "How was the drive?"

"Scary as hell," Ariel replied. "I couldn't relax for a second. They drive like lunatics, the Arabs—trucks, taxis, all going a million miles an hour. And their houses sit right on the road, almost. And where's the army? I had the shakes the entire way. And what if I had taken a wrong turn and ended up in the middle of a hostile village?"

Roni smiled, sat back down in his easy chair, and gestured to his friend to sit beside him. He pulled out a cigarette and offered, but Ariel declined. "Sit, take it easy, man. It's peaceful here. Believe me, I haven't felt this secure since the kibbutz."

Ariel barely heard a word and certainly wasn't convinced. His eyes continued to dart left and right, and every few minutes he frisked the four pockets of his pants to make sure his wallet, phone, and keys were where they should be. Ariel was a large man, with a bald, egg-shaped head that housed thin blue eyes. Those eyes finally fixed on the easy chair alongside Roni, and he sat down.

"You're crazy. I still can't believe you brought me out to this battle zone. I've never been so terrified in my life. What's that camel over there?"

"A camel cow—Sasson's. Forget it, man. Look at the view. Take a deep breath. The Land of Israel."

Ariel's eyes met for a moment with the discerning orbs of the sand-colored camel cow and he attempted a deep breath. To no avail.

They sat quietly and sipped their tea.

"So, they've allowed you to come live here just like that? No questions asked?" Ariel asked.

"Sure, they ask questions. People always ask questions. But the people here are pretty laid-back for the most part. I'm visiting my brother . . . And what about you? How are things at the accounting firm? And what's happening at Bar-BaraBush? Do you still hang out there?"

"For sure, just like always," Ariel said, somewhat distracted by the view of the light-colored hilltops in the distance. "You know, it really is beautiful here."

"Oh, I see someone is beginning to relax a little. Give it a few minutes and you'll be addicted to the quiet."

Ariel took the minutes, closed his eyes, and put his head back. "It's working," he mumbled. "Such quiet."

"Trust me," Roni said, "this place needs a B-and-B. It would make a killing. It's closer than the Galilee, dirt cheap, quiet, the view. You should see the cabin Gabi is building himself on the edge of the cliff. Stunning."

"Are you out of your mind? What lunatic would come here? Are you telling me you want to sell this beauty and quiet and these dirt-cheap prices to Israelis? They'll never come here. Bring it to them."

"As in bring olive oil from here to their doorstep?"

"For example," Ariel responded rhetorically.

"Okay, let's go see Musa."

"Isn't he coming here?" Ariel's pulse rate and blood pressure, which had finally stabilized, reared their heads again.

"Are you crazy? No Ishmaelite ever dares to approach this hilltop. Come, let me first give you a small taste."

The oil pleased Ariel's palate.

"The firmament of the Land of Israel is different from that of the other nations," said Roni, gesturing toward the ancient landscape, after the two men set out.

"Huh?" Ariel responded.

"Don't worry, that's not me. That's the way Gabi speaks. Rabbi Nachman quotes all day and night."

They passed by several of the outpost's inhabitants, Jean-Marc Hirschson, and Josh the American, and Nehama the kindergarten teacher, and the cheerful, singing, babbling toddlers from the day-care center, one of whom, Shneor, Hilik Yisraeli's son, was crying, with snot trickling from his nose. The locals waved greetings at the two men in their city suits, and they nodded in response, Roni with a knowing smile, Ariel with a touch of anxiety.

"Tell me, are they not lunatics, burning with messianic ideological fervor, outlaws and bullies who harass the Arabs and steal land and all that?"

"The only lunatic is my brother, and he's proud of it!" Roni said, and went on to quote Gabi saying things like "Devotion to the Lord requires doing things that may appear like madness."

Ariel laughed and said, "It won't be long before you, too, are reborn." Roni was quick to respond, "God forbid."

"Seriously, though," Ariel said, "aren't there problems here with the army and the Arabs and who knows what?"

"Listen," Roni said, "clearly there are people here who are afraid. And I really couldn't tell you if there are or aren't any Kahanists here who go out at night on raids against the Arabs. But from what I've seen, most of the people here simply get on with their own lives—work, family, school, and prayer and religious studies, too."

"How's Gabi?"

"He reads Rabbi Nachman. Prays like a madman. Rocks and sways like he's on a carousel. He's quiet a lot. He's building a cabin. Who knows. We haven't seen this much of each other since we were kids. To be honest, I'm enjoying it, and I think he is, too. It's a little cramped in the trailer, but I'm trying to get into another one that is currently unoccupied, and Gabi will be moving into his cabin at some point . . . Okay, let's head off here to Musa." Roni turned onto a path between two trailers and drove on in the direction of the olive groves.

"Are you sure?"

"This is what you came for, right?"

The sun burned white over sleepy mountains. The past few weeks had seen the days drag by, get longer, gradually lose their chill. And the hills were covered in a thin film of sourgrass, much to the delight of the goats and sheep of all nationalities. Behind Ariel and Roni, Ma'aleh Hermesh C. faded farther into the distance and ahead of them the village of Kharmish drew nearer. In between lay Musa Ibrahim's stretch of olive trees, absorbing the sun's long rays, which would strengthen over the coming months and bring fruit to their branches, evidence of which could already be seen in the form of tiny clusters, like embryos at their initial stage of development. This year would bring a bumper crop, and if they wanted to close a deal, it would be best to do so now, before the harvest in the fall.

Ariel's brow was covered in beads of sweat, his eyes were now hidden behind black sunglasses that wrapped around his head. "They aren't hostile? Are you sure?" he asked.

"Chill, baby. Musa!"

Musa came over, and friendly greetings and handshakes were exchanged, and Ariel's heart fluttered as he tried not to cast any mistrusting glances. They sampled another dark, bold-flavored oil, and then Roni said to the Arab, "Come, let's see what we spoke about." They walked along the boundary between the village and its groves, and then turned right into the alleyways. Ariel froze, looked neither left nor right, and not for a moment did he take his eyes off Roni, who, for Ariel in that moment, was the only representative of a safe and familiar world.

"So, like I tell you," Musa said, a cigarette attached to a black plastic holder between his fingers, "an oil press like this one, you could find maybe two others in West Bank. The old kind, made of stone. They don't make oil like this today no more. It's the old way."

"Yes, yes," Roni said, spurring Musa on. "Millstones, that's what we want to see."

Musa continued. "My father worked the press for many years, and made oil for whole village," he said. "Two years ago, he got tired, too much work, too many people to manage, too little oil. Someone in the village brought in an electric press and everyone takes their olives to him, me, too. Someone came and offered my father many dollars for each stone. But he didn't want. He wanted to sit back with his *narghile* and said the press must continue to work for the family. I said, Father, take the money, we'll make oil with the electric one. He said, No, the family has worked this way for a thousand years, and you will continue, and your son after you."

"Of course," Roni said. "He was right. It's the traditional way, the real way."

Musa fixed Roni with a tired look. Ariel, still scared stiff, hid behind his sunglasses despite the shade in the narrow alleyways.

Musa produced a large set of keys and opened a lock that hung from a corrugated steel door. The door creaked open. He flipped a switch and a pale bulb on the ceiling lit up. A dank, dusty odor assaulted their nostrils. The room was dark and had a dirt floor. Two millstones stood in a vertical position inside a wide basin, also of stone. Musa explained the process—the harvesting, onto lengths of tarpaulin, was done by hand and with sticks and rakes. From there, the olives went into sacks, which were then loaded onto donkeys and carried to the press—from the tree straight to the stone, *min a-shajar ila ilhajar*, yielded the best oil—the women sorted through the olives, discarding the dirt and leaves, separating the good from the bad and the black ones from the green, then the olives were pressed by the stones.

"What about washing?"

"There's this washing pipe that can connect to water," Musa responded, pointing to a thin brown rubber hose. "But the water in past years too little and weak. And my mother says washing is *zift a-tin*, takes all the flavor and color away. She say the dust and the earth is true flavor. The rain washes good enough. My mother and father aren't willing to taste any other oil. It's the taste of when they were children. They long for it." He pulled out another cigarette and put it in the holder. Ariel anxiously followed Musa's fingers with his eyes. The air inside the oil press constricted his lungs.

"I trust your mother, no washing for us," Roni said, meeting the look of horror in Ariel's eyes with a wink.

The cigarette Musa had lit up made it even harder to breathe, and little help was offered by the tiny barred window, through which they could now see the faces of children, snooping and inquisitive. Ariel was sweating: This is the end, what am I doing here? But then Musa's wife entered with a tray bearing small cups of Turkish coffee, and Ariel accepted graciously and lifted one to his lips—delicious.

"From here, the olives we put on stone," Musa continued. "The donkey we tie to thick beam, and his eyes we cover so he doesn't go crazy. He walks and pulls the beam in circle like this, and the stone crushes the olives, cracks them. This is most natural way and best way, no knives, no shredders, and no machines. The flesh of olives turns into *ajina,* mash, with a good smell. We collect the ajina with special rakes and we spread on the *akalim*"—he pointed out circular, flattened baskets woven from rope with a hole in the center—"and the akalim we put on this pole, one on top of other, and turn screw and press hard-hard, and so the oil seeps out into bath here. It's water and oil together, and we let lie to separate, or separator tool is also possible to use. After we separate, oil goes into pitchers, and there it is good to let sit for a while because it is cloudy, pieces of olives are float in it, and after a week or two, they sink and the oil is clear, and is possible to pour into cans."

Ariel glanced at Roni. Not the most sterile operation in the world. Again Roni winked at him.

"It's the best oil," Musa said. "But no one makes like this any longer because too slow, and gives too small oil, you need healthy donkey, or motor, and many people to work. With new machines, you push button and everything works by itself, clean, and press more oil from olives. You understand?"

Roni looked at Ariel and rubbed his chin. His eyes then drifted to Musa's white mustache. "How much do they cost, the machines?" he asked.

"Six thousand dollar for small Chinese compressor, six manpower. For one hundred thousand dollar, from Italy is best compressor in the world—six hundred horsepower. Extracts most oil from olives in short time."

"But the taste isn't the same taste," Roni said.

"No."

"And that's what matters."

"Yes, a little money we need to fix here because not work for a long time. Electric motor for turning, separator to separate instead of letting settle."

"You said the donkey will do the turning," Roni responded. "I saw your donkey. As for the separating, you said it was best to wait."

"I didn't say best. Letting settle takes two weeks instead of few minutes. I think pity to wait. And donkey has heart problem, is weak."

The eyes of the Israelis met again. Roni's eyes read, I don't have a cent to my name. Right now, I'd rather make a small profit on zero investment than a large profit after an investment—boutique oil. His mouth said, "For now, I say, let's keep things down to a minimum. Original olive oil. Handmade. Boutique. Try with the donkey."

"Okay," Musa replied, "but oil only a little."

On the walk back, Ariel aired out the sweat and clinging odors from his shirt and again frisked his pockets to ensure his wallet and keys and mobile were still there. The fact that he was still alive lifted his spirits, and soon they'd be back on the hilltop, which might have been an outpost in the heart of the occupied territories, but at this point in time, even Ariel felt secure there, surrounded by armed and bearded Jews and soldiers to keep the peace.

"What can I tell you, Roni? I've made several inquiries since we started discussing things. The people at the Olive Boutique on Rothschild Boulevard sent me to see oil presses, the top of the line. The way they do things here, with sticks and stones and donkeys and containers that have been lying around for who knows how long—the world's moved on since then. The production lines from Italy are a different world."

"Forget about it. Nothing beats the old way. The most natural, the purest. A production line means tons of oil a day. We're a boutique, man.

People want that. You tell them it's organic, tried and tested for hundreds of years, made by hand, unrivaled quality, extra-extra-virgin."

"Actually, in Italy, if the oil comes from a press like that, the label shows an illustration of millstones."

"Exactly. You see? We'll mark ours, too!"

"I don't know," Ariel said, returning to his original standpoint. "Didn't Musa look a little tired to you? With machinery, it's more precise, cleaner. There's the washing . . ."

"A waste of water and a waste of space. Those Arab women are better than any machine when it comes to sorting out and discarding the leaves and shitty olives. That's the real flavor, with the dust, and the earth, and the cigarette smoke, and a leaf here and there."

"There are automatic mills . . ."

"And I suppose you also have a hundred thousand dollars lying around somewhere? Leave it, nothing beats millstones. A two-thousand-year-old success story, like the Jews!"

They walked on to Ma'aleh Hermesh C.'s circular road. "Everything in life is relative, isn't it," Ariel said. "When I first got in here, I almost passed out from fear. But after surviving the Palestinian village . . . Now I'm just trying not to think about the drive back." His gaze lingered briefly on a group of children in push cars alongside a mother, and he felt a pang of longing for his own son and wife. His eyes then moved to fix on the damaged windshield of a car—a weblike formation of cracks around a small hole where the rock had struck.

"What's that?" Ariel asked, gesturing with his head.

"Ah, terrorists from one of the surrounding villages," answered the mother, Nehama Yisraeli. "They threw stones at my husband on his way back from Jerusalem. Thank God for the armored windows."

"Armored windows?" Ariel asked in a shaky voice.

"Enough of that now, Ariel," Roni said. "What about our business?"

Ariel, his face now pale, turned to face Roni again. "In a modern oil press, everything is controlled and directed from a central control panel . . ."

"Musa's mind beats any control panel, hands down—just like no computer has beaten Kasparov at chess."

Ariel smiled but remained silent.

Roni stopped. "Listen, Ariel," he said. "While you were out doing the rounds at sophisticated oil presses, I was working on the figures. If there's anything I learned in America, it was to analyze figures, to construct business models, to maximize the dollars. Trust me, I've broken it down to cost versus output at the level of a single olive. You need a minimum of one hundred thousand dollars for a modern oil press, and that doesn't include finding premises, renovations, paying rent. And then you buy the olives and transport them, and what about marketing? Bottles? Labels? More production lines. And then there's dealing with the Olive Board to get a quality control label. Cold-pressed-shmold-pressed, extra-virgin-extra-shmirgin. You need insane loans, and then you have to sit tight for five to ten years until you start making a profit. Is that what you want now? The entire country is filled with them already. What's your advantage over them? Anyway, it's madness to invest hundreds of thousands of dollars in a production plant in the territories and then wait for five years. Who knows what things will be like here even next year?"

Ariel slid his sunglasses up to his head; the sun had set. "So what do you propose?" he asked.

"You already know what I propose. That Musa does everything, that we make a deal with him at a good price and commit to the entire season. We'll label the cans—organic and original, with an illustration of millstones, the mother of all extra-extra-virgin, from the very earth and heart of Palestine. And we'll sell it for twice the price at your Olive Boutique on Rothschild. It'll sell like hotcakes to their sweet Tel Avivians."

"And who says the Palestinians will go for it? Roni Kupper has spoken and the entire village jumps to attention? They hate us, after all."

Roni rubbed his thumb against his forefinger. "Money," he said. "That's all. You pay them in advance, for the whole season. No one else is going to offer them something like that. I've spoken to Musa. Right now, those poor bastards have to cultivate and harvest, and then they go to an oil press that takes a twenty-percent cut, and then along comes some Palestinian merchant who screws them and pays them a ridiculous percentage only if he manages to sell anything. And how's a Palestinian merchant going to sell? Who's he going to sell to? As for the Israelis, they shit themselves every time they need to go through a checkpoint. Musa and his mates know, too, that this is a once-in-a-lifetime opportunity. Honestly, Ariel, Musa told me so."

Ariel bit down on the arm of his glasses. "Okay," he finally said cautiously. "So let's think about our costs: You spoke about paying up front for the olives; a separator; and an electric motor to replace the sick donkey."

"The donkey may be okay."

"Forget about the donkey. Bottles and labels. And we're going to need something for marketing and distribution."

"Minimal, minimal," Roni responded, fully aware he was fighting a losing battle.

"Minimal, minimal, for sure, but we still get to tens of thousands of shekels to begin with. Thirty or forty. Let's play it safe and say fifty. Twenty-five thousand each."

Roni hurriedly lit up a cigarette. He narrowed his eyes through the smoke. "How the hell did you get to twenty-five? You're not in Tel Aviv, you're in an Arab village in the territories. No one here talks in those numbers. Where am I going to get that kind of money?"

"I don't get it. What were you thinking—that it's not going to cost a cent? It's not a whole lot for starting a business with this kind of potential, and with the experience you've had, you know that all too well."

Roni's face took on a look of anguish. "Ariel, I can't go in fifty-fifty with you right now," he said. "Can't you invest the initial capital and we'll sort things out further down the line? I came with the idea. And I found Musa. But when it comes to liquid cash, I'm a little pressed at the moment."

"I'm willing to put in more than you, but you have to come up with something, to show commitment. You can't just leave me in the lurch with this. Don't you have a little in the bank? Didn't you leave something in America?"

The pain etched across Roni's face appeared to intensify. "America's problematic," he responded. He tossed the cigarette to the ground and paused for a long while before stamping it out with the tip of his shoe. "I'll check it out. I'll try to make a plan, okay?" he said. "There's a Fire in

Breslov" began playing on Gabi's phone and Roni fished it out his pocket with two fingers, happy for the interruption.

"Yes, Musa," he said with a smile. "Yes, I hear you." Ariel watched Roni as he listened to Musa, watched the smile fade from his lips, watched as Roni ended the call and slid the phone back into his pocket, watched his morose friend as he said, "The donkey's dead. A heart attack. Just now."

The Trailer

Mobile residential units, known in the vernacular as mobile homes, or transportable homes in government-speak, or precasts, trailers, prefabs, and so on, are more or less of uniform size and proportion—single-story, rectangular units measuring 4.25 meters in width, 11 meters in length, and 2.80 meters in height. The floor is fixed to a metal frame some eighty centimeters off the ground. The outer walls comprise some four to six centimeters of insulation between gray concrete and pale wooden boards with a PVC finish or unfinished drywall. The roof includes a protective layer of aluminum. Four metal steps lead up to an opening on one of the long sides, which also include French windows with sliding glass panes. For the most part, the trailers are positioned with their front doors facing inward, toward the settlement, while the windows open onto the view. The 54,900 shekels required to purchase one is usually donated to the Amana settlement organization by the Housing and Construction Ministry, and rent and property tax to the local council amounts to no more than a few hundred a month. There are, of course, variations on this standard. The chosen manufacturer, English, German, or Israeli, may sometimes change in keeping with the government ministry handling the order, or with the prevailing mood, and thus, over a period of several decades, a mixture of structures that were delivered or produced in various combinations could find their way to the settlements. The two trailers, one of which still served as the basis for the Assis family residence, that Uzi Shimoni brought up to Ma'aleh Hermesh C. in its very first days, for example, measured twenty-two square meters. The *Bar-Onim* were taken from a work site set up by the Americans who built the airstrips in the Negev after the Sinai evacuation.

The trailer that arrived out of the blue in Ma'aleh Hermesh C. on that festive wintry day was still in the exact same spot in the spring and was about to be occupied for the first time. Following the structure's delivery in error to Ma'aleh Hermesh C. and the defense minister's refusal to authorize its relocation to its original destination, Othniel instructed the outpost's Absorption Committee—chaired by his wife, Rachel, with Hilik as her right-hand man—to convene and review the waiting list and invite a new family to move in.

Several weeks passed before the Absorption Committee managed to get together, and in the meantime, the new home remained as good as new, more or less. By the first Saturday night following the delivery of the home, some unknown individual had already managed to overcome the lock on the door, and one by one, solutions were found for faults and problems with numerous other residences throughout the settlement. A rickety shower door was replaced; window shutters; a sink faucet; a showerhead. Even a square, meter-by-meter piece of greenish linoleum from the kitchen floor was removed with a sharp Stanley knife and found its way, with the help of a strong adhesive, onto the floor of another home as a replacement for a piece of flooring already bulging and dirty and rotting from a water leak. Nevertheless, notwithstanding several essential built-in components that quickly became built out, the waiting list for the home had lengthened considerably; and before Rachel even produced the printed sheet of paper with the waiting list, various people, from within and without, began tugging at her sleeve, seeking her ear, whispering to her.

A number of the hilltop residents suggested converting the trailer into a day care for toddlers so that the synagogue could have its own structure and the women's section would no longer have to serve a dual function, with the partition in place during prayer times and otherwise down. The issue had been a contentious one and the subject of many a committee debate since the dawn of the settlement: Who is more important, who is more entitled to their own home—children or God? There weren't many children in the early days, and the synagogue came first, but the number and ages of the children had increased, and a structure specifically dedicated to their education was now a necessity.

Others supported the idea of inviting a family of new immigrants, and some suggested young couples. And parents whose children were without like-aged peers at the outpost tended to look for families with such children. Roni Kupper, Gavriel Nehushtan's brother, who arrived at the outpost at the very same time the trailer was delivered, requested occupancy on a temporary basis, simply to lay down a mattress for a while until the selection of the new family. And then there were the friends of the Rivlins, a young, sweet family from Efrat. The relatives of Jenia Freud, new immigrants from the former Soviet Union who lived in Karnei Shomron and were looking for "a new challenge and a pioneering lifestyle" and certainly ticked all the right boxes for Ma'aleh Hermesh C. Several youths from Ma'aleh Hermesh A. called, as well as an American by the name of Sarah, who had wanted to establish an outpost herself but made do with a spa named after her husband, who, she claimed, was murdered on one of the nearby roads, despite the fact that everyone remembered the incident and recalled nothing more than a regular vehicular accident. And there were more friends and acquaintances and others who had visited the hilltop or were familiar with it—the modest abode, deemed a blessing on arrival, turned into an arena of confrontation among conflicting interests and rivalries, and Hilik Yisraeli, who knew all the families who had come and gone, beginning with Uzi Shimoni, served as the final litmus test to determine and approve the candidates' suitability for the hilltop and its inhabitants.

Roni got word somehow of the meeting and requested and was granted a hearing, in which he tried to plead his case: In light of the unclear status of the trailer, originally designated for Givat Yeshua and still wanted there, and due to the High Court of Justice's rejection of the petition against the military demarcation order—in other words, the entire settlement was slated for evacuation at some stage in the future—it might not be worthwhile to bring in a new family before ascertaining which way the wind was blowing, and until then, "Regardless of what emerges, let me move in. I'm already here. If I need to move out, I'll do so in a flash. Truth be told, I won't be staying longer than a month or two in any case, three at the most . . ."

"Until you tie up your deal for the oil from the Arabs from Kharmish?" came Rachel's question, followed by a chuckle from Hilik, and Othniel Assis fixed him with a look of stern disapproval. Roni had heard that Othniel was a believer in Jewish labor, despite once having employed Thai workers in his mushroom greenhouses for a period of time, and wasn't happy about Roni's business dealings with Musa.

"Yes . . . No . . ."

"Tell me," Othniel said, winking at Hilik, "have you asked him yet about the Kibbutz Movement as a failure-in-waiting for your doctorate?" Hilik's smile turned a little bitter. He hadn't been working on his doctorate like he should have.

Roni lost. The status of the trailer, and of the outpost as a whole, was indeed hanging in the balance, but there was nothing new in that—for that very reason, there was a need to establish facts on the ground so as to tip that balance resoundingly and unwaveringly in their favor. Therefore it would be best, too, for settlers to move in rather than designating the home public use as a day-care facility. The committee thus decided to bring in the Gotlieb family, who came across in their hearing as very sympathetic—precisely the human makeup they were looking for, a young couple with two children from Shilo, the man an optician who wanted to open a store in Ma'aleh Hermesh A., the woman a rabbi's daughter.

"Please tell them," Rachel requested, "to come for a welcoming Sabbath, and as far as I'm concerned, they can move in immediately afterward, with the greatest of pleasure and success. And tell them to speak to me about the home's missing pieces. We'll have a chat with the Settlement Division."

The nerve of them, Roni thought, deeply disappointed. Instead of being thankful that someone normal like me is willing to live in their dirty asshole of a place, what do they do, make fun of me? Bunch of lunatics, they can go shove their trailer. He returned to his bed, Gabi's former sofa, and lay there, morose. The living room had become stifling and oppressive for both of them. He wasn't at ease, and he had noticed that even his brother was struggling with the situation. Gabi was all smiles and love like always; everything, as he viewed the world, was God's will—tests, gifts, whatever he used to say. But Roni knew his brother well, and beneath his smiles, he could see his patience wearing very thin.

The Bulldozers

The bulldozers arrived on a scorching hot day in May, the Hebrew month of Iyar, when Israelis celebrated their independence and their memories. With concerned looks in their eyes, a group of outpost residents gathered on the outskirts of the hilltop and watched as the gray monsters slowly progressed, emerging from the alleyways of Kharmish like enraged chicks hatching from their shells.

"Are those loaders?" asked Elazar Freud, who had been roused from his desk by the noise.

Hilik snickered. "No, they're D-9s," he said. "Loaders have wheels and are smaller. Those ones, with the tracks, are the real mean beasts."

"They didn't dare come here, huh?" Elazar said.

"No," piped in Othniel. "It's because they need to work on their side. The route of the fence runs adjacent to that olive grove over there."

"Yes, Musa's," Roni said. "The bastards!"

"And they also want to move up to our land. Do you realize just how absurd that is?"

Yoni arrived, his rifle at the ready angled across his chest. "Okay, guys," he said, "let's break up this demonstration."

"What demonstration?" The six residents, whose gazes had been firmly fixed southward until then, turned to face him.

Hidden behind his Ray-Bans, Yoni focused for a moment on the beauty mark next to Gitit Assis's ear and swallowed hard. "Listen, okay? I've been ordered to keep you in check if there's any trouble," he said.

"Trouble . . . pshhh, if only someone would make some trouble around here," Othniel snorted, and flipped open his cell phone with his thumb, first dialing Natan Eliav, the secretary of Ma'aleh Hermesh A., and then Dov, the head of the regional council, and MK Uriel Tsur next, and so on—the usual round of calls. They all promised to look into the matter and get back to him. Othniel shut the device, which responded immediately by ringing.

"Yes, Dov," he said to the regional council head, "I understand . . . Okay. And what's the council's stand on the matter? . . . No, not the regional council, the Yesha Council, the council of Jewish settlements in Judea, Samaria, and Gaza."

Othniel noticed that everyone around him had gone quiet and was waiting for the response, so he went over to speaker mode. Dov's voice came through clearly: "At this stage," the regional council chief said, "the Yesha Council's decided not to go with the proposal not to take a stand on the matter."

Othniel stared at the instrument, confused. "What does that mean?" he asked.

"It means that we're going to decide quickly on our position. Either to attack the government for the decision to route the fence through here, and move to reverse it with the help of our friends in the Knesset, or to support the plans to construct the fence through the olive groves, while at the same time opposing any encroachment on the outpost's land, and then prevent the left-wingers from introducing a no-confidence motion. A third option would be to bring down the government no matter what, and to hope that by the time elections are held and a new government is in place, the entire story will be forgotten."

Othniel gave Hilik a puzzled look and then turned to fix his daughters, Gitit and Dvora, with the same. "Just a moment," he said to the phone, "so what did you decide today?"

"To rule out the fourth option," Dov explained, "which was to do nothing at all, to wait and see how things develop, and to hope that we receive post facto approval for the settlement's master plan, which has been with the Planning Council for several months now. In fact, the timing of all this may even present an opportunity to secure its approval. And if it passes, we'll get an injunction based on the approval. *Capisce?*"

"Gotcha," Othniel responded, and smiled at his daughters.

"So, anyway, this morning we ruled out that option—not to take a stand."

"I'm actually all for buying time," Hilik interjected, bringing his mouth closer to Othniel's phone. "It usually pays off. Within two years, the demarcation order won't be worth the paper on which it's printed, less than two years, in fact." He looked at his old analog watch, ivory in color, with a small window displaying the Gregorian calendar date where the 3 would be. He switched to the corresponding Hebrew date in his head and did the math. "A year and nine months, more or less."

"In any event" came Dov's voice again, "let us know immediately if the D-9s begin moving in and we'll send in thousands from the region to stop them. I'm going to try to get ahold of the defense minister, too. I spoke earlier with Malka, his aide on settlement affairs. Ah, yes, that reminds me, how does the defense minister know already that you've moved a new family into the settlement?"

Othniel hurriedly muted the speaker and, running his fingers through his beard, slipped away from the group. "What?" he spoke quietly into the phone.

"Malka said they were aware that a new family had moved in. Even I was in the dark. When did this happen?"

"I don't believe it. They moved in only yesterday, and the decision was made just last week. Are you sure that's what he said?"

"Come now, it's true, isn't it? Someone told them. Do me a favor, try to keep these things a little more under wraps. Malka said the same. It doesn't serve our best interests."

"Sure, sure," Othniel replied, thoughts racing through his mind. "We'll check it out." He turned back to the group. "Come, people, let's go see if the soldiers over there know anything."

"Ah . . . Othni, I'd like you to remain right here." It was the soft-but-somewhat-rasping voice of Yoni. "I've been ordered not to allow you to approach the loaders—"

"It's okay," said Othniel Assis, who, beyond being the oldest and longest-serving resident of Ma'aleh Hermesh C., was also blessed with a deep, authoritarian voice and a piercing gaze that wasn't readily challenged, certainly not by Yoni, even from behind his Ray-Bans. "We're just going for a short walk. That's allowed, right?"

"I'm asking you not to go," Yoni replied with admirable courage. They continued walking.

"I need to have a word with my building contractor, Kamal," said Hilik, who was expecting delivery over the coming days of half a container to expand his family home into a *caravilla* ahead of the upcoming birth of his daughter. Othniel had tried to talk him into finding a Jewish contractor and Jewish laborers, but wasn't willing to loan out Gabi, and hiring a Jewish contractor and laborers from outside the settlement was expensive. So Hilik made an arrangement with Kamal from Kharmish, who would bring along two workers and complete the job quickly and cheaply, without social security or pension payments, travel costs, and all the other hassles and headaches that came with employing Jews.

Othniel, however, was tenacious. "You need to set an example for the youngsters," he said to Hilik while they walked.

"Believe me, Othni, I tried," Hilik responded. "What choice do I have?"

Like others on the hilltop and from Ma'aleh Hermesh A. and B., Hilik would fill his gas containers in Majdal Tur for half price or shop at the Kharmish grocery store. But Othniel was a purist of Jewish labor, and stubborn, too. "I have someone for you. Herzl, an excellent contractor," he said. "He'll give you a good price, trust me. And I'll organize some financial aid for you, too."

"Financial aid from where?" Hilik's ears pricked up.

"A special rate for students, you can count on Othni, old man," Othniel said, "and on Herzl. He's a contractor to die for, he'll do the job a thousand times better than the Arab, and he won't stick a *jambiya* in your back."

Yoni surrendered. He called to update Omer, as he followed the group of settlers, his eyes darting back and forth between Othniel, the loaders, and Gitit Assis's hips and ass encased in their thick denim skirt. Behind them came the clopping of Killer's hooves, and Jehu quietly drew up alongside him.

The two track-type Caterpillar D-9N bulldozers, huge and dusty, weighing in at fifty tons, four meters high and eight meters long, including the front blade and rear ripper, lay motionless like two lions at the entrance to a palace. Alongside their huge, threatening steel limbs that rested on the ground side by side, the work team—two commanders and two operators—had set up a small gas burner and were boiling Turkish coffee. Yoni hurried over to them and quietly relayed the company commander's instruction to refrain from conversing with the settlers. "Why not? All's good, bro," one of them responded. "Let them come. We'll talk to them with pleasure. Tell me, is that a Thoroughbred?"

Jehu, atop his horse, barely acknowledged the soldier with a glance. Othniel glared at Yoni and then smiled at the soldiers. "Hey there, guys," he said. "If you need anything, food, drinks, blankets, anything at all, just come and ask. We're happy to provide."

"We're good, bro, thanks, but there's no need," said the soldier who spoke previously to Yoni. The rank displayed on the sleeves of his shirt indicated he was an operator, not a commander, but he acted like the spokesperson for the group. He was chubby and dark-skinned, and one of his eyes tended to wander when he tried to focus his gaze.

"So what's happening here? When do you begin working?" Othniel asked, putting an end to the small talk.

"We don't know," the soldier said. "We're waiting for instructions."

"And when are you expecting the instructions? Today? Tomorrow?"

"We don't know," the soldier repeated. "Today, tomorrow, in a week. Who knows with this fence? They're waiting for the High Court ruling."

"No, the petition to the High Court was rejected," said Elazar Freud.

Company commander Omer Levkovich's jeep pulled up in a cloud of dust that caused everyone on the scene to cover their faces with their hands and cough. "Don't speak to them, please, guys," the captain instructed.

"We simply wanted to know what's happening," said Othniel Assis. "And hello to you, too."

"Nothing's happening. Let's break it up here. The bulldozers will sit here until the order to begin work comes through. We're waiting for the High Court ruling."

"We lost our petition to the High Court," Elazar reiterated. "Haven't you been informed?"

"Not your High Court petition. A petition filed by left-wingers and Arabs against the damage to the private olive groves."

"Ahhh . . ." Othniel uttered with a smile. He hadn't heard about it. He called Dov, who promised to look into the matter and to provide any assistance he possibly could to the guys from the Peace Now organization.

"Holy crap, so that's what the High Court debate is all about?" said the chubby soldier. "I don't believe it. I don't get why anyone has to ask the High Court–Shmigh Court or the bloody Arabs for permission. Give me five minutes and I'll wipe out all those fucking trees. And if possible, lay down some of those dirty bastards among the trees and we'll wipe them all out together."

Dvora stifled a giggle and squinted at her father. His eyes smiled back at her. Omer, red-faced, stepped out of his jeep.

"Um, excuse me, soldier," he said. "What's your name?"

"Dudu," the soldier replied.

"Dudu, well, first of all, stand up straight when an officer addresses you, Dudu. Secondly, I said no talking, did you not hear me? Are you looking for shit?"

"No, sir," Dudu replied, his chin up straight.

"Who's your commanding officer? Listen, guys, I have lots of respect for heavy-duty engineering equipment and the Engineering Corps, but get ahold of yourselves, and if I tell you to sit tight and wait for your instructions, then that's what you do. You don't make any suggestions you got me?"

The four soldiers nodded.

"Okay, let's break it up," Omer said.

The group of settlers began making their way back to the outpost, and the four soldiers climbed up into the spacious cabins of the bulldozers to enjoy their state-of-the-art air-conditioning systems.

The Birth

Shifra, the midwife, was on call twenty-four hours a day, rain or shine, and there wasn't a single location anywhere in the Land of Israel outside her range. She didn't own a car or have a driver's license, and the word *fear* didn't appear in her lexicon. Everything rests in the hands of God, and with the wheels of the rides she hitched. You wouldn't be too surprised to find her standing at some dark intersection, near hostile villages, as late night turned into early morning, in the pouring rain or even in the snow, her one hand clutching her midwife bag, the other held out straight to hitch, her hair tucked into a modest hat, and her broad, thick spectacles covering those eyes that knew no fear.

And how could God not walk beside a saint like Shifra, who performed such sacred work? Experience had taught her she would always find that one settler, or army jeep, who nine times out of ten would go out of their way to deliver her to her destination. Hundreds of babies had taken their very first breath in this world with her help, her round face the first thing they saw. Hundreds of new mothers had shed tears of pain and joy with their hands held in hers as she soothed them in a New York accent that through the years remained as thick as ever: "That's it, with the grace of God, we're almost there, just a little more, push, sweetie, you are such a trouper. There we go, here's your little beauty. Oh my, if that isn't the most beautiful baby I have ever seen in my life." That moment always choked her up with true emotion, and she closed her teary eyes and thanked God for guiding her there, for watching over her, for giving her the gift of birthing wonderful Jewish babies. When she immigrated to Israel, she changed her name and took on that of Shifra, the biblical midwife from the Book of Exodus, where it is written, about her and her fellow midwife, Puah, "The midwives, however, feared God"—she, too, would fear Him, and He would watch over her, blessed be His name.

The phone woke her at around 2 a.m. It was Nir Rivlin from Ma'aleh Hermesh C. Shifra was familiar with the outpost, where she had previously delivered several wonderful babies into a spectacular desert dawn. A truly biblical landscape. She rose quickly, prepared her midwife case, and walked the five hundred meters from her settlement to the highway in the light rain. On occasion, the fathers were able to pick her up in a car, but Nir couldn't leave Shaulit alone, and no alternative driver could be found. Shifra changed rides twice, but Shaulit's contractions were coming at a good rate and she wasn't needed right away. She spoke with Shaulit on the phone, calmed her down, explained what she should do, how to breathe, how to sit. Then she asked to speak to Nir and gave him instructions on what to prepare and how to alleviate her pain. A yellow Palestinian taxi raced by and she prayed to God and closed her eyes, and she felt soothed and overcome with a sense of absolute tranquility. Menachem Politis from Givat Esther stopped for her. She wasn't sure she remembered, but he insisted. "You delivered my two daughters, you saint. Where do you need to go?"

"Ma'aleh Hermesh C.," she replied.

"No problem, and best wishes to all," he said, and then drove her all the way to the home of Nir and Shaulit Rivlin.

"Excellent, you're well dilated. Everything's going like clockwork. Wonderful. I see a head with curls, oh my, oh my, a charming little boy, little girl?"

"A charming little boy," Nir confirmed. Following two wonderful girls, this was their first son, they knew from the ultrasound.

"So charming, God bless."

"Hallowed be His name," an emotional Nir said softly.

"Nir, Nir, some warm water here, please, not boiling, but a nice temperature, okay? Thank you. I was at the big Ma'aleh Hermesh just last week, it's good to be back. A contraction's coming. Yes, push with the contraction, breathe in with it, you're a star, Shaulit, your third birth, a piece of cake, you're in control, you don't need me. Nir, a cloth, my dear. A small sip of water, sweetie?"

Their second daughter, Tchelet, two and a half years old now, was also delivered by Shifra here on the hilltop. Amalia, the eldest, almost five by now, was born at Hadassah, before they moved here. Oops, a power outage. Shaulit cried out in panic.

"Everything's fine, dear. Never mind. We're almost done anyway. I think he'll be out with the next contraction, here we go, that's it, the head's out, there we go."

Nir tried to recall who was on guard duty now. He was excited, sweating as he scrolled through the list of names in his cell phone. Who could he message? Who was up? The power was suddenly restored, the guard must have noticed and turned on the generator—and there he was, there he was! Caught up in her own excitement and Shaulit's final cry of pain, Shifra went quiet for a moment and prayed to the Holy One, blessed be He, "So God was kind to the midwives and the people increased," and then she spoke again, her voice calm, "He's the most beautiful baby I've ever seen, we thank God for his gifts." Shaulit held her hand, and Shifra embraced her and kissed her forehead, and then she placed the wrinkled, dark pink, bewildered baby on the breathless mother's body, and the dumbstruck Nir thought, Things happen so slowly and yet so quickly, and here I am now, a father of three already. And the sun rose over the mountains of Moab and Edom and a golden light colored the land and a new day dawned on the hilltop.

Shaulit's mother, widowed by an act of terror, stayed home to look after the two girls, and Nir, Shaulit, and the baby left for the city to register the newborn at the hospital. They headed out slowly in the light blue Subaru and were greeted by a gleaming white smile and "Mazel tov!" from Yoni on guard at the gate, and after descending from A. and turning onto the main road, Shaulit said, "Oy, I forgot to tell Mom where I keep the diapers," and Nir dipped into the pocket of his pants, only to find that his phone wasn't there. And then, ahead of the checkpoint, a traffic jam, which appeared to be rather severe, halted their progress. The tension in the car mounted. Shaulit wanted to speak to her mother, Nir would have liked to learn something about the traffic situation, an eight-hour-old baby was in the car with them, and they were phoneless.

"Never mind," Shaulit said, and asked Nir to tune in to Radio Kol Chai. The chatter soothed her and eased her ever-present anxiety, heightened now due to the absent phone. They finally crawled by the checkpoint. Elderly Palestinians peered at the baby. Pregnant Arab women smiled, and Nir and Shaulit flashed sheepish grins in response. The radio cut out and kicked back in, and a sweet odor spread through the car. "Oh God, I forgot that the poop is black to begin with," Shaulit said with a smile that only a mother could display toward a lump of flesh and bones that had just excreted black feces.

The fact that Shifra had been present for the birth didn't satisfy the authorities. She wasn't registered as a midwife with the Health Ministry, and in the absence of a doctor, Nir and Shaulit had to undergo DNA testing to prove they were the parents, another hassle. They eventually collected the infant and the gift packages the hospital routinely handed out to parents of all newborns, freebies from the diaper and baby formula companies, and got back into the dusty Subaru. Nir readjusted his skullcap, stroked his beard, and, with a smile on his face, reached out to tuck in an errant curl that had slipped out from under his wife's hat. That's it, we have a son, who's been duly registered in the computer system of the hospital and the Interior Ministry, approved as a rank-and-file citizen, soon to be receiving mail from the health maintenance organization and the bank. As soon as Nir arrived home and was reunited with his mobile phone, he began dispatching excited text messages about the birth.

The Sabbath touched down on Ma'aleh Hermesh C. like a space shuttle on the moon—purposeful and precise.

The Rivlin family home abounded with chaos and joy. Shaulit and her widowed mother and mother-in-law—the two grandmothers arrived together from Beit El—were hard at work on pastries in the tiny kitchen, and had also branched out and elicited help from the kitchens of Neta Hirschson and Jenia Freud, who themselves were busy preparing their own Sabbath meals, but happily and generously donated the use of an oven and countertop space (in addition, of course, to contributing toward the outpost's customary gift to every family with a new mouth to feed—a fortnight of meals prepared by the women of the hilltop in rotation). Nir had been running around since morning and had bought wine and disposable tableware and pretzels for the children and, of course, the essential *arbes*—soft, savory cooked chickpeas—to snack on. The hilltop was a beehive of warmth and activity, all in honor of the little one, who for his part was interested only in the body part that provided him, in private, in the master bedroom, with his food every two hours, and the crib in which he would then drop off into sweet slumber, spread-eagled and happy.

Sabbath eve. A packed synagogue. The prayer service to welcome in the Sabbath. Humming to the tune of "Lecha Dodi" while meticulously reviewing the pages containing the Torah portion of the week. The evening prayer service. Adon Olam. With the service over, Hilik, in the role of the *gabbai*, the synagogue warden, gave word of a Shalom Zachar gathering at the Rivlin family home, as is the custom in Ashkenazi Jewish circles on the first Friday night after a baby boy is born. After dinner at home, the members of the community rained down on the Rivlins. The women sat with the mother in a separate room, passing the infant from one to the other, and the men occupied the living room, snacking on the *arbes* and drinking arak.

The following day in synagogue, Nir was called up to recite the blessings over the Torah and gave a reading, and Hilik the *gabbai* recited the customary Mi Sheberach blessing over him, and then everyone sang and Nir thanked God for watching over him.

And eight days after the birth, when it was time for the Brit Milah, the circumcision ceremony, the newborn screamed and squirmed to mark the event. Nir, more festive in appearance than ever before, his beard trimmed and neat, his hair brushed, cradled the boy, and the air of anticipation in the room was almost unbearable in the minutes leading up to the naming of the baby:

Zevulun—after Shaulit's father, may God avenge his blood, who was murdered by terrorists in northern Samaria.

Yedid'el—a friend of God, for truly the infant is a friend of the Lord, and he will seclude himself in woods and on rocky plains and call to his friend and be at one with Him.

Shir—song, for although the righteous child may not yet speak, he can surely sing and play beautiful songs and melodies, and rising up from his melodies are praises surely to the Lord, blessed be He. For song is a path intended for each and every individual, and surely for Nir, who sang a song to his son, almost nightly, until he was born into this world, and will continue to sing to him, he promises, until he matures and puts his foot down and says, "Enough, Father!" Until then, however, there's still time, bless the Lord.

And thus, his name in the Land of Israel will be Zevulun Yedid'el Shir Rivlin. Mazel tov!

The Explanation

O n Saturday night, following the Havdalah ritual to mark the end of the Sabbath and usher in the new week, and after reciting the prayer for long life and then the customary melaveh malkah meal to escort out the Sabbath Queen, the Kupper-Nehushtan brothers walked together from the synagogue to the home that could now be called their home. They walked in silence, broken occasionally by the discordant barks of Beilin and Condi. Gavriel was troubled by Roni's desecration of the Sabbath. He wondered whether or not he should say something, or if he should question the rabbi about the extent of his own responsibility. He decided to send a text message to Rabbi Aviner's cellular Q&A service: "When a secular guest comes to stay, am I responsible for his desecrations of the Sabbath, for example, placing a dairy spoon in a meat sink, or turning on a light?" The rabbi always told him to ask, not to agonize over things, not to ponder, because a newly observant Jew has many rules to learn, and he must then decide which of them he accepts. It doesn't come naturally like it does for someone who was raised in a religious home. He recalled an example the rabbi once gave him: It is permissible on the Sabbath to use a pair of scissors to cut open a bag of milk for consumption purposes, but cutting paper is forbidden—how would a newly observant Jew know that?

Roni yawned. They'd be home shortly, and while Gabi read his books, the compilations and deeds and Shulchan Aruch, he'd lie down and stare at the ceiling, and then go to sleep, and still be sleeping in the morning when Gabi was already out at work in the fields or hammering away at his cabin.

"That was nice," Roni remarked.

"What was nice?" Gabi responded, wondering what his brother was referring to—the Havdalah ritual, the prayer, or the Sabbath Queen in general.

"A new boy. Received with dignity and joy. With love."

Gabi's hands were clasped behind his back. He smiled to himself woefully, the pom-pom at the tip of his wide skullcap wobbling as he walked.

Roni glanced over at his brother. "Wouldn't you like another one?" he asked.

Gabi didn't respond. His eyes were fixed to the ground. A familiar pain shot through him—that sharp pain that burned every time he was reminded of his young son, whom he hadn't seen in many years. His Mickey.

"You okay?" Roni asked.

"Maybe. Maybe I'd like another one. I don't know. Everything's in God's hands."

"Only in God's hands? Isn't up to you a little, too? If you want it, if you look for someone?"

"I'm waiting." Roni would never be able to understand that a new child could never be a replacement for a child you once had, Gabi thought.

"You said that Rabbi Nachman preached against despair and . . . what was it? Sadness and sorrow and all that."

"Do I look sad to you? All human suffering stems from a lack of understanding, because when a person has understanding, he is able to see that every single thing that happens to him is sent to him directly from God and that it is all for his own good. And even when he is experiencing some kind of distress, the fact that he knows it is from God helps him to endure and tolerate it and even be filled with happiness . . ."

"Yes, you look a little sad to me," Roni said.

"Look who's preaching now. You're the right one to be talking to me about kids, about a wife. You who ran off to America, for what, money? And even that you didn't—"

"Forget about me for a moment. What about you, Gabi? Are you truly happy with the way things are?"

"I truly am. I'm great. I'm surprised that you ask. It is a great mitzvah to always be happy. I couldn't be a believer without joy. Faith is joy. Sorrow leads to idol worship and heresy."

"It sounds to me like you're trying hard to convince yourself with those quotations."

"Roni, you're behaving dishonorably. You're a guest here, you're getting what you need, a bed, food. All I ask in return is that you respect the Sabbath, kashrut, the mitzvoth. You sometimes desecrate the Sabbath, presumably not deliberately. I accept it and forgive you. But now you're giving me a hard time about it, too? Can't you help yourself? If you don't feel the same passion that burns in my heart, that's fine. But at the very least, don't disparage it."

"I'm not being disparaging." Roni took out his light blue pack of cigarettes as they entered the yard. "It's nice out. Want to sit for a while?" He sat down on the beach chair, alongside a springy Donald Duck ride uprooted from some playground, which now lay there on its side.

"No," Gabi said, and went inside.

Roni smoked. The darkness thickened. He had learned to love the nights on the hilltop. At first he was troubled by the silence and missed the incessant hum of the city when he slept, and sometimes the unknown contained in the silence, the threat that seeped through it, would even wake him. Now he was addicted to the silence of the small hours, to the sense of it enveloping him like a comforter. He replayed the argument with Gabi in his mind and suddenly recalled the last time he had seen Mickey—a blond kid, small and energetic. He felt a pang in his heart. Perhaps Gabi was right. He didn't deserve any flak from Roni.

Roni went inside after finishing his cigarette. "I didn't mean to piss you off," he said.

"Then don't piss me off. Why don't you simply sort out the things you need to sort out and then move on? Resolve your problems and go back to your life?" Gabi asked, raising his eyes to look at Roni. "It's not that I don't want you staying here with me; really, it's for your own good. You sleep all day, you're messing around with that damn olive oil. I don't know and don't even want to know what kind of scheme you are hatching to try to make some money from it. I'm not judging you, it's your life. But perhaps you should try to cure yourself of the obsession, of these vices. I cry out from my heart to God for you, I shout and weep to Him and plead for Him to help you like He helped me."

Roni rested a hand on his brother's shoulder. "Thanks, Gabi," he said. "I know you want what's best for me." He went into the kitchen to make them both a coffee, and they sat together in the living room. And before Gabi had the chance to reach out for one of his books, Roni told him why he had come to the hilltop.

"After the army. After the kibbutz. After Mom Gila. A kibbutz boy in Tel Aviv. The apartment on Shlomo Hamelech Street. The goldfish. The bar in Kikar Malchei Yisrael, Bar-BaraBush. The partnership with Oren Azulai. You remember, right? The good old days, the go-go nineties, the greed. Always more and more and more: more girls, more business, more money."

He told Gabi about his meeting with Idan Lowenhof, who opened his eyes to New York's world of high finance and helped him get there. About his bachelor's degree in Tel Aviv and his MBA in New York. About Goldstein-Lieberman-Weiss investment bank and the private clients and the endless days in front of the screens and the adrenaline of the trading and the money, sums so unimaginable that no matter how many times he tried to explain it to Gabi, Gabi simply couldn't understand how it had all disappeared, and not only that, but how Roni was now so deep in debt that he had no way of climbing out.

It was the monologue of someone who had worked through the story in his own mind on endless occasions, of someone who had analyzed to the point of exhaustion the drive, the goals, the motives, but had yet to get to the bottom of them. The gambles, the successes, the mistakes, that, within the space of a few months during the American economy's most dramatic fall, had pushed his brief and meteoric career into a fatal tailspin and eventually driven him that wintry day in February from San

Francisco straight to the West Bank, dressed in an elegant Hugo Boss suit and worn-out socks, and in possession of scarcely anything else.

Gabi sipped from his mug, but it was empty, and he peered into it, as if to request permission. "Well . . . ," he finally said, "at least you've told me something at last." They had hardly spoken since Roni's arrival, despite Gabi's efforts now and then to question him. Truth be told, they had never been ones for heart-to-hearts.

"And what do you think?" Roni asked.

"You know what I think. Everything lies with God. If He brought you here, then here you should be."

Roni looked at his brother, astounded, but didn't respond. He went to the bathroom, returned, and found Gabi in the same position on the sofa. "You work a lot, don't you, my brother?" Roni said.

"God willing, blessed be His name," Gabi answered, lifting his eyes.

"Good, good, that's great. And tell me, you probably manage to save a little, right? Life here is cheap—this trailer, for example, what did you say the rent is, three hundred shekels?"

"Salaries here aren't the same as in the city. I try to save a little, with the grace of God." Gabi immediately understood the implication of the silence that settled in the room. He had a knack for knowing exactly what Roni wanted. "Roni, I have nothing to give you," he said. "I mean, I'm already helping you, and quite a bit, too: the food, the bills."

"I know. Of course. And what about Uncle Yaron's savings plan? Is there nothing left in there?"

"That's long gone. I live hand-to-mouth. And the little I do manage to save is set aside for a sacred purpose."

"I didn't ask you to forgo any purpose, God forbid. What purpose?"

Gabi wanted to travel to Uman for Rosh Hashanah. He had harbored the dream for several years, and this year, he was going to make it happen. "I will do everything in my power, spanning the length and breadth of the creation, to cleanse and save him. I will take hold of his sidelocks and pull him out of hell," Rabbi Nachman said of all those who come to visit his grave, and Gabi needed that more than ever before. To air out his thoughts, to see green before his eyes, to feel the rain on his shoulders. To get away from where he was and to get as close as possible to the rabbi. To lie on his grave, to pray with the thousands at his tomb and in his *kloiz*, his synagogue. To experience the singing and dancing, and the Torah scroll and the outbursts of joy he had seen on YouTube. To seclude himself in the very same forests and under the very same trees that the elderly Nachman had, that Reb Natan from Breslov had, under the tutelage of the Baal Shem Tov in Medzhybizh, and with Rabbi Levi Yitzchak of Berditchev. Nachman promised eternal salvation to everyone who comes to his tomb, everyone who offers a coin to charity for his soul and recites the *Tikkun HaKlali*, the ten Psalms that serve as repentance for all sins.

"Rosh Hashanah is what, four, five months away?" Roni said. "No problem. By then, I'd have sorted out a proper bank loan and orders will already be coming in. For sure. You won't be missing out on Uman this year, bro, and I'll tell you something else—you'll go again next year, on your brother's dime. So what do you have to say about that kind of bonus? That's what you call interest with interest!"

Gabi didn't know what to say.

And ten minutes later, he had yet to utter a word. Thoughts continued to crash into the roof of his mind. After all, it didn't make any sense whatsoever. The scales weren't even close to being balanced: On the one end, his dream, his money, earned by the sweat of his brow, working the land and building the country. On the other, a dubious enterprise, amateurish, with Arabs, on the part of an irresponsible man, with a chronic propensity for getting himself into a jam, who had cut ties, who hadn't uttered a single word of sympathy during the toughest time in his own brother's life. Not to mention his lifestyle and beliefs on the one hand, and their absolute heresy on the other. Nonetheless, his older brother was in distress, was asking for help; perhaps it was the only way for him to escape his entanglement into the light. Would he deny that to his brother for simply a fistful of dollars? And perhaps Roni was right and it really was a unique opportunity, a safe bet, and the loan really would be repaid quickly and yield the promised interest. Gabi wanted to consult God, the rabbi, his books.

Roni went out into the yard, smoked a cigarette, and returned, waited a while longer, and then asked bitterly, "Why the silence?"

"Silence. As if to say, 'Be silent, thus is the highest thought.' The righteous man is silent."

Roni shook his head. He drew himself some water from the tap and went to sit in the armchair. "You used to be different," he said, "more open, more inquisitive. I don't know."

"And what good did it do me?"

It was Roni's turn not to answer.

"I suppose it's better to manage a bar in Tel Aviv?" Gabi continued. "Or to go to America and lose millions of dollars—your clients' and your bank's and your own—and to shirk responsibility? Or to come looking for handouts for some shady deal with Arabs?"

"I don't feel the need to apologize for doing business and living the good life. Is your life any better? Are you happier? Are your values any nobler? What are those values? To be silent? To pray? To stop using electricity at a certain time on a Friday? I don't get it."

"I know you don't get it," Gabi said.

"Explain it to me, then. What do you get out of endlessly reading and memorizing things said two hundred years ago by some Ukrainian rabbi who told you to be silent, or to sing, or to rejoice, or God knows what?"

"Peace of mind," Gabi replied. "It brings me tranquility, love, happiness. For some reason, it's hard for you to accept that. Maybe you're trying too hard not to see it."

"And maybe you're trying too hard to see it."

"I'm not trying at all. I'm feeling. I feel at home."

"At home? What do you mean at home? Some home! An illegal home, according to the court. Do you feel at home by puncturing the tire of a military jeep that's here to watch over you? Is there a quote about that? What about the law?"

"Disrespect for the law is better than disrespect for God."

"And what about respect for people?"

"Now all of a sudden you care about respect for people? All you're interested in is your ridiculous olive oil enterprise. Don't go thinking that people around here are happy about it. People talk. They ask how long you'll be staying and want to know why we're putting you up if you're working with Arabs. And you want me to lend you money for that?"

Gabi's voice rose. He didn't want this confrontation, but if Roni was insisting, so be it, let him know the truth.

"Ah, so that's what it's all about. I get it. I'm working with the cruel enemy, I'm a cynical shit with no values who only wants to make money. I guess opposing hypocrisy and violence, and working with people who, for the most part, have it pretty rough, means having no values. People are talking about me? Great. Let them come tell me to my face, tell me to go."

Gabi didn't appear impressed. "I see you've adopted the line of the extreme leftists. Do me a favor! The Arabs have it rough, the Arabs are saints, the Arabs, the Arabs, the Arabs . . ."

"The Arabs are to blame, too, for the wife and child who won't allow you near them, right?" Roni yelled. "The Arabs, and secular values, and lust for flesh and money, right? But the sanctity of the Land of Israel and singing praises to God and keeping quiet will allow you to forget Mickey and Anna, won't they?"

Roni had more to say, but the expression on his brother's face stopped him. He went outside and walked down to the edge of the hilltop, to the shining stars carried on the wind, to the dark night. Gabi was asleep already when he returned. But waiting on the table for Roni was a check.

The Suspect

A few days later, in the evening, Gabi's phone rang. "Gavriel Nehushtan, hello," he answered. The name Gavriel still managed to bring a smile to Roni's face. "It's for you," Gabi said. Roni's smile turned into a frown.

An hour later, Roni walked into the neighboring trailer of the Yisraeli family. Nehama made him tea with mint leaves and offered cookies. Hilik gestured toward a chair and Roni sat down.

"I don't understand why you invited me over," he said to Hilik, Othniel, and Jean-Marc Hirschson, who sat across from him on the sofa. "What is this, an Absorption Committee rerun?" He smiled, cookie crumbs clinging to his teeth. He was hoping deep down that they had changed their decision regarding the new trailer and were now going to offer it to him instead of the Gotlieb family.

"Look, Roni," Hilik began, his eyes focused on a point slightly above Roni's head as he scratched his forehead with his fingernail, close to his skullcap. Othniel looked him straight in the eye, while Jean-Marc appeared transfixed by the alligator on his pink Lacoste shirt. "Let's get straight to it. We know that you won't be able to confirm or elaborate on all we have to say to you now, but we invited you here nevertheless because we feel it's important to tell you that we know."

"Know what?" Roni asked.

"Hang on, let me finish. Where was I?"

"We feel it's important to tell him that we know," Jean-Marc said without taking his eyes off Roni.

"Yes, we simply want you to know that we know. Do as you see fit with this information, tell or don't tell your handlers, it's your decision entirely." Roni fixed Hilik with a stupefied gaze. "Now look here, I want to say another thing. We appreciate you guys. Very much. You do a very tough and blessed job, day and night, in order to maintain the security of the country, including in the settlements, the Jewish Division and all that. I mean, the monitoring is a little over-the-top, after all, and as strange as this may sound to you, we are not sitting on the hilltops and plotting the murder of prime ministers or Arabs. But we won't deny the existence of undesirable elements, bad seeds. Let's just call them guys who, in the name of positive goals, get caught up in negative actions, sometimes as provocation, sometimes not entirely through any fault of their own, but we won't get into that now." Othniel nodded. "So we understand the importance, and the need, for people inside the settlements who relay information."

Hilik paused and took a sip of his instant coffee. Shneor called to his mother from his room. Roni cast a bemused look over the three men who sat across from him. He opened his mouth to speak, but Hilik cut in. "Look," he said, "the story with the Gotlieb family. We realize you were offended. We understand that you wanted to move in there temporarily."

"Ah, never mind. It's dead and buried," Roni said.

"It causes problems, you see," Hilik continued, disregarding Roni's remark. "There was a waiting list, and we prefer young families, religious ones, people we can count on for the long run . . ." He looked at his fellow sofa occupants and then turned again to Roni. "We're simply saying, okay, your work is important, do what you have to do, but if possible, at this point in time, hold off for just a little, allow us to get organized. It's not like we've been planning a terror attack! A trailer arrived, we moved a family in, that's it. No reason to run out and announce it to the world."

Roni pointed a finger at himself in astonishment, as if to say, You mean me? Are you saying I was the one who let on? Who would I have inform—

"Anyway," Othniel broke into his thoughts, "good luck, I mean it. You know, Roni, that you're a welcome guest here with us, with your brother whom we love very much, and we wholeheartedly invite you to remain here under our roofs for as long as you want, okay? But when the time is right, let's coordinate our positions, okay?" Othniel tapped his nose with his finger.

"We know you can't say yes or no or admit to anything," Jean-Marc went on. "But we're simply saying that we know, and if you can, be considerate. That's all."

The three settlers sipped from their mugs. Jean-Marc bit into a cookie. "Mmmm . . . apricot."

Roni gathered that the meeting was over and stood to leave. "Okay, I'll be off then, yes? Unless there's something else?"

Othniel stood and placed a broad hand on Roni's shoulder. "We're done, buddy, off you go. Good night, and regards to Gavriel. And Hilik"—Othniel turned to his friend—"perhaps you really should get Roni to help you with your doctorate on the kibbutzim?"

"I'd love to," Hilik responded. "I'm sure I'll have more time after Nehama gives birth."

With the suspect gone, the three exchanged looks in silence.

Roni decided to go for a short walk along the ring road. There was a chill in the night air, but the wind had dropped somewhat and he managed to light a cigarette using his hands as cover. Along the way, he was surprised by his brother, who was beginning the night shift. "What's up, bro?" Gabi asked.

"Everything's cool."

"What did they want?"

"Oh, nothing, really . . . I don't know. Truthfully, I didn't understand, exactly."

"Okay, tell me later. I'm heading in to read some teachings. I've been waiting to do this all day."

Amused, Roni looked at the book in his brother's hand. "Go for it. Have a blast, bro."

A few days later, Ariel called. Roni was still in his underwear in bed, his legs raised. Gabi sat across from him, his face buried in one of Rabbi Nachman's books, his tongue whispering, his eyes aglow, entirely oblivious to any outside disturbance. Roni noticed the bare furrows forming under his brother's broad skullcap, the inevitable beginning of baldness. He ran anxious fingers through his hair, but all was well. It still grew thick, dense and bushy, dark, and at a length that by then justified a quick visit to the barber, had he been living in a normal place, that is. Ariel had spoken to an expert on millstones. He was having second thoughts. He had sent Roni a link by e-mail and told him to take a look.

Roni went over to the old laptop in the kitchen. "The Internet connection here alone is going to break me and send me back to the real Israel," he said to Ariel. While waiting to connect, to the screeching sound of the dial-up modem, the power went out. Lacking a battery in working order as backup, the computer shut down. "Enough already! Enough! I've had enough! I'm sick of this dirty asshole of a place! How can anyone live like this? Fucking hell!" The power returned moments later, and Roni restarted the computer. It rattled and hesitated, went black, lit up, and displayed the Windows logo on a sky-blue background, played the opening tune. A full three to four minutes went by before it had warmed up and booted up and was ready for operation. Roni again clicked on the Internet connection button, and again waited to the sounds of the dial tone and then the engaged signal, the dial tone and then the engaged signal, until the connection attempt was finally snapped up into the shrieking and whistling and rising and falling jaws of the Internet. He opened the e-mail program, which appeared, too, to be in no hurry to go anywhere, and found the desired message and clicked the link that opened the Internet browser, at a snail's pace, until he finally reached the promised land.

His eyes clouded over.

"Are you kidding me?" he asked Ariel, who had been waiting on the line all this time. "I thought we'd settled that issue by now."

"The quality of the oil from millstones is inferior to that from modern presses with centrifuges. My expert says no one uses them these days for good reason. They're dirty, you need more people to operate them, they get moldy, and the oil acquires a more acidic taste, an unpleasant after-taste, it goes bad. He says the Arabs are fixed in their ways, they don't spray against the olive fruit fly—"

"Of course they don't spray! It's organic! Ariel, forget about the pretentious Tel Aviv experts! Despite all their fancy explanations, Musa's oil tastes way better than the lot of them, and precisely because of everything that has touched on those stones over the years. Do you truly believe that anyone gives a damn about centrifuges when tasting olive oil? Who cares? Bring them a flavorful, cheap oil, tell them it's organic, made in the traditional way, tried and tested through the ages. It'll sell like hotcakes."

Silence at the other end of the line.

"What's your problem with the deal with Musa?" Roni asked.

"I don't want to do anything illegal."

"Just a moment," Roni said. He threw on a pair of shorts and a T-shirt, slipped his feet into his flip-flops, went out, and walked to the playground, sat down on a bench. A handful of children were still swinging and sliding before darkness fell.

"We're not breaking any law," he whispered into the mouthpiece. "We're doing business." He felt a tremor of déjà vu down his spine. Someone had said the very same words to him not too long ago. "That's what's so great about the territories," he continued. "There are no rules, you can make them up as you go along. It's so cheap here, it's another country. The Chinese produce for the Americans, but many people don't realize that the territories can produce for Israel. The genius of simplicity."

"You want to label it extra-virgin without receiving the Olive Board's stamp of approval."

"Everyone does it. Didn't you read about it in *Yedioth Ahronoth*? So we won't mention the Olive Board. We'll simply label it extra-virgin. You know what, we'll write it in English only." He removed his sunglasses to gaze at Gitit Assis's long, black hair as she pushed her brother Shuv-el on the swings. Talk about extra-virgin, he thought.

"Did you find a boutique that will buy from us in cash?"

"Are you sure you don't want to do this properly, with books and all?"

The sunset was in its full glory, accompanied by a strengthening wind. Roni scratched behind his ear. "I don't want to get involved with the tax and VAT authorities until we're certain that the business is going somewhere. It's not breaking the law, it's a running-in period, until we find our footing and know if it's worth the effort. What do you want, to get started with all the red tape, and to set up a company, and register, and begin paying taxes to those shits before we've seen a single shekel?"

Silence on the other end of the line.

"Jesus Christ! Lighten up."

"I don't know, Roni. I need to think about it."

"What's to think about? Come visit again. First of all, there's a check waiting here for you—my share, which you rightly requested. Besides, you need to loosen up a little, you know. It isn't so scary the second time, you'll see. Five minutes with the desert spread out before you and you'll be talking differently. You're so, so, soooo tight-assed down there."

"And what if we don't find a boutique who wants to sell it? What if they find out that it's oil pressed by some Arab and his donkey?"

"That's no way to speak about Roni and Musa's Oil. Put a drop on their tongues and then let's see what the centrifuges do for them. Tried and tested for five thousand years, nothing beats millstones!" The last sentence, said in a higher tone, caused Shaulit Rivlin to look up from little Zvuli's baby carriage. Roni smiled and waved at her; she smiled in return and resumed her singing to the infant. "Ariel, you're wearing me out, man. As they say in Spanish, *muqa-muqa*, one thing at a time. Come visit, let's discuss it when we're chilled. Then you can go to the boutiques. I'd like to see the boutique that doesn't take it at this price."

"You know what? Maybe. I'll see when I can come by."

Roni chuckled. "I knew this place had grabbed you, you settler boy, you!" He hung up and thought, It hasn't grabbed me. He was still bristling from the power outage and slow Internet service, and he wanted a haircut and a Diet Coke in a glass bottle and a cigarette and cashew nuts. But where would he get them now? How did people live like this?

The Doubts

E vening settled on the hilltop. Cars passed through the gate and guard post—drivers returning from their daily routines, attending classes and teaching and visits to the hardware store in the city. They waved to the smiling Yoni, pulled up outside their homes, and retrieved their shopping bags from the backseat. The wind picked up when the light faded, in perfect harmony. At this time of the year, the wind can be a real nuisance, rattling the trailers, the swing sets in Mamelstein Playground, the Donald Duck in Gabi's yard, passing under the floors, through the hole where a window once was in the now-torn-up chassis of a Peugeot 104, rocking the traffic sign near the synagogue, flapping the plastic sheeting of Othniel's mushroom greenhouse. The wind carried the lonely, angry barks of Beilin and Condi and the cries of the hungry or tired or hurting infants. The wind smacked against Roni's flesh—he had stepped outside in a T-shirt to take a call—and it caught Gitit's beautiful hair. It blew up grains of sand and dust, formed small whirlwinds in the distance, swirled clouds in the sky, and sometimes carried a few errant drops of wet rain.

Mothers and big sisters played with the little ones and read stories and began bathing them, together or one by one. The men tossed their newspapers on armchairs and sat down for a while, hugged whichever child chose to jump on them, drank a cup of tea. Those who performed manual labor washed off the day's troubles and dirt. Others lifted their fingers from their keyboards and rubbed their eyes.

On the way to evening service at the synagogue, they hugged their prayer books and themselves, stooped but determined. Some attended the late-afternoon service before the sun went down, and then went out for a cigarette break on the wooden bench newly arrived from Jerusalem, made inquiries about the bulldozers, and verified gossip. They raised their voices and lowered their heads against the wind, patted down their skullcaps and hurried back inside, and when the final prayer service for the day ended, they returned home to join their wives and children.

Nehama Yisraeli prepared omelets for her husband, Hilik, and her sons, four-year-old Boaz and two-year-old Shneor. Hilik had promised to help out more with the children ahead of the birth of their new baby, particularly at dinnertime. She had hatched the idea of organizing a biweekly Torah study for the women of the hilltop, and he had urged her on, declaring he'd take care of the boys. But Hilik was caught up with the evacuation threat and the absorption of the Gotlieb family and everything, and feeling sudden inspiration to make some headway with his research, he made several trips to the university. He had started to read an excellent book, Arthur Koestler's *Thieves in the Night*, which beautifully captured the mood of communal settlement and land redemption that swept the Galilee in the 1930s.

And so, in a state of advanced pregnancy, after a day at the kindergarten watching over seven small children, Nehama found herself on her feet beating eggs for an omelet. Everything's in God's hands, she thought, and smiled wearily, recalling how the children that morning, led by her Boaz and Emunah Assis, had tried to sing "Lecha Dodi."

"Just give me two minutes," Hilik said on returning from the prayer service. He lay back in the armchair and the boys jumped on him.

"Take your time, rest easy," she said. "Boys, tell Dad what you did at kindergarten today." They told him. He was suitably amazed. After dinner and with the boys put to bed, she tidied the mess in the kitchen and living room, washed the dishes, and was on her back in bed by nine. "I'm dead," she said to her husband just seconds before sleep took her. He folded his glasses and placed them on the bookcase, then removed his skullcap and placed it folded alongside them, and lay down beside her, and caressed her ball-like stomach, and while deciding whether to read the op-ed page in *Yedioth Ahronoth* or a couple of pages of Koestler's book, he succumbed to his deep breaths and slipped into the abyss of sleep.

* * *

The chaos in the Assis family had reached new heights. Shuv-el was sitting on Gitit's lap and they recited the customary blessing over produce from the land and she tried to feed him salad that he didn't want. All he wanted was "orange juith," and he sipped from it after it was poured. Othniel was eating salad with a spoon and speaking on the phone with his distributor, Moran. "Yakir!" he yelled. "How much *labaneh* is on order for tomorrow? Oops, no, Yakir, I mean cherry tomatoes. How much for tomorrow? What? Both together? Can you all keep it down a little? Hananiya!"

"Just a sec," Yakir shouted back. He was on the Internet, in Second Life, the multiplayer game in which everyone designs a personal avatar that roams through a virtual world, accumulates items—from shoelaces to a home—and interacts and forms bonds with other characters. Yakir's avatar on Second Life was a settler who looked a little like him with the addition of a beard, and he had found a number of friends, like-minded, religious Zionist Jews, and together they'd settled on an island they'd named Revival, and they'd erected a synagogue and prayed and spoke and roamed the world keeping the flame alive.

"Why's Yakir on the computer?" his mother, Rachel, asked his father. "He needs to eat dinner. Yakir! Come eat, get off the computer!"

"Just a minute," Othniel responded. "Moran's on the line. It's important!"

Yakir's friends were about to visit Islam-Online, one of the Muslim sectors on Second Life, to mess with the Arabs a little. He excused himself, logged out, quickly scanned the farm's orders, and made it to the table just as Hananiya pushed Emunah off her chair and her head slammed into the table leg, causing her to burst into tears, openmouthed and exposing a missing tooth. Shuv-el, in a gesture of kindness, then asked to get down from Gitit's knees, and Dvora suggested Yakir try "the excellent salad," to which he replied, "What else is there?" and Gitit said, "Yogurt," and Rachel said, "Hananiya, apologize right now!"

"I don't know what we're going to do this Sabbath about my sister," Neta Hirschson said to Jean-Marc. "She eats only strictly kosher food, *mehadrin.* Do you think I should ask her about it? Perhaps we should ask the rabbi what to do?"

"Or maybe we should simply buy mehadrin," he replied hesitantly. Jean-Marc, in fact, had been born into a completely secular family, in Yamit. His father, a vintner who emigrated from France, and his mother, the daughter of a World War II partisan and a kibbutznik father, were among the founders of Ma'aleh Hermesh A. in the 1970s.

"And what about the dishes?" Neta asked, complicating matters.

"Ask the rabbi."

After dinner Neta made coffee and cut some slices of cake. "Do you think we should introduce her to Gavriel?" she asked.

"Which Gavriel?"

"Nehushtan."

"Gabi? Are you crazy? He's a reborn."

"You're a reborn, too," said Neta, the daughter of the rabbi of Ofra and a mother who helped establish Sebastia, the very first West Bank settlement.

"Exactly, your poor parents. Do you want to burden them with another one? Besides, your parents knew mine, and me. It's not like I was a reborn after a mysterious past."

"I think he's quite sweet, actually. A little quiet. He has faith. How bad could his past be? The story with his son is awfully sad. He looks like a really good guy."

"Divorced," Jean-Marc said, continuing to play the devil's advocate.

"That's life. What's done is done. Look at him now, the way he's taken in that strange brother of his. So tolerant."

"He's a good guy, I'm not disagreeing. But not for your sister. He's too old. She still has time, doesn't she?"

"She'll be twenty-four soon."

"Oh," Jean-Marc said, clutching his coffee mug as he contemplated. "I see. Okay, let me think if I know anyone."

"Never mind. Let's first see what we're going to do about this mehadrin business," Neta said, and then flashed an inviting smile. "I was at the *mikveh* today," she continued. "Instead of a new son-in-law, what do you say to giving my parents a grandchild?" Jean-Marc smiled. But his smile soon faded after Neta turned around and walked into the bedroom. They had been trying since their wedding, for more than a year, and not only had the act itself turned mechanical, businesslike, devoid of any tenderness and intimacy, Neta had begun coming apart at the seams. She so desperately wanted children, and in time her want had become an obsession, consumed her entirely and sometimes boiled over—in the form of complaints against Jean-Marc, angry online exchanges with leftists, verbal abuse hurled at soldiers or other annoying government officials who came to the hilltop. Sometimes—it usually happened the day her period insisted on showing up, an unwanted guest whom no one had invited—silence, a turning in on herself, to the point even of canceling beauty treatments she had set up with clients, closing the shutters, and sliding quietly between the sheets. And now, to the task at hand.

Raya Gotlieb sat on a plastic chair in the corner of the room, unable to hold back the tears. "Is this what we left our home for, Nachi?" she asked her husband. They had just put the children down to sleep. Nachum was half lying, half sitting on the mattress in their bare living room. He wanted to be positive, but he didn't have a good answer. The list of problems with their "new" trailer was endless: the missing shower door caused a mini-flood in the bathroom, not to mention the lack of privacy, and there was no showerhead, which made for an erratic stream of water and yet more flooding. The kitchen sink was missing its hot water tap, and Raya washed the dishes in cold water only. There were no shutters in the children's room, so Nachum transferred the ones from the main bedroom, which was then filled with light every morning at six. Perhaps the most humiliating was the square piece missing from the linoleum floor of the kitchen. Who would think of stealing a piece of linoleum? Nachi Gotlieb stared at the vacant square, the sticky edges of which had already collected bits of dirt. The nerve.

Their possessions were brought in little by little in Nachum's car because Othniel had asked them not to use a large truck so as not to attract unwanted attention at a sensitive time such as this. They had to watch out for the sector's brigade commander and the company commander, who were frequently in the area, the soldiers at the guard post who would report the arrival of a moving van, and then, of course, you had the left-wing groups and Civil Administration inspectors, and—Othniel paused, looked over his shoulder and lowered his voice—we may have an informant in our midst who's monitoring and reporting our activities, and the truth, too, is that the neighbors from Givat Yeshua won't be too pleased to hear that a family has moved into the trailer that was intended for their community and is awaiting a transportation permit from the Defense Ministry. It's therefore best, Othniel explained, to keep a low profile. So Nachi drove back and forth, to and from Shiloh, taking days off work, packing the car to the brim. But some things simply wouldn't fit in the Nissan Winner—the washing machine, for instance. So Raya had been doing the washing in the sink, without hot water, or at friends' houses in Ma'aleh Hermesh B., but she no longer felt comfortable doing so. They were still without a refrigerator and an oven, so they tried to get by with a small icebox and an electric hot plate, which blew the generator every evening.

"But the people are really nice, they brought cakes and toys for the kids, and there was a request in the newsletter to all those who took things to return them," Nachum said in an effort to lift his wife's spirits. "And Shimi and Tili love the playground." Raya responded with another bout of sobbing, and he knew why. Back in Shiloh, their former home stood opposite an amazing playground where the children would play unsupervised for hours every day.

"I just hope and pray this god-awful wind doesn't keep them up tonight, too," she lamented.

Nachum was an optician. He loved the fashion part of the job—an aspect of the business that Raya helped with by choosing the frame catalogs and suiting frames to faces when she was in the store—but he also loved the medical element, helping to mend the body, allowing people to see the world as it is.

"The nature here is stunning," he said, peering into the black night through the torn netting in the window. "You can't enjoy the view but complain about the wind. You have to see the big picture," he added, his voice filled with tenderness.

* * *

Roni went out for a walk and stopped to listen to the radio for a few minutes with Yoni at the sentry post. "Don't you ever go home?" he asked the
soldier. "You seem to be here all the time."

Yoni, paging through an issue of the men's magazine *Blazer*, smiled.
"I'm home this Sabbath at last."

"Where's home?"

"Netanya."

Roni had nothing to say about Netanya. Two minutes later, he stood
up, smiled, and bade Yoni a good night. Outside again, he gritted his
teeth against the wind and thought, Poor guy, he got the worst of both
worlds. An Israeli and an African. God! At least he's still able to smile.

He stopped on the way home at Gabi's cabin-in-the-making and
turned on the pale light. He saw that Gabi was almost done assembling
a wooden bed frame and remembered his brother telling him that once
the bed was in place, he would begin sleeping in the cabin. And though
he had yet to hook up a water pipe, and there was no furniture, and the
roof wasn't finished (Gabi was waiting for tiles promised him by a friend
from a hilltop near Itamar, beautiful green tiles; the friend simply needed
to complete construction of a roof on his hilltop and would then give
Gabi his leftovers), he wasn't concerned at all. On the contrary, he loved
roughing it, he sought that pioneering spirit. Ma'aleh Hermesh C. sometimes felt to him too staid and bourgeois, he used to say, with the stone
cladding on the homes and all. Roni asked him what would happen with
his trailer after he moved. "I don't know," Gabi said. "You'll have to ask
the Absorption Committee." Roni's face dropped. He and the Absorption Committee weren't on the best terms.

Nir rocked baby Zvuli while Shaulit finished bathing Tchelet and
dressed her in a diaper and pajamas. A disaster: Shoshana, the doll without which Tchelet refused to go to bed, had disappeared. The entire
house was turned upside down, mattresses were lifted, furniture was
moved, dark corners were inspected, a flashlight was employed to illuminate the yard—even the search for unleavened food products before
Passover wasn't as thorough. Shaulit finally called Nehama, and after
around ten minutes of idle gossip, the fateful question was posed.

Nehama thought for a moment and then said, "Shoshana may be at the kindergarten."

Nir put on his shoes and exited into the night. He went over to the synagogue, ran into Jehu and Josh in the throes of evening prayer inside, located Shoshana in the day-care area, and returned her to the loving arms of Tchelet, who closed her eyes and dropped off to sleep seconds later. Shaulit raised her red eyes to look at Nir and whispered "Thanks," and he embraced her and caressed her shoulders. She had been feeling down since the birth. Zvuli, she'd say, reminded her of her father, who was murdered by terrorists on the road to Beit El eight years earlier.

"Nehama baked a cake for the Gotliebs," she said, wiping away her tears. "We haven't even been over to welcome them."

Nir made a face. "Get the mixer back from Neta and I'll make something," he said.

Yakir logged on to Second Life again. Because he handled the farm's Internet orders, no one, including Othniel, who knew nothing about computers, dared depose him from his seat at the computer desk. He returned to his virtual character and gazed at the figure on the screen. The avatar pleased him. In addition to a thick black beard, he wore a white skullcap and had a horse called Killer, which King Meir had crowned "supercool." King Meir was—or so he thought, because you can never be sure in Second Life who's behind the virtual characters you encounter—a thirty-six-year-old lawyer from Dallas, Texas, which explained how he was able to lease the virtual island, Revival, for two hundred real dollars a month. The remaining members of the group were, they said, young Jews just like him, mostly Americans, and they all prayed at the Flame of the Revival synagogue that King Meir erected on the island, and they spoke among themselves primarily about Arabs. After all, that's what people do in Second Life, for the most part, talk. You type and your character delivers the words in a cartoon-style speech bubble, and your friends release their words in their speech bubbles. King Meir was the undisputed leader of the group, and Yakir, in all likelihood the only true settler among them, was his favorite.

King Meir, in a yellow shirt bearing the Kach Movement's fist logo and the slogan KAHANE LIVES, wanted to stir things up in the overly tranquil world of Second Life. He wanted to show the Arabs who was boss, cause a commotion in their virtual mosques and their other toxic spaces. He wanted a show of Jewish power! That evening the group spoke about their visit to Islam-Online, where they came across a Palestinian museum that documented "the injustices of the occupation" and "the Palestinian holocaust." King Meir wanted to take action. He wanted the group to plan something that would really hurt the cheeky bastards. Yakir and King Meir and the others—Klaus, the German, and Menachem from California, and several others—threw ideas back and forth in the group chat for quite some time, before Othniel placed a light hand on his son's shoulder and returned him to the real world. "Enough, sweetie, it's bedtime."

The Riot

The massive slabs of concrete—gray, nine meters tall, two meters wide, thirty centimeters thick—the intended building blocks of the border fence arrived on the back of trucks from the Eckerstein plant in Yeruham one day in June, a day of scorching desert winds, with the summer already settled in, past the point of retreat. They were off-loaded near the bulldozers, which for weeks had been dozing in the sun and waiting for their D-day.

Othniel hastily called his regular list of associates at the council, in the Knesset, and in the army. He was told they'd look into the matter, that the alert would be sounded, and that he should continue to report on any developments.

Several days later, the High Court of Justice convened to deliberate the petition—filed jointly by legal counsel for residents of the village of Kharmish, the owners of the olive groves, and the Yesh Din human rights organization—against construction of the fence along its designated route, which would entail the uprooting of the olive groves and the loss of livelihood for their owners. As an act of protest that same morning, many of the village's residents went out and staged a silent sit-in amid the D-9s. Captain Omer Levkovich and his soldiers arrived on the scene to maintain order.

The court heard the arguments of the petitioner and summoned the first witness for the defense on behalf of the State of Israel, a brigadier general with a wealth of security experience who served in the Seam Zone Administration. The officer was questioned on the significance from a security perspective of the location of the fence on that particular ridge, on those private groves. The officer testified to the extreme importance of the fence's location, unraveling a map and pointing at it with one of those foldout rods for pointing at maps. He explained the need to commandeer the land, station guard towers, and erect a high concrete wall to boost security for the settlements, deter enemies, and eradicate rampant and unhindered Palestinian terror.

Testifying for the petitioners was a reserve officer from the very same forces—a major general, with a long history of service in Israel's wars and a wealth of security experience with the Arab enemy in general and the Palestinian foe in particular. And he was asked: The words spoken by the brigadier general who testified before you, were they the truth? And the reservist major general responded, Bullshit. He outlined the futility of erecting a concrete barrier in the location in question, and he illustrated on the map that the region under discussion was quiet and not dangerous, and what's the point of ripping into the landscape like that, cutting off the local population from their source of livelihood and stirring anger and hate where there was none before?

"With all due respect to the beautiful landscape," responded the counsel for the defense, "we are concerned here with a strategic location, with human lives, and with the security and safety of the Jewish settlers—"

"Who have settled there illegally, on private Palestinian land and a nature reserve, with an eviction order hanging over their heads, a petition against which was rejected recently by this very court . . . If you care to pay attention"—indicating with a metal pointer of his own—"the illegal outpost of Ma'aleh Hermesh C. doesn't even appear on the map—"

"The community is absolutely an integral part of the outline plan for the Ma'aleh Hermesh settlement, which appears on the map, and the final permits will be arranged over the coming days . . ."

"The court is surely enjoying this lesson in how one goes about establishing facts on the fly and obtaining permits later—a feast for the mind, the upholding of the law in all its glory—"

"An honorable institution such as this High Court is not deserving of your cynicism."

"Who are you to speak of cynicism? Now I've heard it all. Next you'll tell me that in the name of democracy—"

The presiding justice put an end to the bickering and requested a show of respect for the court. The justices stepped out to deliberate, to clarify, and to consult, and they summoned the legal representatives to their chambers, exchanged words with them, and sent them back into the courtroom. And the justices then reemerged and read out their ruling: The petition was rejected, swallowed up into the void.

Othniel got word of the ruling from the radio and called Natan Eliav. Natan was pleased to hear that the court had for once put a muzzle on the left-wingers and Arabs and was allowing the army to do its job.

"But what about us?" Othniel asked.

"What do you mean, what about you?"

"We don't want the fence to run along its intended route; we have land there. We were actually rooting for the leftists' petition this time."

"Ah, yes. Let me make a few calls."

Natan got back to Othniel within the hour with a calming message. He had been assured that despite the rejection of the two High Court petitions against the proposed route of the fence, it was up to the defense minister to decide on the appropriate timing for the work to begin. And the defense minister was scheduled to travel to Cairo the following week, and then to Washington—and anyway, he was more concerned right now with the northern border rather than the West Bank—he wasn't expected to make a decision on the matter for the next two weeks, at least.

Othniel hung up and scratched his beard. He glanced at his watch.

Time for coffee at home and then off to the dairy. For some time now, he had wanted to reorganize the operation, replenish products, replace machinery, but current events had put everything on hold. Perhaps he'd finally have a few quiet days to himself to get back on track. He had read a helpful book on the subject, *101 Ways to Build Your Business*, by some young American financial wizard, and decided to adopt a number of them. He filled the kettle and flipped the switch. Yes, he'd go to the dairy. And later that evening, he'd speak to Rachel and Hilik, and they'd schedule a meeting of the Planning Committee to discuss the next stages in the development of the settlement—fixed structures, a single-purpose synagogue, a mikveh, the absorption of families. The water came to a boil and the switch dropped and he stirred the instant coffee and sugar and water and milk and brought the mug up to his nose, ahhh . . . the aroma of the coffee. He sat down, and the phone rang.

"The loaders are on the move," Gavriel Nehushtan reported.

"Not loaders—bulldozers. So they're packing it in?" Othniel's mind was still awash with positive thoughts.

"What do you mean packing it in? They're starting to work. They're readying the route, moving dirt."

"What?"

As he reached a spot overlooking the neighboring hilltop, Othniel could clearly see the huge machines in motion and people milling around them. Hilik appeared at his side, and together they headed toward the bulldozers. The telephone interrupted with an update from Regional Council Chairman Dov that the Yesha Council has issued a harsh statement and that thousands had been mobilized via text messages, calls, and e-mails and told to get to Ma'aleh Hermesh C. as quickly as possible.

Othniel's mug of coffee, half full, grew cold on the kitchen table.

At the scene were scores of Kharmish residents, most of whom had been sitting there since morning, about a dozen settlers, the two bulldozer crews clearing a route along the edges of the hilltop, at a fair distance still from the olive groves and the outpost, and Captain Omer with eight soldiers.

"What's this all about?" Othniel yelled at Omer Levkovich.

"Haven't you heard? The High Court rejected the petition. The Defense Ministry gave the order to begin work."

The education minister's aide called Othniel. It turned out that the minister was conducting a tour that morning of various educational institutions in the area, and while he hadn't planned on visiting Ma'aleh Hermesh C., was there any truth to the rumors that the settlement was being evacuated at that very moment?

"Things could go that way very quickly," Othniel responded, recognizing the opportunity. "If the minister could come by to show support and perhaps say a few words to the soldiers and the media, it certainly wouldn't do any harm."

"We're on our way," the aide said, and at the behest of the minister, he placed a call to the prime minister's office to demand a suspension of the work.

Meanwhile, a large military command vehicle, adorned with a range of antennas, lights, and other devices, arrived on the scene. And out stepped none other than the officer in charge of the IDF Central Command, and with him, the brigade commander in the sector.

"Giora!" Othniel Assis called out.

"Othni? Is that you?" responded the major general, smiling behind his sunglasses. "Shit! All I can see is a beard." They embraced. "So, Othni, are you and your buddies making trouble again?" the officer asked.

"Us? Never! We're simply watching. But those monsters dare not try to get anywhere near our homes over there."

"Are you still at Hermesh C.? Really? You're unstoppable, man. Where's Levkovich?"

He approached Omer and spoke with him for several minutes. They wandered over to the bulldozers, whose crews alighted and saluted and exchanged a few words with the officers. Omer's soldiers formed a dividing line between the residents of Kharmish and the settlers. The Palestinians wanted the Jews off their land, but the soldiers ignored the request and wouldn't allow them to cross an arbitrary line drawn by the company commander. A handful of peace activists joined the Palestinians, brandishing placards denouncing the occupation. God only knows how they appeared on the scene so quickly. Roni Kupper cast a watchful eye over them, hoping to find the well-endowed leftist from the time before, but he didn't see her.

The head of the Central Command and Omer returned, and behind them, the D-9s started up again.

"The work goes on," the major general said to no one in particular.

"What do you mean the work goes on, Giora?"

"The work goes on means the work goes on, Othni, my friend. Look"—he turned to point at the bulldozers, which were moving off slowly on their tracks—"the work goes on."

"But what work? Uprooting the olive trees, and then what?"

The major general smiled. "I know what you're driving at, Othni, my friend. Come, let me explain it to you once and for all. Listen, understand what we are doing, and then all of you—settlers, Arabs, left, right, and you, too, pretty horse"—he pointed at Killer—"can turn around and go home to rest." The crowd was silent. Giora adjusted his sunglasses and continued. "As you know, a decision was made to erect the fence along this route here. So we are clearing and preparing the ground for construction."

"But what—"

"I'm not done. And I still know what you're driving at, Othni, my dear. And the answer is yes. In the wake of the High Court's decision today, the unauthorized outpost of Ma'aleh Hermesh C. will be evacuated as part of the preparation for the construction of the fence, and in accordance with the law. That's what 'the work goes on' means. Thank you."

"In accordance with the law?" shouted a square-jawed activist in a Meretz Party shirt who was holding a half-eaten sandwich. "You've taken land and fields away from a village. Why don't you deal with the outlaws over there before you destroy the livelihood of dozens of people?"

"Livelihood?" yelled Neta Hirschson. "You're talking about livelihood? First let them stop throwing stones and missiles, and stop their ax and knife attacks, and stop shooting at cars—then we'll speak to them about livelihood."

Giora looked at the orange-head-scarfed settler, bristling with rage. "All right, everyone," he said. "I've laid it out for you. Now, turn around, go home quietly, and let us do our work. Omer, break up the demonstration. Why are there no riot police here?"

Just then, the education minister's official Volvo pulled up, and his driver jumped out to open the door. Regional Council Chairman Dov emerged from the door on the other side. Following close on the Volvo's heels came two news channel trucks from which crews with shoulder-mounted cameras and furry microphones on long poles spilled out. The minister approached the head of the Central Command. The major general repeated to him what he had just said to everyone. The education minister appeared displeased. He turned to face the settlers and began an impromptu address. The television cameras were pushed in his face. "The government in which I serve will not lend its hand to the uprooting of any settlements," he declared, "and Ma'aleh Hermesh C. in particular, a pioneering and leading neighborhood in the heart of the desert that reminds us of our deep-rooted affinity with this land, that sustains the Land of Israel, the values of settling the land and of work, and the righteousness of our path. This is the true Israel, the Zionist, the pioneering—"

The square-jawed left-winger tried to interject, but was silenced by a TV reporter.

"I've come here on behalf of the government to encourage and bolster the settlers. You are the real heroes of our time, the defenders of the State of Israel. I've come here to say: No to Arab aggression, yes to the settlement enterprise, yes to security!"

Sporadic applause issued from the right of the crowd, feeble boos from the left—both sides had swelled in number. The minister responded to questions from the reporters. They then turned to the head of the Central Command, who said, "I'm a soldier and I'm following orders. I received an order and I am carrying it out." The bulldozers meanwhile continued to flatten and shift the earth; the sounds of their tracks and their blades striking against rocks sent shivers through everyone. Roni's eyes searched for Musa, but he couldn't see him in the crowd. The education minister again asked his aide to get ahold of the prime minister.

"Okay, get moving," Neta yelled toward the opposing gathering. "You heard what the minister and major general said. Go home and let the IDF win!"

"Shut up your mouth," yelled a young Palestinian from Kharmish in broken Hebrew. "Go home, you whore."

"What was that?" screamed Neta. "Arrest him. Did you hear what that terrorist said?"

Two soldiers approached the young man and pushed him to the ground. A sense of rage swept through the Kharmish residents and burst forth in the form of loud shouting and a threatening move forward. The soldiers cocked their weapons and growled warnings.

The major general spoke into one of his command car's numerous communication devices, calling for additional soldiers and riot police. Omer's soldiers tried to control the situation in the interim. A grenade launcher materialized and tear gas was fired at the Palestinian side. The wind promptly carried the terrible smell back to the settlers and soldiers. They all covered their noses and mouths. Frantic hands passed bottles of water.

"Calm down now, everyone," Omer shouted. But his voice, despite the megaphone, sounded weak and high-pitched and less than authoritative.

The education minister hurried over to the major general. The officer made him wait. With all due respect to the minister, he was busy mobilizing forces and restoring calm. Finally he turned to him. "Make it quick, man," he said. "We have a situation here."

"I know you have a situation," the minister said, "and what I am trying to say is that the situation is over. I've just now been informed by the prime minister that he's issued an order to suspend the work."

"Come again?" The noise of the yelling and the bulldozers and the megaphone was deafening.

"I said the prime minister has just told me on the phone that he's issued an order to halt the work of the bulldozers, to suspend the evacuation, to stop everything."

The major general looked at him skeptically. "Just a moment, Ivri," he said into the radio to the officer stationed at command headquarters.

"No one has said anything to me about it," he addressed the minister again.

"Check with the Defense Ministry," the education minister said.

Moving away from the command car, the major general walked toward the commotion. "I don't have time for that now," he said. "If new orders come through, they know where to find me."

The bulldozers began crawling slowly toward Musa Ibrahim's olive trees. Another wave of fury reverberated through the crowd of protestors. Dudu, the chubby operator with the wandering eye, positioned the D-9's blade slightly above the ground, in line with the trunk of a tree, and moved forward. "Noooo!" came the cries from all around. The eight soldiers and two officers attempted to halt the protestors, but three managed to break through the human barricade and ran toward the bulldozer, wildly flaying their arms and calling out "No!" and "Stop!" and "Fool!" The soldiers gave chase, but the three outpaced them—two men and a woman, she in a long skirt and an orange head scarf, one man in baggy pants and a kaffiyeh, and the third in a Lacoste shirt and elegant trousers. The television cameramen darted among the olive trees and over heaps of rocks and dirt; Arab women shrieked; Jewish youths cursed and prayed to their Father who art in Heaven; and settlers frowned and squinted their eyes and asked, "Who the hell . . . ?"

The D-9N bulldozer is equipped with a heavy cast-steel front blade. It weighs more than seven tons, stands two meters tall, and measures almost five meters across. Extending from the edge of the blade are sharp steel teeth, and over them and into the curved blade itself, one after the other, climbed Neta Hirschson, Musa Ibrahim, and Roni Kupper, who moments later found themselves lifted skyward by Dudu, the heavy-duty-machinery soldier, who was oblivious of the contents of his new load.

Frantic arm-waving by Central Command Major General Giora stopped Dudu and bulldozer in their tracks, with the three stowaways panting inside its raised blade. Cameramen descended, but the soldiers drove them back. Reinforcements finally arrived and helped to contain the demonstrators, who shouted slogans against the occupation or against terror, for the settlements or for human rights. Captain Omer

Levkovich made eye contact with Dudu behind the controls of the bulldozer and indicated to slowly lower the blade to the ground. The three heroes were returned to earth, to applause all around from the crowd. Neta said something to Musa, and Musa replied. Roni, between them, said something, too, and the three suddenly smiled—more to themselves than to one another, more surreptitiously than openly, but still.

The Central Command's major general was on a call. He nodded and handed back the phone to one of his officers. A soldier used a zip tie to cuff Musa, and more soldiers escorted his fellow blade-jumpers. The major general then approached his troops and asked Omer to gather everyone around. His briefing was a short one: "Guys, we're out of here," he said, and then turned toward his command car.

The Mixed Grill

Jeff McKinley, the *Washington Post*'s Jerusalem correspondent, stared in rapture at the television screen. Gripped between his thick, chubby fingers was a wonderfully flavorful Jerusalem mixed grill in a pita from the Chatzot grill bar, and he tried, as he did every evening, to follow the Hebrew news broadcast, his tired mind managing to catch perhaps one word in every five or ten. The initial images were pretty standard—bulldozers, soldiers, settlers, Palestinians. But then he began to recognize the faces sprouting from the screen: there was the settler who drove him to the wrong outpost, and the settler woman in the orange head scarf looked familiar, too, what was she so mad about now? And there was his fellow hitchhiker, who was dressed in a suit that day, and also the officer who gave him a ride out of the settlement and told him a few interesting things in the military jeep. Yes, he recalled, that's Mamelstein's outpost, and then, as the report reached its climax with the triple jump into the blade of the bulldozer, his eyes widened in astonishment, and the snort of laughter that escaped his lips sprayed bits of meat and fat onto his desk and the papers that lay scattered across it.

Ma'aleh Hermesh C. God, he had almost forgotten. And now that day months earlier was coming back to him. The editor of the newspaper's foreign desk in Washington was angry about his failure to deliver on the promised interview with the minister. The alternative McKinley suggested—a story about Sheldon Mamelstein and his donation of a playground to the illegal outpost—piqued the editor's interest for about half an hour, but was quickly overshadowed by an earthquake with thousands of fatalities in China and a downed plane carrying a load of Estonian parliamentarians, and the paper's space for foreign news filled up. When McKinley succeeded in rescheduling the interview with the minister for two days later—they met at the Knesset—the story about Mamelstein and the outpost fell by the wayside. Another Jewish American millionaire giving money to another West Bank settlement, not exactly the scoop of the decade.

McKinley rested the uneaten quarter of his pita on the desk, open like a smiling mouth, filled not with teeth but bits of meat yellowed by oil and cumin, and rummaged through the papers until he found what he was looking for: the business card of one of Mamelstein's assistants, on the back of which Jeff had scribbled in pencil the telephone number of Captain Omer Levkovich, whose pink, sweaty face just then faded from the screen in favor of the stern-looking Israeli anchorwoman.

Omer Levkovich was inundated with calls following his television appearance, and they served only to heighten his sense of frustration and disgust in view of what had happened that afternoon at Ma'aleh Hermesh C.—the prime minister's intervention in a straightforward military action designed to enforce a High Court ruling. He sat in front of the television, his bare feet soaking in a bucket of warm water and apple vinegar to combat the foot fungus growing on them.

He would be delighted to speak to the American journalist.

"So what are you telling me, Jeff—that a settler woman and an Arab man conspired to jump onto the blade of a bulldozer to prevent the army from building the fence?" asked Jeff's editor at the foreign news desk in Washington when he called with the story.

This time McKinley was in luck, because not only was the outpost he had visited not too long ago making headlines in Israel in the wake of the bulldozer incident, and not only had he gotten his hands on some additional tantalizing material concerning Sheldon Mamelstein and his involvement in the outpost, and not only did the story tie in with a comprehensive investigative report the *Washington Post* was putting together on contributions made by Americans to shady overseas causes that were recognized by U.S. tax authorities as deductible expenses, but a good deal of space had opened up on the international pages after a big story was pulled.

McKinley spent the next two hours writing at his desk in the small office in Jaffa Street, following the mixed grill with some Oriental cookies he found in a cupboard in the kitchenette and a cup of instant coffee, and after he had submitted the story and surfed the Web for a few minutes in case the editor called with questions, he stepped out into the cool warmth of the Jerusalem night, entered a dimly lit bar in the Machane Yehuda Market, lifted his heavy body onto a barstool, and ordered a glass of Ballantine's with lots of ice from the pretty, short-haired bartender, who ignored the oil stain and cookie crumbs on his shirt and smilingly placed the drink on a cardboard coaster in front of him.

The Backlash

Gabi's morning symphony opened, generally, with the beeping of the alarm clock, and then came the squeaking of doors, the opening of windows, the boiling of water in the kettle, slow at first and then rising to the crescendo until the ping of the switch. The stream of urine, the flush of water to wash it away, a finer stream from the faucet over the basin, the brushing of teeth, gargling, phlegm dredged up from the depths of the throat and spat out, the early-morning fart, and the chirping of the goldfinches. Then the kiss of the vacuum-sealed refrigerator door, the rattle of a teaspoon in a cup, the groaning of a chair under weight. And when he dressed, the oil-starved hinges of the closet door squeaked open and shut, and the springs of his mattress groaned when he sat on the bed to put on his socks and shoes (first the right and then the left) and tie his laces (first the left and then the right). And the clomping steps of heavy-duty work shoes. And the slurping of tea. And the door, the rickety state of which required force to close it properly, slamming, really.

For the first few days following Roni's arrival on the hilltop, Gabi was considerate; he was conscious of the volume of noise he generated upon waking. And then one morning, his toothbrush scraping in his mouth, his ears filled with the cries of ravens and the song of Arabian babblers, accompanied by the whistling of the winds and the intermittent banging of rain on the roof, he thought, That's just nature, there's no changing it. And that's my nature, and I'm not going to tiptoe around any longer. Besides, Roni played an equally impressive nighttime symphony of rolls and groans and snores and farts. So Gabi began to perform all those morning deeds and actions at normal volume, beginning with the alarm clock, and through to the door behind which he disappeared, the sound of his footsteps fading, his tefillin bag in the one hand, on his way to synagogue for the morning prayer service.

Initially, Roni would hear the entire procedure, but his well-oiled sleep habit soaked up the noises and contained them, and he drifted on through the depths of slumber before eventually waking unaided several hours later.

There was a relatively large congregation that morning in synagogue, the first minyan in a long time. The traditionally late risers appeared to be there, too, the rushers, the ones who laid tefillin and recited the Shemoneh Esrei prayer at home. It was as if they all felt a need to congregate, to bolster themselves—they didn't yet know why or what they were facing, but they sensed something in the air. And it would take almost a full day before the full picture emerged. The sun would have completed its journey from the arid hilltops to the east through to its disappearance behind the farthest homes of Kharmish to the west, carrying with it a full day of labor, prayer, and learning—a quiet day on the hilltop, another hot early-summer day in Ma'aleh Hermesh C.

And the sun, the very same sun, pressed on westward. Passing Kharmish, it followed its elliptical orbit over the Judean Mountains and down to the green lowlands, and on to the coastal plain, and westward, pausing not even for a moment, across seas and continents and islands and countries, eventually making its tender mark on the East Coast of the great United States of America and glimmering in the windows of the buildings in Washington, D.C., where deliverymen dropped fresh, steaming, hot-off-the-press editions of the *Washington Post* into yards and onto doorsteps and at the entrances to offices and into mailboxes, where trucks unloaded bound stacks of the newspaper outside stores and from where cables relayed signals that displayed dots on computer screens and mobile telephones around the globe, and where sleepy readers who had just then woken to their own personal symphonies collected their copies from their doorsteps and perused them over coffee, over a slice of toast, over a bowl of cereal, on the subway and in the car and at the office. Only then did something of a butterfly effect ensue, with the rustling of a newspaper in Washington leading soon after to a huge storm over the Judean hills.

"Article? What article? Shuv-el, stop that!" The call from the head of the regional council had disturbed the Assis family's dinner, which included cottage cheese spread on the tablecloth, bits of egg thrown into the air, and orange juice spilled on the floor.

"What are you saying, Dov? Who? Shuv-el, Shuv— Just a minute, Dov, I'll get back to you shortly." But the moment Othniel pressed the red button on his Nokia, the device rattled again with another incoming call. Natan Eliav, the secretary of Ma'aleh Hermesh A., was on the line. "Yes, Natan, yes, yes, I don't understand it. Listen, I need to— I'll get back to you in a— Rachel! Rachel!" he called, and the third time, to signal the urgency of the matter, he stood up and switched from the religious enunciation to street-speak: "Ra-chel!"

A meeting of the Planning Committee, chaired by Rachel Assis, was scheduled for that same evening. Shaulit Rivlin cradled Zvuli in her bosom, Gavriel Nehushtan caressed his sparse beard, Hilik Yisraeli stirred a cup of coffee, and Othniel joked, asking, "Is today Planning or Absorption?" Anyone willing to serve on a committee of sorts did so, and so, for the most part, the same four or five outpost residents were members of all of them.

Hilik dunked a cookie into his coffee just as Othniel asked if anyone had received any current information.

"Current information about what?" Gabi asked.

"I don't know. I got a bunch of calls about some newspaper article. Did something happen in the region? I didn't have a chance to get back to them."

No one knew, and Rachel said, "There's always something happening here. Let's focus on the meeting. I'll read out the list from the previous meeting. I'd like to finally get things prioritized today." She rustled the printed page and began reading in a stern, teacherly tone:

"On the horizon:

"One. Establishing a fixed structure to serve as a kindergarten for the children of the settlement (Housing Ministry).

"Two. Building a mikveh (deputy defense minister).

"Three. Developing a lookout facility on the adjacent hilltop, with an observation point facing the desert and a visitors' center. (Contact the Public Works Department.)

"Four. Construction of fixed homes for existing and future families (Housing Ministry).

"Five. Absorption of families and the expansion of the community's land area (Tefahot Bank).

"Six. An Internet website with promotional videos to help recruit funds and attract new residents (Yakir Assis?).

"Seven. Approaching the Interior Ministry's Names Committee to request a renaming of the settlement to distinguish it from Ma'aleh Hermesh."

"What names have you proposed?" questioned Shaulit. She wanted to propose naming the settlement after her father, may God avenge his blood. Othniel figured as much. When the playground was established, she wanted the park named after him, too. "Doesn't Zevulun Park sound more appropriate than Mamelstein Park?" she had asked anyone who was willing to listen at the time. Her request was denied.

"I haven't proposed anything yet. I'll convene a discussion at another time. We're constantly convening one committee and then we begin discussing issues related to another one, so please, let's maintain a little order."

Silence ensued, followed by a brief discussion about names nevertheless. Then one about a fixed structure for a kindergarten, the issue that had been bumped up to the top of the agenda despite reservations voiced by Gavriel, who proposed building a new synagogue and leaving the kindergarten in its current location.

As always, Shaulit raised the subject of the mikveh for the women. Rachel seconded her. It wasn't easy living in an outpost hundreds of meters away from the closest ritual purification bath and maintaining the laws concerning *niddah*. The women were sometimes forced to maneuver around under the cover of darkness and hide behind bushes and think twice before hitching a ride. It was embarrassing to know that a stranger would immediately smell the fragrance of shampoo and see wet hair under a head scarf and know what they'd be doing that night. Othniel was about to say something, but his telephone rang. He glanced at it and apologized. It was council leader Dov again. He told Othniel about an article about Ma'aleh Hermesh C. that appeared in a newspaper in the United States. He didn't have precise details, but he'd received a call from someone at the Foreign Ministry who heard from someone at the embassy in Washington. The matter was being looked into—exactly which newspaper, small or big, important or not, a supporter or an opponent, remained unknown.

"About Ma'aleh Hermesh C.? In America?"

"That's what they said."

"Are you sure?"

"That's the rumor."

The remaining committee members watched Othniel. The meeting was forgotten. Othniel was bombarded with questions. The phone rang again. He stepped outside and the Planning Committee followed him. Darkness had descended on the hilltop, the stars were out, inviting the Shema Yisrael prayer. A large crowd suddenly materialized and gathered outside the Assis family home. Josh received a call, spoke in English, and everyone stared at him because it sounded like he was getting some interesting information. He put his hand up to his forehead and said things like "No shit!" and "You're joking!" and "Are you sure?" and "Unreal!" and his bright eyes wandered to and fro in an expression that wavered somewhere between puzzlement and astonishment. By the time he said,

"Bye" and pressed the red button, everyone had gathered around him, waiting in expectant silence.

"It's an article in the *Washington Post*," he said, "a big article, about the settlement."

"C.?" yelled everyone en masse.

"C., C., only C. It talks about the playground. And Mamelstein. And the story with the D-9s."

"What does it say?"

Josh had a vacant, pale look in his eyes.

The ring of an old rotary dial phone ripped through the darkness. Othniel removed his hand from his pocket, clutching the device. He looked at the display. "Unknown number," he announced. Everyone went quiet.

"Hello?" Othniel said, and then, "Which ministry?"

And in a lower voice, as he stepped away to give himself some space to facilitate a more intimate conversation, "The Defense Ministry?"

The Article

F amily legend tells that the forefathers of Joshua Levin were Marra-nos, or *anusim*—Jews of the Iberian Peninsula who converted to Catholicism to escape the expulsion of Jews from Spain in the fifteenth century but secretly preserved Jewish traditions. Many years later, in the eighteenth century, some family members decided to make their way to the New World, and journeyed, via Livorno in Italy, to the province of Nuevo Mexico, then in the north of Mexico and today the state of New Mexico in the United States. The legend goes on to say that despite the long years of Catholicism, and regardless of the undisputable fact that foreign blood types infiltrated the family fabric (Irish blood, for example, was responsible apparently for the red hair), they continued to observe customs such as the lighting of Sabbath candles up until the early twentieth century, when Josh's great-grandmother suddenly rediscovered her

Jewish roots, moved to Brooklyn, and married Israel Levinovsky, a young Hasidic Jew who had immigrated to the United States from Lithuania a short time before.

One hundred or so years later, a number of circumstances joined forces to alter the path of Josh Levin's life: achieving the expectant, ripe-for-rebellion age of twenty; the Zionism forced down his throat day and night at the Aish HaTorah yeshiva; a touch of hot-bloodedness (the Irish genes again, perhaps); and the spark that ignited them all, September 11, 2001. The rage burned hotter inside him and told him "to do something."

And so he immigrated and settled in the holy land of his forefathers, and ended up at a religious college in Ma'aleh Hermesh, because one of his teachers in Brooklyn had a friend there. Josh wasn't too taken by the college, but at the grocery store one night, he met Jehu and helped him out with some small change "to make up five shekels seventy" for his shopping, and Jehu suggested he "come take a look at C." Already sick and tired by then of the endless philosophizing with his fellow students, Josh quit college and left for C. that same week, moving in with Jehu to share his trailer.

Now he was translating the *Washington Post* article that Yakir had printed off the Internet. Othniel burst into laughter on hearing the head-line "U.S. Donor Supports Renegade Settlement in 'Wild West' Bank," and he continued to chuckle to himself while Josh, in broken Hebrew, pausing between words to think of the correct translation and not always coming up with one, told the story of the real-estate and money-market tycoon with close ties to the Republican leadership who showed up a few months earlier, in February 2009, at the small outpost on the edge of the desert to take part in a dedication ceremony for a playground he had donated. Othniel remained smiling through the article's description of the place, its homes, its motley bunch of people, and the ceremony and the tour afforded the American millionaire. Hilik, in contrast, wasn't smiling, and even appeared concerned when the piece proceeded to imply the writer's unsurprising political viewpoint: "Mr. Mamelstein neglected to mention in his emotional speech the fact that the Ma'aleh Hermesh C. outpost was established in part on private land that is owned by Palestinians. Another portion of the settlement sits on a nature reserve, where the construction of residential homes is strictly prohibited."

Othniel remained unmoved even when the writer described years of neglected laws and regulations throughout the West Bank. He lost his cool only when the article, with the help of quotes from "a high-ranking IDF officer," embarked on a critique of the outpost's historical background. Like Hilik, he shook his head in the face of the painful inaccuracy of sentences such as "In 2005, they established an office for the farm, and then brought in a trailer for a guard that soon turned into a residence for an entire family," and he started to get really incensed on hearing himself described as "a farmer who grows parsley and organic tomatoes there."

"Parsley? Where on earth did he get that from? And did he say tomatoes? Not cherry tomatoes? Have a quick look." Josh had a quick look and confirmed. "Tomatoes!" cried the horrified Othniel. "Has he lost his mind? It's a different kind of compost entirely, not to mention the seeds . . ."

The details of the political and legal history of the settlements elicited yawns, and as the article proceeded to discuss American legislation—the Clinton administration's Executive Order 12947, which prohibits activities that disrupt the Middle East peace process; the George W. Bush administration's Patriot Act, which, among other things, prohibits governmental funding to educational institutions except for educational or sporting activities; the law concerning tax deductions for American charitable donations abroad—the audience stared up at the sky or shifted uncomfortably and loosened bits of gravel from their sandals.

But when the report explained that by granting tax breaks on donations like Mamelstein's, the U.S. Treasury and the American taxpayer were, for all intents and purposes—and contrary to government policy—actually funding illegal outposts such as Ma'aleh Hermesh C., smiles returned to the faces of the congregation, and some laughter and clapping erupted, too. The journalist's "revelation" that some of the money Mamelstein donated to the outpost went toward the purchase of several pairs of night-vision binoculars was greeted with amusement. "Since when does spotting foxes on guard duty disrupt the peace process?" and "That

Mamelstein is one son of a gun." And toward the end of the article, as the reporter revisited "last week's dramatic development"—the High Court ruling on the route of the fence, and the incident with the bulldozers—everyone again listened attentively to Josh, and even cheered the description of the action. ("The incident climaxed in a bizarre act of solidarity: The Palestinian owner of the olive groves, a religious settler woman, and an Israeli man whose ties to the area remain unclear all leaped together onto the blade of the bulldozer to bring it to a halt.") Even Neta cracked a smile.

When Josh finished, the prevailing mood was upbeat—particularly concerning the role played by Sheldon Mamelstein. The bottom line—"The hodgepodge of laws and conflicting authorities, like something out of Joseph Heller's *Catch-22,* has allowed the Jewish settlers to create a kind of Wild West, where they behave like outlaw sheriffs"—did produce several angry curses from Neta Hirschson and a worried look from Hilik Yisraeli, but there was nothing new in that. Neta was usually on edge, and Hilik was always worried about something.

The Island

Yakir was in his second life, Second Life, on the virtual island of Revival, where he and his bearded friends, in their broad skullcaps and baggy *sharwals,* had established their settlement, off-limits to foreigners—Christians, Ishmaelites, Amalekites, and anyone else who dared to challenge the laws of the place, which declared it holy land, Jewish land, and only for them, no one else. In keeping with the rules of Second Life, King Meir knew, he could close Revival to outsiders.

The day before, his friends had again visited Second Life's Muslim area. "We went to the mosque," said King Meir, the Texan lawyer. "And when we went inside, we didn't take off our shoes like we were supposed to. And we took those veils that they hand out free to women and put them on. LOL!!!"

Yakir smiled and typed: "Cool!"

"It's a shame we can't drop a little bomb there," wrote King Meir. His eyes, hair, and beard were black, his skullcap yellow, and his shirt, with the Kach Movement fist logo, also yellow.

"Maybe we can write some code?" Yakir typed.

"You can do that?" King Meir asked. Yakir explained to him that while it was impossible to damage the belongings or property of another user without his consent, you could make something yourself and then destroy it. For example, you could create a copy of a mosque, and then blow it up, or a Palestinian flag, and then burn it.

"Awesome," King Meir enthused. "That's way better than wandering around with the Uzis and not doing anything with them—like aiming them and saying boom-boom . . . But do they have any rules regarding this kind of thing?"

Yakir did a search and showed him Second Life's Community Standards: "The use of derogatory or demeaning language or images in reference to another Resident's race, ethnicity, gender, religion, or sexual orientation is never allowed in Second Life . . . Physical assault in Second Life is forbidden."

King Meir gestured with his hands. "What a load of crap. Isn't it supposed to be like real life? And what if the mosque offends me?"

Just then, the door to the trailer opened and Yakir heard the thunderous voice of his father, speaking on the telephone. He quickly switched tabs to open the farm's Web page. Othniel came up behind Yakir, gave him a friendly pat on the head, with its thick mop of hair that practically swallowed up his green skullcap, sat down next to him, placed the telephone on the armrest of the easy chair, and rubbed his eyes.

"Sorry, another call came through, can you hear me, Assis?" came a voice from the device.

"I hear you, Dov, I hear you," Othniel said, his head tilted back, his eyes staring up at the ceiling. Yakir pretended to focus on the computer screen.

"So the education minister briefed me on this morning's cabinet meeting. They discussed the *Washington Post* article, too. The Foreign Ministry, and the embassy in Washington in particular, will keep tabs on any White House response to the report, prepared of course with strenuous denials and threats to sue the newspaper for implying that any illegal actions have been or are being committed at Ma'aleh Hermesh C. or any other settlement in Israel, either within the Green Line or beyond it."

"Good." Othniel chuckled, his fingers rubbing his eyes.

"Furthermore," the head of the regional council continued, "a decision has been made to send the defense minister to Washington within the next few days, for the stated purpose of attending a charity event organized by the Jewish lobby, but he'll actually be there to sniff around, drop in on the secretary of state, the defense secretary, and perhaps even the president himself, if and when the opportunity arises—" Just then, the telephone sounded several feeble beeps and died. Othniel gazed at the device, perplexed. Yakir took it from him and immediately understood the problem. He went into the kitchen, retrieved the charger from behind the refrigerator, plugged it into the Nokia, and placed the device on the refrigerator.

His father went to the bathroom, sprayed deodorant under his arms, and tried a little with his fingers to tidy his beard, which had grown hypericum flowers. "Yakir," he instructed, "make a note in the calendar that Herzl Weizmann, the contractor, is coming tomorrow, and that I need to call Motke at the Housing Ministry to discuss a subsidy for the work he will be doing."

Red-eyed, Othniel looked at Yakir, who was typing on the keyboard. "Okay, son?" he said abruptly and stepped outside again. Yakir peered cautiously through the window and watched his father get into the dusty Renault Express, the original color of which few at Ma'aleh Hermesh C. were able to recall—in an effort to conserve water, Othniel hadn't washed it in years.

Yakir promptly returned to Second Life and met up with the small, bearded, skullcap-wearing group outside the Flame of the Revival synagogue. "Ah, Yakir, you're back," King Meir said. Hanging from his shoulder was the Uzi that had cost him next to nothing at an arms store in one of Second Life's commercial areas. "We were just trying to decide where we should go now, after yesterday's successful action at the mosque." Yakir helped him to search for an Arab club. There was the Scheherazade

Club, a nightclub with belly dancers, and the Orient Bazaar, which sells jalabiyas and kaffiyehs, and also Taste of Arabia, an Arab city with palm trees, mosques, and horses. The problem was that not many people hung out there. King Meir finally opted for the large mosque in Taste of Arabia. They'd go in and do some "item spamming" and bombard the mosque with Stars of David.

"If physical violence is out, spam is good. We're smarter than them, let's take advantage of that," King Meir said, and gave everyone the objective's coordinates. Yakir entered the details and appeared in the mosque with his friends. They were greeted with a hearty "Salaam alaikum!" from a woman who didn't appear Arab, and they responded with a barrage of Stars of David: Yakir had used Photoshop to create a Star of David that was compatible with the Second Life graphics, had colored it blue, and had found a simple duplication program. And now, with his mouse, he dragged the Star of David and placed it on the floor of the mosque, where the graphic then duplicated itself thousands of times. The mosque filled with floating blue Stars of David.

"Let's do the same at the Orient Bazaar!" yelled an exuberant King Meir, and he relayed new coordinates. Two minutes later, the bazaar, too, was filled with Stars of David. The bearded, Uzi-bearing bunch rejoiced. Not only had they filled those loathsome locations with some Jewish beauty, they had also messed with the computers of their owners and anyone who visited them. "You're the man, Yakir!" King Meir exclaimed as they returned to Revival. "And you know what the next stage is!"

Yakir laughed. He would try to work on creating a copy of a mosque to blow up and a Palestinian flag to burn. Perhaps he'd have some time that night. He heard his father pull up and park, and a minute later, the door opened and heavy-duty work shoes thumped across the floor.

"What are you doing there, son?" Othniel asked.

"Nothing," replied the son.

"What do you mean, nothing? I heard you laughing . . . Okay, let's go, you coming to prayers?"

"Okay," Yakir said, and clicked on the X in the corner of the screen.

The Campaign

Ariel woke half an hour before his alarm was set to go off. His mind remained clouded for a moment before he snapped to and remembered, and a slight tremor coursed through him, a shudder of anxiety that quickly took flight. He rose, rushed through his morning routine, woke his wife and young son, and prepared breakfast for them.

"What's up?" his wife asked, and he replied, "Nothing, I just woke up early." But she had known him long enough to know better. "Do you really have to go there?" she asked, and he responded immediately with "Oy, don't get started. Yes, I really do have to go there. What's the problem? I've told you a thousand times, it's a safe road, which the army uses, on which—"

"On which no one has been killed in two years—I know, statistically, the chances of dying in a road accident in the center of the country are much higher."

"Look, Daddy," their son said. "Look, Daddy." He pointed at his plate.

"I can see," Ariel said. "That's lovely, a plum!"

"Pum," his son responded.

Do I really have to do this? he asked himself in the car. Why did I take the day off work? He tuned in to Razi Barkai's radio talk show: settlements, the U.S. president, the prime minister. Boring. He switched over to 88FM, cold air streamed from the air conditioner, the sun was still rising in front of him as he headed east.

On Route 443, his confidence started to erode. Roni was right, it wasn't so scary the second time around. But on the 443, there was a real sense of having stepped it up a notch. Not due to the road's history so much, but more so the discernible changes. The outside temperature displayed on the dashboard dropped, the landscape morphed, the hilltops revealed themselves, Arab villages and villagers appeared on the sides of the road. And then there was the checkpoint, and the fence that rose up along the side of the road on both sides, and he had no idea if he was beyond the barrier or inside it, in a narrow corridor between the sides of the barrier itself. The air, too, was different, and past Jerusalem came the sense of being sucked out of a vacuum into the pale yellowish brown, into the desert, with more villages and mosques, more yellow taxis and Palestinian trucks—green-and-white license plates caused a rise in blood pressure, yellow ones were somewhat soothing—and suddenly the radio switched of its own accord from 88FM to Arabic music. His hands squeezed the wheel, eyes darted back and forth between the hilltops and the road. These Arabs drive like lunatics, he thought, and pictured one of the trucks plowing mercilessly into him, not necessarily with deadly intent but as the result of reckless driving.

The telephone rang but he was too afraid to make small talk, his hands remained fixed on the wheel, his mind focused. The descents grew steeper, the ascents more arduous. Don't worry, hundreds of Israelis travel this road daily and no one has been killed here in years, even stone-throwing incidents are few and far between. And yet, unlike those of the settlers, his car wasn't equipped with armored glass. Could they know that, the Arabs? Despite the air-conditioning, he was sweating, and couldn't quite work out why he was there at all, it was just another business idea that would follow in the footsteps of all his previous business ideas. Why couldn't he be satisfied with the not so little he had—accountant, average-size firm, in the center of the country, married, with one kid? But to really make a killing required taking risk, doing things that not everyone would do.

The military pillboxes comforted him, the red-tiled roofs soothed him. He wouldn't have believed he would feel that way, but the turnoff for the settlement was a welcome sight, and outside the yellow steel gate, which opened for his Toyota and its yellow plates without any fuss, he could see the waiting cars of the Arabs and the Arabs themselves, and once inside, he felt secure, as unpleasant as it might have been to admit so. After all, he didn't have a problem with the Arabs, they deserved better, he didn't support the crazy settlers, but he did feel a lot more at ease and safer within their prohibitive boundaries.

"What's up, bro? You look green," Roni said to him.

"Give me a glass of water," Ariel responded, and entered the trailer.

"Okay," he said after he recovered. "Good news. Three boutique stores in Tel Aviv who took samples from me want to place a substantial order for the olive oil. They all say this is the kind of oil that sells these days, heavily flavored, strong-tasting, spicy, with the true fragrance of olives, unlike those yellowish, lighter Italian or Spanish oils."

"Well, of course, it's the real thing." The words rolled gleefully off Roni's tongue. "Not only is it better than the pale, Ashkenazi, overrefined European oils, it's the best in the country, the purest, the tastiest. Better than from the Galilee, better than from Samaria. These are olives from the edge of the desert, it's Bab A-Zakak, the region with the oil of the highest quality! And it's costing us nine shekels a liter, instead of the sixteen shekels you'll pay for the cheapest Israeli oil."

"You can find some for fifteen," Ariel corrected him, but Roni didn't bother to respond.

They sat in Gabi's yard, which overlooked the olive groves of Kharmish.

"What's a substantial order?" Roni asked after a few moments of thought.

"A thousand liters and more."

"A thousand and more . . ." Roni nodded, and released smoke from his nostrils. "Multiplied by three, you say. I hope Musa can handle that. We're a small enterprise, after all, not an industrial farm."

"He has to cope. Anything less, and it's not worth my while to leave the comforts of my office. But now that we've bought him that wonderful electric motor to replace his dead donkey, I'm not worried. And just so you know, you can boutique me all you like, I still haven't given up on my dream of a sophisticated oil press and mass production. After we've established the brand, we can invest in an Italian production line, and then, within five years, we'll have made it."

Roni laughed to himself. The words "God willing" were on the tip of his tongue, but he refrained at the last second from blurting them out. He waved to Othniel and Yakir, who were walking along the ring road toward the synagogue.

"Now take a look at this," Ariel said, and glanced around for his black briefcase. He reached for it, couldn't get a hand on it, cursed, stood up, and went over to retrieve it, patting down the pockets of his pants to feel for his wallet and keys and mobile phone as he walked. He removed several printed pages from the briefcase, glanced at them, and handed them to Roni without a word. Roni took them, then took a final puff on his cigarette before stubbing it out in the ashtray. He browsed through the pages and a broad smile slowly appeared on his face. He nodded intently.

"Initial drafts for the ad campaign," Ariel said with a sense of satisfaction. "I also want a draft with the headlines from the newspapers. People will be floored."

"Or I'll be floored. What will people who know me think when they see me like that in an advertisement?"

"They probably won't see you. It's not going into national newspapers or anything like that. You know, local ads, signs at stores, that kind of thing."

"Well, if they do, you can say it is 'an Israeli man whose ties to the area remain unclear.' "

"What's that?"

"Nothing," Roni said, "just the *Washington Post* article. That's what the son of a bitch wrote about me. I was pleased actually that they had no clue who I was or what the hell I was doing jumping onto the blades of bulldozers."

"I heard about the article. That's why the defense minister went to America, right? We may be able to leverage the story for our own needs. Perhaps for exports," Ariel said, scribbling down a note to himself in a small notebook.

"Why not? Leverage as much as you like." Roni browsed through the pages again and looked contentedly at the photograph of himself and Musa on the blade of the bulldozer. "Just a sec," he said, and paged back through the photographs. "Isn't there something missing here?"

"The religious woman," Ariel confirmed. "We Photoshopped her out. I was of two minds about it, but the settlers are daunting."

Roni nodded. "'Together, we'll press on?'" he read out the slogan under the photograph of the bulldozer.

"They're only initial drafts. We have lots of options for slogans. You won't believe the brochures I'm having made—quotes from the Bible, symbols, Arabic verses, heritage, ties to the land, uses of olive oil. You'll be blown away."

"Great, great. And get the Golani Brigade in there, too, with the olive tree on the brigade tag—Roni, the former Golani fighter who went from being a fucked-up soldier with an olive tree on his shoulder to producing olive oil in partnership with an Arab. Know what I mean?"

Ariel smiled politely, his silence clearly implying that Roni should leave the marketing and branding to him. "Okay, dude," he said, "ask Musa when he can get us some oil."

"I'm on it," Roni responded, putting a hand up to shield his eyes from the sun and dialing the Palestinian's number. "I'm on it."

The Summer Camp

The summer was suddenly at its peak. The month of July arrived and the long summer vacation began, and on some of the days, Nehama Yisraeli organized activities for children of all ages (a day at the swimming pool, a hike, a day spent working at Othniel's livestock pen, a day of building), entrusting the older ones with various responsibilities and tasks. She called it a summer camp.

On one such day, the children left to go hiking through the Hermesh Stream riverbed. Nehama showed up at the kindergarten at 8 a.m. with her two sons, Boaz and Shneor, one in each hand, and a huge rounded tummy. Elazar Freud brought along his son, Nefesh, and went into the men's section of the synagogue for morning prayers. And Amalia Rivlin arrived with her baby brother, Zvuli, in a baby carriage, her younger sister, Tchelet, at her side, and their mother, Shaulit, a few steps behind, talking on her cell phone, laughing and gesturing intently with her hands, saying, "Insane, insane."

Along for the day, too, were Shimi and Tili Gotlieb and all the Assis children aside from Yakir—Gitit, who served in the summer as a teacher's aide, Dvora, Hananiya, Emunah, and Shuv-el, and Beilin the dog as well. At the request of Nehama, they were accompanied by Jehu, his butt firmly fixed in the saddle of his horse, Killer, and his Jericho 941 pistol tucked into his holster, and when the merry bunch exited through the settlement's gate, Yoni the soldier surprised them and asked Nehama, "Can I tag along?"

"Sure," she said. "But don't you have to remain here at the gate?"

"There are other soldiers here," Yoni said, pointing into the guard hut. "And it's a quiet day."

"Praise the Lord," Nehama responded. The fear of running into an Arab was always there; having another soldier with them could only boost everyone's sense of security.

The group walked slowly, hats on heads, water bottles and sandwiches in colorful knapsacks. The older children hurried ahead confidently, the younger ones and pregnant kindergarten teacher waddled like penguins, and the tiny tots sat in a wheeled crib pushed by Gitit. As a treat, the kids were lifted one by one onto Killer's back, where they rested securely in Jehu's strong arms. They all made their way down the dirt road to the lowest point in the wadi, between the hills of Ma'aleh Hermesh C. and Ma'aleh Hermesh B., where the path turned toward the Hermesh Stream riverbed. A vulture soared overhead, one of two that could be seen almost daily from the hilltop. Nehama pointed at the bird and asked, "What's that?" The response came in the form of excited cries from the children.

Some fifteen minutes into the hike, as they neared the cave, they stopped for a sandwich break in a small, withered field, alongside a modest Jewish National Fund sign bearing the words *The Jennifer Shulman-Zimmerman Wood*. They washed their hands and recited the customary blessing, and then, after the blessing over the bread, they dove in. Nehama pointed out various plants—white wormwood, thorny saltwort, prickly alkanet, Dominican sage, Jerusalem sage—"And what do you think about that chubby little mourning wheatear resting there in the shade?" The children turned to look wearily at the bird. Tili Gotlieb and Emunah

Assis, both missing a single bottom front tooth, the one in a white dress and the other in a yellow one handed down from her sisters, were holding hands and singing "Kol Dodi Hineh Ze Ba," and Yoni clapped for them until they started giggling shyly and began all over again.

Nehama lowered her burdensome body onto a rock. Her denim skirt wrapped around her swollen ankles and beads of sweat appeared from under her black head covering. "Let's go, guys," she said. "We'll go on from here a short way into the cave, cool down a little inside, and then turn around and head back." The children stood. "Just to remind you, hold hands when we're inside the cave and be careful not to slip. Yoni, you're bringing up the rear. Jehu, tie up your horse and come inside with us."

The opening to the cave revealed itself after a short descent into the steep ravine, which sloped sharply on both sides—white limestone and sand-colored rocks, with thorny burnet and Israeli thyme growing among them. A quiet pair of Nubian ibexes roved farther down the incline, and the rustling sound of bats rose from the crevices, and Chukar partridges skimmed across the ground in the color of the earth, and an alarmed snake-eyed lizard zigzagged away at the sound of their footsteps. They reached the entrance to the cave, one of several large caves in the side of the mountain that had served as hideouts for the Maccabees and Romans, for monks and bandits, for shepherds and commando unit fighters and Crusaders; also for foxes, and for porcupines, and for leopards and snakes—for any living creature that passed through that desert at some point in time.

On reaching a wide slab of rock at the mouth of the cave, Nehama called a halt and asked everyone to cast their eyes farther down the ravine. She quoted a verse describing a landscape from the book of the Prophet Amos—"New wine will drip from the mountains and flow from all the hills"—and warned: "We're going in now, so I'm telling you again, everyone hold hands and take good care, because the floor of the cave may be slippery."

"Mommy, I want to go wee-wee," came the sound of Shneor's voice.

"Shhh . . . Shneor, I'm talking. Go with Yoni to find somewhere."

She told the children about the history of the cave and its size, and in they went, stepping hesitantly into the murky, low-ceilinged, dank interior.

"Mommy, Mommy," Hananiya Assis said, and he tightened his grip on Jehu's hand. Jehu lightly stroked the back of the young boy's neck in an effort to soothe him.

"Pay attention," Nehama continued in her teacher voice, "the cave has twenty-three rooms, and it splits up and branches out, so it's very important to walk slowly and not to let go of the hand of whoever is next to you."

Hananiya trembled. The light from the outside grew ever weaker, blocked out by small bodies. It was cooler and more pleasant inside. Hananiya whimpered, "I want to go back out, go back out."

"Quiet, Hananiya, everything's okay, we're going back soon," said his sister Dvora. Contrary to the explicit instructions of the kindergarten teacher, she let go of his sweaty hand and entered one of the side rooms, fearlessly feeling her way.

"Dvora, Dvora!" came the high-pitched voice of her brother, Hananiya, and Nehama followed suit, "Dvora? Where are you? Dvora?"

There was no response. The sound of a sob rose up, followed by a second, and then a third. Nehama raised her voice in the darkness, "Children, don't be afraid, just keep holding hands," but the hands were sweaty, small, smooth, and the floor was smooth, too. "Older children, pick everyone up and go back to the entrance!" Nehama commanded, afraid to lose control, her heart pounding now. "Dvora? Are you here? Dvora?" That was the key, the source of the distress, she sensed, she could feel the silence that failed to offer a response. "Dvora?" The whimpering of the little ones died down, Yoni and Jehu and Gitit comforted and caressed, and everyone returned to the mouth of the cave.

Dvora stood rooted to the spot in one of the inner rooms. Nehama heard whispers, entered the room, placed a hand on her narrow shoulder, and peered into the darkness beyond.

"I don't know, something drew me here," whispered Yakir's twin.

"Did you hear anything?"

"No, I didn't, not with my ears, at least."

They stood and looked, not sure at what, exactly, but they were sure it was something unusual, it was hard to see in the dimness, a heap in the corner of the room. Had someone been here recently and forgotten something? What is that? Dvora approached and reached out her hand to touch, it jingled . . . Coins?

Dvora turned her head and gave Nehama a puzzled look, and then, a few seconds later, her ears pricked up, because a new sound was heard in the room. What was that? Water? Nehama turned her head to listen, too, they stood next to each other, their heads tilted in opposite directions. Could there be water flowing through the cave? After all, there'd never been water here . . . The water sounded very close, and Dvora asked, "Nehama? Can you hear it?" And Nehama said, "Yes," and only then did she get it—it was from her. Her waters, the life fluid of her third daughter, flowing between her legs in the middle of the cave, and she said to Dvora, "Go—slowly—slowly—to the entrance—of the cave—and tell—Gitit—and Yoni—to come—get—me—out—and Jehu—to ride—to the outpost—and call—Hilik—with the car—urgently—now." And then she sat down, exhaling deeply, and Dvora went on her way.

And there Nehama remained, on the verge of motherhood, tenderly embracing her belly, her cheek pressed against the cool wall of the cave, her lips moving in prayer, and the young maiden Dvora made for the mouth of cave in measured steps, and cried out. Jehu spurred Killer into a gallop, and the youth's hair and thick sidelocks flapped in the wind under his broad skullcap, and the two ascended through the field and along the dirt road to the settlement, and Killer whinnied, the steel gate opened, and rider and horse raced to the fifth property on the right on the ring road.

Out in the field, meanwhile, Yoni and Gitit remained as the only adults. Despite the heat, both were dressed in long, thick clothing, Yoni in his green army fatigues, Gitit in a white cotton shirt and dark skirt that hung ten centimeters below her knees. They exchanged meaningful looks and swallowed a smile, and Yoni said, "Go into the cave, and find Nehama, and help her out, because she needs air. We'll get her to the road." To the children, he said, "Sit, boys and girls, drink some water from the bottles and water flasks, eat fruit and sandwiches and candies from the knapsacks, and let me try to get ahold of . . ." He looked at his phone and used his finger to browse through the list of names, found Hilik's number, and pushed the green Send button, but there was no signal in the ravine. He brought the device closer to his face and, peering through his Ray-Bans, observed that the antenna icon displayed zero bars.

"Everybody up," he announced to the children. "We'll head up to the top field with the white wormwood, the prickly alkanet, and whatever she called the hyssop earlier." Shneor burst into tears, asking, "Where's Mommy?" And Yoni said, "Mommy will come right along, Gitit is helping her." And up came the good, quiet, well-behaved children, and even Shneor stopped crying, although he did turn to look back from time to time and ask about Mommy. "What's Daddy's telephone number?" Yoni asked Shneor, attempting to confirm that he had the correct number. "I don't know," Shneor responded, but his elder brother, Boaz, intervened and recited the number, and Yoni entered the digits and pressed the Send button. This time the cellular signals caught up with Hilik, and Yoni relayed the news just as Hilik heard the sound of Killer's hooves outside the window. His face dropped, his mustache drooped, and he jumped into his car.

Hilik stopped at the point on the dirt road where the path led to the cave. He left the engine running and raced to his wife, whom he found leaning on Gitit's slender shoulder. Together they hoisted her up the steep ravine and across the length of the field, for all the children to see, and Boaz asked, "Daddy, what happened to Mommy? Is Mommy dead? Did terrorists kill her?"

"No, Boaz, heaven forbid," Hilik answered. "Mommy is fine, bless the Lord, and Daddy will take her to the hospital now and we'll return, God willing, with a baby sister, just as we promised you. Isn't that right, Boaz?" Boaz nodded and followed the slow progress of the three grown-ups. Nehama tried to smile at her son and the other children, and to say a few words of farewell, a comforting word or two, but suddenly, in the middle of the field, a contraction struck, and she burst into a stifled wail that turned into a moan.

Hilik looked at the alarmed children and said, "Don't worry, kids, everything is fine, everything— Yoni! Can you—" Nehama bit down on the lapel of her blouse, and Gitit poured water from a bottle onto her hands and, with her wet fingers, gently caressed Nehama's sweaty brow.

Only in the evening—after the children were dispersed to their homes, and Gitit and Yoni were left standing together on her doorstep, where they again exchanged a look, and then a feeble "See you," because Gitit had to look after her brothers and sisters; after Jehu, aboard Killer, in all his splendor, circled the ring road to ensure that all were safe and sound, and after the sun set again in the depths of the west; after an emotional Hilik called to tell of the lightning birth of a beautiful and healthy baby girl, bless the Lord; less than an hour from the time Nehama landed on the hospital bed and following a few waves of contractions on the frantic drive to Jerusalem and several verses from the book of Psalms along the way and by her bedside; after dinner and evening prayers and the reciting of the Shema; after Roni Kupper's after-dinner cigarette, smoke from which drifted through the netting on Gabi's window; after the excited tales of the children, who relived the dramatic moments in the cave—only then did Dvora Assis recall the odd heap she and Nehama had discovered in the corner of the cave, and told her mother and her father and her brothers and her sisters about it, and Othniel looked at her sharply and asked, "Coins, you said?" And the green-eyed Dvora nodded. And Othniel said, "I'd like to go over there to have a look. And perhaps we'll ask Duvid to join us, too, he knows about coins," and he lifted a piece of his fried egg to his mouth.

The Meeting

The defense minister was back from Washington, where he successfully wormed his way into a brief meeting in the Diplomatic Reception Room and tried to minimize the damage caused by the McKinley article in the *Post*.

"McKinley went too far," the minister charged. "We're talking about a small, insignificant outpost with a handful of families. You can't possibly make the claim that the American taxpayer or U.S. Treasury has had to foot the bill for anything there, for the simple reason that no one at all has spent a dime there. Apart from Mamelstein, a private individual, and what, after all, did he donate? Nothing but a small playground."

"But what about the water, the electricity, the military protection?" asked the U.S. president, who, much to the regret of the minister, had been thoroughly briefed. "What about the road that was paved there? That was the work of the Public Works Department—U.S. satellite photographs prove that—not a private donation."

"Yes," the minister responded. "It's complicated, because we have to protect our citizens against Arab aggression even if they have settled there only temporarily, and the young people who have grown up in the settlements don't have anywhere—" He tried not to stumble over his words, but the president interjected, "I've actually been reading about immigrants from the U.S., Russia, France, and not merely extended families. It's unlawful. And what's this about giving in to the people who were protesting the evacuation because they jumped onto a tractor? I don't get it," the president said. "I don't understand how you run things there. Is there no law?"

The defense minister stared at one of the president's socks. "It wasn't a tractor, Mr. President," he said. "It was a D-9 bulldozer." The minister subsequently claimed, in off-the-record conversations that were then widely quoted, that the president wasn't up to speed with all the particulars.

The minister had expected the meeting to be his most difficult moment, after which he'd be able to breathe a little easier, but he was in for a surprise. On his return to Israel, his office was swamped with daily calls from the American ambassador, and even the U.S. secretary of state called for a progress report. He decided to go to Ma'aleh Hermesh C. to show the Americans he was doing something.

He convened a meeting with the head of Central Command—the de facto prime minister of Judea and Samaria—and the head of the Shin Bet security service's Counter-Subversion Department, commonly known as the Jewish Division.

"What are we to do with them, Giora?" the minister asked, turning to fix the major general with his sad-bulldog gaze.

The major general shrugged. "I'm supposed to know?" he responded. "Whatever you decide, we'll make it happen."

The minister closed his eyes and shook his head. "I know that, Giora. But I'm asking you to tell me what the decision should be." The major general remained silent.

The minister continued, "What happened there with the bulldozer? Why did you give in to a handful of lunatics? How do you think the rest of the world sees us? I've got the president asking me, 'What is this? Is there no law there?' Can you comprehend the shame in that?"

"What happened was that the prime minister called and told us to stop. You know that. We had no part in the decision. We would have continued with the work of clearing the area. Those three clowns didn't change a thing. But the education minister was there, and he called the prime minister, and they brought in hundreds of demonstrators . . ."

"What do you have to say, Avram?" The minister looked at the Shin Bet official as if he had just then remembered his presence in the room. "Can't they be removed so I can get the Americans off my back?"

"Ummm . . ." The Shin Bet man pressed the fingertips of his one hand to the fingertips of the other. "Look—"

The door opened and one of the minister's aides said, "Sir, it's the ambassador again."

"Tell him we're in a meeting at this very moment to prepare for a trip to the outpost. Tell him he can join us, we're going next— You know what, don't tell him any— One moment. Okay, just put him through."

The head of Central Command, who had been standing, took a seat and sipped from a glass of soda water. At his request, Avram from the Shin Bet passed him the Sports section of *Yedioth* and he paged through it, but in the summer of an odd-numbered year, there's nothing interesting. Only tennis and swimming and cycling and athletics.

"Yes, Milton, yes. We are now sitting here preparing to go to the place next week. Don't worry, yes, I'm sitting here with good people from the army and the Shin Bet. They know exactly what to do, sir, yes." He smiled and nodded. "Listen, if you want to join us next week, talk with my assistant. Of course, yes. No, we don't know yet . . ." He raised his eyes to look at his two guests, and they nodded with raised eyebrows. "Yes, yes, early next week, maybe Sunday." He winked at the head of Central Command and retrieved two pretzels from a bowl on the table in front of him. The major general smiled. He knew just how much the ambassador hated working on a Sunday.

"So what do you say, Avram?" the minister asked after hanging up.

"Look, our informant at the outpost, she said—"

"A woman informant?"

"She says there are a number of elements there who could spark unrest. We saw the last time that they can fire up the situation pretty quickly."

"Fire up?"

"Be serious, Avram," the major general said. "That's not exactly firing up—"

"One second," the head of the Jewish Division continued, "let me finish."

"Let him, Giora," the minister said.

"In short, it's a sensitive issue. They'll fight. I'm not saying lives will be put at risk, I'm not talking about a subversive organization, but fierce resistance, the rallying of supporters, violence—without doubt. A mess. Not to mention the fact that the prime minister and half the cabinet will back them. I'd advise against an evacuation at this specific point in time, if that works for you."

"Have you read the article? Nothing there is legal, none of the permits, as if . . . If we can't take action there, then where—"

"There are newer places, ones that are more makeshift. I can draw up a list for you. In the same area, too. Perhaps they'll appease the president. Those guys at Ma'aleh Hermesh C., after all, have been there for several years already. The place actually received a permit as an agricultural farm and has since developed. Other settlements can't even say that."

"Okay, okay. Let's do it. Arrange a visit for us there, Giora. Sunday morning. Early. Pini, inform the ambassador and the media, particularly the Americans. Giora, you'll be joining us, of course. Avram, thanks."

"But what are you going to say there?" Giora asked. "That we're evacuating? Leaving them be? We need to prepare accordingly."

"We do, too," the Shin Bet official echoed.

The defense minister fixed them both with a weary look. "We'll see," he said to them, and left the office in the direction of the bathroom.

The Heat

T he heat was oppressive. The month of July had come and gone and they were in the midst of the Three Weeks, the period of mourning to commemorate the destruction of Jerusalem—long days, devoid of festivals, a recipe for troublemaking. Freshly squeezed lemons, cold water, and sugar yielded cool lemonade. The children spent all their waking hours outdoors. Fans and air conditioners, for those who had them, worked at full tilt, and the windows of the other homes were left open to the breeze—Gabi claimed that his cabin was built in such a way so as not to require air-conditioning, the positioning of the windows and doors ensured that during the summer the breeze coming off the edge of the cliff would stir up the air in the room. He forgot to mention that in the winter, the winds were capable of blowing the cabin into the Hermesh Stream riverbed.

It was the eve of Shabbat Hazon, the Sabbath before Tisha B'Av, the day of destruction of the Temple, pointless hatred the cause of its devastation. Preparations ahead of the Sabbath were in full swing, cooking and the chirping of telephones and the groaning of wheels on the outpost's dirt and gravel and tarred roads, and new tableware shipped off to the mikveh for purification. Gabi returned from the Ma'aleh Hermesh A. grocery store with heavy bags filled to the brim with Sabbath goodies. He found Roni sitting in the living room, shirtless, in front of the fan.

"Bro," Roni called out from the living room. "Did you get any Diet Coke?"

"No. Did you ask me to?" Gabi said.

"Do I need to ask?"

Gabi distributed his haul among the kitchen cupboards and refrigerator to the sound of the rustling of the plastic shopping bags. His eyes wandered to the sink, which overflowed with dirty dishes. Since arriving some six months ago, Roni hadn't washed a single fork. Gabi left the kitchen and stood at the doorway to the living room, pressing one hand up against the lintel. "What are you doing?" he asked.

Roni didn't look good. He was sitting in the armchair, his legs spread, in front of a fan, gazing—tired, or sad, or simply bored—out the window. He spent hours sitting in the trailer, and the highlights of the day for him appeared to be his conversations with Gabi, which usually spiraled into sermonizing and arguments where Gabi ended up on the defensive. Gabi didn't enjoy that but found himself sucked into the exchanges anyway, as he justified himself. Perhaps he felt a sense of obligation to help Roni unload his frustrations, or perhaps he, too, needed the confrontations, because he was angry.

"What am I doing?" Roni responded. "I don't know."

Gabi smiled at him. "Enough, my brother, it's the eve of the Sabbath. It's a great mitzvah always to be joyful."

"Yes, so I've heard. Keep saying that, you'll convince yourself in the end." Roni sank deeper into the armchair.

Gabi turned to leave. Roni shut his eyes. "One moment, don't go." He sighed. "I'd like to be happy all the time," he said. "Who wouldn't? But it's not as simple as that. It's naïve to claim that just by saying it, it'll happen."

"It's naïve to merely say it. But it's something else to truly believe it."

"I don't see the difference. If you truly believe it, will the sorrow disappear? And where exactly will it go?"

"You can't see it from the place you are in. I know you like to make fun of everything I say, but you are in a place of sin, of folly, not a place of faith. And because it scares you to think differently, all you can do is ridicule." It was the same conversation, with slight variations, time and again. Gabi never intended to fall into the endless loop, but did so every time anew.

Roni shook his head. "You weren't raised religious, you know it's just talk, the clichés the religious have about secular people. Where's the value in coerced praying and rejoicing? And desire is folly? Isn't the body deserving of desires?"

"Those are not the values of Judaism. Those are the values of Hellenists. Earthly desires are like rays of sunshine in a dark room. They appear to be of substance, until you try to grab one."

"But they brighten the room, they warm it. What's wrong with that? Why do you need to grab them?"

"To have more depth to your life. Light and warmth are the superficial. That's all very well, but there's more, a lot more."

"And where do you find it? In forcing yourself to be happy? You, after all, are not happy. And we both know why. Did you think you'd be able to forget about your son by going to the end of the world, secluding yourself, putting a piece of cloth on your head, and swaying wildly in synagogue? Do you think you'll be able to forget Mickey?"

Gabi closed his eyes. Of course he'd never forget Mickey. "We like to think that forgetting is a problem, but I believe it's an advantage. Knowing how to forget means letting go of the troubles of the past."

"Well, that's great. A quote for every occasion." Roni sniggered bitterly. "Forgetting is an advantage for someone who is afraid to confront his memories. What do you mean by 'letting go of the past'? Is that your excuse for never in your life having seen anything through to the end— army, university, being a father? Perhaps you should deal with the troubles of the past, instead of looking for refuge in quotes and sayings."

Gabi could almost taste the sting of Roni's sarcasm on his tongue. His brother spoke like someone bent on being offensive. Their arguments had turned increasingly mean. "The only frightened one here is you. Why is it so hard for you to accept that your world doesn't suit me? I've been there. It's not for me. Why don't you trust me to know what's good for me? I trust in the Holy One, blessed be He."

"It's hard for me to accept it because I know you, perhaps better than anyone else, and you know that. I know what suits you. I can smell what you are truly feeling from a mile away. I know how long you lasted everywhere else, and I wonder how long you'll last here. How long you'll continue to spin yarns to yourself. You tell yourself that you're strong— Nehushtan, like copper. But I checked on the Internet, the name Kupper has nothing to do with copper. It's someone who makes barrels."

Gabi went into the kitchen and began washing the dishes in the sink.

"I've heard about the barrels," he said. "But a rabbi, an expert on Jewish names, told me that it's probably copper." Several minutes of silence went by, nothing but the water from the faucet and the hum of the fan and the banging of a hammer in the distance. Gabi stopped washing and returned to the living room with an unwrapped Twist chocolate bar in his hand, and another that he tossed over to Roni.

Gabi sat down on the armrest of the sofa. He adjusted the position of his white Sabbath skullcap with the pompom and bit into his Twist. "Take a look at yourself," he said quietly. "Think about why you are here, about the condition you were in when you arrived. You're the one stuck in this house for hours on end, doing nothing, feeling down. So how come you always turn things against me?"

Roni threw the Twist wrapper onto the small table. Gabi got to his feet, picked it up, and threw it, together with his own, into the small triangular wastebasket in the dairy sink. "It's so hot," he said, opening the refrigerator and retrieving a jug of water.

"And what about bringing more children into this world?" Roni suddenly asked, in a softer tone.

"What?"

"Why don't you get married? Aren't Breslovs supposed to have many children?"

"It's not easy to find someone in a small place . . ."

"You don't even try, Gabi. I see you. You aren't interested in anything aside from your Nachman and your noble values and this small place, which, I have to say, reminds me a lot of the kibbutz—a hole at the end of the world, a small idealistic society, shut off and holier-than-thou, where everything is more just and better than anywhere else in the world—the forerunners of the tribe. You've simply returned to your childhood, even your Arabs are like the Katyushas back then—"

"This hole takes you in, and look at your attitude toward it. You're spitting into the only well that is giving you water. Just so you know, people here at the settlement aren't comfortable with this olive oil story. And the same goes for me. People make an effort here to preserve the concept of Jewish labor. An Arab almost never steps foot in here, even though it costs us money. And you show up, as a guest, and do business with them . . . It's not as if I am personally—I did give you the loan, after all—but how do I appear to the people—"

"You'll get the money, don't worry. Rosh Hashanah, right? Sure, it's being taken care of."

"I'm not speaking about the money," Gabi said. But he wasn't speaking about anything else. They both went quiet, tired.

"Are you incapable of saying Musa?" Roni finally asked from within the heated silence. He *did* want to talk. "The man has a name. Do you know what they did to him after the episode with the bulldozer? Was Neta Hirschson arrested? Was I arrested? We did exactly the same as he did. But they went to him, took things, smashed, pushed, arrested. If I hadn't intervened, they wouldn't have released him. Your Jewish labor thing sounds all clean and nice, but this insistence on not having anything to do with them—where's the logic in that?" Roni looked at his brother, then yawned, almost swallowing up the trailer. "And it's not that I'm a leftist or anything like that, you know," he said from within the yawn.

"Of course you aren't a leftist, you simply recognize an opportunity for some wheeling and dealing and suddenly the Arabs are your friends."

"What exactly are you saying? You want me to leave?"

"Heaven forbid, that's not what I said," Gabi said, returning from the kitchen with two glasses of cold water with ice.

"Thanks," said Roni—who throughout the conversation hadn't moved an inch from his position in front of the fan, or offered to turn it to face his brother or switch on the rotate mode—"although it's not really a substitute for Diet Coke."

"You can stay for as long as you like," Gabi said. "I've grown accustomed."

"Me, too." Roni laughed. "I'd no longer manage anywhere else." And then he stretched and said, "I'm dead tired." Gabi looked at the clock and stood up. There was more to do before the Sabbath came in—cooking, laundry, calls to make. Truthfully, however, he wouldn't mind resting for a few minutes himself. He went into his room and looked at the bed, at the disheveled sheet, the crumpled pillow, and thought, I'll lie down for just a brief moment, and then . . .

The Stray

On the Sabbath, even the stray felt the heavens and the earth weighing on his shoulders and eyelids, which narrowed into tiny slits to stave off the sun's glare, survey his surroundings, ensure no danger lurked. His nostrils flared, his nose was wet and primed, and his small brain processed the data and the odors, the sights, and the sounds.

He grew up not far from here. Folks in the outpost didn't know if he was of Jewish or Arab origin, a settler or an Ishmaelite—but he did. He knew, in his capillaries and DNA, and even in fragments of memory that flashed through his mind from time to time, he was Palestinian through and through, a native of Hebron, one of seven brothers and sisters, most of whom had remained in the city of their ancestors—two with their mother and her family, two down the street with cousins (one of them a known criminal), and two to wealthy brothers in the village of Yata. One brother was a doctor with a clinic in the city who showed up one day with his daughter—saw the sweet puppies and simply had to have one—and the other a university lecturer whose daughter became jealous of her cousin. And thus the stray's six brothers and sisters were scattered, whereas he—cross-eyed, with a partial second row of teeth on his bottom jaw, who on first impression appeared far less cuddly than the others, less useful—belonged to the street, and there he remained, tried to survive, followed the scent of the food in the market, and fell in with a street pack.

One day his nose and paws led him to the Jewish enclave in the heart of the city. And he—what did he know, what did he understand about borders and checkpoints and nations and soldiers, he knew smells and nothing more—he followed his nose to the black army boots, which kicked him and cursed him and yelled, "Piss off, you filthy mutt!" He sounded an offended yelp but stood his ground and sniffed the air, a mournful look in his eyes.

"Hey! Didn't you hear what I said? Motherfucker!" came the voice again. And the army boots drew nearer. "Piss off before I—"

"Hey, hey, hey, Lichtenstein! What has that poor thing done to you?" Lichtenstein's boot froze in mid-swing of a particularly hard kick that probably would have broken a rib or two and perhaps even left him dead, and the second voice, the voice that saved him, Yaakobi's voice, whispered in his ear, "Come here, sweet boy, what have they done to you? What does Lichtenstein want with you, huh?"

Yaakobi took him into the military base. And gave him food. And petted him. And allowed him into the barracks when it rained. And stood up for him when Lichtenstein and the others made fun of his cross-eyed stare and his odd teeth. He was Yaakobi's friend, and if it had been up to him, he would have remained with him all his life. But when Yaakobi's platoon commander returned from leave on Sunday morning, he told Yaakobi that the dog couldn't stay. Yaakobi requested, pleaded, argued a case for animal welfare, but the platoon commander said he was sorry but those were the rules. As a favor to Yaakobi, who was a good soldier, the platoon commander agreed to allow the dog to remain on the base until Thursday, when Yaakobi would then be able to take him home. The problem, Yaakobi explained to the platoon commander, was that he already had a dog at home. Anyway, it's a Palestinian dog and who knows what diseases it's carrying, it's almost certainly never been seen by a vet, after all. Yaakobi wanted it to be his army dog, not his home dog. He told the platoon commander the dog would be happy, the soldiers would be happy, everyone would be happy. Looking after the dog wouldn't be a problem, he'd take care of it himself—so Yaakobi promised.

"Know something, you're right," the platoon commander said to him. "Who knows what he's carrying—a Palestinian dog that showed up out of nowhere. He's never been seen by a vet. I've changed my mind. He can't stay until Thursday, he needs to get outta here right now." Yaakobi fixed the platoon commander with a look of disbelief, and the dog laid its head on the rug in the barracks and abandoned itself to its cherished and pleasing caress. "Right now!" the platoon commander reiterated.

Lichtenstein, who had just returned from the showers with a towel around his waist and a khaki-colored toiletries bag in his hand, laughed.

"Go on, Yaakobi, get rid of that cross-eyed mutt, I told you he's stinking up our room." Yaakobi remained silent.

Yaakobi managed to get the dog onto an armored Hummer that left for Jerusalem, and he asked the driver to drop off the dog in a safe-looking neighborhood. It was the least he could do for the dog so that it wouldn't have to return to the mean streets of Hebron.

The Hummer driver, a friend of Yaakobi's, agreed. The platoon commander agreed, too. Even Lichtenstein bade the dog farewell when the armored vehicle exited the camp gates. Yaakobi said his good-bye with a kiss on the nose and a whispered "You'll be okay, I know, right?" The dog nodded.

Had his friend Yaakobi not implored him and asked explicitly, the Hummer driver would have left the animal anywhere on the side of the road, abandoning it to its fate and the mercy of the elements. But he restrained himself and tolerated the smell and discomfort of his motionless, cross-eyed companion, and when he passed through the Har Homa neighborhood on the outskirts of Jerusalem to stop by his uncle's place to collect a Beitar Jerusalem soccer club season ticket, he took the animal and left it by the side of one of the new roads under construction, some distance from his uncle's house.

The dog watched the heavy-duty vehicle pull away with a roar of its engine—and sat there puzzled. Around him, he saw buildings and half buildings and the skeletons of buildings and heaps of sand. He saw an empty pool that had filled with rain, and he dipped his tongue in and lapped from its fine waters. He walked over to the framework of a building, found shelter from the wind, curled up in a corner, and went to sleep.

He opened his eyes at the break of dawn, to the calls of the laborers. One gave him a small piece of pita bread and a pinch of cheese, and water in a cottage cheese tub. Several nights and several days went by, and the dog lazed in its spot or went out on nighttime walks around the neighborhood, never running into a living soul other than a random fox, which raised its tail and fled.

Othniel, at the time, was adding on to his home at Ma'aleh Hermesh C., and was covering it in Jerusalem stone, and he needed cement and stones. A good friend discreetly informed him that he had taken out a mortgage on an apartment in Har Homa, construction there was going ahead at full steam, and construction material was plentiful, and Othniel was welcome to drop by one evening and load up his Renault Express with whatever he needed. The streets and houses had no signs or numbers yet, but the friend gave directions and said that even if Othniel failed to find the right building, it was no big deal. The materials were there to build up the country and its settlement, the government was all for it, the contractors were are all for it, and the home owners, too.

With Gavriel Nehushtan along for the ride, Othniel followed his directions to the new neighborhood, where they loaded the materials into the car. They saw a small dog, with a second row of teeth on his bottom jaw and a cross-eyed stare, but bright and friendly nevertheless, and Othniel said, "Whoever preserves a single soul of Israel is said to have preserved an entire world, God giveth and God taketh away, blessed be the name of the Lord." They took him, and he was named Beilin, a stepbrother for Condoleezza, who had turned up a year earlier from Ma'aleh Hermesh A. Beilin grew, and grew stronger, and he tied his soul to the soul of the Assis family and became one of its children, and soon it was as though he'd been there all along.

The Word

C aptain Omer Levkovich woke to the beeping of the alarm on his phone in his tiny Jerusalem apartment at 5:45. Early. The headache came on moments before his recollection of the previous night—too much beer, a short-haired girl, a student at Hebrew University's Mount Scopus campus, studying something strange that he couldn't recall, and he had consumed beer and talked about the ex who'd dumped him. When they left the bar, the student declined his invitation to come over and look at photo albums.

After a shower, he fixed his light hair with his fingers in the mirror. His gray-green eyes were shot with red streaks of weariness. He made himself a coffee in a thermal mug, got into his jeep and drove to the base, collected his crew, and headed to Ma'aleh Hermesh. The Situation Room was already abuzz with activity, he heard on the radio. Yoni was waiting at the outpost, having been summoned back for duty on Saturday evening the moment the minister's visit was approved. Yoni got into the jeep and they went for a drive.

"What's that all about?" Omer pointed at the sight of the people walking silently along the ring road at the early hour.

"Morning prayers," Yoni answered.

"But so many? They always struggle to get a minyan together," said Omer.

"Lots of visitors," Yoni explained in a slow, scratchy voice.

The motorcade began arriving a little after nine. The defense minister's adviser on settlement affairs had shown his boss newspaper headlines that spoke loudly of the minister's "capitulation" to the U.S. president, and op-eds scoffing at his efforts "to suck up to" and "curry favor with" the U.S. administration. Up in front, in a command car bedecked with antennas that climbed the narrow and steep road to the hilltop, sat Giora, the head of Central Command. Toward the back, behind several other security vehicles, appeared the long silver car of the American ambassador in Israel, Milton White. And bringing up the rear, behind the security vehicle that followed the ambassador's car, came a beaten-down and dusty line of vehicles covered with stickers from the corresponding end of the political spectrum.

Standing on a mound of dirt, his arms folded across his chest, Roni followed the convoy's progress. Perhaps due to his position, elevated above the crowd, coupled with the defense minister's constant need to demonstrate conviction, Roni attracted the attention of the minister, who exited his vehicle with his familiar sense of urgency, stretched out his hand, and firmly grasped and shook Roni's, to the clicking of the photographers' cameras. But the moment Roni said, "What's up, bro?" the minister realized he had erred—not only in his choice of target for the handshake, but also in his estimation of the heat outside the air-conditioned car. He was dressed in a jacket and tie, and to remove them now would appear hasty—a surrender to the conditions, a capitulation. Beads of sweat covered his brow, his sunglasses abandoned somewhere in the car. His baseball cap would have been the ideal solution, but he had been instructed not to wear it at public events following the unfortunate photo op at Kibbutz Zikim last month.

Othniel Assis hurried over to welcome his friend Giora, the Central Command major general, who of course hadn't forgotten his sunglasses, and who in turn quickly introduced the minister to the more typical settler. "I'm pleased you came here to show us, to show all the Jewish people and the American president in particular, that you are behind us and won't lend a hand to the uprooting of settlement, minister, sir," said Othniel, smiling as he held Shuv-el, who was clad in a white Sabbath shirt. Othniel knew what would look good in the papers. The minister smiled briefly at Othniel and, from the corner of his eye, glimpsed the lanky figure of Milton standing behind him. The ambassador was leaning in to ascertain whether the minister's response to the settler corresponded with his promises to the administration. Regrettably, the minister spoke in Hebrew.

"Come, I'll show you around," Othniel said.

The minister looked around in an effort to locate his adviser on settlement affairs. The visit wasn't going as planned. He didn't feel in sufficient control of the way events were unfolding. A walk would only serve to intensify the heat and the sweat and the discomfort, and he hadn't had a chance yet to relieve himself of his suit, not to mention the large circles of sweat that must have formed by then on his light blue shirt—he peered down as if to brush away a fly from his tie and noticed its light color—and removing his suit would surely involve a fair amount of embarrassment and yet another opportunity for the cynical photographers to go to town at his expense. He spotted his aide, Malka.

"Come here, Malka," the minister said, and Malka turned away from a warm handshake with Othniel and an embrace with Elazar Freud (one year his senior at their pre-military service yeshiva) to confer with his boss. Othniel's tour wasn't going to happen.

"Malka, find me somewhere to say a few words and we'll get the hell outta here. I'm drowning in sweat." The ambassador approached, and the minister tried not to roll his eyes.

"Milton! Good to see you." He smiled. "What's got you out of bed so early on a Sunday morning?"

"Ha, ha," Milton chuckled. "I guess my bosses really do believe it's important." The minister, his right hand still in the right hand of the ambassador, broke into a loud laugh and slapped the American's shoulder with his free hand.

"Just look at him licking the Americans' asses," Neta Hirschson whispered into the ear closest to her.

"Disgusting," agreed Jean-Marc, her husband.

Beyond them, the Central Command major general was in conversation with the sector's company commander, Omer Levkovich, who then briefed the platoon of reinforcements.

Ambassador White, meanwhile, was asked by reporters what message he expected to hear from the defense minister that morning. "A message of peace, and of progress, within the framework of the law and the vital agreements reached between the countries in recent months," he responded. The defense minister, his back to the ambassador and still speaking to Malka, heard the words and his body responded with another wave of perspiration. Everyone then walked the short distance from the synagogue, where the throng had formed, to the Mamelstein playground. The security guys led the way, followed by the aides of the dignitaries, the dignitaries themselves, the crowd, and the soldiers. Malka instructed the minister to stop alongside a yellow swing set. Ambassador White, Central Command Major General Giora, and the outpost's longest-serving resident, Othniel, then lined up alongside him—click—that was the photograph that appeared the next day in the morning papers: bright, almost overexposed, the minister visibly uneasy and squinting his eyes against the high sun, the Central Command major general authoritative and sure of himself in sunglasses, a tall and content ambassador, and Othniel displaying the ease of a landowner. Close behind, but out of range of the cameras, stood the minister's aide, Malka, and Omer Levkovich. Jehu and Killer trotted jauntily back and forth along the edge of the park, and one of the bodyguards kept a constant eye on them.

"Good evening, everyone, excuse me, good morning," the minister began. Sporadic laughter rang out.

"Shame on you!" shouted Neta Hirschson. "Coming here as the emissary of the American president—"

"Shhh . . . Let him speak," someone said. Two soldiers approached Neta.

"I'm not here as the emissary of any president, please hear me out and be patient—"

"Patient? How can you expect us to be patient when you're selling out the country to foreigners and screwing us over?"

"Excuse me, madam, you focus on abiding by the law and the Americans won't make any demands on us." He diverted his gaze away from Neta Hirschson to a nonspecific point above her, beyond her, catching sight of the white desert hills, the crevices of the Hermesh Stream riverbed. "It's beautiful here," he continued, almost in surprise, "and there's no denying our rights here. But we must respect the law. Mistakes have been made, by the government of Israel, too. There are many legitimate settlements, but there are also some that have been established in places where they shouldn't have been. What I've come here today to say . . ." He cast his eyes over the gathering. The sun had brought out large beads of sweat across his brow. The tie practically choked him. Malka handed him a bottle of water and he sipped from it. ". . . is that we are going to make a few adjustments. And these adjustments will come at a price—"

"How dare you?" Neta now yelled. "What adjustments? What price? What's he talking about?"

"Madam, allow me to finish."

"Let go of me!" the cosmetician shouted at the soldiers now holding her by the arms. Her husband, Jean-Marc, screamed at them in French, mentioning the Holocaust.

"Guys, guys, let her—" the minister tried, turning to look at the major general. "Giora . . . Madam, allow me to finish. There'll be adjustments, there'll be a price to pay, but the government of Israel won't stop supporting—" His address was then interrupted by the intensely loud barking of a large, angry sand-colored dog.

"Beilin! Quiet, Beilin," Gitit shouted in an effort to silence the dog. "Beilin! Beilin!" The defense minister, his eyebrows scrunched up, looked at her, and then, unable to restrain himself, a half-smile appeared on his lips.

"Woof! Woof! Woof!" Beilin roared incessantly, drowning out all conversation, and Condoleezza joined in, running to the scene and barking loudly, and Killer started snorting, and the goats at Othniel's farm down the slope bleated in panic, and Sasson's camel cow looked up inquisitively from somewhere near the sentry post at the gate, chewing vigorously on some vegetation. But Beilin appeared to be directing his barks at one of the soldiers, who stared back at him.

"Beilin?" The soldier laughed. It was Yaakobi, who was part of the squad of reinforcements that was brought in from the base in Hebron. "Is that his name? What's up with him?"

Neta Hirschson, no longer in the clutches of the soldiers at the instruction of the major general, began yelling again. "Shame on you, coming here with the American ambassador and talking about adjustments. What adjustments? You've got a nerve!"

The minister threw in the towel. Much to his dismay, he wasn't going to get to the line he had intended to make the day's sound bite—a catchy, original phrase to come at the height of his address and later make the news headlines, to be relayed by the ambassador to his secretary of state, who would then convey the same to the president, a phrase he was particularly proud of, because he had thought of it himself. He turned and began walking toward his car, surrounded by bodyguards, sweating, reaching up a finger to undo the knot in his tie, and not caring who took his picture or what would appear in the newspapers. Grumbling to himself quietly, he removed his jacket and deposited it in the hands of Malka.

Neta Hirschson continued to shout, and approached the dignitaries. "Tell the American president that he doesn't stand a chance against us, because the king of the world is on our side!" she yelled as the ambassador walked past the slide. "What do Americans understand about the Israeli people's struggle against Arab brutality? Who asked you to come here? Have you come to weaken the Jewish people, who've returned to the Land of Israel after two thousand years of exile and persecution and wars and pogroms and the Holocaust? Are you forcing us out of here—here, God's sanctuary, the land of our forefathers? You're throwing us out of here? And you dare to call that peace? Chutzpah!"

"Will someone shut that dog up!" barked the major general of the Central Command.

As the defense minister walked past, Neta Hirschson gathered up saliva in her mouth and spat. She hit one of his bodyguards. The minister observed the spit land on the bodyguard's shirt, turned his head toward Neta, and the next sentence to escape his lips—which, aside from one unmistakable word, wasn't picked up by any camera or recording device—became the subject of endless debate, consuming liters of ink and creating mountains of words and commentaries over the following days and weeks, and it, instead of the phrase he had thought up, became the sound bite heard round the world.

According to Neta Hirschson, the defense minister said: "Scram, you insolent savage! You and all your dog friends, scram!"

According to associates of the defense minister, he said, "Insolent savage," and then turned to face the other way and said, "Scram! Will someone make those dogs go away already!"

And Beilin and Condoleezza said, "Woof, woof, woof! Woof, woof, woof!" and bared their teeth.

And at that moment, it dawned on Yaakobi from the reinforcement squad: The extra row of teeth! The cross-eyed look! He was a lot bigger than the puppy Yaakobi had cared for a year earlier on the streets of Hebron, the one he'd sent away on the Hummer bound for Jerusalem, but it was him, no doubt about it.

"Holy shit!" the soldier cried out. "You named him Beilin? I don't believe it! Come here, sweet boy. Remember me? It's Yaakobi, from the base in Hebron." And Beilin stopped barking and wagged his tail and walked toward Yaakobi with his head bowed and his tail wagging and snuggled into his embrace, abandoning himself to his caresses. And Condoleezza followed suit, happy and wagging her tail, and the commotion died down. The dignitaries climbed into their official vehicles, which immediately sped off, creating a cloud of dust on their way out of the outpost, and the residents dispersed to their respective homes, the soldiers to their bases, the reporters to their offices. But as for the reverberations caused by the minister's visit, and as for the incident that would long be remembered as the "Scram Affair," they had just then come to life, and wouldn't die down for a long time to come.

The Handyman

"There's never a dull moment with you guys, huh, Doctor?" said Herzl Weizmann when he turned up at the outpost that same afternoon. Though he was dark-haired and dark-skinned, the man's defining feature was albino-white eyelashes over one eye, which added a mysterious dimension to his every stare.

"Despite all the hoopla," Herzl continued, "I wanted to come before Tisha B'Av. I've let you down too many times. Come, let's have a look. Oh my, what a sweet child! What's his name?" He stretched out a finger, with its blackened nail, to touch the nose of the tiny baby girl on Hilik's forearm.

Hilik lowered his gaze to his infant daughter and smiled at her under his mustache. He had almost forgotten she was there. "*Her* name," he said, "is Yemima." He didn't bother revealing to Herzl her full name, Yemima-Me'ara, with its reference to the incident in the cave. He didn't have the energy to go into the whole story. His memory drifted back to Simchat Habat, the naming ceremony for newborn Jewish girls. How long ago had it been? Two weeks? Three? After the birth of a child, the days and nights all seem to run into one another, a sweet jumble of constant fatigue, adapting to the new family structure, wondrous moments of awareness of the existence of this new living, demanding, nagging being, of efforts to somehow maintain a semblance of normal life—a meeting with the adviser at the university, reading books for his doctoral thesis, the appointment with Herzl Weizmann to move ahead with the renovations. At the naming ceremony, the blessing after the Sabbath morning prayer service, Nehama and Hilik had explained their choice to the community: Yemima, Job's beautiful daughter, the Hebrew expression *yamim-yemima*, days gone by, which evokes historical and deep-rooted ties to previous generations, the words *yam* and *mayim*, sea and water, which occur in succession in the Hebrew spelling of the name; and the second part of her name, Me'ara, the Hebrew word for cave, the place where she chose to emerge into the world.

Hilik showed Herzl around the trailer, all the while wondering why he had allowed himself to get involved with the handyman in the first place, why he had given in to Othniel's pressure. With all due respect to Jewish labor, Hilik wasn't planning on building a villa. He was merely adding on half a shipping container, due for delivery any day now—a simple job that Kamal could complete within a few days and at a cost of next to nothing. Now this Herzl Weizmann guy, after rescheduling his visit several times, was talking to him about ideas that appeared to be too complicated and far too expensive.

Why had he given in to Othniel? Why should Othniel care if a local Palestinian got some work and made a little money? Kamal wasn't a terrorist, he was a good guy. There were some good apples, too, and they'd really had it rough in recent years. Hilik had talked with Roni the previous day. He wasn't about to speak out in favor of Roni's olive oil business with Musa—another good guy, as far as he knew, despite having jumped onto the IDF's D-9—but he was willing to admit to himself that he did agree with Roni on occasion. Herzl Weizmann from Mevasseret certainly talked the talk, but who knew if he was any good, or if his ideas were worth considering, and how much time and money would be involved. All Hilik wanted was a little more legroom and for the children to have space to grow up.

What struck Hilik the most about Herzl Weizmann, more than the black curls and white eyebrow and odd gaze, and more than the heavy shoes that Hilik suspected were fitted with insoles to compensate for the man's small stature, were his plaster-casted forearms—two tubes of plaster, no longer white, from the wrist up to the elbow, equal in length.

"It's nothing, don't worry, it doesn't bother me. An accident," Herzl Weizmann said in response to Hilik's stare. He didn't elaborate and changed the subject. "Forget about the container, we'll get lumber from the guys down there"—he pointed out the kitchen window in the direction of Gabi's cabin—"and we'll build a great little extension for you."

"Who says he has enough to give me? His entire cabin is about the same size as the extension I'm planning."

"So, we'll ask. And if there isn't enough, we'll order from his supplier. Or I can arrange something for you through my carpenter. No problem." Herzl squinted and took in a panoramic view of the settlement.

Yemima-Me'ara, meanwhile, had fallen asleep, and Hilik set her down in her crib and went with Herzl to Gabi's cabin to ask about the lumber. The wood boards, it turned out, had come from the carpentry workshop at Ma'aleh Hermesh A. at a price that Herzl defined as "not bad, not bad at all—relatively speaking." They returned afterward to Hilik's trailer. "Whoa, looks like that camel has escaped from the Bedouin!" Herzl exclaimed on the way back, pointing at the animal.

"What Bedouin?" Hilik said. "That's a camel cow, Sasson's camel cow."

"Tell me, Dr. Hilik," Herzl said once they were back at the house and were sitting in the living room sipping coffee, "what's the name of that guy at the cabin? He looks so familiar to me."

"Who? Gavriel?"

"Gavriel?"

"Yes, Gavriel Nehushtan."

"Gavriel Nehushtan." Herzl rubbed his chin and pondered. "Gavriel Nehushtan," he said again, as if repeating the name would somehow jog his memory. "No, the name doesn't ring a bell. Has he been here for long?"

"A few years, I can't recall exactly."

"A few years, huh?" He rubbed his chin some more.

After the coffee, he got into his car and placed his plaster-casted arms on the wheel. "I'll call you with a quote," he promised.

"Thanks," Hilik responded indifferently.

"Okay, hang in there," Herzl said, and stepped on the gas.

That evening, Gabi ran into Hilik at the evening prayer service. "Your handyman looks familiar to me," Gabi said to him. "Is he from the Galilee or something?"

Hilik chuckled. "Not at all, from Mevasseret," he responded. Gabi frowned and returned quickly to his prayer book.

The Shed

Nir Rivlin, with his red hair and beard, sat at the kitchen table and sipped from a large bottle of Goldstar beer. Tears flowed from his red eyes. Between sobs, he mumbled sentences like "I don't understand. What have I done?"

"You haven't done a thing," Shaulit said while Zvuli suckled from her ravenously. "And that's part of the problem."

Nir had come into the kitchen from the porch a few minutes earlier to retrieve the bottle of beer from the refrigerator—his third that evening, and they hadn't even sat down to dinner. He had been sitting on the porch for the past hour with his guitar, trying to compose a new song. But aside from coming up with the line "All pain is but another scale in the armor," which he ended up repeating to himself over and over, and consuming two beers and a joint, he didn't make much progress—until he finally gave up and began playing "Berta."

Shaulit, at the same time, had bathed Amalia and Tchelet, had made them dinner and then fed them with Zvuli in her arms, and the infant, too, demanded attention and his own food. Amalia wanted to help but she was too small to hold him, too impatient to play with him or watch over him for more than two minutes. After dinner, Shaulit put the girls to bed, read them a story, and returned to the kitchen to wash their dishes and begin preparing dinner for herself and Nir. All the while, the flat chord had repeated itself, the pain and the scale in the armor. For her, every slap in the face—or simply every minute of the day—was a scale in the armor. But tough armor could sometimes crack, too. And then things were said. Threats were made. And Nir, whom she knew well enough, would immediately revert to acting like the small child within him, that was his defense mechanism, and the beers didn't help things, weakening the walls of defense and self-awareness of the man he was meant to be, and then the tears would come, and she'd be expected to apologize, to take pity on him, but she had reached her limit that evening. She knew what was coming—an admission to the fact that he had been wrapped up in himself of late, that he didn't know what had come over him, that he was struggling terribly with his culinary studies (What's so hard? she wanted to scream. Inserting a piece of cucumber in a sushi roll? Peeling a yam?), and with all this uncertainty concerning the outpost, no one knew if their home would even be there for much longer, the evacuation was on one day and off the next—he wasn't one for fighting battles, but just let them decide already, all this stress. Nir believed it would soon pass and he'd be able to be of more help to her. He felt that this phase he was going through would spark new creativity and that he'd be able to record these songs.

She knew he'd never record those songs anywhere at all, it was a waste of time, his and primarily hers, but she didn't have the heart, despite the anger and exhaustion. She didn't have the heart to yell at him and to tell him that—and perhaps it wasn't a matter of heart but of years of habit and upbringing. He could do as he pleased, while she kept the household functioning. And after the tears and the admission and the promise and the hope—she knew, expected it, readied herself—his spirit would be renewed, and with that would come the transfer of the blame.

"Perhaps it's postpartum depression?" he offered. At that stage, she had already tapped her hand lightly on Zvuli's tiny shoulder to encourage a burp and then placed him in the rocking chair, broke eggs into a frying pan and sliced tomatoes and cucumbers, removed hummus and cottage cheese and cream cheese from the refrigerator and bread out of the bread box, and set the table.

"Perhaps you should go speak to someone? Perhaps we should consider seeking help? Perhaps someone like Gitit could come over to help out for a few hours every day?"

She responded with nothing more than a weak "Perhaps," but she knew that Gitit had her hands full with her five younger siblings, and that they didn't have the money to pay Gitit, and that the whole idea was stupid anyway—she only needed *his* help from time to time, goddammit. He couldn't even say, like most men, that he didn't know how to cook—he was studying to be a chef, for crying out loud! And as for the postpartum depression, who knew, maybe. Or perhaps they simply weren't suited to each other. Perhaps they married too young, in their teens, without really getting to know each other and without knowing anything about life.

The strange thing was that their marriage didn't come about through an arranged *shidduch*. They had known each other from a young age, they both grew up in Beit El, and they were members of the Bnei Akiva youth movement together. She remembered him from her father's shiva, which he had come to every day with his own father. It was as though they had gotten together as secular people do. But after six and a half years and three children—the last one conceived after the onset of this tension, perhaps as a remedy, a distraction—one could now definitively say that it simply wasn't meant to be. More proof that the secular way of life didn't work. Shaulit had repeatedly put herself through the mill and agonized, in conversations with herself, and between herself and God, but had come to realize that it wasn't simply Nir's help or support that she lacked. After all, she managed somehow. It was more than that. She didn't know the man, didn't truly love him. Not that she really believed in the notion of falling in love, but she *really* didn't love him. She couldn't fathom spending years by his side. And as for the songs, well, there were one or two pleasant ones, but she hadn't heard any breakout hits being cooked up on the wide swing in the yard. She wasn't holding her breath. His music was not about to save them.

They chewed on slices of bread with cream cheese for several minutes in silence, their eyes fixed on arbitrary points on the table, and Nir sniffled every now and then and poured beer down his throat. When he was done, he dropped his fork with a clatter on the glass plate. He glanced at his watch. He was due to report for guard duty in forty minutes, he informed her, and left—without a guitar or any religious literature this time, and without another bottle of beer or something to smoke, either. He walked along the settlement's ring road. The evening sky was huge, and despite it being late July, there was a pleasant breeze, and he stopped, closed his eyes and sucked it in, and spread his arms to allow the air to reach his fingertips from the inside. They must not crack, he thought. There are ups and downs, there are rough patches. But they had to hang in there.

Shortly before reaching the Assis family home, he heard a door close and footsteps on the path. He pressed himself to the stone wall, disappearing into the darkness. It was Gitit Assis, who looked right and left and set out quietly on foot, hunched over. The manner of her gait, the urgency and the furtive glances, suggested she wasn't out for some fresh air at the end of the day. Nir followed her, sticking close to the fences, hiding behind whatever he came across—trash bins, cars, heaps of construction material, or empty refrigerators. With the contents of three bottles of beer swirling inside him, Nir could admit to himself—after trial and tribulation and begging forgiveness from his wife and from his God (He knew that "one who is slow to anger is better than a mighty man, and one who rules over his spirit is better than one who conquers a city." He remembered Joseph, who resisted temptation. He knew that a man who is drawn to the temptations of the world and resists those temptations is no less a righteous man than one who is not tempted at all)—that he was attracted to Gitit. It wasn't a coincidence when he suggested that Shaulit have her help out with housework. He'd gladly pay for the privilege of seeing her in their home from time to time. Nir entered the playground and stepped on a soft toy, which squeaked. He froze. Gitit stopped and turned. The breeze picked up. Where's she going? he wondered.

The moment passed. She turned and continued on her way. He released the air from his lungs and slowly lifted his foot off the plastic duck, which, thankfully, didn't squeak. He watched from the playground as she walked into the wind, her long hair flapping, her dark dress billowing. The next trailer was the last before the guardhouse at the gate, the army's trailer, Yoni's. And instead of walking by it, she turned onto the entry path. Had she found something that belonged to Yoni? Had her father asked her to relay a message to him? Had her mother sent a cake, perhaps? Nir crouched down on one knee. His shift was scheduled to begin in twenty-eight minutes.

Gitit knocked three times on the door to the trailer, turned around, and began walking toward the playground, toward Nir! He looked around for somewhere to hide. At the far end of the park stood a small wooden shed where the laborers stored their tools and building materials. Yoni's door slammed shut, and his dark figure began making its way toward the park. Just then, a huge bang sounded and a wedding firework from Kharmish exploded in the sky, shaking the outpost from its slumber. Taking advantage of Gitit's and Yoni's surprise, their gaze skyward, the barking of the dogs, Nir regained his composure, made a dash for the shed, and ducked in. It was hot inside, and stuffy, with the smell of sawdust and varnish and synthetic paints and turpentine. He hoped they hadn't spotted him.

Where were they? All he could hear was his own breathing, the beating of his heart. He focused on his discomfort and on the awful heat in the shed, which had absorbed the rays from a long day of sun, with hardly the smallest crack for air to slip in. He could feel his glands pumping sweat, onto his forehead, under his arms, onto his lower back (Shaulit would ask him in the morning why his shirt was so wet and smelled of turpentine). He pressed an ear to the door. Are they there?

A thump on the side wall a few centimeters to his right startled him. He heard whispering he wasn't able to decipher and then Gitit giggling. "You're crazy, be quiet."

Yoni responded in a low tone, Nir couldn't make out the words, only the monotone hum of an accent.

"No! Are you crazy?" she said. "Not now." Another short monotone hum. Nir waited for a response from Gitit, but none came. Suddenly he heard a familiar sound—lips smacking, teeth knocking together, the suction of mouths uniting for an instant, quickened breathing, voices soft, purring, shy. Nir listened intently, pressing an ear to the wall against which they were leaning, sweating from every pore, inhaling toxic fumes but failing to notice them because of the sounds coming from the other side of the thin wooden wall. The teenager, the daughter of the settlement's most senior resident, was kissing the Ethiopian soldier. The image filled his mind, hampered his breathing, thrilled him, disgusted him. What's she thinking? he wondered. How dare she?

Another monotone murmur, and a breathless "No. Are you crazy?" from her, and a giggle, and then their mouths must have locked together again because Nir could hear nothing apart from their bodies moving against the wall, snatched breaths, another smacking of lips, another wet suction. And then "No, not there . . ."

Where?

"Yoni!"

More shuffling against the wall, groping, clothes rustling. The click of a buckle? A button undone? A zipper tugged? The sounds swirled in his head, mixing with the odors and the humidity, and he was no longer sure what he was imagining and what was really happening. "Yoni, no!" Another whisper, and then Nir asked himself if he should go out and help her. Was the brash soldier forcing himself on her? And what exactly was he trying to force? And then silence.

Nir's breathing was labored. Nausea rose up in his chest. He tried to lean on something in the dark, to sit down perhaps. He needed water. Beer-flavored burps filled his throat. And still not a sound from outside. He couldn't see the time but assumed his shift should be starting any minute now. He was the first guard on duty that evening, and the first guard needs to report to and update—and suddenly it dawned on him— Yoni. Had the Ethiopian done something to her? Strangled her? Then came another of Yoni's monotone hums, and Gitit burst into laughter, which started out loud and was then stifled, a hand over her mouth, and then the sound of more movement and rapid breathing— What are they doing there?

"No," he heard Gitit whisper. "Not today. I have to go. Next time." Another distant firework made them jump, and then stifled giggling, and then a monotone hum. "Next time, I promise." A hum that sounded like a question. "Yes, I promise," and a brief kiss. The thin wooden wall groaned and clothes rustled, and then came the sound of receding foot-steps, with another soft giggle from Gitit.

Nir's face was hot from sweat, from heat, from shame. After a few minutes, he turned the handle and inhaled as though it were crisp Alpine winter air—not that Nir had ever been in the Alps in the winter. He made sure they were gone, stepped out from the shed, and circled the structure to the place where the pair had been moments earlier, sniffing around, looking for proof, clues that would perhaps add substance to the audio experience, but aside from a faint smell he couldn't quite put his finger on—his brain was awash with odors and chemicals—there were no clues as to what had just happened there.

He walked to the center of the playground, spread his arms, and allowed the breeze to cool his wet clothes, his forehead, the back of his neck, and all the remaining sweat-soaked areas. He inhaled deeply, sighed. And then he crossed the road to Yoni's trailer to let him know that the night shift was starting.

"You're ten minutes late, dude," Yoni said. "Don't let it happen again, okay? I was just about to call you." Nir nodded, ran his hand over the telephone in the front pocket of his pants, and then over the butt of the pistol tucked into his pants at the back—and left without a word.

During his shift, Nir returned twice to the scene of the incident, trying to reconstruct it, to find evidence, and the more his mind sobered up from the beer, with the help of liters of water and the passing of hours, the more he wondered what really had happened. While snooping behind the shed for the second time, he heard footsteps and a voice, and the love scene that had been playing over in his thoughts made way for a new show. He pressed himself to the wall of the storeroom and froze again, again tried to blend in with his surroundings. At least he was outside now, breathing in fresh air and the smell of the wooden boards, a far more pleasant odor than that of turpentine. He could hear better, too, the sounds were less muffled—undoubtedly an upgrade in conditions.

Someone was speaking on the telephone in a low, self-conscious voice. He caught the sound of rope straining under the weight of a body, of a gentle movement slicing through the air—a swing in motion. Thank the Lord, it had yet to start creaking and squeaking, as it would in time, when rust and dirt have accumulated in its joints; still new and well oiled, it coped just fine now with the body weight of an adult woman, who quietly said, "Is there not names list?"

Nir's ears pricked up. What did she say? And then "No, I no check. I what you say to me. No find. Roni Kupper, no. No talk to Roni Kupper, but . . ."

Nir peered into the darkness. Were the beers and the joint still messing with his head? What was going on here this evening? He slowly shifted his position, peeling his body from the wall of the shed to turn to look at the woman. He had of course recognized her voice the moment he heard her first word, but he had to see with his own eyes, and now, under the faint light of the stars, he saw her, Jenia Freud, swinging on a swing too small for her dimensions, her left hand gripping the rope, her right clutching a phone to her ear. Why is Jenia talking on the phone, in the playground, at night, about Roni Kupper?

She resumed talking quietly. "No, before minister come, I not hear talking, nothing. After he say scram, also no. Jehu and Josh I watch. Yes, I know I said they can make problem. But no, there are nothing. Okay. Okay, I talk with Roni Kupper. Yes, with Arab, but I no see anything there. Yes, okay. Kupper I check."

Nir slid his back down the wall of the shed until he was sitting on solid ground. He closed his eyes and then opened them again, and turned his head to look at Jenia, who was holding the phone in the air, swinging and deep in thought. The world froze for thirty seconds, a chill wind blew through the playground and rustled the leaves, the Arabs and their fireworks went quiet in deference to the moment, and even Condi, who was barking earlier, fell silent. Jenia blurted a few words—a curse in Russian?—got off the swing, and went into her home across the road.

Nir remained where he was for several minutes, his eyes closed, his back to the wall of the shed, his butt on the ground. Finally, he gathered himself, stood up, and headed off to patrol the ring road. When Gabi Nehushtan relieved him, he barely said a word, merely nodding, his eyes low, and went on his way. Gabi watched him, puzzled, stroked his sparse beard, and went up into the guard tower to recite the Tikkun Chatzot prayer.

The Attack

Duvid, an expert in ancient artifacts and a longtime settler whom Othniel knew from his early days in Samaria, and also from reserve army duty, came to the outpost a few days after Dvora Assis found the coins in the cave, and after her father, Othniel, "popped over to have a look." Duvid combed the cave's rooms with a metal detector and found a total of thirty-eight coins. His initial conclusion: they had been unearthed, thanks, probably, to a rock rabbit that had been digging in the cave in the hope of finding water or food, and come across the coins instead, buried under the sandy earth and soft limestone.

Othniel invited Duvid back on a number of occasions, and he repeatedly declined, citing various reasons, until Othniel, annoyed, instructed Yakir "to check his Internet" to see if he could find any information about ancient coins in the area.

For Yakir, delving into the archaeological archives of American universities was an intriguing challenge. The research project offered him an excuse to remain awake and chat with people in American time zones— or so he explained to his father—and so he was left with plenty of time to spend on Revival with his friends. Because they were in the midst of the long summer vacation, and because Othniel was bent on looking into the matter of the coins and not relying solely on Duvid, Yakir spent many hours at night in front of the computer undisturbed.

Duvid, meanwhile, finally succumbed to Othniel's pleas and came again to visit. After a cup of tea and some small talk about the defense minister, the Central Command major general, and the other obligatory niceties, Othniel asked about the coins.

"What can I say, Othni, you need patience with this type of thing. I know you'd like to know right away, but it takes time. We're cleaning the coins, we'll send them for various tests, we'll get an accurate dating, and then we'll see. I'd also like to send a few to expert colleagues of mine. There are several distinguished researchers in the field of ancient artifacts—most of them Jewish—who are located at Duke University in America. And I have someone in Australia who knows more about these things than anyone else. Show a little patience and we'll eventually have trustworthy results."

"And then?"

"And then we'll know if the coins are authentic. We'll know what period they come from. We'll be able to identify the symbols that appear on the bronze under the greenish layer of patina. If they're Roman dinars or Hellenistic drachmas, it won't be worth the effort. If they're from the Hasmonean dynasty, and we know the Hasmoneans inhabited these caves, they could be worth a little more. The most valuable are the ones from the rebellion era, in particular the silver shekels from the Bar Kokhba Revolt. If that's what we're dealing with—and my initial hunch with the naked eye tells me no—then you can sell to collectors or museums via an antiques merchant or public auction. That's where there could be big money."

"And what do we get from the big money?"

"Ha, ha, ha, ha," thundered Duvid.

Othniel wasn't amused. His brown eyes were locked on eyes that were practically swallowed up behind the glasses on Duvid's chubby face when he asked, "What's imprinted on coins from the revolt period?"

"Jewish symbols—pomegranates, chalices. A little like the ones that appear on shekels today. And the year of the revolt is imprinted on them too. Every year has a different value."

Othniel rubbed his chin through his beard. "Listen to this, Duvid. My son Yakir did some checking on the Internet. He found something interesting. Yakir! Yakir! Come here for a moment!" he called. Yakir rose from his seat at the computer and came to the living room. There he found Duvid—fat, bespectacled, with silver hair and beard and a look of disdain in his eyes.

"Listen, Othni," the visitor said, "there's lots of crap on the Internet, I'm telling you, it takes time, let us—"

"Listen to what the kid has to say," Othniel interjected. "And then do with it as you please." Duvid reached out for his cup of tea and sipped.

"What was the name of that monk, Yakiri?" Othniel egged on his son.

"Saint Onuphrius."

"Saint Onuphrius. Heard of him?"

Duvid motioned with his head in a manner that could have been construed as a yes, but he was clearly unmoved by the information being fed to him. "Yakir found an archaeologist in America who once lived in Ma'aleh Hermesh A.," Othniel continued. "I remember him, an American, from the first days of the settlement, a good guy, despite being a good friend of Shimoni, that son of a bitch. Anyway, he did his doctorate on this Onuphrius guy. He— Yakir, you know more about this than me, tell Duvid."

"Saint Onuphrius was an Egyptian-born monk who lived as a hermit in the desert, in this area, for several decades during the fourth century," Yakir recited. "He was abducted by bandits along the road and taken out into the middle of the desert, and returned naked, with only his long white beard covering his shame, and for the remainder of his days he lived as a hermit, enduring extreme thirst, hunger, and discomfort. According to the archaeologist from Duke, Onuphrius lived in the Hermesh cave and had a trove of coins that he hid, that he probably received for safekeeping from nomads who passed through the area."

"Well, okay," Duvid said, coughing slightly, "the Internet is full of stories like this—too many, if you ask me." His fat lips smiled at Othniel and he forced a laugh.

Troubled by Duvid's apparent apathy, Othniel joined Rachel in bed earlier than usual. He soon fell asleep. Gitit was asleep already, too, and so were all the little ones, naturally. The house fell silent, with only the buzz of Othniel's snoring providing the rhythm, casting a subconscious sense of security over the members of the household tucked away in their beds.

Yakir logged in to Second Life and hurried off to meet his friends on Revival. The Star of David spam attack had stirred stormy reactions in the virtual world—Arab solidarity demonstrations, the establishment of new mosques, increased anti-Semitic sentiment and expression, and even a botched retaliation attempt at a synagogue. Reactions had filtered into the real world, too, and images of the mosque flooded with Stars of David popping up on blogs and websites, and even on Ynet. King Meir was pleased. He wanted to move on to the next stage—a real terror attack. Yakir retrieved a jam cookie from the box, took a bite, and waited for his friends Klaus, Menachem, and a new recruit, Harvey, who had told Yakir that he was a follower of Rabbi Kook, and King Meir himself, too, of course.

They were standing alongside the Flame of the Revival synagogue, chins adorned with tapered beards, Uzis on their shoulders, a Kach T-shirt stretched across King Meir's chest, the others in flannel shirts, light blue tzitzit peeking out from under them to always bring to mind the Holy One, blessed be He. King Meir was smoking a virtual cigarette.

They teleported themselves to Taste of Arabia, which was teeming with people, Muslims who had come to demonstrate solidarity after the Stars of David spam, and various other curious and bored Second Lifers who had heard about the controversy and had come to check it out. The Revival gang entered the large mosque. A bearded Arab man welcomed them and asked them to remove their shoes. They ignored him and went in. Yakir's heart was pounding. King Meir gave the order and they pulled out Palestinian flags they had created and, with the click of a mouse, set them alight with a flame-making application Yakir had downloaded for free. They stood there holding the burning flags, and then in came the Arab characters and their supporters, enraged, shouting, ordering them out, to cease the desecration. There were many non-Arabs, who were carrying placards and shouting with angry faces. King Meir spoke to Yakir. He wanted the mosque then and there. But the computer was acting strange. Its fan was working and stopping every few seconds. Yakir bent down and looked at the computer case. He couldn't figure out what was happening, it had never acted like this before. Don't crash now, he pleaded.

Yakir punched some keys, and from his Second Life User folder, the Inventory, he retrieved the mosque he had built—an exact copy of the mosque they were in moments before, the big mosque in Taste of Arabia. He felt a pang in his heart when he thought of all the hours he had spent at the computer building the beautiful mosque, complete with its arches and colorful adornments. He positioned it, and the two mosques stood there side by side, the original in its place, the replica Yakir had built on a sandbox—a nonrestricted public area—beside it. Curious onlookers turned up to see what and why, exchanged bewildered looks, someone asked if it was a gift, recompense for the violence, an effort to bridge the differences between the religions. King Meir laughed. He gave Yakir the signal and Yakir ran Particles, the explosion simulation software he had bought, with the replica mosque as its target.

The first boom destroyed the walls. The fire was impressive. Passions flared. People yelled. King Meir raised his arms. The fan in Yakir's computer labored. Yakir dipped his hand into the box of jam cookies and found crumbs. His brother Shuv-el started to cry, but stopped and slept on, a bad dream. On the screen, meanwhile, the nightmare of the Arabs and their leftist friends continued. Flames filled the mosque. King Meir pushed for more. Yakir ran another explosion program and the mosque's column broke and fell. Klaus and Menachem were dancing. An Arab brandishing a sword approached Yakir, but he could do him no harm. Yakir sent him the only curse in English that he knew, and in mid-sentence, the computer froze.

The Japanese

The days grew short. August flowed into September. Darkness fell a little earlier, accompanied by crispness in the air. During the day, a gust of air would occasionally rise up, as if to declare, It won't be long now before the summer gasps its final breaths.

The babies grew steadily, their rounded bodies drew in fluids from every nipple, plastic or human, that agreed to provide them, and immediately translated them into additional grams. Filled with anticipation, their brothers and sisters were driven into the city and returned with colorful notebooks and shiny writing implements, ready for a year of hard work. The Ki Teitzei weekly Torah portion passed, and the Ki Tavo portion arrived, and soon the season of new beginnings was on the doorstep, white shirts were pressed, and new dresses were acquired. And the synagogue was cleaned and rejuvenated and readied, and rose to the occasion. Verses of the Mishnah were memorized and commentaries lengthened and the festive mood filtered in and took over. The days were beautiful and the nights clear, and clouds gathered, increasingly darker and thicker. The curses of one Jewish year perished and a new one—5770—began to the sound of the shofar and with the turning back of the clocks and the Days of Awe.

Musa Ibrahim looked up at the sky. He could feel the expectancy in the air. The wet days awaited their turn, were assembling just around the corner, and after the first rains came, and washed the olives, swelled them and cooled them and darkened them a bit, they'd be ready for the next stage. His nostrils widened, a hint of excitement. It was his favorite season. The Jews were quiet and focused on their holidays; the skies, Allah willing, would bring their bounty, and the entire family would pitch in on the harvest, assemble in the grove from all corners of the village, spend long days there, collecting olive after olive.

Standing by his side was his son, Nimer, fair-skinned and balding. Musa smiled and laid a hand on his shoulder. "Soon," he said. Nimer had told him of the talk among the people in the village about the business deal with the Jews. They weren't too happy about it, particularly after the story with the bulldozer, when Musa was arrested and soldiers showed up to snoop around and harass them. A good boy himself, Nimer nevertheless had a few hotheaded friends. He trusted his father. He wasn't crazy about that Jew, Roni, but after learning he wasn't a real settler, wasn't a religious lunatic, that all he intended was for everyone to profit from his initiative, and that he had also helped to retrieve the equipment that was seized, he gave him a pass.

"Here comes your friend," he said to his father. Musa chuckled.

"Hey there, Musa, Nimer, how are you today?"

"Allah be praised." Musa smiled and shook Roni's hand. The two villagers accepted cigarettes from the outstretched light blue box, with Musa inserting his into the plastic holder, and the three lit up in silence, casting their eyes over the grove.

"How cold was it last night, huh?" Roni said.

"The wind is beginning," Musa responded. "Soon the first rains will come. And then we . . ."

Roni nodded. "Is everything ready?"

"What is there to be ready? We're waiting. There's many canvas from last demonstration of settlers. And sacks, and sticks, and 'luminum rakes. We need only first rain, to wash olives and give them good color. And you ready?"

"Definitely ready. We've got a bunch of boutiques in Tel Aviv just waiting for the oil. They love it, they know it's the real thing, and not that light machine-made piss. Ariel is doing a good job with the marketing, with a picture of me and you on the D-9, and the whole story. He says it's going to create a stir."

"Boutiques?" Musa wondered out loud.

Roni was there to finalize the deal. Ariel wanted a signed agreement. He had prepared the paperwork and had even had everything translated into Arabic. Musa had said there was no need, and Roni had apologized and made fun of his meticulous partner, but Ariel had insisted and Musa consented.

Roni gestured with the envelope. "Should we go sign this?" he said.

"I must first to read paper, so I understand what says," Musa replied.

"Sure, sure. Take your time. Sit and read. I'll smoke my cigarette meanwhile."

"No, no cigarette. I give to someone from the village. His brother is lawyer in Bethlehem."

Roni's gaze wandered from the father to the son. An impatient sigh escaped his lips. "Okay," he said. "So we'll meet again tomorrow, then?"

"Allah willing," Musa responded.

The afternoon of that same day saw the arrival of the Japanese, along with a few grayish clouds and currents of air moving at a speed that finally crossed the barrier between a breeze and a wind. A gleaming black Toyota with dark windows—one of those upscale urban jeeps that serve businessmen on off-road trips—stopped at the guard post at the gate, and Yoni, somewhat taken aback by the slanted, smiling features that appeared in place of the dark window sliding down with an electronic hum, waved them in without asking questions. The vehicle cruised along the settlement's ring road, attracted several curious stares, and then turned off onto the dirt path and headed down toward the edge of the cliff. The Toyota pulled up on the gravel, and from it emerged an elegant-looking man, attired in an expensive silk suit, sporting a dark tie, wearing wide-rimmed sunglasses, followed by two other men. They stepped cautiously, perhaps to avoid dirtying their shoes or to escape a sprained ankle, and then gestured and gazed in the direction of Kharmish.

Jehu noticed them and rode up and halted alongside them without saying a word. They bowed with their heads. Jehu waited, slipped two fingers into his pants pocket, and withdrew a cigarette.

"Kamish?" asked the man who had emerged from the vehicle first, repeating the word several times. "Kamish? Kamish?" Jehu turned his head toward the settlement in search of help from someone. The man pointed again at Kharmish. Another anti-Semitic, so-called peace delegation? Lost tourists? Businessmen who had taken a wrong turn?

Roni, who was returning from his visit with Musa and Nimer, approached, an unpleasant and sweaty expression on his face. The Japanese man smiled at him and said, "Kamish? Orive oi?"

"Huh?" said Roni. "Josh!" he yelled. "Come here and see what these guys need!" His eyes remained fixed on the visitor and he grumbled quietly to himself, "That's all we need here now—as if Jews and Arabs and Americans and Russians and French aren't enough. Now these guys are joining in on the fun. Fantastic." He smiled ungraciously in response to the hesitant, don't-understand-a-word grin on the Japanese guy's face.

Josh understood a little better. "Olive oil?" he asked.

The Japanese man nodded excitedly and pointed toward the olive groves of Kharmish.

"Kupper, they're asking something about olive oil," Josh said to Roni. "Isn't that your game?" He looked at the Japanese, pointed at Roni, and said, "Roni Kupper." The Japanese man responded with a sheepish smile. "Gabi Kupper?" Josh tried.

The three Japanese men burst into laughter and repeated, "Galy Cooper, ha, ha."

"Are you looking for Arabs or Jews?"

And still the Japanese failed to comprehend.

Roni lit a cigarette; he started to feel uneasy. What are three spruced-up Japanese men, in suits from another world and an immaculate Toyota jeep, doing here asking questions about olive oil and pointing at Musa's groves?

Efforts to communicate ran aground. The Japanese tried to move the Toyota closer to the olive trees and soon learned that even the four-by-four was unable to blaze a path. Following a series of smiles and handshakes and the presentation of business cards and bows, they got back into the vehicle and headed away from the hilltop, leaving behind a few confused faces—but only for a brief moment, because odd visitors showed up on the hilltop almost daily, and most were erased from memory mere seconds after the last of their vehicles' exhaust fumes were spat out into the hilltop air.

Roni tossed his cigarette butt and held the three business cards closer to his face. The Japanese characters that covered the cards meant nothing to him. He turned one over and found more familiar English letters. Matsumata—Heavy Machinery Division, it read, along with a Japanese name and a job title. Josh poked his nose in and read it, too, and then shrugged and departed. Roni stuffed the cards into his pocket and walked off toward Gabi's trailer. Perhaps he'd ask Ariel to check on the Internet.

The Sting

Nir Rivlin was tormented. What he had heard during Yoni and Gitit's encounter left no room for the imagination, it embarrassed and thrilled and disgusted him, and the shame and curiosity had not waned several weeks later. He knew he should talk to Othniel, but what would he say? That he had listened in like some kind of depraved voyeur? Why hadn't he stopped them? And how would Othniel bear the shame, knowing he had witnessed his daughter's wantonness? Nir thought about speaking to a rabbi at Ma'aleh Hermesh A., or sending a text message to Rabbi Aviner's cellular Q&A service, but after managing, or so he thought, to formulate a question, he hesitated and changed his mind. He wanted to confer with Shaulit, but the situation at home had gone from bad to worse, they were drifting further apart and their conversations had devolved to the bare essentials: payments, kindergartens, schedules, shopping. They didn't speak about their own feelings for each other, so how were they going to tackle a large moral dilemma?

Nir sat down with his guitar one evening and tried to compose a song inspired by what had happened. He closed his eyes and tried to reconstruct the feeling inside the storeroom: the pungent smell, the heat, the stuffiness. What he had heard.

In a small wooden square
The smell of paint and glue filling the air
Standing alone and . . .

His daughters were crying inside the house, but he had to focus. His hand felt under the hammock for the box of grass. He thought he had a joint already rolled in there, but there wasn't. Tchelet screamed from inside. Shaulit yelled, "Nir! Nir!" He strummed on the guitar and tried to come up with a rhyme for the third line. Hair? Dare? Wear? He gave up and launched into a rendition of Kaveret's "Natati La Chayai."

The yelling stopped, and with it the crying. A good time to go inside and ask if everything was okay. He put down the guitar and went in. The look he got from Shaulit—red-eyed, despairing, accusing—told him what he already knew. He had already asked for another chance, had already promised to be more attentive, more helpful, more supportive. But it wasn't working. Her stare drove him away, forced him to say, "I'm popping over to Othniel, something important," and to turn around and purposefully walk the few meters to the trailer on the other side of the street, knock on the door, and say, "Othniel, I need to tell you something."

The sense of urgency was clearly visible in Nir's eyes. Othniel took him by the arm and led him outside, to a bench in the yard. He didn't offer tea, didn't open with small talk, just sat Nir down and turned to face him and waited. Nir opened his mouth and closed it and closed his eyes and opened them and looked at his bearded neighbor and pictured Gitit and Yoni the Ethiopian soldier in a small wooden square, with the smell of paint and glue filling the air, standing alone and stripped bare. He recalled the sounds, and nausea rose in his throat, how could he tell a father something like that about his daughter, why had he come, what a mistake, it was simply an excuse to escape the house and Shaulit's look, which again appeared in his thoughts and bore into him mercilessly . . .

"What's up, Nir? You look worked up. Is everything okay?" Othniel placed a hand on Nir's freckled, suntanned arm, and Nir almost cried but bit his lip and held back. "What's up?" Othniel repeated, his voice soft.

"No . . . It's . . . Okay, look. A little while ago, in the evening, on guard

duty, I passed by the playground, and suddenly I heard something . . ."
He went quiet again for long enough to get Othniel to prompt him with
a "Yes, and . . . ?"

"I don't know. You know what? Leave it, I'm just . . . It's nothing, I'm
probably . . ." Nir placed the palms of his hands on his knees, like someone about to stand up, but Othniel again placed a hand on his arm to
calm him.

"Say what you came here to say. It's good you came. Sometimes we
hear and see things we don't want to, that we aren't sure of what they
are, but it's important to share, you probably know you heard something
important, even if now it suddenly seems trivial."

The stuffiness in the closed shed, the smell of the paint, the animal-
like noises of the stooped nigger, the soft whispers, or maybe the distress
sounds of the victim? And also—the confusion in his life, the tension at
home, Shaulit's rebuking . . .

"Jenia Freud," he finally said, and looked up at Othniel.

"What about her?"

"I don't know. It was weird. She was speaking on the phone all quiet-
like, or the playground, like she was hiding from someone. About Roni
Kupper. About Arabs. I don't know. It was weird. Perhaps I shouldn't
have come." He placed his palms on his knees again and stood this
time.

Othniel didn't stop him but looked at him in earnest. "Do you think
she's the Shin Bet informer?"

"What?" The idea hadn't crossed Nir's mind. He was still thinking
about Gitit. "Umm . . . I don't know . . . Do you think so?"

Othniel screwed up his mouth in thought. "Listen. Elazar Freud may
have been an officer in the army and may have grown up on a settlement, but big idealogues they are not. He does something in computers,
he explained it to me once, Google something, searches, advertisements,
truth is, I didn't understand a thing. Do you have any idea what he
does?"

"I only recall that he told me once he was sick of being a teacher and
traveling every day to Jerusalem. And Jenia is a math teacher, right?"

"I have no problem," Othniel said, "with residents who came here for the landscape and the quiet and rent—every Jewish settler is welcome. But to say I'm in shock that the evil stems from there?"

"Well, we're not sure, I don't want to . . ."

"Thanks, Nir." Othniel placed a hand on his shoulder. "You did good. Are you willing to help me check it out? I simply want as few people as possible to know about it right now, so let's keep it between us."

Hilik Yisraeli struck up a conversation with Jenia the following afternoon, on the Sheldon Mamelstein playground, while the children ran wild around them. He approached her after a seemingly coincidental clash of heads between his Boaz and her Nefesh (Hilik had lightly pushed his son into Nefesh) and joint pacifying on the part of the parents and the initiation of small talk about this and that.

Hilik glanced over his shoulder and said to Jenia, "Did you hear about the Japanese who were here yesterday?"

"*Da*, I hear Japanese here," Jenia said. "They wanted something olive oil."

Hilik lowered his voice. "Olive oil is just the cover story. There's talk that they're collaborating with radical elements. They spoke to Jehu. That kid could get us all into trouble. Do you know what he is up to? That guy sometimes disappears for entire days."

Jenia appeared very interested. "Moment, Jehu . . . You think that . . . But what Japanese have to do with it? The Japanese no have olive oil?"

"There's no shortage of crazies in Japan, right? They have underground movements, lunatics of all stripes, I don't know. I understand they may be passing weapons on to Jehu." He stroked his mustache and leaned in closer to her. "Not that it's any of my business, but we've had enough drama in the settlement. We've been under the spotlight ever since the defense minister was here. We don't need any more trouble." He tapped his finger twice under his right eye and whispered, "An eye that sees and an ear that hears."

When Hilik returned to Othniel's place from the playground, he apologized for his bad acting and said he was sure Jenia had seen through him and that there was no chance that she, or any self-respecting Shin Bet agent, for that matter, would fall for it. Less than twenty-four hours later, however, the sector's company commander, Omer Levkovich, turned up to visit his friends at C.

"Well, well"—Othniel smiled at him—"who do we have to thank for this visit of yours? Something happened?"

"Just a routine visit," the pink-cheeked captain said, and glanced around. They both knew the visit wasn't routine. Ever since the newspaper article, Omer was a rare visitor at the outpost. The settlers hadn't appreciated the hostile quotes of the "high-ranking officer."

"Anything happen here of late? Have you come across anything suspicious?" Omer asked.

"Suspicious?" Othniel played dumb.

"An unexpected visit, anyone unfamiliar hanging around?"

"Unfamiliar?" the veteran settler wondered out loud.

Following Omer's departure, Othniel ran into Yoni outside his home. Yoni appeared anxious, and Othniel seized the opportunity to press him. It turned out that Omer had questioned Yoni at length about the Japanese, and ordered him to report in immediately if he saw them in the area again. He also told him to keep an eye on Jehu, because there was talk that he was involved with a group of right-wing extremists. To finally tighten the screw, Othniel made a call to his friend Giora, the head of Central Command, to sniff around. The Shin Bet's Jewish Division, he knew, was as slippery and elusive as an eel. His fellow settlers had tried for years to plant countermoles and find a way inside, but Othniel had learned that Giora was the go-to man when it came to matters of urgency.

This time, the first thing Giora said after his secretary transferred the call was "Othni, what's this I'm hearing about Japanese kamikazes running around over there?"

Jenia Freud was summoned to Othniel's home that same evening. Together, he and Hilik had constructed a detailed action plan, a stage-by-stage takedown of the mole, the good cop and the bad cop and all that. Jenia cracked in the first minute.

Othniel and Hilik glared intensely as the math teacher sobbed in front of them, spouting fragmented apologies and excuses.

"Jenia," Othniel demanded, and she raised frightened eyes. "Go on home. We'll do some thinking and figure out how to right this situation. Meanwhile, you stay quiet."

She left the trailer in tears, her hands covering her face, and Hilik and Othniel exchanged meaningful looks.

The Soul

Gabi returned to the trailer, pricked up his ears—was Roni around? The silence reassured him, but then he heard the toilet flush. He sat down in the living room and took a religious book from the shelf. He didn't look up when Roni sighed and lay down on the sofa, his bed.

For several long minutes, not a word was said between them.

Gabi thought about Uman, the trip he had forgone. The dream. How much he craved the experience, the closeness to Rabbi Nachman. Abandoned for the sake of his brother. Man is the fruit of joy, and without joy there can be no faith, but where, where's the joy? Gabi went to Jerusalem that day, thinking he could manage to find a way after all. He visited the travel agency, the bank. Realized he didn't have a hope. It was $1,265 for a basic five-day vacation package, plus a visa, plus transportation from the airport, plus food. It would cost less if it were not Rosh Hashanah, but Rabbi Nachman said, "My whole mission is Rosh Hashanah . . ."

He couldn't and also didn't want to take out a loan. He didn't want to have to work the entire year to cover the cost of the trip. He added up all he had given Roni. He was his brother, flesh of his flesh, he shouldn't think that way. He tried to read verses from the Mishnah but couldn't concentrate, rested the open book on his chest, and closed his eyes.

Roni picked up on the energy flowing from Gabi. When he chose to break the silence, the first thing he said was "I'll get you the money, don't worry. It's on the way. Shame you didn't mention that Rosh Hashanah comes early this year . . ."

Gabi, in response, reached out his palm and waited. Roni looked at him without speaking. Gabi waited. His palm remained empty of money. "If you want," he finally said, "put four thousand shekels down here right now. But without talking. Without saying 'soon.' Without promising that orders are about to start coming in or that you're going off to the bank to arrange a loan or that Rosh Hashanah comes early this year."

Roni looked at the outstretched hand.

"Put four thousand shekels down here," Gabi said. "Now. You're always telling me that I should be doing the things I truly want to do, so here goes. That's what I truly want. Show me the money, and if you can't, get out of here. Because if I don't go to Uman over Rosh Hashanah, I won't be able to live with you in this trailer for a single day more. This is my home and you invaded it and I accepted you without a word and with love and maybe I'm not good enough, not strong enough, not loving enough, but I can't take it any longer. Either I go to Uman or you leave me be."

Roni looked into his brother's tearful eyes, his outstretched hand, and stood up. He put on a shirt, pulled down the suitcase he had stashed on the top shelf of the closet, and began tossing his belongings inside. Without a word, he collected them from around the house, put them in the suitcase, and zipped it shut. Went into the kitchen and drank a glass of water. Gabi remained in the same position, his hand out in front of him, as if he was giving him another chance, wasn't retracting the offer. He should have told him to stop, to stay, but he couldn't. After the glass of water, Roni returned to the living room, gripped the handle of the suitcase, and started wheeling it toward the door. Not another word was said. A gust of wind slammed the door shut, shaking the trailer's slender frame.

There are some days when enough is enough, when the waters rise up to flood the soul, there's something in the air, something in the wind—and something, of course, in the waters and the soul. Because at the same time the waters slowly rose up in Gabi's soul; at the same time Roni headed out, wheeling a suitcase along Ma'aleh Hermesh C.'s ring road, without a clue as to where he would go; at the same time the waters collected and trickled into the soul of Shaulit, and as a result—and only as a result and in that order—the soul of Nir, leading them both a bleak assessment concerning the future of their life together; at the same time the defense minister of the State of Israel received yet another angry call from the State Department and realized that the waters had risen up to flood his wounded, war-scarred soul.

At the very same time, the waters approached like those of a swift-flowing alpine river after a sweltering summer has melted the last year's snows, and would soon come crashing down like an ill-fated waterfall on the tender souls of Nachum, Raya, Shimshon (Shimi), and Tehila (Tili) Gotlieb. Roni was still walking down the road as an old edition of the *Washington Post*—the same infamous edition—tumbled along in the quiet twilight wind. Roni didn't notice the newspaper, but he might have heard Tili Gotlieb's cries.

"What happened? What happened?" Raya cried as her daughter and son came crashing through the door like a gust of wind in a storm. Tili opened her small mouth, which was missing two front milk teeth along its bottom jaw, gasping for air. "What happened? What happened?" Tili finally found the air and released it in the form of a long and violent sob. "What happened, Shimi? What happened to her?"

"Condi bit her," Shimi said.

"What, where?" She picked Tili up, wiped her tears away, soothed her. "Where, show me, sweetie." Tili pointed to her ankle. Raya raised her eyes and encountered the gaze of her husband, Nachum. Her head shook from side to side in despair. He responded with a somber stare and knew the waters had arrived.

"That's Othniel's dog," he said to her, the implication being, Listen, there isn't going to be a state commission of inquiry into this, there isn't going to be an apology, there isn't going to be any quarantining or punishing or educating about pets, because it's the sheriff's dog, and no one lays a hand on the hilltop sheriff.

Raya dressed the wound. Tili's sobs subsided into snivels. Shimi went off to play with blocks in a corner of the room, struggling to erect towers on the uneven floor. Talking about waters rising up. They hadn't had rain for months, but a thin and persistent stream of water from a leak in one of the pipes had made its way to the same corner, and the PVC flooring had swelled and cracked and warped into mountains and valleys. Nice perhaps for a game with a train, but not for blocks, or for positioning a sofa or lampstand.

"She needs a shot," Raya said to Nachum, implying, Look, this place, with all due respect, as if the fact that it's harsh and basic isn't enough, the fact that we as newcomers are on the bottom rung of the status ladder and that if we've been bitten by the dog of the man on the very top rung we have no right to complain; as if it's not enough that the work is hard and the traveling long and the people few—it doesn't even offer basic services like a clinic.

Nachum didn't respond. What could he have said?

"I want to take her to the clinic."

"Where will you go at this time of the day?" he asked, and looked at his watch.

"I can't take it any longer, Nachum." That was the moment the waters found their way and completed their journey to Raya's soul. "I can't take it any longer. Just give me a clinic. Give me a village administration, Nachum."

The husband looked at his wife and daughter. His hair and beard were scruffy and dense, both cropped just beyond what could be considered short. His face was narrow and long like his body and nose, which served as a base for a thin aluminum frame—selected as suitable by Raya—that surrounded the lenses of the glasses. The optical store he was trying to establish in Ma'aleh Hermesh A. wasn't taking off. He was patient, but sometimes he wondered what for. He motioned in a manner that shifted the glasses on the bridge of his nose without actually touching them and said, "Give me rabbis. Give me a daily portion. Give me three prayer services with a minyan."

Tili was smiling by then. Her parents looked at each other.

"Give me a grocery store. Give me a bus into town. Give me a kindergarten and a preschool and a school."

"Give me an air conditioner. Give me stone walls. Give me hot water."

Nachum looked out through the screen window toward the Hermesh Stream cliff face, and beyond it to the homes of the Yeshua settlement. This kind of life didn't suit everyone. They supported them wholeheartedly, their right and its realization. But from afar—at demonstrations, in petitions, at the polls. The newspaper continued to tumble in the wind down the road along the edge of the cliff face.

"Give me a library. Women's evenings. Proper parties for the holidays.

"Give me a community center. Give me a swimming pool.

"Give me shows for the children. Dancing classes and judo.

"A babysitter.

"Yes, a babysitter."

Raya Gotlieb smiled at her husband. She knew the business wasn't going to work. She had been in the store twice that week, helping with the office work, waiting with Nachum for customers to come in. They were told they'd get some from the settlement, from neighboring settlements, from Jerusalem, even. The percentage of people with glasses among the religious was twice that of the general population. But there were only a handful here. And they were thrifty, went to the Halperin Optics discount center at the Malcha Mall. They were told they needed to be patient, that thousands of new settlers were on their way. But this government, those Americans. Raya shifted her gaze from her husband to the tiny kitchen.

"Give me a normal kitchen. With a normal-size oven. A normal-size fridge."

"And a normal floor?"

"Definitely." Raya looked at the linoleum-free square on the floor of their kitchen. Over the past months, the glue that had been under the linoleum had attracted dust, leaves, webs, and nests. Life-forms could be detected in there. Raya gave up on cleaning it. She grew accustomed to the sound of shoes sticking and releasing. She accepted the empty square, the void, as an integral part of her abode. The mystery had been solved just a few days earlier: she was talking to Shaulit Rivlin on the playground, and the conversation went on for quite some time—the usual topics, children and kindergartens and breast-feeding and cooking—and when the heat rose and the two women looked for shade, they slowly began pushing their baby carriages from the playground to the ring road, and when they approached the Rivlins' home, Shaulit invited her to stay and they sat on the swing bench in the yard while the older children played inside and sounded content.

Shaulit didn't tell Raya about her moribund relationship with her husband. And Raya didn't say a word to Shaulit about her general despair with life on the hilltop. The two enjoyed the conversation, supported each other with more than just words, just by listening. And then, while in the middle of breast-feeding, Shaulit needed a diaper and a pacifier and explained to Raya where she could find them inside the trailer. Raya went in and noticed a square of green linoleum that had been stuck down in the kitchen, cleaner and newer than the rest of the linoleum around it. She moved closer and checked and measured the length and width with her thumb and finger so she could compare later at home, though it wasn't necessary, it was obvious.

She didn't say a word when she emerged with the diaper and pacifier, but back at home, after confirming her measurement with her finger and thumb, she told Nachum and he looked at her in disbelief and then grew angry and said, "I'm going over there right now. I'll rip it off their floor. I'll show that scoundrel."

Raya, however, smiled indifferently and said, "Let it go, Nachum, it doesn't matter now," because by then she knew they wouldn't be staying long at that outpost, in that trailer, in that kitchen, with the partial floor.

The Vomiting

"Yakir!"

"Yes, Dad?"

"Do me a favor, do a search on your Internet for some Japanese sect or group that . . ."

"That what?"

"That . . . I don't know. Supports the idea of a Greater Israel? Likes Arabs? God knows, is looking for something here . . ."

Yakir did a search. There's the Makuya sect in Japan, they're Israel lovers. But Othniel had met some nice tourists from the Makuya, and those businessmen didn't appear to be connected to the sect. So Yakir searched some more. There were all sorts of right-wing neo-fascist movements.

There were several terror groups. There were organizations opposed to the regime, opposed to minorities of various kinds, including Arabs. When he typed in the word *Japanese*, followed by *Judea* and *Samaria*, he found, among the slime that Google presented, a short report on an unfamiliar website, with fluctuating numbers and green and red graphs at the top and bottom of the page. He showed the report to his father, and Othniel narrowed his eyes, trailed a thick finger—callused and yellownailed from the work in the fields—across the small flickering letters, and mumbled as he read:

Japanese Farming Machinery Company
Penetrates Israeli Olive Oil Market

Japanese company Matsumata (MATS—Dow Jones and Nikkei) has announced plans to enter the Israeli olive oil market. The Japanese giant, whose operations include the manufacture of electronic devices and engineering and agricultural machinery, has branched out into the field of food imports and exports. Olive oil has become popular among the middle and upper classes in Japan, Korea, and China. These countries have also seen an increasing consumer awareness of the advantages of organic food and the benefits of olive oil in terms of reducing cholesterol and fighting cancer. Matsumata employees reviewed olive groves in various locations in the Mediterranean basin, and the company has displayed particular interest in Palestinian groves. The European Union and the Japan International Cooperation Agency previously announced a special program of support for the Palestinian economy, wherein investors receive tax breaks and favorable financing. Thanks to this program, Palestinian olives may be cheaper than the European olives, despite the security situation. Furthermore, for millions of Christians in East Asia, the significance of olive oil from the Holy Land . . .

Othniel's finger moved away from the screen. "It's killing my eyes," he said to his son. "Where does it mention Ma'aleh Hermesh?"

"Ma'aleh Hermesh isn't mentioned. Only Judea and Samaria."

"So what's it got to do with us?"

"I didn't say it has anything to do with us. You did. It only says they're looking for olives from Arabs in Judea and Samaria."

"Anti-Semites," Othniel said. His phone vibrated in his pocket and he took it out and went into the yard to talk. Yakir continued to browse quickly through the article—the phrases *machine equipment, regional olive presses*, and *cans of tuna* jumped out at him from the screen, but the financial terms exhausted him. He listened to make sure his father was still engrossed in his call and, heart pounding, returned to Second Life.

He went into Revival virtual region. King Meir rushed over in welcome. "Where've you been, champ?" he asked, and reached out for a handshake. If sensations could be conveyed on Second Life, King Meir would have deemed Yakir's handshake weak and limp.

"You won't believe it," continued the bearded and yellow-T-shirted character in the speech bubbles floating above his head, "things have gone crazy, there've been demonstrations, they want to kick us out. I think the people who run Second Life are looking for me."

Yakir panicked. Looking? Soon would come the days of repentance and the Day of Judgment, but King Meir was rejoicing, and the other friends were excited, spoke about the ban, the curses, the Arabs' pathetic attempts at retaliation. They wanted to continue, to intimidate, to blow things up, to show the Arabs who they were. But Yakir couldn't share their fervor. He was worried. He didn't want to get into trouble. Didn't want anyone showing up at the door, or anything arriving by e-mail, accusing him of causing destruction, disturbing the peace, breaking Internet rules of conduct. Not only that, as hard as he tried, he derived no joy from the bombing of the mosque. He struggled to understand why he had done it, and for whom—who are these people, his so-called friends, an odd collection of guys from where? Texas? Germany? The neighboring settlement? Why blow up a mosque, a place of worship? He was a person of faith, who visited a place of worship all the time.

King Meir must have sensed something because he asked, "What's up, Yakir? Everything okay?" If Second Life could have displayed facial expressions, Yakir's friends would have been looking at a pale, agonized face. He heard his father bid farewell on the phone with wishes for a good

year and inscription in the Book of Life. Inscription in the Book of Life—
how would he look his Creator in the eye? How would he be rewarded
with inscription in the Book of Life? He had committed a crime, sinned,
and now his punishment would come. If you could have seen someone's
eyes on Second Life, the exultant, messianic Jews on Revival would have
been looking at frantic eyes, racing back and forth like a lab rat's.

His father's footsteps approached, and Yakir left Second Life, fled, shut
down the computer, dropped to his knees, and quickly disconnected the
Internet cable, the power cable, and just as he was asked, "Yakir, what
are you doing down there? Something happen to the computer?" a light
brown stream speckled with bits of meat, pasta, potatoes, and chunks
of fruit shot out of his mouth, and another, and another, with his chest
heaving violently and a terrible tightening of his throat. His eyes welled
with tears as the waves rose up and burst forth from within him, emp-
tied his stomach until nothing remained, and he continued to retch and
cramp up and eject awful-tasting bile, and Othniel laid his large and
warm hands on his overwhelmed son, one tenderly stroking the back
of his neck, the other offering a glass of water, and all he said was "Small
sips, small sips, small sips."

The Departed

A few days after Shin Bet informer Jenia Freud emerged from the dark
into the light, Othniel invited her and her husband, Elazar, over for
a private chat. Initially, Othniel asked all those in the know—Nir Rivlin,
Hilik Yisraeli, and his wife, Rachel—not to cause a fuss and not to spread
the word. He consulted with Hilik—perhaps it would be a good idea
to use Jenia as a double agent, a mole? Perhaps through her they could
obtain information about the security forces' plans for the evacuation,
the building of the fence, and so on?

But when rumors began spreading across the hilltop, Othniel realized that the affair wasn't going to remain under wraps for very long. He
decided to inform the residents himself in order to avoid unnecessary

tension, and to warn against falling asleep on their watch. The talk with Jenia and Elazar was a precursor to his briefing of all the residents of the outpost.

"Elazar, explain to me again what it is you do, something on the computer, right?" Othniel began.

"I run ad campaigns on Google for a number of companies, some in Jerusalem and some in America, most of them in the field of printing . . ."

Othniel nodded, but was distracted because just then Rachel placed on the table a pot of coffee and a cake Jenia had baked. He wasn't listening. Jenia was rubbing her fingers together. She smiled as a sign of gratitude when Rachel poured her a cup of coffee, her red eyes betraying sleepless days and nights. Elazar appeared even more stressed than she did, his Adam's apple particularly active. Silence fell. Rachel left the living room and went into the kitchen. Othniel sipped.

"Why did you do it, Jenia?" His tone, much to the surprise of the Freuds, was soft, not accusatory.

A shrug of the shoulders. Pursing of lips, lowering of eyes. A hesitant hand running through a mass of blond hair. And again the broad shoulders hunched up. "I don't know. I . . . Someone talk to me at ride station. She speak Russian. Not remember what we talk about, maybe recipes, cookies." She looked up with hesitant eyes—perhaps he didn't want to hear all those details, perhaps he was impatient? But Othniel's eyes conveyed a sense of ease, and his hands gestured to continue. If he was in a rush, or angry, it didn't show.

"She gave phone numbers. Don't know how happened, a long time we are in contact. She was my friend . . ."

"I met her, too," Elazar intervened. "Daliah, her friend from the ride station. Sure."

"Did you also speak to her regularly? Meet with her?"

Elazar shook his head. "I don't know Russian. And she never visited us."

"And after a while she started talking about politics," Othniel said.

"*Da* . . . You know how it works?" She looked up at the leader of the outpost.

"I know, I know. I know them well," Othniel said. "She probably told you she's a settler herself. And lauded the settlement enterprise. And complained about the government and about the army and about the Arabs. And then started talking about the extremists. About the price-tag incidents. The lunatics who give us all a bad name. Who have to be stopped because they're damaging the settlement enterprise. That if we don't stop them, if we allow them to run wild and carry out their extreme actions, then the Palestinians will also take revenge on us, and the army, too, will retaliate and evacuate us—she frightened you."

Jenia and Elazar looked at him, stunned. They weren't expecting this. Weren't expecting a show of understanding for what Jenia had been through. What Othniel was displaying here was a lot more than under-standing. He had described exactly what had happened. But then his benevolent face stiffened, and Jenia's and Elazar's hearts skipped a beat. "But that's still no reason to spy on your friends."

"True," she quickly agreed. "I . . ."

"We can't tolerate such betrayal."

"They told me you follow only Jehu. That it bad seeds, youth of hill-tops. I not betray outpost. Not look for others."

"We heard you said something about Roni Kupper, too."

"They ask Roni Kupper but I don't know. And he's not from residents. I don't give them anything about him! And about residents! I only Jehu!"

"Jehu is one of us," Othniel calmly responded. The kindness in his voice had disappeared. "You shouldn't be reporting anything about him to anyone, either."

"Of course, I not report anything anymore."

"And no more trying to play it smart. No matter what happens, how it happens or who it happens to—you come straight to me."

She nodded. "Of course, of course."

"I'll be letting everyone know now," Othniel summed up. "I've been in this business long enough. Those bastards know how to latch onto and attract weak elements, how to confuse and get things out of people with-out them even realizing what they're saying. We'll let you off the hook this time, Jenia. This time." He turned to fix Elazar with a stern look. "Take her home and explain it to her. Next time, we won't be so forgiv-ing. It's your responsibility, man. Take charge of her."

Jenia shot an anxious look at her husband. "*Chto eto*, 'let you off the hook'?" she asked in an effort to understand. Elazar trembled. His Adam's apple turned circles. He lowered his eyes. "Yes, of course, Othni, trust me, you have nothing to worry about." He took hold of his wife's arm and gently prompted her onto her feet. "Thanks, Othni." He nudged her toward the door. Elazar clearly wanted out of Othniel's trailer before the latter changed his mind.

The revelation sent shock waves through the outpost's residents. Gavriel Nehushtan bore the hurt of everyone, and Neta Hirschson fumed with rage, and Yakir felt a touch of compassion for the tall woman who had been sinisterly manipulated, and Jehu disappeared again for several days. Elazar Freud, so consumed with panic and shock, did absolutely nothing for days, couldn't look his wife in the eyes. But after she tearfully but determinedly tried to get him to explain to her what was going to happen, he fell into her arms and sobbed, without saying a word.

Nachum Gotlieb knew that the Ki Teitzei Torah portion, read recently, dealt with going to war and not with going from slavery to freedom or from one place to another, but during those hot days, with the year coming to an end, he couldn't help but think of Ki Teitzei as a sign, a directive from above, that it was exactly what he and Raya and Shimi and Tili their children should do—go. After making the decision, they informed Rachel Assis, began the formal process of closing down the optical store in Ma'aleh Hermesh A., let the tenants in their apartment in Shilo know that they'd be returning, reserved places for the children at kindergarten, and so forth. Nachum and Raya felt a huge weight lift off their shoulders, and they began filling their Nissan with belongings to transport load by load back to their previous lives.

Yakir, too, got going—away from Second Life, with no intention of ever returning, but he continued to mull over the stormy events he'd experienced there, their significance and implications. His sister Gitit began to depart from her innocence with the generous assistance of Yoni, delving blindly into a new and intriguing darkness, discovering fresh and wondrous feelings and emotions. Shaulit Rivlin, depressed by the bleak mood at home, despondent over her husband's insensitivity and selfishness, also pondered setting out on a new path. Not to mention the outpost of Ma'aleh Hermesh C. itself, its people, its crops, and its structures . . . it was becoming increasingly likely that it, too, would be departing, or cleared out, at the very least, in the wake of moderate yet consistent pressure from the secretary of state and the United States ambassador, who would probably end up breaking the strong back of the defense minister.

Meanwhile, after departing from Gavriel's house, Roni had walked and wheeled the large suitcase alongside him, turning things over in his head. Maybe he'd look for somewhere on the hilltop to crash for the night. Like his brother's almost completed but not yet occupied cabin? Spread a blanket in the Mamelstein playground? Lay his head down on the unkempt woolly coat of Sasson's camel cow? Perhaps he'd simply leave altogether and head to the plains, where he hadn't been for years, and where there were colorful lights and densely packed buildings, filled with people?

No and no and no and no and no—those were the answers. He walked on and turned southward off the ring road, crossed through Othniel Assis's fields, and went down to the terraces and up through Musa Ibrahim's olive trees. His friend. His business partner. He was going to put his trust in him and ask if he could stay with him. And screw Gabi and his settler friends who weren't capable of living in peace with their neighbors. As far as he was concerned, he didn't mind even sleeping in the olive press, near the olives and the large millstones, wrapped in the fragrance of oil. Why not? If this is his new life, if this is the source of his income from now, he should live as a true worker of the land, who feels the earth and its fruits.

He knocked on Musa's door. His wife opened the door, looked in surprise at the suitcase, said "Hi, Roni," and ushered him in and served up Turkish coffee with cardamom. Musa will be here soon, she promised. Roni sat in the humble living room, wanting to feel more at home there than at his brother's. It's just a matter of time, he assured himself. And anyway, this isn't his new home, the olive press is.

Musa arrived. Roni stood up and smiled. They shook hands. Musa looked at Roni's large suitcase, and then looked up at him with smiling eyes. "The first rains are coming soon," Roni said, "aren't they? You feel it in your bones? You can already see the clouds. You can see they want to, right?"

"Sit, Roni, sit," Musa said. "You got coffee?"

"I got."

"Yes, the rain comes soon. Soon the olives. The whole village is waiting."

"We are waiting, too, Musa, we are, too. I want to be in the thick of it already. To harvest, to work, to make the oil."

Musa gazed at him. Roni gazed back.

After a few moments of silence, Roni asked, "What?"

And Musa said, "Has no one spoken to you?"

"Spoken to me about what?"

The Decision

The Defense Minister's Bureau. The session of the Knesset's Foreign Affairs and Defense Committee had ended, and they were now meeting in a more restricted forum, and briefly—or so at least they hoped—the minister; Malka, his adviser on settlement affairs; Giora, head of Central Command; and Avram, head of the Shin Bet's Counter-Subversion Department. The director-general of the Defense Ministry had notified them that he'd be there in seven minutes.

"Yes, Malka," the defense minister said. His eyes were red from lack of sleep, his nerves shattered from the Foreign Affairs and Defense Committee meeting, where, as usual, they had come at him from all directions—a Palestinian inadvertently killed in Nablus, a breach in a stretch of fence along the border with Lebanon, barriers torn down on Hebron's Shuhada Street, the acquisition of computer systems for tanks, the sale of computer systems for Chinese submarines, a demand to pave a stretch of road in the territories, opposition to the paving of a stretch of road in the territories, the suspension of work on the separation fence, revelations concerning abuse at an officers' training course . . . there wasn't a single decision made by his ministry or incident that had occurred that would fail to give cause to someone on the committee to attack him, berate him, sully him in rivers of slime and muck and contempt, and the minister would be forced to explain, and justify, and go on the defensive.

"What are we discussing?" He picked out two pretzels from the bowl on the table in front of him; he always ate them in pairs.

"Approval for the laying of Route 991." Giora stood and elaborated on the map. Avram tapped uneasily on the table with a box of cigarettes. The discussion dragged on. Giora outlined the strategic significance of the road. Malka gave a briefing on the political pressure for and against the road. The minister was well aware of Malka's opinion, and knew by then how to relate to his briefings and alleged objectivity. He had even developed a mathematical system for calculating and understanding what truly lay behind his assistant's position, by determining an average between what Malka said and the opinion of the ministry's director-general and the decision of the head of the Finance Ministry's Budgets Department. Regarding the road, everyone was actually of the same opinion.

From time to time, his aide informed him of an incoming call or a visit. The minister was hungry, and earlier, on the way from the committee meeting to the office, he had a little accident in the bathroom and wet his pants when his stream of urine split into two, and he didn't notice it until he felt the wetness.

"Okay, bring me the documents for signature," he ruled with lowered eyelids. He knew he'd come in for a lot of criticism for the road. He knew he'd get calls from Ambassador Milton White and from the secretary of state and from the leader of the opposition and from representatives of the left-wing parties on the committee the following week, not to mention Army Radio, the UN, and the peace movements. Well, let them fly off the handle. Let them call. One's got to move ahead in life. "Anything else for this forum?" he asked his aide while signing the paperwork.

"Yes, something small, actually. Just came in."

All eyes turned to Malka. "What?" the minister asked.

"The Japanese ambassador has submitted an official complaint about that story with the Japanese anti-Muslim underground sect that's passing on weapons to radical Jewish elements in the territories."

The defense minister's eyes widened. "The sect that . . . What was that? A complaint about what?" He turned to look at the head of the Shin Bet's Jewish Division, who appeared to be trying to bury himself in his cigarette box. "I don't understand. Will someone explain to me what is going on?" the minister demanded. Malka reached out to drag the bowl of pretzels a little closer and fished out two, in a perfect impression of his boss.

"Forget it, it's a ridiculous story," Avram said, fruitlessly trying to evade the issue.

"What do you mean, ridiculous? I have a complaint from Japan here on the table. Do you realize who we're dealing with here?" the minister said. Curious now, too. "Get the director-general," he said.

"Some Japanese company is getting involved in the territories in an olive oil project. They've closed deals with Palestinian growers throughout the West Bank. They're setting up a large olive press near Ramallah with their own equipment, a state-of-the-art—"

"Ah, Matsumata," the defense minister said. And to the surprised eyes that stared at him, he responded, "I read about it in the *Marker*. With the support of the EU and JICA, tax breaks and all that." He knew more than that, of course. Pressure from Japan had played a part in the suspension, for now, of construction work on the separation fence along that route; something that few knew about, aside from the prime minister, the defense minister, and the director of the Fence Administration. Perhaps Malka, too.

The minister glanced at his aide skeptically, feigning innocence. "So why are they complaining?"

Avram exchanged a look with Giora and sighed. "Someone played a prank. On one of their visits, the Japanese ended up at one of the outposts in error. And someone at that outpost spread a rumor . . ."

"Which outpost?"

Malka swallowed hard. Avram lowered his gaze. "Ma'aleh Hermesh C.," he said.

The defense minister stopped chewing his pretzel. Malka feared the minister was choking and extended a glass of water. The minister's eyes were steely and red. He swallowed, sipped from the glass, and, seemingly at ease, he focused for several seconds on a random point on the other side of the room. The images rose in his thoughts again, and with them came the feelings. The fucking "Scram" that had stuck to him and wouldn't go away. The ingrates. He went there to support them, and they spat on him. In any normal country, the outpost would have been dismantled and they would have been thrown in jail. He didn't care that he and his predecessors had provided permits or turned a blind eye, as Malka took the trouble to remind him sometimes. That's no excuse. No longer.

"Ma'aleh Hermesh C.?" he asked. "Them again? Just as the Americans and Peace Now finally get off my back a little on that place and move on to Route 991 . . . Hasn't there been a High Court ruling regarding them?"

"Still under deliberation," Avram said defensively. "The state prosecutor submitted a response to the petition, on your behalf, on behalf of the commander of the IDF forces in the West Bank, on behalf of the head of the Civil Administration, and on behalf of the commander of the Judea and Samaria police district. You all confirmed that the outpost in question is illegal, but because the required resources are currently occupied elsewhere, you've requested a delay in the evacuation."

"Okay," the minister said, and extended two fingers toward the pretzels. "So, someone was looking to have some fun, you said?"

"And spread a rumor that the Japanese from Matsumata are actually some kind of underground terrorist sect that's supplying weapons to extremist Jews in the outposts. They even gave the name of some hilltop kid whom the Japanese supposedly visited at the outpost to make a deal with. Something like that."

"Okay, so some settler made up a bullshit story. How does it get to this?" He picked up the Japanese fax that Malka had placed in front of him, waved it in the air.

"The person who heard the story was our informer at the settlement. She relayed it to us. And there was some kind of misunderstanding. The story wasn't connected to Matsumata, no one connected the dots, and we issued an alert, and our guys were involved in a small incident with the Japanese." The defense minister hung his head, his right hand supporting his forehead. "And our informer was exposed," Avram continued. "That in fact was the essence of the prank, because they suspected her, and . . ." Avram's voice trailed off.

The minister remained in the same position. The room was quiet. The muffled ring of a telephone came from the other side of the door. The past few days hadn't been easy. His beloved dog, Soldier, had passed away over the weekend after a lengthy illness. Soldier had in fact lived with his ex, his first wife, but his death stung nevertheless. His second wife called that morning to tell him that both toilets were blocked. And he felt uncomfortable in his wet pants, and a faint smell of urine seemed to be emanating from them. But even all that wasn't what prompted him to say what came next when he resumed speaking. Nor was it the stress and the questions and the demands and the accusations that rained down on him from every direction at the meeting of the Foreign Affairs and Defense Committee and every day and every minute, in conferences, at meetings, on the telephone, in the newspapers. Nor was it Route 991, the laying of which he had just authorized with his signature, as a gesture, so to speak, to the settlers and the right-wing parties, and which perhaps he now needed an action to offset, to appease the critics, a little candy for the Americans and the leftists and the attorney general—after all, almost every action is designed to offset, to appease, to serve as a gesture toward someone who's been offended . . .

No. None of those factors were behind the sentence that came from his mouth, but rather the law, the plain and simple law. The law from the book of laws of the State of Israel, and the international law, which the minister felt himself entrusted to uphold.

He raised his eyes, cast his gaze over his three colleagues around the table, placed the fax sheet on the dark mahogany surface, positioned it so that its edges lay parallel and flush to the edge of the table, and said, "Giora, evacuate that outpost. I'm serious this time. No games. Remove that thorn from my ass. It's been digging into me for way too long. Way, way too long." He handed the fax to Malka, stood up, and left the room.

FEEDING ON CARRION

The Takeoff

The realization came on the eve of Shavuot. He was sitting in the dining hall in a white shirt and felt ridiculous. Some families sat together, but he didn't want to sit with Dad Yossi; he never sat with him in the dining hall. Children were singing about the first fruits and he knew neither the children nor the songs. Roni was in Tel Aviv, bumming around, living in the apartment of his girlfriend's father and raising goldfish. Working in some pub. It didn't sound very appealing to Gabi, and anyway, his brother never invited him to tag along when he came for his monthly visit. Here, too, no one invited him to tag along. He could see his childhood friends Yotam and Ofir, sitting with their girlfriends, joining in on the sing-along. He could see the soldiers with their drooping eyelids, the volunteer girls with their smooth skin and blue eyes.

He was no longer an outcast at the kibbutz. The years since he left the army had passed in relative peace. After wandering for a while from one kibbutz enterprise to another, he finally managed to settle down—in the bananas. The groves were on the shores of the Sea of Galilee, about a forty-minute drive from the kibbutz. The banana boys spent long days out in the open, on the shores of the large lake, under the broad leaves, meals in groups of four or six in the peaceful picnic corner, cruising along the lake in kayaks when they felt like taking a break. It wasn't light work—bananas are a pampered fruit with a short life cycle that requires digging new furrows every winter, uprooting the groves and planting new ones every spring, endless weeding. Even that morning, the eve of the holiday, with the banana fingers green in their palms and the palms clumped together in their bunches and the sun heralding the first days of summer, he sweated like a pig while digging an irrigation canal with a hoe. But Gabi didn't shy away from hard work. After all, manual labor wasn't what broke him at his previous jobs—it was the overpowering smell of tomatoes in the field crops division, the allergic itching caused by the grass in the factory, the condescending treatment from Dalia, who was in charge of the food supply department. His ejection from the army, too, wasn't brought on by physical hardship, but rather because disrespectful cooks refused to feed him.

Suddenly, in the middle of the holiday dinner, he realized who he reminded himself of: Ezra Dudi. When they were children, Ezra Dudi, who was ten years older, would always sit alone in the dining hall and eat the same meal—yellow cheese, tomato, and a slice of bread. And he'd always shoot basketballs alone in the gym, for hours. And in the factory, Gabi recalled, he operated the forklift in silence and with precision, transporting the ready segments of lawn to the packing hall and the packed parcels to the delivery trucks. He showed up at the dining hall alone every day, in work clothes and with a somewhat dirty face, adorned with an ever-thickening beard.

Gabi thought about the fact that he never once saw Ezra Dudi exchange more than a word or two with anyone. He lived on the kibbutz with his mother, who arrived there from Europe after the war on her own and didn't speak much about her past, but from here and there— her accent, her pale skin, a passing reference—people pieced together a patchwork of stories and came to the conclusion that she was originally from Ostland, the eastern territories. She may have spent several years in a Siberian gulag; may have been released from there under a repatriation agreement. Whatever the case, she arrived at the kibbutz alone and destitute and ten years later her son, Ezra Dudi, was born. And in this case, too, there was more to the story than met the eye: she became pregnant and gave birth to a dark-skinned and cute baby boy, of that there was no doubt, but no one knew the identity of the father.

There was always something slightly off about Ezra Dudi. His hair was the wrong length, his beard too wild. His eyes were black and large with a soft, though somewhat dim, look in them. He looked a little like Theodor Herzl, the father of Zionism, only a kibbutz version, and curly-haired. His clothes somehow didn't sit well on his large frame. And his name, too, which no one understood—why two names? Both first names? And if one's a surname, what kind of name is that?

From the looks he got from the kibbutz's young children, Gabi could see he risked becoming another Ezra Dudi—with his odd isolation in the dining hall, with his silence and aimless wanderings, and perhaps even in appearance, rarely shaving his beard or cutting his hair, and remaining for the most part in his work clothes and shoes. He was overcome with regret. With the festival of the first fruits in full swing he felt like an onlooker, disengaged, out of place, and he arrived at the realization: that's the problem. He knew, of course, that he wasn't really Ezra Dudi, who suffered in all likelihood from a mild mental disorder of sorts. His mind and soul were more or less intact; the short-circuits in his brain over the years were deviations from the norm—the psychiatric medical officers he met with during his military service confirmed that, and added that he was blessed with a high level of intelligence and judgment. But he didn't have money to leave the kibbutz, and Tel Aviv wasn't appealing. He didn't feel comfortable discussing things with Yossi, and when Roni came to visit, he felt his brother wasn't really interested.

As in the case of previous significant junctures in his life, Uncle Yaron helped to steer him. Gabi went to visit him at the kibbutz on the Golan Heights the weekend after the Shavuot holiday, enjoying as always the cool air and heavy smell of cow dung while lying on the large ragged hammock.

"It's like being in another country." The nephew smiled at his uncle, and the uncle responded, "How would you know, you've never been overseas."

"True," the nephew said, "but it's the closest to overseas I can get, so let me say it's like being in another country."

"You want to go overseas?" the uncle said. And the nephew stopped for a moment—not the hammock, because that moved by the force of inertia—but on the idea, because he had never before considered the option. Then he recalled why he had never considered the option. "How can I go overseas?" he said. "I don't have a cent to my name."

Uncle Yaron, with his balding egg-shaped head and glassy eye and half-chopped-off ear, appeared older than ever. Gabi had never thought about it, but Uncle Yaron Kupper had never married, hadn't raised a family; he was hitched to the kibbutz, or more precisely, the Golan Heights. He paid homage to it with his eye and his ear, and it to him with earth and basalt and fresh air. He looked at his nephew and said to him, "Listen." Gabi listened.

Uncle Yaron recounted that after taking care of all the matters related to the death of his brother Asher and sister-in-law Ricki—the funerals, the shiva, finding a kibbutz for the children, the sale of the house in Rehovot, locating the savings and closing the bank accounts—he was left with a significant amount of money in hand. With the blessing of Ricki's father and sister, he opened a savings account for Roni and Gabi, for when they each reached the age of twenty-one. He concealed its existence from their kibbutz. Anyway, the kibbutz received a handsome sum as part of the absorption package. They don't have to get it all, decided Yaron and the grandmother and the aunt. The savings grew and accrued interest and swelled over the years, and Uncle Yaron continued to monitor the account and keep it on the right investment tracks and top it off with his own money, because over and above his natural sense of responsibility, Uncle Yaron felt terrible guilt. He was the one who'd invited Asher and Ricki that week, he was the one who'd persuaded them to return home at night and not in the morning. And his sense of guilt manifested in his sweat and his money—insofar as he had any, as a member of a pioneering kibbutz on the Golan Heights—into the savings account. When the grandfather, Ricki's father, passed away, another good dose was injected into the savings plan.

"Why haven't you said anything until now?" Gabi asked.

"I was waiting for you to come to me when you'd need it. I knew the day would come. It was the same with Roni."

"Roni?" Gabi raised his head at an angle from the hammock.

"Roni got his when he reached the appropriate age and needed money. How do you think he paid for his studies and went into a partnership in the pub? Only by virtue of hard work and drive?"

"He's a partner in the pub?"

"We withdrew a tidy sum for him and he invested it in the business. Otherwise he wouldn't have received the share he did."

"But what will I say at the kibbutz, how come I suddenly have money to travel?"

"Say it's a gift from your uncle Yaron," the uncle said.

Gabi went quiet and rocked on the hammock. Overseas. Did he really want that? What would he do there? Was that what his parents would have wanted for him to do with the money? What about university? He had thought about that, too, recently, but had no idea what to study.

Uncle Yaron seemed to read his mind and said, "Come on, just go. Stop agonizing. It's exactly what your parents would want you to do. And me, too."

"Are you sure?"

"Sure I'm sure. I can hear Asher telling me in my head to give you a good slap and put the money in your hand and give you a kick in the butt to get onto that plane. Asher talks to me in my head all the time."

"Send him my regards," Gabi said. He was on the plane a week later.

The Landing

He was cold. He saw another passenger ask the flight attendant for a blanket and did the same, and he wrapped himself in the thin blanket but was still cold. He was filled with doubt. What did he need this for? Why had he been swallowed into this strange metal tube, what was he looking for? What was so bad about his peaceful life among the bananas, in his warm and familiar room? Perhaps going to university would be a better option after all, like Roni had? Perhaps he'd ask Roni with more resolve, more confidence, to join him and try living in Tel Aviv. Or at least ask to spend a few nights in the kibbutz's apartment there, to check out the possibility, to see what the university had to offer. But Gabi knew what it had to offer, he had read through the almanac in the kibbutz library, list upon list of courses that didn't mean a thing to him and didn't explain what kind of future they would offer him and what he would do with himself afterward. He shivered under the blanket, glanced into the darkness outside, stroked with hesitant, alien fingers the smooth cheeks he had shaved in honor of the trip, after months of wild growth.

He got a nice send-off: Uncle Yaron, of course, who came to the kibbutz and drove him to Ben-Gurion; Roni, who met with them at a coffee bar in Tel Aviv for a quick meal, a little stressed out, because he wasn't able to go with them to the airport; Dad Yossi, who appeared to have had a weight lifted off his shoulders; his friends from the bananas, who on his last day at work staged a festive lunch for him; and Yotam, who stopped by his room and hung out with him for an hour and smoked four cigarettes while Gabi packed and didn't stop talking about Erez, his cousin from Kibbutz Manara, who worked as a mover in New York and whom Gabi was supposed to contact when he landed, and at the same time had tried to lay his hands on half the things Gabi left behind.

Wide-eyed, he stared at the human chaos of a large American airport. At the thousands of directions in which a million people were bustling. At the colorful whirlwind of suitcases, clothes, skin. Human forms he had seen in movies and on television and now for the first time face-to-face: Asian businessmen with polished glasses and smooth briefcases and pressed suits; a huge African lady in bright yellow that fell down around her like a veil; American cops with belts packed with a full array of goodies in the form of clubs, pistols, handcuffs, and notebooks, with precise mustaches, with menacing eyes; small Indians and large blacks and fragrant women and youths in reversed baseball caps and huge backpacks and small children, sweet like they always are.

He wasn't offended or intimidated, because he barely sensed the threatening severity with which the customs officials examined his bag. He looked at the sheet of instructions in his hand and found the way to the subway. He swayed to the metallic rattling over bridges and underground, the colorful lines that Johnny the American had told him about at the kibbutz now jumbling before his eyes into a mass of spaghetti. One hand remained firmly attached to the bag, his eyes fixed constantly on a new target: huge billboards, stretches of tenement housing as far as the eye could see, two black men in baggy clothes, endless graffiti. Someone in a suit spoke to the person alongside him in that accent, Johnny's, from the movies. A chubby and unattractive young girl with a blank expression, headphones from a music player wrapped around her head, which was wet at the top. Orange and yellow seats emptying and filling. Doors sliding to open and close. An intercom system that scrambled the words. A hot and stifling smell, and different, everything was so different.

When he emerged from the bowels of the earth, the sheer size stunned him. The city rose up above him, made him feel like a stinky black beetle on the kibbutz path in summer. He marveled at the steam billowing out from under the sewer covers and the masses of people and the height of the buildings.

He stopped outside McDonald's. He had heard about it. He rummaged in his pocket and examined the green bills and went in. Standing in front of the picture-heavy menu, he remembered it was a place for hamburgers. He hadn't touched meat in almost ten years, since the abduction at the kibbutz. But suddenly it no longer deterred him. He was too hungry, too tired, and didn't know of anywhere else. He decided to try. The soft bun, the sour ketchup, the crispy fries, the meat patty, too—he loved them. His head spinning, he finally made it to the small apartment of Erez, Yotam's cousin.

They didn't click. Erez wasn't pleasant. Didn't take an interest. Gabi felt Erez didn't really want to be hosting anyone in his apartment, which was small and home to another Israeli roommate, who didn't say a word. Gabi slept on a futon in the living room, and on the first morning Erez and his roommate spoke next to him as if he didn't exist and then left for work. Gabi went out and wandered the streets around the building for a while, ate at McDonald's because it was actually nice, went into stores and looked around but wasn't wanting for anything so he returned to the apartment. Johnny had recommended that he go see Central Park, the Statue of Liberty, and several museums, but he didn't really feel like it.

Erez asked him if he'd like to work the following day. They were looking for workers at his moving company. He woke Gabi at six the next morning and took him on the subway to the office. He told him on the way that he was leaving to do a three-day move. When they arrived, he referred Gabi to another guy, also by the name of Erez, and he got into a truck with his crew and left.

Like the city, the place was large and chaotic and crowded. Drivers and workers dressed in red shirts raced back and forth. Dozens of red trucks fired up noisily, pulled in, pulled out, people yelled in Hebrew. The second Erez was a little more pleasant than the first, but he, too, wasn't much of a talker. He asked for Gabi's signature on a contract, gave him a red shirt, and led him to a truck where a driver with a dark complexion was already waiting, tapping impatiently on the wheel with his right hand, and smoking with his left. His name was Victor.

Cardboard boxes. And more cardboard boxes. And more: sofas, tables, chairs, dressers, from upstairs to downstairs, from downstairs to upstairs. From outside the apartment and into the lift and out the lift and out onto the street through the back door and from the sidewalk into the belly of the truck. The boxes weighed less than a banana stem but were harder to grip and less pleasing to the touch, or more accurately, Gabi knew how to load and grip and carry banana stems, how to enjoy the feel of the fingers of fruit on his back. Probably, if he carried the boxes and furniture of Americans long enough, he'd come to feel a similar intimacy with them, too. But on that first day, all he asked himself was why he was overseas carrying boxes when he actually wanted to travel around, and see things, and who knows what, but not work like this, certainly not when he had the money he'd gotten from Uncle Yaron.

He returned to the apartment and the silent roommate who was glued to the television, and went out and down to McDonald's, already knowing he'd order a Big Mac. He felt the tense urban atmosphere around his shoulders, heard the sound of loud youthful laughter, of customers at restaurants, smelled the oil and his own sweat and the grime of the city. He returned home and showered and waited in the living room for the roommate to finish watching television—and after the roommate went to his room and Gabi converted the couch into a bed and arranged the sheets and lay down on them, he remained awake for a long time, hours perhaps, and felt more alone than he had ever felt on his bed at the kibbutz.

In the morning he called the office and they told him there was no work. He spent most of the day at home, went out only to eat. The next day they told him to come in. This time, he worked with a foreman by the name of Itzik, who spoke to him like a commander to a soldier and spoke to the driver—the same Victor—in a loud voice about parties and girls. They did a small move from the company's storage facility in Queens to an office in New Jersey. Afterward they went to load up an apartment in Manhattan.

The apartment—spacious, a high floor, spectacular view—was home to a middle-aged Israeli by the name of Meshulam, who was dressed in a suit and flip-flops and didn't say much. Gabi followed Itzik's orders and began taking the boxes downstairs to the truck. Victor waited in the truck's cargo compartment and arranged the boxes inside. They worked like that for about half an hour, and then Meshulam replaced his flip-flops with a pair of polished shoes and informed them he was going out to a meeting. Gabi sensed an immediate drop in tension on the part of Itzik. Every time he returned to the apartment after a trip down to the truck, Itzik had made himself more comfortable, until eventually Gabi found him stretched out on the sofa, Meshulam's cordless telephone pressed to his ear while he snorted loudly with laughter.

When he heard Gabi enter, he signaled with his fingers for him to wait a moment, continued talking for another three minutes, and then said, "Listen, I'm going down to get something to eat with Victor. Stay here to keep an eye on the apartment. I don't want the owner to return and find no one here. If he gets back before me, tell him we're on a short break. We'll take over afterward and you can go down and grab something."

The owner returned. Gabi passed on Itzik's message. He nodded, loosened his tie, and sat down in an armchair. Then he sighed and turned away from the view to look at Gabi. "Been in New York for long?"

Gabi shook his head. "Three days."

The man smiled. "It shows. You aren't managing very well, are you?"

Gabi wondered what he meant, what showed. "Not managing what?"

"The city. The work."

Gabi looked at the man. Considered whether to be loyal to the company or to tell the truth. He smiled. "It shows?"

Meshulam laughed. He asked Gabi about his background and Gabi responded with an appropriate summary. He gave Gabi a can of soda from the refrigerator and Gabi drank appreciatively and glanced out at the canopy of clouds and the sun that struggled to break through them from above, and the tall buildings that tried to pierce them from below. "This city is so huge," he said.

"You'll like the place I'm moving to more," said Meshulam. "It'll remind you of the kibbutz."

"Where?"

"Hollywood, Florida."

Gabi was confused.

"It's not the Hollywood you've heard of. It's a different Hollywood. Nicer. You'll see when you go there to unload."

"It won't be me." Gabi smiled. "We aren't supposed to do long-distance in the first month."

The Fund

Hollywood, Florida, was much nicer. According to company regulations, Gabi shouldn't have been on the truck, but company regulations stipulated that at least one worker who was there for the loading must also be at the unloading, and because Itzik and Victor were called in to help with a huge twelve-truck job down on Wall Street, the dispatcher bent one rule to stick to another. Or he simply didn't have any people.

They went by Meshulam's apartment one more time to load a few more new items he had purchased. When they told him they were continuing on from there straight to Florida, Meshulam told the foreman that he was also about to leave, and offered to give Gabi a ride in his car. That wasn't in keeping with company regulations, either, but worked best for everyone: for Meshulam, who clearly needed company and help with the driving on the long journey southward; for Gabi, who was worried at the thought of spending two or three days in the truck's cabin with the two imbeciles he'd met ten minutes earlier who were treating him like he wasn't even there; and most of all for the foreman, the ruling authority, who couldn't believe his luck—not only had he managed to get out of the huge job in lower Manhattan but he could also head down to Florida with a friend and with extra room in the cabin.

One thousand, one hundred and eighteen miles is a long way to go, lots of time, lots of nature, lots of air. Leaving the big city, Gabi felt the tension drain from his body—the few days he'd spent in New York were the longest of his life in a city. Within hours he got used to the pace of the journey, the softness of the Chevrolet's beige leather seats, the regularity of the American road, the open spaces and rest stations and roadside diners. He ate something other than a Big Mac at last. And the English from the kibbutz began rolling off his tongue naturally again—the rust finally fell away.

One thousand, one hundred and eighteen miles is sufficient distance for deepening an acquaintanceship. Meshulam Avneri had been in the United States for eleven years. He had a student son, a soldier daughter, and one ex-wife in Israel, another daughter who was traveling in Ecuador, and a second wife who had been living with him in New York until two weeks before and had returned to Israel. Her father had fallen ill, but that was probably just an excuse. He didn't know if she'd be coming back. She wasn't too keen on the move to Florida, and claimed, anyway, that Meshulam had promised her they'd go back to Israel, although he didn't remember making such a promise. So now she was there and he was here and who knew what would happen. Besides, he traveled a lot and didn't get to see her half the time, so things hadn't changed much. On the other hand, he should have been doing less traveling from Florida, that was part of the improvement in the terms of his employment, his promotion. The New York office was the company's main office in the United States, and it was good to be close to the honeypot, the tail of a lion rather than the head of a dog, and all the other clichés. But being handed the North Florida zone, Palm Beach County, the region with the highest concentration of Jews outside of Israel, and what Jews, too, Jews of the perfect age and social status for his kind of work—that isn't an offer one refuses, and Nira could say and do whatever she pleased. When Meshulam said that, his words were tinged with bitterness, and his eyebrows scrunched up into his graying face.

Meshulam worked for the Keren Kayemeth LeIsrael. Gabi recalled that it was the organization responsible for the forests in Israel, but Meshulam explained that that was only one of its activities. In America it was known as the JNF, the Jewish National Fund, and they were involved in raising money, which went toward all aspects of land development and land maintenance in Israel. Meshulam arrived as an emissary, and a few years later, after receiving a green card and subsequently an American passport, he became a local employee. His main job in Florida was to find people who would bequeath their money and property to the State of Israel, to make contact with them and to nurture the connection.

"How do you find people who want to leave their money to Israel?" Gabi asked.

"Ah, it's complicated. A JNF person needs to be well rooted in the Jewish community and the synagogues. He'll present brochures on the JNF activities and offer people the chance to adopt projects. He'll give lectures, leave business cards. Sometimes he'll hear of candidates in advance and make contact with them. Sometimes the donors themselves make the approach. We also publish ads."

"And then what?"

"You set up a meeting. They're usually elderly Jews. Sometimes they have a family or friends or other organizations, and we get a portion of the inheritance. But the really big fish are people with money and assets who don't have a family, no heirs, and then we step into the picture. That's the real work."

"What's the work?"

"I meet with them for lunches. Call to maintain the relationship. I show them the work the JNF is doing, and befriend them, try to make them feel that the State of Israel cares about them. There are financial arrangements, too. Sometimes they're complex, with lawyers and accountants. Sometimes it's simpler. The details are finalized over time: the size of the bequest, the validity of the will, the precise wording, where exactly the money will go, what will be done with the property."

They drank coffee at a truck stop. Meshulam, who insisted on wearing his suit and tie the entire journey, suddenly sighed, and Gabi wondered what he was truly feeling. "So your work is really just making friends with old people, sucking up to them, making sure they don't pick up the phone to a lawyer to tell them they've discovered some distant relative whom they've decided to leave everything to, and waiting for them to die."

Meshulam smiled. "Not all the work, but that's a part of it."

"Not bad."

"You're away from home a lot, you eat with them, listen to them, treat them well. It's not that simple."

"Actually, doesn't sound too bad to me."

"It's tough with those people sometimes. They're not the most interesting. Or they're angry with someone, or something hurts them. You have to be there for them all the time."

"Better than carrying boxes and sofas on your back."

"I guess. And also, don't forget, it's Zionism in the end. We're building the country. We need that money."

They resumed their journey. Gabi drove. Meshulam drove. Gabi drove and Meshulam slept. They stopped to spend the night in a city called Charleston, and at dinner Meshulam told Gabi about a client he once had in that city, not even a Jew, but he contacted the organization and decided to bequeath his home, a beautiful house with a large garden in the heart of town. Meshulam met him for dinner, at an amazing fancy seafood restaurant. It was a fascinating evening, the man had an interesting life story, he was a CIA agent in Italy for many years. They finalized all the details, the man was supposed to call his lawyer the following morning to change the will, but before he had a chance, he suffered a heart attack and died of food poisoning, and Meshulam himself spent all day hanging over the toilet throwing up and having diarrhea.

As he slowly emerged from sleep after the night at the motel, Gabi thought about Meshulam's work. He didn't like the parasitic element of it, the way the State of Israel sent emissaries to hover like vultures over human carcasses, or worse, even, over living people, waiting for them to become carcasses and then swooping down and scavenging whatever they leave behind the moment they die. There was something disturbing about the cold and calculated process by which they found candidates for death, secured their bequests, waited for their demise. On the other hand, he thought, they offer the caring and warmth that's missing from the lives of childless people who've come to the end of the road. Even if the motive is a selfish one, it's still caring and warmth that no one else offers, and who says the warmth and caring offered in more conventional ways, by family members or friends, stems from less selfish motives?

The next morning they continued in driving rain. Gabi liked rain, but quantities like that were too much even for him, and in the month of June as well. Meshulam smiled and said it was the norm in this part of America, there were hurricanes sometimes, too, which was a lot crazier. They drove slowly, a bit pensive and withdrawn, the wipers working vigorously and noisily, the rain slamming down on the metal.

After one more night at a motel, they arrived at Meshulam's new house. The foreman called to say the stormy weather had slowed the progress of the truck, which wouldn't arrive until evening, thus leaving Gabi and Meshulam with an entire day to wait in an empty house. Hollywood, Florida, did indeed remind Gabi of the kibbutz. The contrast with New York surprised him. In front of every house was a well-groomed square of lawn, the houses themselves were tidy, spacious. The storm passed, maybe didn't even reach that part of Florida, and it was the most sun-filled day since he'd landed in America. He sat on a deck chair someone had left in Meshulam's yard, sipping the coffee in a paper cup that Meshulam got from around the corner.

Meshulam took him on a tour of the neighborhood. Gabi got into the Chevrolet and three minutes later caught sight of the most beautiful sea he had ever seen, a deep and intoxicating turquoise, and long white beaches, and the girls . . . He took off his pants and went into the sea in his underwear, and couldn't believe how gratifying and familiar it felt when the water engulfed him. Like the kibbutz? The kibbutz wished. It was a hundred times better; it was like the kibbutz, only without strange looks in the dining hall and with the most beautiful beach you'd ever seen, with all due respect to the Sea of Galilee.

He lay on the sand and said, "This is paradise, Meshulam. This is what I dreamed of when I dreamed of overseas. Not about a million people and tall buildings in which I go up and down with furniture." Meshulam smiled. He took him to eat at a restaurant on the beach, and when they returned home, he showed Gabi the small apartment adjacent to the main house. It had a separate entrance, one small room with a kitchenette and bathroom.

"I've been thinking about renting this out, what do you think?" Meshulam asked. He meant, what did Gabi think of the idea of renting it out, and of the unit in general.

But Gabi said, "I'm in."

Meshulam looked at him in surprise. "You're in what?"

"I want to live here," Gabi said.

Meshulam laughed. "Are you serious?"

"Totally."

"And what will you do?"

"Don't you need an assistant?"

The Bar

While his brother left for the United States, and many of his friends for the Far East and South America, Roni remained in Tel Aviv. It was far enough for him. He had ended up there almost by chance. Started dating a girl from Ra'anana, an economics and philosophy student at Tel Aviv University, whose father had an office in an apartment on Shlomo Hamelech Street with a vacant room, and the girlfriend suggested to Roni that they take over the room. During work hours they shared the apartment with the office, and because Roni didn't feel comfortable, he preferred to go out and frequently just went with the girlfriend to the university, started sitting in on classes, and discovered that the courses interested him.

In the evening and on weekends they had the apartment to themselves. They bought a fishbowl and two fish for a few shekels from a pet store around the corner. Their "rent" was to clean the apartment and wash the dishes of the office employees, usually three mugs with the remains of coffee or water. He decided to register for studies—if he was already investing the time in lectures, why shouldn't he glorify himself with a degree? But just a few months later the girlfriend told him she was pregnant, which ended in an abortion and despair and a teary breakup.

The girlfriend left the apartment while Roni ended up staying, and continued to share it with the father's office. But now he had to pay rent, and tuition fees at the university, too. Roni spent a few days wondering how he'd manage, until the day the fish died—from overfeeding, they explained to him at the pet store. He went to a pub on one of the corners of Malchei Yisrael Square—it was a few years before they stopped calling them pubs, or the square by that name—and drank so much that by the end of the evening he barely managed to notice the small "Kitchen Help Wanted" ad posted near the toilets.

He washed dishes, and then helped the chef, and then became a barman, and eventually a shift manager. He discovered at university that he was able to breeze through the basic statistics and math courses. A year later Roni was for all intents and purposes already managing the pub when the owner, Oren Azulai, made him an offer. He was about to open a new place and wanted Roni to run it for him: the setting up, décor, renovations, team, inventory, menu, wages. Oren didn't want to spend a single minute there. Roni would earn twice his current salary.

"And here's your real incentive," Oren threw his way at the end of the conversation. "To give you another shot in the arm, I'll give you a bonus of two percent of the after-tax profit at the end of every month."

The offer left Roni stunned for several moments, but he maintained a cool façade and said, almost matter-of-factly, "Let me come in as a partner, it'll be more worthwhile for you."

"Partner?" Oren asked, and tried to suppress the patronizing smile. "Do you have money to invest?"

Roni didn't, but he said he'd check. He checked. The banks he went into showed him the door within minutes. But Uncle Yaron, whom he called without a glimmer of hope, surprised him with the savings account he had opened with the inheritances of his parents and grandfather. Roni went in with a 20 percent share.

He set up the new place from scratch: from the exhausting red tape of the Tel Aviv Municipality, through to the last tile in the bathrooms. All he knew, he knew from running one conventional pub in a square in Tel Aviv, from years of drinking at the kibbutz pub, and from a handful of courses at the university; but he also knew, from intuition, from common sense, that he wanted something different. More appealing, more fun. He started with the name. He wasn't the first proprietor in the '90s to drop the prefix "Pub" and swap "Bar" in its place, but he was certainly a pioneer of sorts when he named the place Bar-BaraBush, after the wife of the not-so-long-ago president of the United States. He then moved on to the design of the sign and façade, the inviting and comfortable interior, paying strict attention to cleanliness, selecting the staff and training them. His most impressive innovation was his approach to the food. Unlike most drinking establishments, which served fries and chicken wings with their beer, Bar-BaraBush offered good food: filling and also diverse, simple and also fresh, inexpensive, and available at all hours. Roni hired a sous-chef who designed a menu, which was gradually perfected and adapted to suit the place and the mood. In time more and more people were converted: a bar that offered not only good drinking but good eating, too.

The business began turning a tidy profit. And despite the skeptical look on Oren Azulai's face, Roni insisted that the two owners draw a modest salary and invest the rest back into the business. Oren went along with it because he could see the results, and realized that Roni's vision, which was backed up by hard work and admirable diligence, though it might not have been precise and clear even to Roni himself, would take them forward. Azulai was smart enough not to intervene, a great business decision in its own right.

Prosperity and growth were the signs of the time, and Tel Aviv teemed with young people and tourists and foreign investors and Russian immigrants and frazzled soldiers, each in his or her own way needing a glass of something, which Roni happily and competently provided. He moved into an apartment in a high-rise on Basel Street with a view of the sea and a sixty-square-meter balcony with a wooden deck, scored the best weed from acquaintances who did reserve military duty in Lebanon, and puffed sweet smoke into the warm skies of the Middle East, usually in the company of a pretty young girl. He cultivated a trendy beard and allowed his curls to grow.

He worked hard—harder than he had ever worked before. Being a boss was a learning curve for a kibbutznik: managing finances, wages, income tax, and social security. Being tough, unpleasant. Maintaining a daily routine. In the morning, after a coffee and cigarette on the deck, he'd arrive alone, sit in the office, and go over the bills, the orders, and the calls, and receive suppliers. The first workers showed up toward noon, and the initial customers began trickling in. Afternoons he freed up for his studies. His second year suffered significantly due to the workload at the bar, but he didn't want to stop school entirely and focused his efforts on those hours. He returned to the bar in the early evening, made sure everything was ready, and at some point lost track of time. Time stretched and whirled like a small tornado that came through the gates of Bar-BaraBush a little after nine and exited its doors after midnight: shards of memory, a conspicuous incident or two—usually shouting in the kitchen or a celebrity customer—and a general buzz in the air, sore feet, the smell of frothy beer at the pouring stations. The time he liked most came just before one. The pressure eased, but the place still teemed with people, who continued to pour in from cinemas, from restaurants, or after a long day at work. Those were his favorite customers. They had more time on their hands. That was when Roni took charge of the bar, poured, chatted, flirted. Invited customers to join him for a chaser on the house, and at some stage turned to fill his glass with water. If things were really quiet, he'd move to a barstool and cradle a glass of Scotch on the rocks between his fingers.

The Drinkers

He didn't have friends. But in the small hours, the quiet ones, people came to sit with him. Customers he met there and who became regulars, random customers who passed through and whom he'd never see again. Colleagues from the restaurant and hospitality industry who talked business. And faces from the past: from the commando unit, from his kibbutz, from the surrounding kibbutzim. How they knew to go there, Roni didn't have a clue. But they drank. And after they drank, they rambled on.

Yifat came in one night. His sweet Yifat from high school who'd broken his heart. She was with another guy and ignored Roni, apart from a few glances. She came in the following day and apologized. She didn't want to have to explain things to her boyfriend. They were serious, she said, and she didn't want to jeopardize anything. She really hoped it would work out this time. She ate lunch and drank a little wine and told Roni that she was doing well. She had "found herself" in Tel Aviv, studied fashion at Shenkar, didn't miss the kibbutz.

"And I think that Yoav," she said, "is the best thing that has ever happened to me. He has a band. Wow, it's so weird for us to be sitting here and talking about it. You don't mind, right? I'm sure you have lots of girlfriends." She giggled.

He glanced at his watch, bored, and told her he needed to head out for a while, she could join him if she liked.

"Out for a while?" she asked.

He showed her his apartment with the wooden deck and poured her another glass of wine. At some point she told him she wanted to tickle his funny beard, and they spent the next two hours in bed—since her childhood she had learned a few things, loosened up—until she looked at the alarm clock and said, her hair disheveled, "Wow, I have to get home," and he never saw her again. He didn't care.

A few weeks later, as the night was winding down, Baruch Shani came into the bar. Holy shit, what happened to him? was Roni's first thought. Baruch from the cattle, from the commando unit, Roni's mentor, who'd transformed a few young girls on the kibbutz into women. Now—balding, unkempt, a strange twitch at the corner of his mouth— he drank with an unhealthy disposition. Not an end-of-the day drink to air out the thoughts, but drinking for the sake of drinking. He appeared to have been through a rough time; however, Baruch didn't want to talk about it but rather about days gone by, and Roni didn't press him, he had learned not to press, whoever comes by is welcome, whoever wants to talk can talk, and whoever wants to can keep quiet.

After a few beers, Baruch recounted how he had slept with Orit from Roni's class at school, when she was fourteen and Baruch twenty-three. It wasn't news to Roni—he remembered seeing Orit slipping into Baruch's sleeping bag at the summer camp—but he was curious now to hear all the details. Baruch told him that Orit was now happily married with two children in Kiryat Ono, and that efforts he'd made to renew the connection, including recently, were met with stubborn resistance. "She's still beautiful," he summed up, as if to explain the reason behind her refusal.

Baruch came to the bar from time to time, always looking the same, swallowing words and drinking and rambling on about the past. Roni wasn't able to understand what he was doing with himself. He mumbled something about a job in insurance, but Roni couldn't imagine him selling insurance to anyone in his state.

Kibbutz old-timers who were vacationing at the kibbutz's apartment in the big city showed up on occasion, until financial problems forced the sale of the apartment. They always spoke about Tel Aviv in relation to the kibbutz: different worlds. Sometimes pretty young girls would turn up and tell him they were younger sisters of his former classmates. Ezra Dudi came in one day, with his thick beard and sullen Theodor Herzl–lookalike face. Roni enjoyed those encounters, so surprising and haphazard. But most of the nights were simply pleasant Tel Aviv nights, and most of the customers were anonymous until they started talking and went back to being anonymous the moment they left.

One night after midnight, a good-looking, well-built man in his twenties entered, walked in, and sat at the bar and ordered a gin and tonic. The song "Tarzan Boy" with its "Oh ho oh ho oh ho oh ho, oh ho" Tarzan calls was playing in the background. Roni placed the glass on the bar. "You don't recognize me, huh?" the customer said. Roni looked at him again. Focused his stare. The buzz cut, the gleaming eyes, the askew smile. Just a sec. The askew smile. No, not the askew smile, the askew jaw. Hang on a sec, no, yes, it has to be, those were the eyes, for sure, how had he not recognized him right away?

"Eyal?"

By then he was already smiling, his head rocking back and forth on the fulcrum of his neck. Eyal's father, Yona, had been sent to Buenos Aires on behalf of the kibbutz's instant-lawn enterprise when Eyal was fifteen, and they hadn't been seen since. Eyal was now telling him about the two years in Buenos Aires, followed by two years in Paris, at the end of which his parents, Yona and Yona, got divorced, and he stayed with his mother and studied architecture in a small French town, and then the kibbutz factory decided to scale down its operations abroad, and his father went to live in a village in northern Spain with his secretary from the office. Dad was back in Israel now, alone, and trying to regain membership of the kibbutz and his job at the factory, and Eyal had come to help him.

In the background Haddaway was asking what is love and pleading for his baby not to hurt him no more, and Eyal asked if his was the craziest story Roni had ever heard here at the bar.

"No," Roni replied, "but it's not bad." Eyal's father came in the following day at the same time. This time Roni recognized him immediately, though Yona also no longer looked the same as he used to. Fatter, grayer.

"What can I get you, Yona?" Roni asked, and reached out for a handshake.

The evening was the antithesis of the previous one, at least one aspect of it. The evening before—as Roni had quickly picked up—Eyal grabbed the attention of almost every girl at Bar-BaraBush: those there alone, with friends or partners, waitresses or clients. When Roni pointed it out to Eyal, he smiled and gestured with his hand, as if he no longer noticed it. This evening, his father was the one who shot imploring looks at all of them—those there alone, with friends or partners, waitresses or clients. And they, of course, acted as if he didn't exist, and he was used to it, but couldn't stop.

"Did he tell you he's a homo?" Yona asked Roni, and that explained a few things to Roni, but he wasn't able to work out if the disappointment on the father's face was related to the women's disregard for him or his son's tendency to disregard women. "Are you a homo, too?" Yona asked. "What's that little beard?"

Yona drank more than Eyal. Roni got tired of the man's ramblings about Argentina and the kibbutz and the bastards who had forgotten all he had done for them. When Yona began chatting in Spanish with a tourist girl, he seized the opportunity and slipped away to the storeroom. When he returned, Yona signaled to him with a finger.

"Yona," Roni said, "haven't you had enough to drink for one night? Should I call you a cab?"

"Just a moment," Yona responded, his voice low and gravelly from exhaustion and alcohol.

"It's just that we're going to close soon. Would you like me to find Eyal, for him to come get you?"

"Did he tell you he's a homo?"

"You told me," said Roni, and cast his eyes over the clients still at the bar. It was nothing out of the ordinary, naturally, a drunk who needs help at the end of the night, but Roni felt a twinge of pity for the kibbutz member. Yona mumbled something in Spanish.

"What?" Roni asked.

"A homo is what I ended up with," Yona concluded, and stood up on shaky legs.

Roni could have said good-bye and gone about his business, but he came out from behind the bar and said, "Come, Yona, I'll call you a cab. Where do you need to go?" Yona didn't respond. "Or should I call Eyal?"

"The homo?" the father asked, resting an arm on Roni's shoulder and stumbling along beside him.

The acrid air of the bar was replaced by the heavy night air. And there they stood, the inebriated adult and the uncomfortable youngster, one arm on a shoulder, a second arm having no alternative but to be around a waist, waiting, in silence, and then Yona cleared his throat, and then spat out a curse in Spanish, and then asked, "How's your loco brother doing? He's okay? Recovered?"

Roni was thrown for a moment, and then said, "He's fine. He's in New York now."

"New York? Very nice, very nice."

Roni lifted an arm to signal a passing cab. It didn't stop.

"I'll never forget how we took him, Yona, Eyal's mother, and I, how we stuffed those stinky beetles into his mouth."

"You?" Roni stepped away from the embrace and stood facing Yona.

He could fall, for all Roni cared. But his balance was better than it appeared to be. Another lesson Roni had learned—people who appear to need to lean on others, leave them be and you'll be surprised by just how well they manage.

"Me and Yona, Eyal's mother. That kid, your brother, the loco—he was a bad kid. Wait, what's with him, he's recovered?"

Thoughts flashed through Roni's mind. "But how . . . What about the hairy arms?" Gabi's only clue from that night. That, and the fact that there were at least two people, and lots of decomposed legs in his mouth.

"Hah . . ." Yona broke into the slow and beaming smile of someone who is completely wasted. "That was Yona's, Eyal's mother's, idea. She wanted everyone to think it was Shimshon Cohen. Because look, I have smooth hands, look." He held out his arms.

"But wasn't Shimshon Cohen a friend of yours? Why did she want to incriminate him?"

"Ooh. A long story. We'll have to save that one for another time."

The thought of having to spend another evening with Yona made Roni shudder.

"Taxi!" Roni shouted, and when one appeared and stopped out of nowhere, Yona chuckled and said, "God's on your side, kid."

He got into the back and closed the door, and after the cab pulled away, the window came down and he yelled, "Regards to your brother the loco. Let's hope he recovers."

Only after the cab disappeared did Roni realize that Yona hadn't told him how Yona and Yona had given the father hairy arms like those of Shimshon Cohen.

The Assistant

When Roni told Yona that Gabi was in New York, he had no idea that Gabi had left New York in favor of Hollywood, Florida. Roni wanted to call Gabi to tell him of his discovery. He got the number of a kibbutznik who was working in the moving business in New York, but he told Roni that Gabi had been there with him for a few days and had then disappeared. With only this flimsy lead to go by, Roni decided on second thought that he didn't want to inform Gabi of his discovery. What for. Why pick at old sores.

Gabi Kupper returned to New York on one occasion. It was to meet the daughter of Cyril Zimmerman, a millionaire from Boca Raton, an important client of Meshulam Avneri and the JNF branch. Zimmerman had agreed to leave a significant portion of his estate to the Jewish National Fund, and was about to amend his will to arrange the bequest. Meshulam had met with him several times, some together with Gabi, and made a note to himself that Zimmerman fit the profile of a candidate who could very well come up with a large contribution, if they could maneuver around a number of obstacles on the way.

One such obstacle was Jennifer, Zimmerman's fifty-nine-year-old daughter, who lived on Manhattan's Upper West Side. The elderly man told them about her one day. He said she was asking questions about the JNF and the inheritance. He didn't believe it'd be a problem, but he didn't want to create unhealthy tension, or as he put it, "to leave this world on a discordant note," and therefore wanted to give her the answers.

"What's she asking?" Meshulam pleasantly inquired. He had told Gabi about such cases. The children of a potential donor ask questions, particularly when it came to an inheritance. Meshulam stressed the need to display understanding for the suspicion, and to propose a series of confidence-building measures—a presentation, lecture, meeting, even an invitation to Israel, so the children could see with their own eyes the work being done. There were cases in which children had secured a post facto annulment of the will on the claim that their lonely parents had been exploited, and there was no point in butting heads over such incidents, as it would tarnish the image of the organization. All such problems had to be resolved in advance.

"Well, what could she be asking—how come all of a sudden I plan to give half my money to people I don't know?" Zimmerman said, and sipped his white wine. He had pinkish skin, glasses, and a full mane of white hair. He'd made his fortune as a lawyer. "I say to her, Jenny, it's the JNF, it's the State of Israel, it's what's written in the will, the text is being scrutinized by a thousand pairs of lawyer eyes, including mine, everything's kosher, everything's been defined and reviewed, the bank accounts, the money will go to recognized institutions. So she says, with all due respect to the State of Israel . . ."

The thing is, Zimmerman said, Jenny doesn't even need the money. She married, and then divorced, a Jew who's even wealthier than me, Shulman, the steel magnate, know him? They didn't. She had a lot more than she could spend in her lifetime even if she tried, and she's also still supposed to get half the inheritance of her father, as his only daughter. Her intentions are good, she only wants to protect him, to make sure his head isn't being turned, he said. So all that needs to be done, in his opinion, is to send this young man to see her—he pointed at Gabi, who had been sitting there in silence through most of the dinner, eating politely and slowly, smiling at all the right times—so she can see that the money really is going to the "good guys" and not some Israeli swindler. Gabi sat up straight when Zimmerman said that, with a piece of wonderful rustic bread in his mouth, which he tried to swallow whole. He looked at Meshulam in surprise, and noticed a glimmer of recognition in his boss's eyes. A flight to New York was scheduled for the following week.

A few months had passed since Gabi moved into the separate apartment in Meshulam's Hollywood home. He felt comfortable there. It wasn't really like the kibbutz, he soon realized, but there were the yard, the single-story homes, the nearby beach, with its grains of white sand on the backdrop of warm turquoise water in which beautiful-looking girls waded and splashed. He often visited the cinema and wandered among the theaters, which screened the same movies over and over again.

He was fortunate—two junior positions had just opened up at the local JNF office. They were supposed to be reserved for local employees, Americans, but he was able to land a temporary work permit that would tide him over until all the visa paperwork was completed. He began by getting to know the local staff and their work: establishing ties with Jewish institutions in the area, organizing gatherings in homes, identifying donors and keeping in contact with them, putting together delegations to Israel, distributing and collecting the blue collection boxes. He sometimes accompanied Meshulam to meetings, and the rest of the time he spent in the office. The first project he handled entirely alone was a lecture tour by former Israeli justice minister Dan Meridor to a pair of local retirement homes.

The work was interesting, easy. He did the math and found that the moving business had actually paid more, but the JNF salary was still pretty good, and his expenses were minimal. The constant brush with the wealthy, people who all their lives chased after money and attained it but were left alone, not knowing what to do with so much, taught him something, namely that in the end almost everyone shrivels and fades away with only a few family members around, at most, and the money they've worked so hard for lies scattered around them like fallen leaves that someone's forgotten to rake up.

Even after months, he remained unable to get a full grip on Meshulam. His family status, and the motives behind his willingness to offer a job and a place to live to a young guy he barely knew. Or what exactly he did in his free time. Sometimes Gabi heard muffled noises, the footsteps of more than one person on the hardwood floor, or the turn of a key in a lock in the early hours of the morning—Gabi was a light sleeper and he'd raise his head, glance at the clock—three, four—and go back to sleep, but they always met up at eight thirty to leave for the office, and Meshulam always looked well groomed and fresh. Gabi tried two or three times to engage him in conversation—to ask about the situation with his wife's father or what chance there was of her returning to the United States, or if he had done anything interesting the night before. But Meshulam wasn't forthcoming, and Gabi gave up. He sensed that Meshulam was a loner. That he possessed a bitter side.

Jennifer Shulman-Zimmerman owned a large apartment with an enormous balcony. Every corner was filled with purple—cushions, picture frames, drapes, even the shirt she was wearing. They sat on the balcony and sipped cold lemonade. Her eyes were blue and large and her hair strawlike—a full-figured woman, nothing much to look at, but amiable and funny, too. She barely spoke about money, simply asked questions about Israel, the kibbutz, the army. Gabi did as Meshulam had instructed: responded to the point, joined in the small talk, asked about the apartment, about her fondness for the color purple, about her childhood and her father, about her children and grandchild. Gabi marked her down to himself as yet another lonely individual, like her father, with too much money and luxury and lacking the ability to enjoy it all, who for the most part wanted, like so many of the donors, to spend a few hours in the company of someone who'd fawn over her.

But then her partner arrived. She introduced him as "my young boyfriend," a sprightly man by the name of Irving, three years her junior, the resident psychiatrist for the New Jersey Nets basketball team, short, with curly hair and beard and thick lips. The three of them went out for dinner to a wonderful Italian restaurant, and Gabi enjoyed himself so much that he didn't know where the time went. He had been too quick to judge Jennifer, he realized. And New York, too. The city was different from the one he had encountered during his first days in the United States. It was light, thrilling, funny, and the more the wine flowed, the more Gabi developed a fondness for the two.

Gabi and Irving discussed the drug problems of the NBA players, and the latter promised to arrange tickets for Gabi when the Nets next visited Miami. They told Gabi about a tour they once went on in the Galilee, about wonderful olive oil made with age-old millstones, about the graves of departed righteous Jews in Safed, about a good restaurant in Rosh Pina—Gabi, a Galilee resident all his life, knew nothing of any of it, but told Irving that on his next trip he should come see the kibbutz's basketball team. They asked him about the JNF and he told them what he knew, what he had learned from Meshulam, but the wine had loosened his tongue and he confessed at some stage that he was new to the job, that he didn't know much, that he had always known they planted trees, not that they looked for rich donors in America. Jennifer said she wanted to donate a forest in her name, irrespective of her father's gift, at a new settlement where friends of hers from Brooklyn who immigrated to Israel were living. She called someone from Irving's cell phone—it was the first time Gabi had seen a device like that in real life, and although Jenny had to repeat sentences and turn up the volume, he was amazed by its very existence—and wrote down the name of the settlement on a paper napkin and, after she ended the call, tried to read it out—MAALE HERMESH?

"What?" Gabi leaned forward, narrowed his eyes, tried to sharpen his hearing amid the commotion of the New York sidewalk. In his hand was a teaspoon with the remains of a crème brûlée. Jennifer tried to pronounce the words. "Ma'aleh Hermesh?" Gabi repeated. "I think I've heard of it. I'll look into it. No problem. Where is it?"

Jenny called again. "Judea and Samaria," she said when she hung up. Gabi nodded with a surprised smile on his lips. His mind suddenly threw up the image of a settlement he had arrived at in a Susita years ago, on his escape journey from the kibbutz. The only time he had been in the territories.

"Oy, don't tell me . . . It's those crazy settlers from Brooklyn?" Irving said. Gabi liked Irving. He reminded him of the actor Elliott Gould, with his bushy eyebrows and conquering smile, only with a beard. He eyed Jenny cautiously. The boyfriend's remark didn't faze her.

"So you want to buy a forest and dedicate it in your name?" Gabi asked, giving her one last chance to opt out. She nodded and smiled. Her blue eyes flitted from the wine and Gabi couldn't tell if they held a trace of flirtation—he was never good with that stuff—so he turned to Irving with a bemused look, and Irving rolled his eyes and shrugged.

"Sure, I'll take care of it," Gabi said, and downed the rest of his wine in a single gulp.

They invited him to sleep over in the guest room, but at that stage, he was feeling bewildered by Jennifer's blue eyes and the boyfriend's bushy eyebrows, and besides, Meshulam had told him not to cross any lines in relationships with the donors and he feared he had already crossed them. When they offered to drive him to a hotel, he said, "What are you talking about? You live here, go up home, I'll manage." They hugged and parted. They'd made him swear he'd take a cab and he swore, but only after walking the streets for a few minutes, soaking up the atmosphere, seeing the big city. Gabi walked for a long time, block after block, people and cars and yellow taxis and restaurants. He wanted to ease the buzzing in his head, but the buzzing intensified, the wine pumped in his temples, and his eyes and mind were left agape by the sheer quantity of stimuli to which he wasn't accustomed. He eventually saw a subway station and went down the stairs and bought a ticket and went in and stood on the platform. He had nothing against taxis, he was simply enjoying the New York experience so much and wanted to round it off with a ride on the subway. He stood on the platform, and a loud thundering rolled in from the mouth of the tunnel and approached, and lights crashed onto the platform with a bang and a rattle and a roar, and an incomprehensible announcer bellowed from concealed loudspeakers, and the silver train slowed and the doors along its length parted, and out from the carriage in front of him, cautiously, stepped Anna.

The Surprise

It comes when you least expect it, when you aren't paying attention. Behind the back, over the shoulder, stepping cautiously in front of you. It catches you unawares, startles you with the speed at which it comes, with its fortuity. It puts things in place, explains courses of action that seemed inconsequential, incidental, inadvertent. It offers a reason, looking back and looking forward. It mostly hits you smack between the eyes and blinds you for a few moments. In that instant you aren't thinking. The thoughts will come later, years later, on a small hilltop in the heart of the mountains, before a barren desert and freezing winds. Only then will you be able to ask: If I had known what was going to happen, would I have forsaken love?

He saw Anna, and unlike back then, in Sinai, this time he approached her. They began talking on the platform of the nameless subway station, and didn't stop. For two hours they sat on a bench, the thundering comings and goings, the small hours creeping in.

He told her about that day in Sinai. The day that started with the earthquake while he lay on the sand, and continued with him seeing her arrive with a group of teenagers. How he had panicked, and dressed, and hurriedly left the beach and started out for home. Escaped the escape. Was afraid she'd recognize him and expose his secret. Had always wondered if she'd seen him. She hadn't. And hadn't felt the earthquake, either. Even if she had seen him, she certainly wouldn't have put him at any risk.

She vaguely remembered him disappearing, a search for him. But at that time, in Sinai in particular, she was too caught up in herself to notice what was happening around her. She was in love with a German volunteer named Luther, quit school for a few months because of him, hung out with him, smoked with him, did everything with him that a sixteen-year-old girl discovering the world outside the kibbutz does. They stayed in Sinai for two months, she thought, and as far as she remembered, all she did was love Luther. Gabi laughed. He had been so panicked by her appearance, and she wasn't the slightest bit interested. You're so focused on yourself sometimes, he said to her, that you forget that for others you aren't the center of the universe. He told her about running away. The Golani uniform. The crazy rides he hitched. The settlement—it hadn't crossed his mind for years, and now for the second time that evening he could picture it in his thoughts: the small homes, the family who put him up in the crowded children's room, the terraces and mountains. It happens like that sometimes, Anna said with a dreamy look, something comes out of nowhere, a memory, a thought, and there's a reason for it. She shifted her gaze from the opposite platform, the wide steel girders, the rats wandering between the tracks, to Gabi. And then she smiled and her eyes remained fixed on him. He almost reached out a finger to touch the cute dimple on her cheek.

He told her about the short-circuits in his brain, the fits of rage, the solace he found in Sinai. Anna apologized for ruining the solace and just then a train thundered onto the platform and he said, "Want to take a ride a little, a different vibe?"

They boarded the train and sat on the orange seats.

"So what's with Luther, is he still in the picture?" he asked.

She frowned for a moment and then laughed out loud. "Idiot," she said, and he liked the way she called him that.

He told her about the ride with the three Arabs in the Peugeot, about the darkness he felt the moment he got in. How they tore his shirt and frisked him and touched him between his legs and spewed their dirty breath all over him, realized he was just a kid dressed as a soldier and didn't have a weapon, and threw him out into a ditch at the side of the road. He was with them for mere minutes, but the chilling terror, the sense that this was the end, that this was how someone who's about to be murdered feels. He remembered every second, remembered thinking about Anna, too, and the blue-eyed man from the settlement. And how he lay stunned in the ditch with his life restored to him, and in his mind the sentence he still recalled—the eye sees, the ear hears, through the valley of the shadow of death I will fear no evil—the tides had shifted and he began viewing the strange day he had experienced not as a mistake but as a blessing, a sign of good things to come.

And then the news of the poor soldier who got into the Peugeot after him. Gabi cried when he told her, and she cried with him, two near-strangers in the middle of the night on an empty train, and she rested a hand on him and said, "It wasn't your fault, they would have found him without you, they were looking for a soldier to kill," and Gabi held her hand and between his sobs tried to say "Sorry" and "I don't know what's come over me," and she caressed his hand and soothed him.

They emerged aboveground and walked in silence. It started raining. They stopped, looked up, and at each other, and walked on. The rain came down harder. She giggled and he smiled in response and she snuggled up to him and he held her, shielded her, and she said, "I think any second we're going to have to run and find a place to hide," and he answered, "Don't worry, it'll soon pass." And the period at the end of his sentence was the loudest and closest clap of thunder they had ever heard and a deluge washed over them, and they stood like that, rooted to the spot, hugging, helpless, breathing in the smell of a wet sweater, fading perfume, faint alcohol, washed avenue leaves, until Anna said, "We need to do something," and Gabi responded, "Why? It's fun . . ." And she, hidden in his arms, bit her lip and smiled and admitted that, yes, it really was fun, but he didn't hear, so he asked, "Isn't it?" And she simply nodded into his armpit and that was enough to make him happier than he had been for years.

The rain eventually eased off. They looked around. They were the only ones on the street, aside from two homeless people under an awning at the entrance of a tall building and a man smoking in a car with squeaky wipers. They returned to the subway and rode two more stations to Gabi's hotel. Showered and dried and got into one bed—Anna in the only clean pair of underpants and T-shirt left in Gabi's suitcase, tomorrow's clothes; Gabi in dirty ones, but dry at least, yesterday's—and fell asleep before even having a chance to think about what happens next, because they were so tired, so dizzy, too much had happened to the two of them in one night, all energy depleted.

But in the morning, as nature would have it, the energy was restored.

Anna left Luther, the German volunteer, after a few months in Sinai and a few more days on the kibbutz. Maybe she feared replicating the life of her mother, who married a volunteer who returned to his country of birth two days after Anna's fourth birthday. She continued to see her father every two years on vacations, and decided at eighteen to forgo the army and go stay with him for a year in Hartlepool, a small town in northeast of England. It was a nightmarish, freezing-cold year, in which she figured out the vast distance between genetics and environment. She learned most of all that love doesn't conquer all, and certainly when it cannot form a bridge between two such different worlds—that of a kibbutz girl born to two frightened Russian Jews who were thrown in their teens into a foreign and hot land and began growing tomatoes, and that of a roughneck from northeast England with parents who had never in their lives left the area and at the age of seventy still spent evenings at the pub drinking beer and talking about horses.

"Sex can bridge everything," Anna said, "and I'm the proof. But love? No way." Gabi thought about that magical night and continued to think about it often over the days to come and over the years come. What determines a good match, how can you tell? Does love win out? That night they both thought it did. Anna clearly spoke about her parents who were foreign to each other precisely because she and Gabi were the very opposite. They grew up in the same environment, were made of the same stuff, saw the world through the same prism. Anna spoke about her unfortunate parents as if to say to Gabi in nonexplicit terms: We're not like them.

The Analyst

Roni felt he already knew all he needed to know: about girls, about drinkers, about former fellow kibbutzniks, about the big city. And about business, or at least about running a business like that. The sour smell of beer, which he'd once inhaled with gusto, made him sick to the stomach after two years. Sometimes he'd observe the patrons and wonder, Why do people go to bars? What is it that they find in the mix of noise, alcohol, and strangers in a single room? The evenings on the deck with sweet smoke spiraling up into the sky as the sun sets into the sea—still pleasant, still "the good life," as everyone he invited there gushed—but no longer new. Fewer people were invited. The urge to impress lessened. A touch of distaste crept into his nights, and boredom, and the feeling that he was destined for bigger things. He continued his studies and was close to completing a second year, endeavoring to stimulate the soul and the mind, but the business was demanding, required that he keep working long hours to maintain their success: seven days a week, practically around the clock, seizing opportunities, big loans on improved terms, reinvesting revenue into the development of the business. And thus it grew and expanded—he opened a second Bar-BaraBush with Oren, this time as equal fifty-fifty partners, and then he sold a franchise for a third Bar-BaraBush. Roni had a successful chain of bars, but he wasn't content. He wanted out of the partnership with Oren Azulai, who turned out to be lazy and arrogant. He thought about opening new places, his alone. But the Tel Aviv night scene now appeared stifling and stained with the smell of dried beer. From his place behind the bar at Bar-BaraBush, he caught glimpses and heard mentions of more distant worlds, bigger opportunities. In time, his distaste was directed toward new challenges, processed and metabolized into a new type of drive.

Ariel was one of his bar's regular customers, one of the after-midnight people with whom Roni enjoyed talking. Ariel didn't hit on girls, earned a living from accounting, and spoke about business ventures that mostly sounded to Roni flighty and impractical: importing soup-vending machines from Japan, a factory for personal portable air conditioners, a bar-club that would be called Kindergarten After Hours and would function at night out of a real kindergarten, when it was closed. Roni listened, somewhat amused, semi-convinced that a good idea would emerge at some point.

One wintry evening Ariel showed up with a friend. It was a quiet evening at the bar and Roni wandered over to their corner. The friend had come to Israel from Boston for the Christmas holiday. He worked there for a strategic consulting firm. Roni didn't really understand what the friend did at his job, but after he left, Ariel quietly told him how much the friend had earned that year, and how much he'd earn next year, and Roni looked around at the bar and felt pathetic.

He would have forgotten about that episode had Ariel's friend from Boston not come in the following day in the company of someone else, someone whom Roni recognized immediately. It was Idan Lowenhof, who'd served ahead of him in the commando unit. They shook hands and smiled. He had studied business together with the other guy and was now living in New York and working as an investment manager for Goldman Sachs. "What about you?" he asked Roni and looked around. "Cool place. Yours?" Roni nodded, and felt just as pathetic as the evening before. He was again drawn to their corner of the bar, again failed to understand half of what was said, and this time, when Idan went to the bathroom, heard in a drunken whisper from his friend the size of the yearly bonus Idan had just received.

He was captivated not only by the sums but also by the sense that these guys were living real lives, not some phony bullshit. They were at the very heart of things, at the pinnacle of the world economy. Were involved in real matters, serious business, were responsible for portfolios worth billions, consultants to leading companies. Just as the two were leaving, Oren Azulai replaced them at the bar and began talking to some guy from the Haifa suburbs about opening a megaclub in a hangar at Tel Aviv Port. Azulai appeared so bloated with self-importance and so small.

Idan, the army commando–turned–Wall Street analyst, continued to show up at Bar-BaraBush every evening for a week. His mother lived around the corner, and after having dinner with her, he had to escape for a while. Sometimes he came with friends, sometimes he came in late, after a night elsewhere, but during the course of that week, he and Roni connected. He told Roni of the path he had followed, and Roni lapped up his words. Law school and a quick rise through the ranks at a large firm in Tel Aviv, a loan of tens of thousands of dollars, MIT's Sloan School of Management in Cambridge, an internship at Goldman Sachs while still at school, a job offer from the same firm after graduation, a gradual rise up the ladder and a move to New York. The work also sounded interesting, a competitive world filled with risks and opportunities. Endless hours of work, mountains of money. Idan used terms that were Greek to Roni—*private equity, hedge fund, margin call*—but he was mesmerized. And Idan said if Roni wanted, he'd help him.

"Your business experience is impressive," Idan said. "A chain of bars, new concept. We could piece it all together in an application just the way they like—an entrepreneur in the food and entertainment industry. Dressed up nice and pretty." He chuckled. "And we'll include the whole story of the kibbutz, the humble socialist background, they'll love it."

Roni smiled. "They'd probably like the fact that I'm an orphan, too, right? A real Cinderella story."

"You're an orphan?" Idan cried out. "You're kidding me! Awesome, you're in without doubt, we'll weave them a heart-wrenching personal story." Roni smiled, until Idan said, "But you have to finish your degree with good grades. What are you studying? Economics?" Roni nodded but felt as if the wind had been knocked from his sails. He was far from completing his degree, and not all of his grades were high. "Listen," insisted Idan, who saw the expression on Roni's face, "there aren't any shortcuts here. You need to put in the effort, work hard. But it will repay the investment, big-time. It's a different world. You'll love New York, it isn't Tel Aviv, it's the real deal. And half of our commando unit's already there."

Roni was busy behind the bar that night, caught up in that whirlwind of activity, but Idan's words echoed in his mind while he rushed back and forth to the kitchen and the bar and the tables and the customers. Idan arrived the following evening, as usual, and asked Roni if he'd already downloaded the application, if he wanted to go through it together. Roni said he hadn't had a chance yet. He didn't know if it really suited him. It would take him at least another year to complete the degree, and if he wanted good grades, he would have to devote more time to school. Then another two years of studies in New York, all in English, not to mention the fact that he didn't have money, and a loan of that size stressed him out.

"I haven't got it too bad," he said. "Why are people always hungry for more? I have a successful business, an income, a good life."

"Yes, people are apprehensive about the loan thing," Idan said. "It's a lot of money, but with hard work, you pay it back in five years at the most, and then you are left with a job on Wall Street. On top of the world." Idan flashed a white smile and said, "And you know, after having worked with the cattle and completed the commando training course and established this business, you can handle hard work with ease. I'm telling you, you can."

"And all that time? And the English?"

"Your English is just fine," Idan responded. "I heard you earlier with the tourists. And I'm not going to say anything about the time, because the time will go by whatever happens. But if you're content with your life, that's cool, forget it."

Roni didn't respond, he simply towel-dried a beer glass and stared at Idan, and did the math in his head and said to himself, God, it's been ages since I last spoke to Uncle Yaron. Just then a pretty customer signaled him, and he hurried over with a smile to serve her. Even Idan, who hardly knew him, noticed something amiss in the smile.

The Dinner

Meshulam was pleased with Gabi's success in New York. He'd received enthusiastic calls from Jennifer Shulman-Zimmerman and her father, and was happy about the additional donation of the forest. It was a promising start, he said to Gabi one evening as he grilled steaks on the small barbecue in the yard and sipped beer from a bottle. Gabi simply had to want it, and he'd be able to move up in the organization. "What's most important," the boss said as he flipped a bloody steak with a pair of tongs, the drops of blood and fat fueling the flames under the grate, "is that you're doing something for your country. Zionism, right?"

Gabi himself would admit perhaps, albeit only years later, that Meshulam's talk about a career, and certainly Zionism, must have struck a chord in his heart. But at that precise moment his heart was elsewhere, seized for Anna. The aura of the twenty-four hours they'd spent together enveloped him. They had soared together to unscaled heights and struggled to come back down to earth—and time froze there, from their perspective, and their thoughts fanned the fire like the fat that dripped onto the orange coals of Meshulam's barbecue grill. Gabi asked Meshulam if it would be okay for him to have a female friend come stay, and kept a close eye on the expression on his boss's face—surprise? disappointment? apprehension?—as he responded, "Certainly." Three weeks later, Gabi and Anna shared an excited embrace when she landed at the airport with a large backpack filled with everything she owned, everything she needed.

And Gabi, all he needed was her. The following months were a perfect honeymoon. Florida's pleasant weather, the freestanding house with the yard, the warm turquoise sea along which they walked hand in hand every evening, taking in movies at the cinema. Most of the time they made dinner together at home, then stretched out on the sofa to watch a video. Sometimes they borrowed Meshulam's car and drove around Florida: sea, alligators, sleepy Southern towns that appeared to have stepped out of old movies.

Anna worked as a waitress at one of the beach restaurants and sometimes went along with Gabi to his meetings with donors. Meshulam was happy to pass that sort of meeting on to Gabi after the success in New York, and Gabi was happy to get away from the routine of the office, which included endless phone calls to Jewish institutions and potential or existing donors, and arranging in-home meetings or similar events for

Meshulam. There was something refreshing about the one-on-ones with the donors, and Gabi discovered that he was fond of many of the old folks and enjoyed listening to their stories. Meshulam was all for the idea of Anna tagging along to the meetings, because he knew the old men loved the company of a young, pretty woman, a typical born-and-bred kibbutz girl (the volunteer father wasn't mentioned), and Anna and Gabi were pleased because they got to spend time together at dinners, some of them excellent, with wine flowing freely, for which they paid not a cent, and Gabi also received a salary. The old folks were for the most part likable and harmless gentlemen, happy to have the opportunity to spend an evening among youth. Only one tried to ask her out on a private second date, and even offered to transfer a portion of his inheritance into her name. Meshulam managed to find a dignified way out of the awkward situation.

One evening they had dinner with Samuel Lax, a Jew born into a wealthy family. His father had done very well for himself in the real-estate business in Chicago after World War II, and the son went on to diversify the business among several additional fields in which he did no less well for himself, like the manufacturing of paper products, primarily paper take-away cups—for a long time he was the leading producer of the cups in the United States, until people discovered China.

The main topic of conversation at these meetings was, naturally, the State of Israel: its future, its internal politics, foreign relations; the donors were ardent Zionists, and it was Gabi's job to fan those feelings. But Gabi enjoyed trying to identify the personality types hidden behind the Jewish-Israeli patriotism: the ones caught up in themselves and their successful business biographies, who spoke endlessly about money; the bitter ones who focused on family members who had annoyed or abandoned them; and the open ones, the ones who showed an interest, who knew a great deal, were full of fascinating stories about trips around the world and surprising encounters, and displayed a lot of curiosity. Lax was of the last type. He asked about their kibbutzim, their families, their childhoods, and told them about his visits to kibbutzim in the '60s—he even tried to establish a paper-cup manufacturing plant in the Galilee, but at that time, drinking coffee from a paper cup was unthinkable in Israel.

After inquiring about the background of the young couple, Lax asked about their plans. They looked at each other. They had discussed the future several times. Gabi was happy to stay here for a while. To save a little more, and at some stage down the line return perhaps to the kibbutz, or maybe to Tel Aviv, to join his brother, who knows. Anna said she was thinking of going to university, but she didn't know where or what she'd study. At Tel Aviv University, Lax said, there was a business school named after his father. His family donated a lot to the university, the next time they were over, they had to go see the sign on the building. After Lax said that, he looked at Anna with his kind eyes and said, "Why don't you go study there? I think it would suit you. I'm good at recognizing people with the right instincts, with intelligence, and with courage. And those are the three most important things in business, in the end, although there are those who are successful without them, too. I think we're lacking female entrepreneurs in Israel. I like to see girls at our school."

Anna's fork had just slipped a portion of creamed potatoes into her mouth, and she froze and stared at Samuel. She drew the fork out of her mouth, laid it gently and attentively on the table, fluttered her eyelids, and lowered her gaze to the plate. Lax and Gabi watched her all the while in silence. "I . . . I didn't think about . . . I mean, thanks . . . I . . ." She smiled. When her gaze found Gabi's eyes, in them she saw question marks and a tinge of sorrow.

When they returned home later in the night, with several glasses of wine throbbing in their heads, they made love, after which they lay there sleepily in each other's arms.

"Interesting, what he said," Anna said.

"About what? He said lots of interesting things," Gabi responded.

"About going to school. Business. I've never thought about taking that road, but some people are perceptive. Don't you think?"

"Maybe he's simply got his eye on you? Another dirty old man trying to make an impression with his money, buttering you up. He also looks relatively young for these old folks, no? His hair is black."

Anna laughed. "Fool. Didn't you get that he's gay?"

"Gay? How am I supposed to know?"

"It was obvious, by the way he looked at me. And at you. And the fact that he didn't mention family. And his hair was dyed, yes, he's better groomed than most of the old folks we meet."

"Are you sure?" Gabi asked.

"Pretty sure," she said. "But you didn't answer me. What do you think about me going to study business?"

Gabi caressed her flat stomach and thought for a few moments. He hadn't liked hearing Lax say those things to her. Now, though, with the possibility raised that courtship wasn't the millionaire's motive, how did he feel? He still wasn't enamored.

"Particularly because of that," Anna continued before he answered, "like he didn't have a vested interest in saying it, it's more flattering, right?"

"Yes, it sounds good," Gabi said. "If you think it suits you." And after staring at the ceiling for a few minutes, he asked, "So we're going back to Tel Aviv?"

"You want to?" she asked.

He wanted anything that included her in the plans, and said it. She turned toward him in the darkness and held his face between her small hands. "I love you so much, Gabi. I'm so lucky you fell into my lap." Her voice trembled a little. She kissed him on the lips, a brief kiss. "I fell into your lap? You're the one who fell into mine," he responded. "So lucky," she repeated, and now her voice squeaked, and the tears began to flow, and he sensed a huge wave was threatening to drown him, and he sniffed, too, and hugged her tight, and didn't say a word. He wondered sometimes what she found in him, what she loved about him. She could very easily attract the attention of many men, and did. The answer he gave himself was that they simply had good chemistry. They were happy together, and that was that, and there was no need to go searching for any other explanations. With her at his side, he felt complete.

The Return

Living in Tel Aviv is living among power lines and solar water-heating systems and peeling plaster and plentiful young people, trees and stores that are open sufficient hours of the day and night to allow you to feel that you're not at a way station to the real thing. Anna went every morning to university and returned in the evening. Gabi got up late, tidied the house, did the shopping, prepared lavish dinners, and thought about what he was going to do with himself. One of Roni's former classmates from the kibbutz had opened a flyer-distribution business, so three days a week Gabi shoved flyers into mail slots, or threw escort agency calling cards onto the windshields of cars, using a technique he believed he invented—ambling along the sidewalk alongside the parked cars and throwing the calling card, in an arc, so that it landed in the center of the windshield and slid down under the wiper. Before long he became an area manager—no longer did he shove flyers or throw calling cards himself, but instead handled five young guys who did it. The work brought in a bit of cash, and together with Sam Lax's support for Anna's studies and the remains of Uncle Yaron's savings plan, they lived comfortably.

Anna brought home the university catalog and they spent a few nights going over the list of courses, many of which appeared interesting: history, criminology, economics, film. But Gabi kept asking himself the same questions: Does it suit me? What would I do with a degree like that? Do we have enough money to be two full-time students? And mostly—is that what I really want to do with my life? The answer was always no.

Anna said he was making too big a deal of it. "You're not being asked to decide the rest of your life," she said. "You're going on a journey, and even if you study something for a few years and go nowhere with it afterward, what's the problem? Few people our age know what they're going to do with their lives, but most of them go to university because a degree is a degree, because studying is an enriching experience, because—"

"Because that's what everyone does and they have no idea what else they could do and their parents push them," Gabi said.

"No one pushed me," said Anna.

"You were lucky. You realized what it is you want. I don't know what I want."

He nevertheless registered as a criminology student, because it sounded exotic, and interesting, with potential employment opportunities in the future. But Tel Aviv University didn't offer an undergraduate degree in criminology, so he registered at the College of Management Academic Studies. He continued with the flyer work while he completed high-school courses for his matriculation certificate and took the university entrance exam, and began his first year as Anna started her second at business school. Because they were studying at different institutions, they saw less of each other than during the previous year, too rushed in the mornings, too on edge at night. On rare occasions Gabi managed to get to the university and meet Anna in the cafeteria.

Gabi's life, until then peaceful and laid-back—albeit filled with questions and fears concerning the future—now turned busy and stressful and cluttered, and still full of questions and fears. The quality of life dropped. The dinners were more simple, the home somewhat neglected. When he worked with the flyers, he felt guilty about not studying, and while he was studying, he stressed about not earning a decent living and not being able to focus on the reading or find it sufficiently interesting. The chapter in the catalog that outlined the criminology courses—social situations related to crime, detection, codes of ethics, conflict theories, analysis of topical crime incidents, tours of prisons and the courts—left him in no doubt that it was a fascinating field. But after getting down to the nitty-gritty, after spending long hours in the library reading endless sociology and anthropology and biology papers, all written in neoclassical, pompous, and boring academic language, he began asking himself what the hell was he doing and where his time was going.

And then Anna got pregnant. And all the stress until then—it was like someone twisted a knob and turned it up way higher.

They agreed to see the pregnancy through. Anna thought about her mother and her father, the volunteer who disappeared, but it wasn't the same thing. Gabi was her man. And Anna was his woman. They had been through enough to know that, insofar as someone can ever really know something like that. True, they were students who were scraping by, but Anna had always thought she wouldn't wait until she was much older to have a child. They didn't believe the home pregnancy test, were convinced they were the lone percent against the 99-percent accuracy rate the test boasted on the box. By the time they walked out from the first scan, which showed a minute beating heart, they were both spooked and excited, and in the middle of the street Gabi stopped and gripped Anna's shoulders, and she looked into his eyes, and they both smiled in amazement, as if to say "Wow!"

Gabi completed his first year and announced he wouldn't be returning for the second. Not now, anyway, maybe in the future. One of them had to bring in money. Anna didn't argue. It was clear to both of them that her degree was more important than his. That, unlike him, her goals were clearer—a degree, then integration into business. That she owed it not only to herself and the faculty but also to Samuel Lax. And in some way, they both felt, to the baby too, to the livelihood of the family.

The Wallet

Two days after landing in New York, Roni found a wallet in the snow. It was a fat, bloated wallet, a woman's wallet. It contained almost two thousand dollars in cash. For Roni it was simply the natural progression of his life: the world smiled at him. He recalled something Baruch Shani once said to him at basketball many years back: Fortune favors the good. A few minutes earlier he'd seen an apartment on the Upper West Side that appealed to him, but it was a little expensive and he left without deciding. After finding the wallet, he returned and signed the lease. He felt worthy of the apartment and it of him. And just like success came easily to him on the basketball court, with the cattle, in the commando unit, in the bar business, and eventually with his undergraduate degree—there was no reason why it shouldn't continue to come easily in New York as well, and as proof of that—a nice fat wallet in the snow two days after landing. When he fished through it, he found a driver's license bearing the pleasant face of a black woman. Her date of birth was close to that of his brother's, he noticed. Thoughts of his brother seeped into his mind, but he chose to focus on the wallet. He wondered about returning it without the money, so the sweet-looking black woman would at least get back her license, credit cards, various club cards, and the rest of the junk that filled the wallet. He found her address and decided he would mail her the cards. His kindheartedness pleased him. Yes, fortune favors the good.

The MBA was harder and more competitive. He got used to listening to the lectures in English pretty quickly, but in the first months he struggled for hours on end with the mountains of reading assignments. On the other hand, he didn't have to work at the same time, like he did in Tel Aviv. He had money, thanks to the loan he was automatically eligible for as an MBA student. He was shocked by how simple it was to take the letter from the university to a branch of Citibank and immediately open an account containing $120,000.

His last year in Tel Aviv had started out nightmarishly: university in the morning, Bar-BaraBush at night, tons of material to study and absorb for his research seminar paper, Oren Azulai, who showed no consideration for his partner's time constraints—he simply couldn't understand why Roni bothered with university—until, in the middle of the year, with New York appearing sufficiently close and alluring, with the smell of stale beer coming out of his every orifice by then, he sold his share in Bar-BaraBush and dove headfirst into completing his degree and applying to an MBA program in New York.

In Tel Aviv he'd met other Israelis who were going to business school in New York on the way to a career on Wall Street, and with most he didn't connect. Spoiled rich kids whose paths were padded by their parents' money, who didn't know what hard work was, who gave off an air of arrogance that rested on sharp intelligence, an indulgent mother, and an easy life. Two of them, Meir Foriner from Savyon and Tal Paritzky from Kfar Shmaryahu, were accepted along with Roni to the same university in New York. But in his cluster, in class, he befriended other foreign

students—a Japanese, an Italian, and Sasha the Bosnian in particular—
and observed the efforts of Meir and Tal to ingratiate themselves with
the American WASPs. Roni understood them, he wasn't there to seclude
himself among foreigners, either, and realized that to fit in, he had to
make connections and do some aggressive networking—the word that
everyone mumbled dozens of times a day—the spinning of a spiderweb
of contacts, primarily with Americans. But when he saw Meir and Tal
partying and playing drinking games like beer pong, just like the Americans, talking music and football just like the Americans, copying them
in dress and gestures and accent, he felt uncomfortable and returned to
the warm embrace of his foreign gang.

Idan Lowenhof guided his progress and served as his mentor. Together
they had put together the perfect admissions essay, spinning a narrative
about his groundbreaking business initiative, which changed Tel Aviv
nightlife and created the first chain of gastro-bars in the country; the
success story that began in tragedy—the path of the boy who lost his
parents in a horrific car accident, from a simple life on the kibbutz to the
commercial success story, on his own steam, with hard work and per-
sistence. Idan continued to help Roni in New York: advised him on what
courses to choose based on the topics and the lecturers, led him through
the degree's maze of politics, and hooked him up with several graduates
and professors. Most important—he showed him the ropes when the
cocktail season started during that first autumn.

The cocktails: dozens of financial firms hunted talent from the ranks
of the leading business schools. Already within the first weeks of the first
year, the companies staged cocktail receptions on school premises, and
sometimes at bars around the city—up to three different cocktail receptions in an evening—and invited students to watch presentations about
the firms, drink alcohol, and try to convince their representatives that
they were the right fit for them. After the cocktail receptions, the students sent the representatives ingratiating e-mails, in the wake of which
came one-on-one meetings, after which the candidates received invita-
tions to formal interviews. At the end of the process came an offer of a
summer internship in the break between the first and second year, and
the internship generally led to a full-time job following graduation.

Roni didn't like it, but Idan insisted he play the game and coached him ahead of the meetings and interviews. Roni embarrassed himself at the initial receptions. When the small talk turned to sport, he didn't have a clue about the rules and names of baseball players. He tried to steer the conversation toward basketball, but didn't do too well with that, either. He mentioned Nadav "The Dove" Henefeld and Doron Sheffer "The Iceman," names of the most successful Israeli players in the NCAA, who Roni was sure were well known in America because that was what the Israeli newspapers claimed, but no one knew what he was talking about.

Roni worked to improve his conversation skills, and at the same time pressed Idan Lowenhof to set him up with a personal interview at Goldman Sachs. Idan promised he was working on it, but the development came unexpectedly from elsewhere. He received an e-mail one day from Dalit Nahari. Dalit was in the same year as Gabi at school, four years younger than Roni. She was a friend of Anna, Gabi's partner, and Anna had told her that Roni was in New York. Dalit had been living in the New York area for many years, ever since the post-army trip with Anna. She invited Roni to dinner. Anna had told him in an e-mail that Dalit was married with three children, so Roni wrangled his way out of it. He saw no reason to go all the way to Plainsboro, New Jersey, to devote a precious evening to Dalit and her family at the expense of his studies. But she insisted until he consented. He recalled her as a small and pretty Yemenite girl, and in a moment of loneliness he imagined that she was bored, that her husband was away on a business trip or something, and that she was looking for an adventure with no strings attached.

The door was opened by her husband, a round-faced Indian man, potbellied and thick-lipped, with jet-black hair parted at the side. The fantasy crashed in on itself, and went on crashing when from behind his broad back appeared Dalit—small and pretty she was no more. As he walked into the huge home, he began formulating excuses to leave early. He never would have imagined that he'd be leaving the apartment after two in the morning, coming away with the most effective piece of networking he ever could have achieved.

Jujhar Rawandeep, Dalit's husband, was a Punjabi. He was also a Muslim. And a senior executive at a hedge fund that belonged to a small investment bank, Goldstein-Lieberman-Weiss Investments. Juj, as his wife affectionately addressed him, admired kibbutzniks, particularly kibbutzniks from the Galilee, and soon became an admirer of the Galilee kibbutznik whom Dalit recalled as a talented basketball player and brave soldier, and who offered a wealth of amusing stories about childhood on a kibbutz and the nightlife in Tel Aviv. Jujhar promised at the end of the evening to look into job placements at the investment bank, and the following day Roni received an e-mail invitation to a Goldstein-Lieberman-Weiss Investments recruitment cocktail reception.

One of the bank's headhunters at the cocktail reception was Alon Pilpeli, a hook-nosed and green-eyed Israeli. Biting down on small shrimp sandwiches and sipping cava at a trendy bar downtown, he and Roni Kupper got on, as the Americans say, like long-lost friends: Roni could tell that Pilpeli was less staid, was wilder and more of a go-getter than people like Idan Lowenhof, and Pilpeli was enamored of Roni, because, so he claimed, he chilled at Bar-BaraBush whenever he visited the Holy Land. The formal process of submitting an online application was completed a week later and then came personal interviews that the well-prepared Roni passed with flying colors. Shortly afterward Roni was offered a summer internship.

The Ages

Mickey arrived on a cold and clear day, sounded a brief wail of shock, and went quiet. While a nurse helped his mother wash herself in the adjacent shower, Gabi held him on his knees, bundled up in a sheet, looked at his tiny, moist chin, and said, "You're twelve minutes old," and then "You're nineteen minutes old," and then "Twenty-three minutes." Those were the first things he told his son, because he didn't know what else to say.

Gabi was Mickey's nanny. He very quickly found his footing. He continued to tell his son his age, it became a habit. He'd say, "Mickey, today you're three months and two days old, and we're going to the park." Anna took a short maternity leave, and when she first returned to school she kept shorter days, especially when she was still breast-feeding, but she slowly began spending long hours on campus again, like before the birth. Gabi and Mickey continued to count the days and learn how to move arms and smile and roll over and crawl and sprout teeth and swing on swings and go for walks in the park and hear remarks about the Norwegian or Swedish or Finnish kid, which to begin with annoyed Gabi a little but slowly turned into a source of pride for him—as if the compliments about the beauty and distinctiveness of the baby mirrored a compliment about his own beauty and distinctiveness; as if the attention were intended for him, and the jokes ("Specially imported?" "Where can I buy one like that?" "Diplomat parents?") were designed to impress and amuse him, and not the ones who made them. They shopped at the minimarket and greengrocer on the way home for the afternoon sleep, and while Mickey napped his two hours, Gabi prepared dinner like in the good old days before his studies.

He didn't have any free time, but he did have time to think. Was he missing the criminology degree? A little, but it certainly wasn't a burning passion. He planned to read the material from the first year that he hadn't gotten to, but the heap of papers didn't budge from the bedside table during the first year of his son's life. What he did read, while paging through a magazine one day in a pediatrician's waiting room, was an article about Apple CEO Steve Jobs, who recounted that he went to university because it was expected of him, and decided after a year to leave because he didn't know what he wanted to do with his life and couldn't understand how studying would help him find the answer. In retrospect, Jobs said in the article, it was the smartest decision of his life. Gabi liked the article—Jobs even grew up with adoptive parents.

Anna would get back late—sometimes after Mickey's dinner and bath and sometimes after he had fallen asleep. It seemed a little strange to Gabi, but when he tried to raise the subject, Anna called the line of questioning chauvinistic, because when fathers work hard and get home late and don't see their children, no one says a word, but when a woman does it, then there's something wrong with her.

"I didn't say there's something wrong with you," Gabi parried. "A father who doesn't see his children is also something strange to me." But she was angry. He understood that the demands and responsibilities of motherhood were hard on her. She asked for a little more freedom for herself, and he accepted it and gave it to her.

He said to Mickey, "You're five months, two weeks, and three days old," and took him for a long walk by the sea. He offered to dress him in long-sleeved shirts in the fall and winter, but Mickey insisted on short sleeves all year round, and because he never got the flu and the confrontations were exhausting, Gabi gave in. He said, "You're six months and six days old," and took Mickey on a rare visit to Uncle Roni, who was always busy and under pressure. "It's your eight-month birthday, mazel tov," on the way to an activity class for babies that accomplished nothing other than to pass time for the mothers—they were all mothers aside from him.

"Today you're ten months and one week and one day old," he said the day he found out that Anna had been lying to him. He was out walking with Mickey at Tel Aviv Port and a pretty young girl smiled at Mickey and made faces at him. It was nothing out of the ordinary, of course, Mickey attracted a lot of attention from strangers and loved it; Gabi frequently brought the stroller to a halt and allowed his son to babble with the nameless female admirer.

But this girl, after the obligatory coochie-coo, said, "Just a sec, is this Mickey?" She studied together with Anna. She recognized Mickey from a photograph Anna had shown her. She continued tickling and caressing and making sounds and eventually looked up and asked, "Where's Anna?"

"Anna?" Gabi questioned, like it was the first time in his life he had heard the name.

"I mean, what's she doing on the day off?" Anna hadn't said anything about a day off school. Gabi shrugged disconcertedly. "Ah, hang on," the girl continued, "didn't she go with Sami to Afula?" Sami? Afula? Gabi was about to open his mouth to respond, but Mickey shrieked in order to recapture her attention, and got it. And then her phone rang and the father and son continued their walk, and she waved good-bye while talking to some "darling." Gabi didn't get her name.

When Anna returned late that evening, Gabi didn't ask, and she didn't say a thing. Years later he'd think, if he had asked, perhaps she would have explained. But that evening he looked at her as she slept and felt something unfamiliar, a new wind blowing. What do we say to ourselves and to the world? he thought. We think that love is good and life is good and all that, and still. He didn't confront Anna. Didn't investigate and didn't probe and didn't question. Didn't check her cell phone while she was sleeping. Didn't look through her notebooks for inadvertent doodling, telephone numbers, or reminders. He didn't want to hear about the anguish and the excuses, didn't want to play along with self-pity and give her a chance to blame him or to make him responsible for her actions, for denying her the warmth and passion that she went elsewhere to find. Perhaps he feared that if he allowed her to explain, he'd understand. And he didn't want to understand. So he told himself again that Anna was asking for time for herself, more freedom.

He took Mickey in the stroller to the swings and merry-go-round in the park and told him he was ten months and two and a half weeks old. Drove him to a swimming lesson for toddlers at the age of eleven months and nine days, and dressed Mickey after the pool in his short clothing despite its being the rainiest day of the year. As usual, the boy didn't catch a cold, but was suffering during that period with pain caused him by his sprouting teeth. When he cried, Gabi would lay him down on his chest and gently stroke his yellowish, soft hair, until he dropped off and slept like an angel.

On his first birthday, Mickey suddenly waved his arms like a butterfly: rapid movements, for several seconds. Anna looked at Gabi with a smile and shook her head in wonder. Her eyes shone with pride. The boy uttered a syllable and started walking. The first step merged into a fall, which merged into a wail and brief sob, and a gleeful crawl until his father picked him up and sat him on his knees, and everyone burst loudly into a melody of Israeli birthday songs for children and a Hebrew rendition of "Happy Birthday to You" to the traditional English tune. And then the boy got to taste chocolate cake for the first time in his life, and loved it with passion.

They were at Anna's kibbutz, at the grandmother's (the English grandfather sent a greeting card, had yet to see his grandchild). The step-grandfather, Yossi, who now had a girlfriend, came from the kibbutz, and Uncle Yaron, the brother of Asher, Mickey's long-since-dead grandfather, was there, too, was very excited by the antics of the blond toddler. Uncle Roni didn't come.

Where Mickey got the blond from, no one could say. The grand-mother thought it came from the English volunteer, she was certain he once told her he had Nordic roots, although he himself was ordinarily pink-cheeked and brown-haired—the entire area of northeast England was once a colony of Norwegians and Swedes who set sail westward in their Viking boats until they struck land. That's why the northeastern accent, the most difficult to understand in the English language, aside perhaps from certain variants of its Scottish neighbor, sounds similar in tone and emphasis to Nordic languages. There've been studies about it, you can check, the grandmother said, and Gabi made a note to himself to look it up on the Internet. The blond, whatever the case may have been, remained, and only Mickey's eyes were, without doubt, the almond-brown eyes of his father.

After the sugar high sparked the energy level of a Duracell bunny in the birthday boy, he crashed into a deep sleep on the hammock in the yard, brown crumbs and fresh drool encircling his mouth. The adults rounded things off with coffee and adult talk. Neighbors and childhood friends came over to wish Anna well and marvel at her son and her stories about the business management studies. Gabi sat mostly with Yossi and his new partner and Uncle Yaron. He thought about the possibility of making a quick visit to his kibbutz, but couldn't think of a good reason. He was pleased, however, that Uncle Yaron invited them to spend a day at the far edge of the Golan Heights.

Mickey was happy at Uncle Yaron's kibbutz, and when a one-year-old is happy, babbling syllables, crawling all over, trying to put excited wob-bly steps together, his parents cannot help but smile. Anna agreed that the place was stunningly beautiful, that the cool wind and basalt land-scape offered the pleasant sense of being in another country. They had planned to return home in the afternoon to beat the Saturday-evening traffic, but Mickey was having so much fun, and they felt so at ease, that

322 • ASSAF GAVRON

after lunch all three fell asleep on the large bed in the guest room, and decided when they woke to take advantage of the daylight hours and head home after darkness fell. The birthday boy would sleep on the way south well fed, bathed, and exhausted after two action-packed and exciting days.

When Uncle Yaron bade them farewell on the road outside his house, the tears fogged the lenses of his thick glasses. "Almost thirty years," he sobbed, "but I remember it just like it was the day before yesterday. You were right there." He pointed toward the car seat in which the little blondie nestled. "There weren't car seats, but you were sleeping, too, worn out from all the wild running around on the kibbutz. You were exactly a year old. And next to you, your brother the troublemaker, tired but fighting off sleep to show he's a big boy. And in the front, Dad and Mom . . ." Gabi rested a hand on Uncle Yaron's shoulder, and afterward Anna hugged him and told him how much she'd enjoyed herself, how much everyone had enjoyed themselves, and he hugged her back and continued to cry.

"Drive carefully, slowly-slowly," Uncle Yaron said when they were sitting in the car, and Gabi replied, "For sure. We'll watch out for stray cows. Worse comes to worst, you'll know by now what to do with Mickey, you've been drilled."

"Don't you dare," the uncle responded, and patted the roof of the car as if it were a shoulder, to send it on its way. A lone IDF flare some forty minutes into the drive made their hearts skip a beat and raised goose bumps on their skin, but they reached their rented apartment in Tel Aviv safe and sound.

It ebbed and flowed like the tide, he noticed, like spring and fall. There were times he felt that Anna had time for him again. Returned earlier. A sense of warmth emanated from her then, and he felt close, too: when he heard her laughing at something on the television from the other room, saw her piecing together a puzzle with Mickey with a degree of patience he himself didn't have, stole a glance at her with her nightgown above her head, on its way to draping over her white skin.

He continued to tell Mickey his age, and Mickey continued to grow: a year and one month; and three months and two days; and seven months and nineteen days. He grew and walked and talked and demanded, and Gabi was at his side all the time, and Anna was at the university, close to finishing her degree, looking into options, seminars, job fairs, a year and nine months and three days. Fall winds, and again Anna disappeared, and again she blamed the studies, and again turned her back, and again from within his sleep Gabi heard the door opening and closing gingerly and the water in the shower turned on and off discreetly, and he glanced at the clock and continued sleeping, and woke with the rustling of the comforter, conscious enough to notice that he didn't get a kiss or caress or embrace, and he didn't ask her in the morning, but she summed up the evening in two sentences and specified a return time different from the one he saw on the clock.

They thought about putting Mickey in day care. The long hours with him were no longer smooth sailing for Gabi. The sweet and ever-smiling baby had turned more demanding, more frustrated, sometimes on edge. Gabi lost it sometimes, too, in return, and with time Mickey learned exactly which buttons to push to anger his father. Gabi wondered about what would become of him, and about what he was giving up by devoting most of his time to the child. He knew at some point he'd have to decide what he wanted to be when he grew up. On the other hand, Mickey gave him an excellent excuse to delay his decision. He couldn't honestly think of a better way to spend his time. And he loved his boy, enjoyed most moments in his company.

The problem was, they couldn't afford to live without salaries. Anna wasn't going to land a job immediately, it would take her some time to find the right fit. During the adjustment period, would she be able to spend more time with Mickey? Gabi asked. She appeared to recoil at the thought. Gabi got angry, felt used. It was decided: day care.

Gabi dropped Mickey off every morning and missed him from the moment he closed the day care's gate and went to work. The friend from the flyers business welcomed him back gladly and gave him an office job in sales and marketing, with short hours and modest pay. Mickey adjusted. Anna attended lectures and conferences and supplementary courses and job interviews. On one occasion, when she told him about an offer from a factory in Afula, his ears pricked up.

"A factory for toasting sunflower seeds?" he asked, referencing the snack the town was famous for producing.

"No, funny guy," she answered. It was a municipal garbage recycling plant, one of the most sophisticated in the world. They had an opening in the business development department, and they liked her CV and had invited her to come in for an interview and get a feel of the place. She'd probably have to spend a night there at a hotel at their expense.

"Afula has hotels?" he asked. She laughed again. "And if you get it, will you travel to Afula every day?"

She turned serious. "We'll see," she said. "Maybe we'll move to one of the kibbutzim in the area? There are wonderful kibbutzim in the Yizrael Valley. We've always said we'd like to give Mickey the kind of childhood we had, instead of the soot and the buses and the closely packed apartment buildings and the parks full of dog shit." We said that? Gabi tried to recall, but couldn't place the conversation. He didn't "want to give" and didn't wish a childhood like he'd had on anyone, certainly not his beloved son. And what she said about Tel Aviv, maybe there was something to it, but he was pretty surprised by the contempt Anna suddenly expressed toward the city in which they had lived for three years, felt a little offended on its behalf. When he tried to play things back, he remembered her speaking differently. Once upon a time they'd enjoyed going to the beach, the long evening walks along the boulevard on the way back, stopping on occasion at a café. Until Mickey was born.

Ebb and flow, spring and fall. She returned from Afula enthusiastic. That weekend he noticed that she held his hand when they walked along the boulevard, smiled at him and kissed him on the cheek every now and then for no reason. She felt good, was excited about the new job. It wasn't a long-term thing, she said, she'd like to start a small business of her own one day, but it was an excellent starting point: a sophisticated and innovative plant, a product that benefitted the environment and nature, nice people she clicked with from the first moment. Gabi began to imagine life in the valley, despite his aversion to the kibbutz idea. But perhaps he'd be able to continue his studies remotely. Perhaps he'd be able to get involved in an interesting kibbutz industry. Mickey would love it. And then Anna said that if he wanted to remain in Tel Aviv, she could maybe find a room at one of the kibbutzim, stay in the north a few days a week, and return to Tel Aviv for long weekends. The idea blinded him for a moment, he couldn't see a thing around him. It sounded to him like a suggestion—albeit delicate, veiled—to separate. Not only from him but, like her father thirty years earlier, from her only child, too. The ebb and flow of the tide are intrinsically linked. He looked at her with moist eyes and she smiled and said, "Don't panic, it's merely a suggestion. In the event you want to stay in Tel Aviv."

"You're two years and eight months and three days old," he said to Mickey on the way to day care. And Mickey said, "Yes, Daddy?" and Gabi said, "Yes, Mickey."

Anna worked in Afula. She was given a company car and drove there and back three days a week, and on the fourth day spent the night in a guest room at one of the kibbutzim in the area. She was content, and Gabi discovered that all was not doom and gloom. He took Mickey to day care in the morning, collected him in the afternoon, and in the interim sat in the office and missed him and tried to interest potential customers in advertising on flyers that were distributed in mailboxes and under the windshield wipers of cars.

"You're two years and eleven and a half months old." Two weeks later the three of them took time off and spent a day of fun at the beach and the café. Ate schnitzels and fries, and brown ice cream just like Mickey loved. And played on the playground. The experiences of that day were etched in Gabi's memory: The sweaty, happy expressions on Mickey's face. The sand that stuck to his forehead. The mouth adorned with a dry brown crust. And the annoying kid who tried to snatch the wolf doll Mickey brought along on the walk, an older kid, curly-haired, bored, and cheeky.

What are you doing here, you annoying little boy? Where's your father where's your mother where are your friends? Why do you insist on running to every ride and every game that Mickey wants to play with, pushing in front of him, stamping your feet? How dare you lay your filthy hands on Peter, my boy's wolf? Why do you insist on making my blood boil? My blood's boiling, the air's streaming from my nostrils, my child wants to climb this ladder, so I stand next to the ladder and physically block the annoying kid, once, twice,

and a third time, when he tries to push forcefully with his small body and
again touches Peter, I give him a little one with the tip of my shoe in the
kneecap, pinching and fiercely twisting his ear at the same time, and hear
the shocked, the pained cry, and clench my teeth in response to the angry look
directed upward at me at foreseeable speed, in terror, to the accompaniment
of undulating howls, and say to him, "Don't mess with me," and look around
discreetly to ensure that no one saw.

When Gabi and Mickey returned from a turn on the slide to the bench
where Anna was sitting and speaking on the phone, she looked up and
asked, "What happened there?" Gabi simply mumbled, "Nothing," but
was surprised by the short-circuit in his brain.

In time, Gabi stopped telling Mickey his age almost entirely. The relationship between the father and the son cooled. Anna added another
night in Afula and now slept there two nights a week, said she was under
a lot of pressure at work, but she told him practically nothing about the
work. He sensed that on weekends she simply waited for the time to pass
and for Sunday to come around, and she'd go back to her Afula, with
her Sami or whoever she had there. There was someone there, of that he
was sure. He persisted nevertheless in not investigating, not prying, not
asking. He simply knew. And Mickey perhaps recognized the weakness
in his father, and sank his teeth into it—don't wanna dress, don't wanna
go to day care, don't wanna eat, don't wanna wash hands after pee-pee.
Gabi's patience wore progressively thinner, his frustration increased. No
longer could he boast of quality time with the boy, because there was no
quality to the time with him. No longer could he offer an excuse for the
absolute sacrifice of his advancement, of whatever kind—a career, studies, self-fulfillment. He was chained to the little shit, lived for him, while
she managed to live for herself. When Mickey began resisting Gabi's
cajoling with his silences, his improving intellect, his increased physical strength, too, Gabi responded in kind. A shove was rewarded with a
shove back. A kick was rewarded with a counterkick. The rationale was—
this way Mickey would learn that violence is not an effective means of
achieving goals, and also, that his father would not allow him to twist
him around his little finger. Gabi was swept into a dangerous cycle.

The Ladder

R oni sometimes saw the Moishe's trucks driving around Manhattan, the Israeli salesgirls in the shoe stores, his basketball teammates from the Sunday pickup games, and snorted to himself with an air of self-satisfaction. He looked at all those Israelis, who came to get into America through the back door, to crawl slowly upward from the lowest rung of the ladder, and felt pride. He'd entered through the front door. He'd gone straight to the top. And he didn't even have to take the money from his own pocket to get there—the bank financed it, and the bank would get the money back within . . . ? five years, Idan Lowenhof said? So Roni decided—four years at the most.

He allowed himself to take his foot off the gas a little in his second year of studies. The summer internship at the Goldstein-Lieberman-Weiss boutique investment bank was a success, insofar as "a success" was the correct epithet for two months in which he wrote up the minutes of meetings, prepared Excel tables and PowerPoint presentations for analysts and managers, collected suits from the dry cleaners, and made a particularly good impression with his extraordinary ability to repair printers that malfunctioned. One way or another, his people inside the company, Alon Pilpeli and Jujhar Rawandeep, with whom he made a concerted effort to nurture a relationship, promised him that a formal job offer for the following August would soon land on his desk.

An offer was indeed extended, and a contract was signed, and the first $45,000 was transferred into his account, a signing bonus, and close to $3,000 of it was promptly spent on a shopping spree at Hugo Boss and Brooks Brothers and Barneys, during which the tune of the "Who Knows One?" Passover song played over and over in Roni's head: Ten are the socks, eight are the shirts, five are the ties, four are the pants, three are the shoes, two are the suits, one is the belt, the belt, the belt, the belt, the belt, in heaven . . . although he did in fact buy two belts.

So, by the start of year two he was already guaranteed a job, like most of his fellow students—2005 was a good year for job seekers on the pendulum of crisis and growth of the financial world since the '90s—but Roni continued to attend lectures, especially the math ones, which delved into the obscure particulars of bond derivatives, for example, where he sat next to quiet geeky Asians, because he had the chance to learn from the finest lecturers, to get tips for a rookie financier who was just starting out in a very competitive and sometimes cruel world. From time to time he was invited to dinners with the Goldstein-Lieberman-Weiss team, and even received handsome gifts from the company for his birthday and for Christmas.

One summery Monday, neatly wrapped in a light, casual Hugo Boss suit, Roni spilled out of the 3 train onto the platform of the Chambers Street subway station in lower Manhattan, and from the station onto the street. He stopped for a moment among the chaos, flexed his broad chest, and held his head up high. He inhaled the salty air from the Hudson River into his nostrils, and started walking, initially west along Chambers Street, and then south down West Street, passing by the Battery Park sporting facilities, until he reached a tall office building. He stopped again for a moment to survey the entrance and then looked up—somewhere there, on the thirty-first floor, lay the offices of Goldstein-Lieberman-Weiss Investments. He stopped because he knew that from then on he wouldn't notice those details, would simply walk in for another day at work. Look where Roni Kupper is now, he thought, and look where Oren Azulai and the rest of the small fries are. He spat on the sidewalk, and then walked into the building.

Roni crowded into the 3 train every day in the company of hundreds and thousands of suited-and-tied financiers just like him, who, from a few blocks in lower Manhattan, managed global deals worth billions of dollars. While he continued to prepare Excels and PowerPoints and write up the minutes of rather dull meetings, he didn't really feel a part of that nerve center, but Alon and Juj and others said that in a small and diverse institution such as theirs, the opportunity would come quickly. So he waited, continued to weave more strands into the expanding network, kept his eyes open, efficiently carried out whatever was asked of him, and tried to be charming.

At the start of 2006 the opportunity arose. Two traders—stockbrokers—retired from the hedge fund's trading desk, and one day when Roni walked into the office of one of the senior partners, Eliot Lieberman, to deliver a pitch book he had requested—a presentation on a potential client—he said to Lieberman at the end of the meeting, "Let me sit on the desk. You won't regret it."

Lieberman stared at him with watery blue eyes and remained silent for a moment. And then he asked, "Do you have experience in sales and trading?"

"No," Roni responded, "but I have common sense and the ability to focus. I'm an Israeli, I have a tough mentality and know how to make quick and sharp decisions." He smiled and added, "I've read many books about trading." He didn't add that he had also learned a lot from the characters of Gordon Gekko in the movie *Wall Street* and Jack Bauer in the TV series *24*.

Lieberman asked his secretary to summon Jujhar Rawandeep, and in the meantime asked Roni, "Are you aware of the implications? You won't get much sleep, you'll wake up in the small hours of the morning with the markets in Asia, spend the morning with the ones in Europe, and then you'll start working. You won't go to the toilet during trading hours between nine-thirty and four, and then you'll meet with teams to analyze the day gone by and prepare for the one to come. In the evenings you'll go out with fellow workers from the desk and meet colleagues and drink a lot and go to sleep late and get up at five for a new day with Asia. Relationships, family, a life—you'll have none of those, only colleagues who aren't friends but predators, and you'll love and hate every minute with them and you'll feel constantly sick to the stomach from shitty nutrition."

Roni had heard about Eliot Lieberman's elliptical speeches. He looked him straight in the eye throughout his address, and didn't lower his gaze when he responded, "I'm aware of the implications, sir, and they don't deter me. To the contrary." Jujhar had entered in the meantime and Roni spoke of his passion for the stock market, told of an account he had managed for himself that produced handsome yields. He spoke about the stock of an Israeli company, not very well known, and analyzed its performance. Jujhar smiled with satisfaction. And then Roni repeated what he said at the start: "Give me a chance, you won't regret it." Jujhar and Lieberman looked at each other, and Jujhar said, "Dale Savage needs a trader."

So Roni Kupper worked at an investment bank on Wall Street—a rung on the ladder. And soon achieved the position of trader—another rung. He knew by then that every rung of the ladder would appease him only for a time, until he would cast his eyes upward to the next one. That's human nature, he thought.

The first decade of the century began with a crisis, then came a recovery. America went to war, the Dow Jones index reacted positively, the mood was good—the world was a playground filled with opportunities. Roni learned quickly. His seven computer screens—two for the stock prices, two for making deals, one for the Bloomberg channel, one for e-mails from brokers and the team, one for chatting—were burned into his retinas, the columns of financial commentators passed under his scrutiny, he sat in meetings with partners and analysts and traders and clients. Spoke with brokers, studied products, and compiled tables and presentations about them, deepened his understanding of the various aspects of the market, and in particular honed his expertise in the field of technology stocks.

The Israeli social club, or as Idan referred to it, "the Thursday Hummus Forum," was Roni's most important networking arena. There he not only met dozens of other Israelis who were scattered among key positions in the New York finance and corporate world, expanding the web exponentially, but also participated, when he had the time, in seminars the forum organized for its members: methods of establishing connections ("How to Be a Networking Ninja"), better dress sense (at Barneys' menswear department), and a workshop on "Accent and Refinement," to smooth over the Israeli coarseness of speech and style. It was a diamond-polishing plant, which Israelis on Wall Street went through and emerged from a little less Israeli and a little more American, on the exterior, at least.

Despite his aversion to some of the Israelis in New York, Roni enjoyed

Thursday nights at the forum, and understood, too, that it was an inexhaustible source for connections and work. There he took off the jacket, loosened the knot in the tie, opened two buttons in the shirt, ate hummus and drank Goldstar beer that someone took the trouble to supply, and spoke in his mother tongue. Got a good dose of home, which was actually better than home itself—he realized that on a visit to Israel over Christmas, while he wandered the streets of Tel Aviv and didn't know what to do with the direct and pure dose of Israeliness that struck him. He was there for a week and did nothing aside from soaking up the sun's winter rays during the day, and going to Bar-BaraBush in the evening, as just another customer.

One evening he bumped into his friend Ariel. He looked the same, slightly balder, perhaps. Still an accountant, but had married in the interim.

"What about the soup-vending machines from Japan?" Roni asked.

"Ah," Ariel responded, and waved his hand. "I'm working now on something new. A mousetrap that doesn't poison and doesn't kill. A humane solution, clean, effective. Look"—he retrieved some papers from a case—"it's a tube of sorts, which opens here . . ." As he explained, Roni looked at him without hiding his sense of amusement. People don't change, he thought, they carry on doing the same things over and over again. He was thinking the very same thing a few hours earlier, during his visit to Gabi. All that his brother had been through in the past years was pretty surprising, after all, when you thought about it. All the yuppie trappings—university, a wedding, a kid, an apartment in the Old North of Tel Aviv—who'd have believed it of his little brother? And then, just as you had grown accustomed to the new Gabi, more upheavals and dramatic changes. And still, with all those changes, Roni asked himself over another beer alone at the bar, after Ariel had gone on his way with his revolutionary mousetrap, had his brother really changed? Is the Gabi of today different from Gabi his little brother, the somewhat detached, somewhat impressionable, somewhat searching Gabi? The detachers, the impression-makers, and the search objectives change, the set changes, like in that English learning show on educational TV when they were children, with Sheriff Goodman, who would drink a glass of milk while the stagehands changed the backdrop—but was he a different person on the inside?

It was late at Bar-BaraBush. Roni looked around. Everyone here, he felt—at this bar, in this city, in this country—is pathetic, is swimming in the shallow waters of provincialism, doesn't realize what world is out there. He diverted his attention to a girl left alone at the bar.

"What do you say, Ravit," he said—he'd caught her name earlier, when she said good-bye to a friend—"can people change, or do they always remain the same?" And when she merely looked at him and didn't respond, he added, "In your opinion?"

The Bus

I n the end, only a few persistent memories remain. They manage to achieve prominence and survive from among the infinite medley of life, from among the hundreds of daily events, the vast majority of which sink and remain forever in the depths.

One memory: Gabi, Anna, and Mickey, surely just a few months old because he's lying in a baby carriage, and it's winter, they're out walking. Gabi and Anna are arguing. She's wrapped the boy in layers and all-in-ones and blankets, and Gabi thinks he's probably too warm—it was before Mickey put his foot down and stubbornly refused to wear warm clothing at any time of the year—because it's not that cold, the rain's stopped and wind's died down and what's all the fuss. And Anna, not only was she insisting on all the layers but she was now kneeling down and removing from the small basket under the baby carriage the plastic covering against rain and starting to attach it.

Memories usually come with footnotes of context, time, frame of mind, and the footnote accompanying this memory would explain that this was a time of tension between the couple. They fought a lot, almost every day, often yelling, Gabi in particular.

"Why are you putting that on?"

"Because it's cold."

"But he's already got a million layers. That's for the rain. It isn't raining now. Look at the sky."

She didn't look at the sky. The sun breaking through the clouds could be felt without lifting one's head.

"It's for the wind. There's a strong wind."

"Strong wind? Where's the strong wind?"

She didn't respond, simply stretched the plastic cover over the carriage, packaging the well-bundled baby in a thick plastic wrapping.

"You're going to suffocate him! No air will get in! For God's sake, Anna!"

Memories usually come with a punch line, a line or thought or high point that offers meaning, and for Gabi in this instance it was the thought that settled in his mind at that moment and whispered, If only he would suffocate. If only he would die. And then she'd have nothing more to say. Then she would spend the rest of her life feeling sorry for all her wild exaggerations. She'd stop arguing about every little thing. She'd be eaten up inside. Gabi would return to that thought many times, the death wish on his son, simply to win an argument with his wife.

Other memories: Mickey's silences. Sudden, without apparent cause. Something he didn't like, something that was said, or any slight change in the way his toys were arranged in his room or the living room. It pushed Gabi over the edge, and Mickey soon mastered the technique and used it as a weapon, without restraint or accountability, as is the wont of children. Gabi tried various tactics—repeating the question, raising his voice, using logical explanations, yelling, threats of punishment, tempting with rewards, countersilences, leaving the room. With every attempt he turned increasingly helpless, and the ever-increasing helplessness saw Mickey become more and more entrenched in his silence, and that led to gritting of the teeth, tightening of the jaws; to rage, which always clutched Gabi to its bosom with open, comforting arms. The rage, which evolved into a small debt-collection department: the forcible removal of clothing, twisting arms and legs and pinching at the same time; ear tugging, firm pressure on the head, squashing up against the wall while growling, shoving a heaped spoon into a gaping crying mouth. *You're not talking? Take that, you little hero, take that into your silences, cheeky thing.*

And the adrenaline pumping inside him while he did so, and the screams of the crying child, and the deep sense of regret five minutes later, the mutual apologies and the oath to himself not to get to that point again, not against his toddler son.

Alongside the memories, the mitigating footnote, which says, We spent too much time together while Mom was studying and traveling to Afula, we got on each other's nerves, we learned to live together, we were just learning to live together, we were in the throes of the process, and we would have made it, it would have worked out, if only we'd had the chance. But the stern footnote says, You didn't deserve to be a father, and you never have. The role was too big for you to play, and thus the role was taken from you. You were put to the test, and you failed.

When Gabi would come to learn sometime later about the power of silence ("Silence—as if to say, 'Be silent, thus is the highest thought.' The righteous man is silent"), he'd appreciate his son even more, he'd see in his silences the legacy of the strong man, the righteous man, who left the weak behind to learn and improve himself.

A red traffic light—often it's merely a suggestion. When you're young, and brimming with confidence, and look right and left like you were taught, and don't see a car on the horizon, you cross on red, too. Once, in your childhood, at the Tiberias central bus station, a policeman stopped you and gave you a token fine, but you haven't heard of a fine like that in years and you assume the police no longer bother with such trivialities. It begins with an empty street at a crossing, and moves on to crossing a street not at a crossing, and gets to decisions to cross not only when there are no cars, but also when you see them and judge that you can make it. Once or twice it's a close call, you get honked and yelled at, on rare occasions your heart will race or your skin will bristle and your brain will think you need to watch out, because it could end badly. You think about that word, *almost*. You even imagine sometimes what would have happened if that car had hit you, if you hadn't noticed it at the last second, or it you. A wheelchair? A complete life change? But when it remains "almost," those thoughts drift away with the flow of life. Because it hasn't changed, because nothing happened. So what's the point of waiting for green?

And then you have a son and you walk with him in a stroller through the streets of the city and become responsible. You stop on red. When it comes to the life of a child, there's no playing around and no taking risks, even if you've looked right and left and there's no real danger, and the road is empty. Because it's a child, and it's a stroller, and it moves slowly, and if suddenly out of nowhere there comes a car traveling overly fast, you won't be able to hustle out of the way like you're used to doing. You discover alongside you the people who wait at a red light. You've always seen them, when you were younger, you thought about them, obeying the rules, not cutting corners, not questioning them. People who would wait at a red light even if they were to come across one in the middle of the desert with the nearest living soul several days' journey away. Now, stopping and waiting alongside them, fists gripping the handles of the stroller, you come to respect them.

Bottom line, however, you are not one of them. With time, the defenses drop and the self-confidence rises. You walk with the stroller day after day, learn it, and if you've become more responsible now that the life of a toddler and not only your own life is in your hands—fuck it, the road's clear, what's the point of standing around? It's a matter of principle, after all. When you, too, were alone, you didn't want to risk lives, you crossed when you felt sure no harm would come to you, so what's actually the difference? So you begin to cross with the stroller and with the baby, too. Even when from time to time you almost get caught up in an unpleasant situation and regret crossing, and your thoughts wander to What would have happened if?—they vanish into thin air as usual. Because it's only "almost."

The last age that Gabi told Mickey was three years and two months and twelve days. He collected him from day care and asked, "How was preschool today?" And Mickey responded, "Fun," and asked, "Where's Mommy?" And Gabi answered, "Mommy's in Afula, she'll be back in the evening." Mickey hummed a song. Gabi listened, tilted his head, and narrowed his eyes and brought his ear closer, and eventually recognized it, a birthday song.

"Was there a birthday party at kindergarten today?"

"Yes."

"Whose?"

"Ido's."

"And did you have cake?"

"Yes!" And he began singing again, and Gabi joined in. They walked like that, leisurely, the weather was pleasant, there was no reason to go home.

"When I have birthday I wear crown," Mickey said.

"What?" Gabi said. And the boy repeated the sentence and the third time his father understood and asked, "A crown? What crown?" And Mickey said, "With red flowers," and Gabi remembered there's a crown like that lying around at home somewhere, and said, "Sure, sure, when it's Mickey's birthday, he'll wear the crown with the red flowers," and added, "But that's only in another nine months and two weeks and three days, so there's time."

Mickey pointed at a small hopping bird and said, "Birdeeee!" stressing the *deeee*. Gabi asked if he'd like to put a sweater on, but knew the response would be "No." A chilly fall wind was blowing in a clear sky dotted with a handful of clouds, and darkness was about to fall on the day.

Gabi pushed the stroller in the direction of the park and asked Mickey if he'd like to see the ducks on the lake.

"Ducks on the lake!" Mickey repeated excitedly, and bounced his small body up and down in the stroller.

Gabi smiled to himself. They came to the crossing. The light was red.

"Ducks on the lake!" repeated Mickey, and continued to bounce his body, which was restrained by the stroller's safety harness.

Gabi looked right and left. The road was clear, almost. A blue bus was driving at a safe distance and was signaling to stop at a station.

But it didn't stop at the station. And Mickey was no longer buckled up. Had somehow freed himself from the safety harness, jumped quickly off the stroller, and ran into the road, heading for the ducks.

When Gabi turned to look straight ahead again and saw Mickey in the road, he screamed, "What are you doing, you fool!" and ran into the road after Mickey. The bus approached and Gabi could already hear the air brakes breathing down his neck. Gabi afterward wasn't able to reconstruct exactly what he did, the bus driver and his passengers either, the entire situation remained strange and unexplained, but a review of the outcome tells the following story. The blue bus braked but hit the stroller, which for some reason Gabi had carried on pushing into the road, and sent it crashing into Mickey, and the blow from it and from the resulting fall broke the boy's right arm and cut into the flesh of his thigh. A light injury, very light, even. Lucky. Almost. Another almost, one that does indeed shake the heart more than a run-of-the-mill almost, but is likely nevertheless to subside and grow faint before long, after the cast is removed and the sutures dissolve. Gabi, meanwhile, exactly how remains unclear, completed his part in the scene some distance from the stroller, leaning over Mickey and showering him with hysterical screams, harsh curses, which frightened and offended the boy more than the blow, the fall, and the pain.

Mickey was a superhero that afternoon: on the drive to the hospital, the setting of the plaster cast and the stitching and the infusion. And perhaps it wasn't heroism but shock. He didn't cry, and he didn't speak, but he understood what was said to him and carried out the instructions efficiently. Gabi, for his part, sat hunched over next to him in the ambulance and shook, and was furious with Mickey, and furious with himself for being furious with Mickey, and felt terrible nausea. And when Anna arrived in a panic from Afula, he wasn't willing to say what had happened, left it for Mickey to describe, because he was furious with her, too, and since he left it up to Mickey to recount the manner in which the events had unfolded, Anna deemed him solely responsible for the injury to her son, and perhaps she was right.

They made up a few days later. Anna returned to Afula after Gabi promised he had calmed down and everything was okay. He went back to ferrying Mickey to and from preschool every day, they went back to walking around and laughing together on the way home. There was one moment that he recalled, when they were sitting at an ice-cream parlor and licking happily and Gabi thought, That's why you have children. At moments like these, what difference does it make if Anna's not here, or if I complete my degree, or what I end up doing with myself? This is what I am doing with myself. These are the moments you live for. But it was a rare moment. The laughter diminished. Mickey persisted with his silences. Gabi gritted his teeth. He enjoys it, he thought, enjoys bringing out the anger in me, the violence. He's mastered it and now he's playing with it and he's testing me. Mickey was now humiliating his father: When Gabi came to collect him from preschool, he refused to leave, screamed, and planted himself on the floor, lay down in the sand. Every morning he refused to dress. Every evening he refused to eat. It was a tough battle, one of the toughest in Gabi's life, and Gabi was determined not to get drawn in. To leave him be, to disregard the insults and humiliations. Mickey was a different child when Anna returned on the weekends—obedient, considerate, happy. There was no sign of Mickey the rebel, the provoker, the boundary-tester, the angerer-on-purpose, and Anna therefore, absurdly, tended not to believe Gabi's stories.

Mickey's skills improved as he neared the age of four—the ability to express himself, the scheming, his physical strength. He got into the habit of pushing his father away when he tried to forcibly dress him, yelled at him when he tried to ignore him. For days on end Gabi gave up trying to ready Mickey for preschool and simply remained with him at home. But then the preschool teacher called Anna and told her that Mickey hadn't been coming. And Anna called Gabi to ask what was happening. And one week she remained in Tel Aviv and took Mickey to preschool, and of course everything went smoothly.

It's inevitable, because that blond creature has learned in three and something years better than anyone else, better than Eyal in the dining hall and Alex from the groundskeeping team, better than the cooks in the army, better than any cheeky shit who's ever dared to approach me askew and has been dealt with, how to push my buttons. How to draw out the monster. He knows how to draw it out, and he wants to see it, because when he kicks and screams after preschool and doesn't allow me to carry him, he knows I'm left with no choice but to squeeze him, to pull his ear, to bite his shoulder until he lets out a yelp and calms down. He knows I have no choice, he wants to take me there. So here goes, if you want it so much, then take it, I don't care who you are, and I don't care about the norms. The norm for an animal like you is to shove it into a cage.

The preschool teachers informed Anna. And a nosy neighbor from upstairs recorded something on video. And bad luck left marks in various places on the small body, the remnants of pinches and dry blows, bruises, and swellings. Everything he got he had justly earned, that's what Gabi wanted to say to Anna when she confronted him, and it's all your fault, you left us alone, you pushed us into this, you're the irresponsible one of the two of us! You, and your Sami, and your Afula, and your bullshit!

The final morning from hell was rainy and cold—Tel Aviv hadn't seen snow since 1954, but if there was a day out of all those that Gabi spent living in Tel Aviv that came close, it was that one. Strong winds swayed the palms along the avenues, the rain crashed down almost vertically, mixed with sudden bouts of hail.

No. No-no-no, Mickey. You're not going to take your coat off now.

Mickey, I said no. Are you crazy? On a day like today you . . . ?

Mick-ey. Mickey! Put the coat on right now. Leave the boots. Have you seen the puddles . . . Mickey.

Don't you dare struggle! Ow! Hitting now? Yes? Okay. Here-we-go. This-is-how-you-put-on-a-coat, got it? Like this with the arms, like this to close the zipper. Like this.

Excuse me? Madam, please don't interfere in my . . . Get outta here. Go!

Do you see what you're causing? Shut up. Shut up. Baby. Cry baby. Know what? Cry. We'll see if that helps you. Yes. Waaaaah-waaaaah-waah, baby!

Don't you dare take off your boots! I swear to you, Mickey. I. Here. Like this, like this, you understand, right? Ow! Cheeky-thing-you'll-learn-it-doesn't-pay-to-hit!

Cry, cry, no problem. Here, you little shit, like so. We'll see what your mother has to say. Here.

I'm asking you, mister, to mind your own business . . .

I don't care if you're a policeman! Because you're a policeman, does that mean you're allowed to interfere in my . . . Excuse me, piss off before I . . . So what if you're a policeman? Does that mean you understand anything? I'm the one who's been living with him for three and a half years. Shut it, Mickey, you little shit . . . Let go! Let go of me, I told you, I'm warning you. I said . . . Take-that-here-I'm-twisting-your-ear—yes—you-don't-like-it, huh? Here. Shut-it-take-that-and-shut-it, ow! You're biting? Now-you'll-get-it-

cheeky-motherfucker—Here! Take that! Take a kick in the mouth. Cheeky-biting-mouthing-off-shouting—kicks aren't fun, are they? You see what kicks can do? Here's another one! And take that, too!

That very winter, his wife was no longer his wife, and his son—no more his son. Under court order, she took him to one of the kibbutzim near Afula, Gabi wasn't allowed to know which, he was banned from coming into contact with him or even calling. In court he adamantly rejected the definition "murderous blows," expressed profound and teary remorse, successfully argued against the bus accident being criminal negligence, and was eventually convicted and sentenced only to community service and a suspended prison term.

In the holding cells, bearded men in hats urged him to lay tefillin, shoved pamphlets with titles like "Why Suffer?" into his hands, and he had nothing to do except wait, and think, and get angry, and read those pamphlets—"Why Suffer?"—and again when he was released from detention they persuaded him to lay tefillin, and the feel of the black leather straps on his skin comforted him and continued to comfort him each time the rage within him rose to the surface. They were the only people who didn't view him as an outcast, the only ones who offered him redemption and solace, who took an interest in his well-being, who found an answer to his questions. The only ones. Dad Yossi didn't come to visit. Roni in New York didn't call, and the few friends Gabi had at work and school vanished into thin air. So he went to one Torah class, and to several more, laid tefillin, and listened, and wondered—Why suffer?—and opened his eyes to the light: Though I walk through the valley of the shadow of death I will fear no evil for Thou art with me.

The Light

His brother, Roni, saw the light, too, in New York. Two thousand six was a good year for him. He enjoyed the work, Eliot Lieberman had been a little over-the-top with the cryptic warnings, but Roni's days were indeed stressful: long hours in front of seven screens, almost without breaks during the New York trading hours, and half an eye squinting in their direction while trading was going on in the rest of the world, not to mention the dozens of e-mails from brokers and team members, to which he replied only after getting home, sometimes at midnight or one in the morning, after an evening out with colleagues. Those evenings weren't for having fun, it was work; the never-ending effort to establish a social standing, glean gossip and tips, keep a finger on the pulse. Roni didn't sleep much.

Roni's trump card was his Israeli connections. They were networked across the entire continent, not only in the world of finance but also in industry, the energy firms, and of course in tech. He established his ties quickly and diligently, made sure to cultivate them and secure information before it was published, and to convert that information into deals. He then went on to trade himself, too—and after he made a name for himself as a gutsy, quick-witted, and mostly profitable trader, a fair number of Israelis, from the Hummus Forum and others, entrusted him with their investment portfolios. For the bankers and techies who knew nothing about stocks but had money to invest, Roni was the right guy, he spoke the right language and yielded the right profits.

Someone noted during one of the first seminars Roni attended at the Hummus Forum that a talent for winging it—a skill Israelis always prized—wasn't held in high regard in the United States. There was no cutting corners with them, they said, everything was by the book. They respected everyone, everyone got an equal opportunity, and they expected everyone to play fairly by the rules. That was the reason, it was said, why the American economy was so prosperous and attracted the finest minds from around the world, including ours. Wheeling, dealing, and scheming Israeli-style may sometimes help, in the short term, but there was no substitute for fair play and orderly work. But as he gained experience, Roni's opinion began to change. He learned that while perhaps many Americans don't cut corners, the Indians and Koreans and Croats—and some Americans, too—did in fact cut a corner or two, and he came to observe that on more than one occasion those corner-cutters left the honest Americans lagging far behind.

At one of the Hummus Forum gatherings, Idan Lowenhof asked Roni, "Remember Bronco?" Idan squeezed the shoulder of a short, pug-nosed guy. "Should I remember him?" responded Roni as he shook a firm hand. Bronco was part of Idan's team in the commando unit, was wounded and left for the 8200 intelligence unit before Roni arrived. Nevertheless, two or three minutes of conversation was all it took for them to find enough common acquaintances to share some laughs. In the army Bronco was Yoni, but now he called himself Jonathan and worked in Silicon Valley, at an Israeli-owned company that provided location services. He regularly traveled the San Francisco–New York–Israel circuit, and would stop by the Hummus Forum once every few weeks. Once, after Roni and Bronco spent an evening drinking beer, Bronco said, "I have a craving for sushi."

Roni took him to Sushi Yasuda in Midtown, and after topping up the beer in their bellies with warm sake, they hopped into a cab to the Ulysses pub and chilled the sake with Guinness. They were in an advanced state of drunkenness when they began shooting pool. In the middle of the game, Bronco picked up a red ball and said, "You know this was once the tusk of an elephant?" Roni chuckled. "Once," Bronco continued, "they used to make the balls out of wood." Roni hit the white ball into a red one, which shot into one of the pockets.

"You know where I saw wooden balls?" Roni paid no attention to the drunken jabbering, and Jonathan answered his own question. "At Googleplex. They have this amazing old-school table."

Roni, bent over the green table, raised his eyes. "What were you doing at Google?" he asked, his curiosity drawing him momentarily out of the fog of the Guinness.

"Oops, I didn't say a thing." Jonathan Bronco giggled and mimed zipping his mouth shut. "My turn now?"

That same night, despite his inebriation, Roni canvassed the Web and reviewed the data, and he came to an unequivocal conclusion: Google was set to purchase Bronco's location services company. The following day he traded and invested accordingly. He spoke with the manager of his portfolio, Dale Savage, and received a onetime approval to exceed his trading budget. Announcement of the acquisition came the following week. To the Goldstein-Lieberman-Weiss clients, and to his Israeli friends, it was worth a lot of money.

Over the next year Roni received a few more tips from Bronco and from others, some inadvertent and alcohol-based at Ulysses, some with greater intent. The gamble he took on Google's negative fourth-quarter earnings report was based on a mixture of sharp wits, luck, and the balls of a bull. Bronco dropped something he had heard, Roni crossed it with reports he read and with a conversation he'd had with a classmate who worked at an investment bank in California. This time he didn't request approval, and traded in sums that exceeded his ceiling. The bank and its clients earned $8.5 million from the short-position gamble on a drop in price that he took on the Google stock.

One evening in January, Eliot Lieberman called him in for a talk. When he walked into the office, Dale Savage was there, too. Roni could feel his heart in his throat. Employees had been told that an announcement on the bonuses for the previous year was expected only in February, so he figured he'd been summoned on some other matter. They both appeared stern-faced. He was sure they were onto him, that they'd reviewed his portfolio and realized that he wouldn't have achieved the successes he had achieved without inside information and without deviating from his trading budget. That the supervisory mechanisms entrusted with ensuring fair trading had picked up on his activities.

"Sit," Dale said, and ran a hand through his straight blond hair. Roni sat, ill at ease.

"You've caught our attention, Roni," Dale continued. Roni noticed out of the corner of his eye that Lieberman was nodding. "You had a nice year. Several impressive deals that earned us a decent sum."

"And more importantly," Lieberman said, "you've shown you know how to manage risks; you don't panic when the market goes crazy."

Here it comes, Roni thought, and lowered his head slightly, almost ready to raise his hands to defend himself.

"Your bonus for two thousand six is two hundred and seventy-five thousand dollars. Just so you're aware: it's one of the biggest bonuses

we've given to traders in their first year with the company. You deserve
it." Roni waited for the "but" that was about to come, but it didn't come.
"We've decided to increase your investment budget," Dale Savage went
on, "and to give you more freedom to be aggressive, in order for you to
present us with an even better number next year. So go out there and
own that desk, big man, pull the strings you pulled this year, work your
fine network, go out and grab them by the balls!" By the time he got to
the last sentence, Dale was shouting, and when he was done, he stood
and began clapping. Lieberman joined in, although he remained seated.
Roni didn't know what to do, so he smiled and looked from one executive to the other.

He continued to shine in 2007. Jonathan Bronco showed up at the
Hummus Forum less and less, and Roni's efforts to contact him were met
with a somewhat chilly reception, but other opportunities arose. One, to
Roni's surprise, came via Meir Foriner. Foriner—the guy from Savyon he
had studied with, and who had turned Roni off with his rich-boy blue-
eyed arrogance and his groveling at the feet of the Americans. Foriner,
like Tal Paritzky, Roni's friend from Kfar Shmaryahu, was a regular at
the Hummus Forum. As time went by, Roni got the feeling they wanted
to cozy up to him, which wasn't surprising—his success at Goldstein-
Lieberman-Weiss and in managing the investment portfolios of a number of the forum members wasn't a secret.

"One more drink at Ulysses before calling it a night?" Foriner asked
one evening.

"Sure, why not?" Roni replied. They went to the Irish pub; Roni drank
a Guinness, and Foriner a Ballantine's on the rocks.

Meir Foriner worked at a credit-rating agency on the West Coast.
Roni was aware of the importance of such companies, which determine
the risk levels or viability of an acquisition or investment in companies or
countries. Most important, Roni knew, was that the rating agency people
were in the picture during the lead-up to acquisitions and mergers, and
knew which way the wind was blowing long before the public at large.

What started out that evening as a veiled and alcohol-driven tip turned
into a measured and consistent stream of valuable information. Foriner

dropped blunt hints ahead of large acquisitions, taking care always to do so in person, in Hebrew and in code, unmediated by electronic communication, because all the phone calls, e-mails, and chats between traders and clients and brokers were recorded. Roni knew that after several such gifts thrown his way by Foriner, he'd come calling for payback: Foriner asked Roni to open a fictitious account for him, and in that account Roni managed investments to the tune of millions of dollars that came via a convoluted and complex transaction from a Swiss bank account.

Foriner worked cautiously, maintaining a low profile for months until opportunity arose. One time he showed up at the Hummus Forum and with a whisper in Roni's ear arranged a meeting that Saturday, at a barbecue restaurant in Williamsburg. The small piece of information he gave Roni at Fette Sau's bar—the acquisition of an international hotel chain by a Texas-based holding company, a deal to be announced within days—had huge financial implications. Roni had to act with caution to ensure that he didn't attract attention or leave behind any traces. But to realize the potential of the deal, he again broke through his investment budget ceiling by forging Dale Savage's signature. The tightrope he was walking this time was thinner than ever.

He chalked up another success. Another rung on the ladder. And after that success, smoke still rising from the skid marks it left on the trading room floor, he gazed upward and searched for the next rung on the ladder. He increased the sums, upped the risks. (Once he took a $300 million position instead of $30 million. If someone asked: The extra zero sneaked in by accident. He wasn't asked.) Dale Savage and Jujhar Rawandeep allowed him to continue, and even encouraged and fired him up and at a certain point demanded success from him and entrusted him with investment budgets in the hundreds of millions—he no longer had to add zeros at his own discretion. He knew that they were playing the game alongside him. Other brokers bought him drinks on their companies' expense accounts, and so did his own coworkers, and of course his Israeli clients, whose numbers grew, and who increased the sums they invested. Of that he was particularly proud, the trust they placed in him, his standing in the Hummus Forum, among the wielders of power and influence—a fleeting recollection of the wooden deck in Basel Street flashed through his mind for an instant. He ended the year with a bonus of close to $600,000. He paid back his school loans well before the four years he had allotted to himself were up, and moved into the penthouse in his building—a few more rungs on the ladder. He felt invincible.

The Crash

The bad omens, which had been evident in the market for quite some time, began making their mark. Two hedge funds folded. People lost jobs. Rumors were rampant about an approaching real-estate crisis and liquidity problems at banks and investment firms. All this served only to ramp up the pressure to succeed and the demand to bring in more profits. Falling markets and losses also had the potential to yield significant profits if you played your cards right.

Idan Lowenhof approached Roni at one of the Hummus Forum gatherings. The two had drifted apart of late—both were too busy for socializing and rarely went to the forum. That evening, when Idan asked how he was doing, Roni felt a little uneasy. He was indebted to him—Idan had introduced him to this world, encouraged him, helped him with the application forms and admission interviews. Moreover, Idan symbolized for Roni the right kind of success story. He was infinitely likable and a straight shooter. Roni was certain that every single dollar of the millions Idan must have already earned was squeaky clean. Idan and Roni weren't cut from the same cloth. Idan got to Wall Street and felt at home. He adopted the American accent, embedded himself in the culture, went with the locals to baseball games, mastered the rules. Roni refused. Way back when he was still a student and talking to the companies' recruitment people about Doron Sheffer and Nadav Henefeld, he felt that his way in would be on his terms, not theirs.

They were both smart enough to understand the divide between them. Roni noticed at the time that Idan wasn't in any hurry to help him get into Goldman Sachs. Idan didn't recruit Roni into his company, but tried to look out for him, to warn him not to stray off course. In all likelihood, Lowenhof had heard of Roni's success. And from his knowledge of Pilpeli and Goldstein-Lieberman-Weiss, he must have figured out things weren't entirely kosher. So, after inquiring into his well-being, Idan said, "Let's go get a drink." Roni couldn't get out of it.

"Listen, Roni," Idan began, as if he had prepared a speech. "I've thought highly of you ever since I showed up at your bar in Tel Aviv. I saw what you did there and recognized the potential. I knew you'd be successful here, too."

"What's this, a pep talk?" Roni tried to joke, but he knew where it was going, and knew he had no choice but to sit and listen. He scratched at the label of the Mexican beer.

"I feel responsible for you, in a way . . . ," Idan said.

"You're not. I'm a grown man. I'm responsible for the things I do."

Idan ignored the remark. "I know the temptation is huge. The connections and information. That you see all these insane sums of money and you know you can simply reach out and grab them."

Roni looked at him. "What do you want, Idan?"

"I know you're not a criminal," Idan continued, gazing into Roni's eyes. "I know those people. They aren't people who were raised badly, who have no choice but to be criminals. It's merely greed. There are two principal behavioral patterns that make people operate within the law, a sense of right and wrong, or the fear of being caught, going to jail, losing a lot of money. I'm telling you this because it's easy to forget this stuff in this line of work, and because I care about you. I've seen people trip up. It's not pleasant. I don't know what you've done or haven't done. But I'm not stupid. Whatever you've done, you did well. But stop here. And be careful. I know you trade for many Israelis, and some aren't exactly the nicest people. If they fall on the ground because of you, you'll be in trouble."

By this time in his career, Roni was trading almost exclusively in options. With the options, he bought or sold the right to purchase a share at a designated price by a predetermined date. The options were cheap—hundreds of thousands of dollars—but the opportunities and the risks inherent in option trades are exponentially greater than trading in the share itself. A slight fluctuation in the value of the share could have a significant impact on the value of an option. A deal that costs ten thousand dollars can yield a profit of hundreds of thousands but can also run into a huge loss. An option is a gamble that's been raised to the power of itself: Juj once said to Roni that if trading on the stock market is roulette, trading in options is Russian roulette.

To counter such risks, the investment bank had several safeguards. One was the requirement that they maintain a special account, a margin account, with sufficient money to cover the risks. A debt could swell to terrifying proportions and have to be paid immediately, so the bank didn't permit going into the red. A second safeguard was the company's risk-management department, whose job it was to control and oversee transactions to prevent mishaps—to stop a trader from buying a large amount of options of the same kind without spreading the risks. Roni made an effort to get to know the department's personnel at Goldstein-Lieberman-Weiss.

He continued to make moves and yield profits. His network of ties at that stage was extensive enough to snare interesting snippets of information and translate them into cash almost every week. It was safe, because his informers were also invested in the fund. Everyone shared the same interests. But there were scary moments. There were fluctuations that momentarily carried him to the edge of debt. At those moments, Idan Lowenhof's words flashed through his mind. As the market turned more and more insane, people were being fired en masse, and the pressure he was under to turn a profit became overwhelming.

The story with the options of RIM, the company that manufactured BlackBerry devices, began at the Sunday pickup basketball game with some Israelis on the Upper West Side. He still went there whenever possible, to stay in shape and sweat a little, and also because he liked most of the guys.

A chance remark by one of them at the end of the game initiated the ballistic path that would end in Roni's crash: "Fuck this motherfucking iPhone, what a piece of shit."

"Is it new? You don't like it?" Roni asked as he browsed through the e-mails on his BlackBerry.

"Yeah, I got it a week ago. The Internet connection is a joke, never works. And look at this." He held out the device to Roni and turned it over. Pink stains had appeared on the smooth white plastic backing. Roni took hold of the device and frowned. "What's this, is it blushing?" He smiled.

"Can you feel how hot it is? I've read a bunch of complaints on the Internet. They said they'd exchange it for me at the Apple store." He looked at the device in Roni's hand. "Fuck it, I don't understand why I gave up my BlackBerry. This iPhone is nothing but noise and ringtones."

Roni didn't give it much thought when he got a call the following day from his Bosnian friend from school, Sasha. Sasha was working now at a large consulting company in San Francisco. He was in New York for a few hours en route to Bosnia for a visit—his grandfather had died—and asked Roni if he had time for a quick lunch, for old times' sake.

"You've gotten fat!" Sasha said on seeing Roni. They ate at Mister Mei, an Asian bistro they'd enjoyed back in their school days. "You're not doing any sports?"

"I played basketball yesterday." Roni examined his increasingly round stomach. Spending hours in front of monitors year after year was not a recipe for a healthy, slim body. Many of his colleagues went to the gym a few times a week after trading hours, but he couldn't be bothered. "What's happening in San Francisco?" he said, changing the subject.

Sasha was working too hard. "My grandfather was always good to me," he joked, "and now he died at precisely the right time."

Sasha's team worked with a company from San Jose, a manufacturer of microchips for digital cameras. They did business with some of the leading camera manufacturers in Korea and Japan. The company had hired Sasha's consulting firm to streamline procedures between the manufacturing plants in China, the development center in San Jose, and clients in Japan, Korea, and the United States.

"You can't imagine just how boring the work is, and hard. No one wants to help us help them improve the way they operate."

"What about the U.S.?" Roni wondered. "Aren't there manufacturers of digital cameras in the United States?"

"There's Kodak," Sasha replied, "and now Apple has brought out the iPhone, with their camera. Turns out the chip heats the devices more than they expected, and everybody's complaining, and that's why the guys there are freaking out and have zero time for us."

Roni froze in the middle of shoving a forkful of General Tso's chicken into his mouth and looked at Sasha wide-eyed. He recalled the weird color on the basketball friend's device from the previous evening.

"What happened, did you choke?" Sasha asked.

"No, no," Roni waved his hand, "go on. So, the thin telephones aren't coping with the cameras?"

"Don't know. All these devices that are trying to be everything, maybe it won't work. A strong communications device with telephone, e-mail, SMS"—he picked up his BlackBerry and gestured toward Roni's—"I don't believe there'll ever be a real substitute for it, as long as it works as well as these. Steve Jobs hasn't always been right, you know."

When Roni got to work, he set one of the monitors to keep track of the Apple and RIM stocks. Apple had remained pretty fixed, but the fluctuations of RIM were interesting. From late June to mid-July it lost some 20 percent of its value, but then regained the same over a similar period of time. From late August to September, it fell sharply again. He read a commentary in *Business Week* that concluded that "the iPhone will never be a threat to the BlackBerry," and articles about intrinsic faults with the iPhone—*MarketWatch* dubbed the device "a ridiculous idea."

Roni messaged Meir Foriner on the chat screen, in Hebrew: "The Maccabi game?" The Maccabi game was code for a landline-to-landline call from home at nine in the evening.

Foriner replied: "With the grace of God."

Roni called him that evening and spoke to him about his ideas. Foriner came back the following day with information he'd managed to gather at his credit-rating company. The sales figures for the new iPhone in the first three weeks were indeed a little disappointing. The BlackBerry remained strong, encouraging reports and favorable reviews had been published about new devices released in response to the iPhone. Google, too, Foriner added, was a player worth keeping an eye on. It planned to release its own operating system for mobile phones that fall. Which would also adversely affect the iPhone, at some point, Meir assessed. It could be worthwhile going with Google against Apple.

Mid-September. Roni and his colleagues watched, astonished, as Lehman Brothers collapsed and the entire market entered a downward spiral. Roni spotted an opportunity. People were fleeing banking and insurance company stocks, he analyzed, but there was no reason for that to affect a manufacturer of mobile devices—on the contrary, people would be looking for real, working, successful products. Roni took a combined position. The RIM share was trading at a price of 105. He assessed that within a month the smoke would have cleared and it would rise to somewhere in the region of 125–130 and perhaps even 140, its value three months earlier.

He played his gamble two ways: by purchasing "call" options, which would allow him in a month to buy the share at $115, which was lower than the value he assumed it would be. And by selling "put" options, which required him to buy the same share for $80, an even lower value. The expiration date for the options was a month into the future: Friday, October 17. From Roni's perspective, it was a good bet. In addition to his theory about people fleeing the bank shares in favor of commodity stocks, he believed the faults and complaints concerning the iPhone and the disappointing sales figures would be all over the financial news, and maybe even the mainstream media, and that BlackBerry would go to town over it and pump out publicity for its new products and good sales. It was a rather confident position—Roni gambled in one direction only and didn't hedge his bets. He was one thousand percent sure of himself, and he took money that belonged to the bank, the bank's clients, Foriner and the rest of the Israeli clients, and his own, and he invested it. The position, according to the complex mathematical models he ran, had the potential to yield millions in a single month.

In the first week the shares lost almost a third of their value and fell to $70. The second week saw the drop continue, but more moderately, and Roni believed that the parabola would now swing upward again. He stuck to his gamble, waiting until the expiration of the options. But the curve upward never came. The whole of Wall Street shook. It was hard to find a single stock that didn't fall sharply.

When the option expired, Roni's position wasn't covered. Far from it. The shares were trading at $55, the sums he had invested were wiped out, and worse, he was obliged to cover the put option and buy tens of thousands of shares at $80, now twenty-five dollars above their market value.

Roni got the margin call from the bank—a telephone call to warn that the margin account was in the red, and he was instructed to pay up immediately: two million dollars. To cover the debt, he transferred cash from the company account and the accounts of his private clients— again forging Dale Savage's signature—and purchased more options with a similar position. His rationale: After the fall in June came a correction. So the current drop must culminate in a rise. That's what the pundits were saying, and what Roni told his friends in the risk-management department who came sniffing around. He turned forty that week but didn't bother to celebrate. His nerves were too shattered for partying, and he didn't have anyone to celebrate with anyway. He received the expected call from Gabi. It came during trading hours, and Roni told Gabi he was in the middle of something and would call him back in a few hours. He forgot.

A month later, the stock continued to plummet, by then to below $40. A large round of layoffs hit Goldstein-Lieberman-Weiss, and one of the people dismissed was Dale Savage. Roni survived the cut. He saw it as confirmation that he knew what he was doing, and that management knew it. Roni withdrew more cash from the accounts of his private clients and the bank and purchased more options and evaded calls from the risk-management bosses and the clients, who were already in a panic regardless of what he was doing. The position he opened this time was worth millions. He continued to gamble on a rise in the RIM price, and also threw in shares of Google, which did indeed launch its mobile operating system, as Meir Foriner had predicted. This time Roni was dead sure he wasn't going to fail. The market had been falling for two months already, all the historical data indicated that after the market tanks comes a leveling out, which is usually followed by a climb. He received another margin call and, left with no choice, withdrew $1.5 million from his private account to cover the risk. By November, the RIM stock had already shed $100—two thirds of its value. Google plummeted to a low not seen in three and a half years.

In mid-November Roni stopped going in to work. He didn't answer the calls from Jujhar Rawandeep, from Meir Foriner, from Alon Pilpeli, from Idan Lowenhof, and from others. While all of them did indeed have their own problems, Roni Kupper was one of their problems. Every time his BlackBerry rang, he felt it was making fun of him. He couldn't pay rent and began to worry that his superiors and Israeli clients would show up at his apartment, so he took the Mercedes he'd purchased in better times and left New York. He traded it in for a cheaper vehicle at a car dealership in Ohio and lived on the twenty-some-thousand difference for two months—all his bank accounts and credit cards were blocked the moment he disappeared, and there wasn't much in them anyway. He drifted from one motel to another, didn't contact anyone (he took apart the BlackBerry and threw it into a garbage can at some gas station), and thought about what he was going to do with himself. In January he arrived in San Francisco. He couldn't remember the telephone number of his Bosnian friend, Sasha, or his address, but went into the offices of the consulting firm where he worked and they helped him locate Sasha. The first thing Sasha said to him when he saw him was "You've gotten thin!"

Roni stayed with Sasha for five days, until one evening the Bosnian's phone rang while they were watching a DVD and eating Chinese takeout. Sasha answered and then paused the movie and looked at Roni and signaled with a finger to his lips. "Shhh . . ."

He ended the call and said, "It's some private investigator. People are looking for you. The Israelis whose money you looked after. They asked if you've been in touch with me recently. You didn't tell me you lost millions from private portfolios. They want to take legal action."

"I lost? They lost. Everyone lost. What do they want to charge me with?"

"He said something about unauthorized trading, exceeding credit ceilings, lies, forgeries. He said there are also witnesses to insider trading . . . Listen, Roni, I'll help you as much as you need, but I don't want to get into any trouble."

Roni looked at Sasha and said, "Let's finish the movie, and then I'll decide what to do."

In the early hours of the following morning, Roni dressed in his smartest Hugo Boss suit, put on a tie, polished his shoes, drove to the airport, purchased a ticket to Tel Aviv, and breathed a sigh of relief when his name didn't pop up on the no-fly list. The first flight was to Los Angeles, where he boarded an El Al flight direct to Tel Aviv. After paying $3,600 for the ticket (business class, because after all, if he had to leave, at least let it be in style) and fifty dollars for two light blue cartons of cigarettes—he was left with two hundred dollars in cash in his pocket. Almost twenty-four hours later, he arrived at Gabi's trailer in Ma'aleh Hermesh C.

BACK TO BASICS

The Ninja

The black asphalt that stretched and wound through the hills had seen a lot: the tires of cars and the tracks of armored personnel carriers and the clopping of donkeys and the patter of goats. A merciless sun had melted it and angry rain had crashed down on it and snow had softened it; rifle bullets and old Jordanian mines and large boulders and the teeth of D-9s and the concrete blocks of checkpoints and mud and stones had formed potholes and bumps. It had been painted a thousand shades of gray, it had been opened and closed to traffic. And that Thursday morning: an apocalyptic yellow in the skies, winds of such force that it seemed even the ancient trunks of the olive grove had yielded and were bending, and then relentless rain, which washed over everything regardless of gender, race, and religious faith, thundered on the windshields of cars and their metal skins, eventually drowning out the political babble on the radio, and the hands-free conversations went quiet. And even the in-car debates, for example the loud argument that was under way in Othniel Assis's battered Renault Express between his daughter Gitit and his son Yakir, paled and surrendered and made way for silence, and contemplation, and admiration for the uncompromising power of nature and God, and a slight sense of fear of that same power, and, in the case of Captain Omer Levkovich, a frustrating uneasiness. Not only was he traveling in a David jeep, which was supposed to be brand-new and airtight but was allowing in cold air like an air conditioner in August, and not only was the deluge mocking the excuse for a roof and dripping onto selective parts of his anatomy—in addition to all that, when the jeep passed below Majdal Tur, its tire went over a ninja: two six-inch nails that had been bent and welded together. Omer sat on the wet seat, waited for the rain to subside, and said to himself, You won't lose your temper, you'll take a deep breath, you'll fix the flat in no time and move on.

The military vehicle with the black license plates wasn't moving, and the vehicle with the yellow plates passed it. Othniel slowed, considered stopping; he had traveled that road long enough to know that another ninja had exacted a price. He actually believed that the ninja layers were not Palestinians hostile toward Jews and opposed to the occupation but instead the sons of Younis, the owner of the tire repair shop in Majdal Tur, where most of the punctured tires went for fixing. When Othniel recognized Omer, he drove on. He had given the sector's company commander the cold shoulder ever since the *Washington Post* article that quoted the "officer" badmouthing the settlers. Omer tried to claim that his statements were taken out of context, but Othniel hadn't forgiven him, even all these months later.

The rain turned down the volume a little, and Othniel said to his children, "At least the car will be clean!" He laughed and stroked his beard. They didn't laugh. Despite the pause in their argument thanks to the rain, they were still in an agitated mood. When they drove by the officer, Gitit echoed her father's sentiments and cursed, "Bloody traitor."

Yakir responded, "Watch your language, you should be ashamed of yourself."

"I should be ashamed? You should be ashamed. And shame on the army that sends us those ingrates and then they give interviews and badmouth us. Screw him, the bastard." Othniel searched for a radio station but got static.

"You're a hypocrite," Yakir said, "they're protecting us. Guarding the roads, the settlements. Dad, why didn't you stop, I think he drove over a ninja."

"Guarding?" snorted the big sister. Ever since she was sent to the all-girls' religious high school in Samaria, she'd adopted more extremist views, and every time she returned for a holiday, she sounded more adamant and aggressive. Othniel and Rachel had conferred between the two of them about the changes in her.

"Yakir," Gitit continued, "I really hope you won't enlist, and if they force you, then God forbid, only a *hesder* yeshiva, a year and four months instead of three."

Yakir responded that the army took precedence over everything, that if everyone were to dodge their service, there'd be no army, and then who would protect the country and us? Othniel stroked his beard and remained silent. The windshield wipers provided the rhythm. Yakir wouldn't be enlisting for another three or so years. Who knew what would happen by then? Who knew what was going to happen by next week? His children joined in his silence. The rain slowed but didn't stop. Who would protect us? Yakir's question reverberated through the silent car. Perhaps the image of Yoni, the Ethiopian soldier, flashed through their minds. Rage flared in Gitit's eyes. "You know that Yoni gets discharged next week?" Yakir asked. Gitit shot him a look.

An engine emitted a huge roar and propelled a large truck past the sputtering Renault. The Assis family turned their gazes to the rear of the large vehicle, which was emblazoned with a decal: *Weizmann Bros. Renovation & Construction.* Herzl Weizmann waved a plaster-casted arm and flashed a broad smile from the driver's compartment during the passing maneuver. Othniel smiled back. "The road belongs to everyone, pop, be my guest."

Captain Omer Levkovich stepped out into the rain. He went to the back of the jeep and removed the spare tire and the tools. He shouted to the driver and medic to come out. The driver was new, he wasn't familiar with the jeep. Omer barked instructions in the rain.

A car signaled and stopped next to them. "Need some help, sir?" asked a bespectacled gentleman with graying hair. When he stepped out with a large black umbrella, Omer saw the dark suit he was wearing.

"Excellent, hold that umbrella here over us," Omer said, and loosened the wheel nuts of the flat tire.

The man stood over him and the driver. "What rain, huh?" he said. Omer's face was flushed red. He continued to instruct the driver. "Tell me," the man tried, "do you know where Ma'aleh Hermesh C. is?"

Omer turned his head up toward the man with the umbrella. "Why, are you a journalist or something?" he asked, a glint of apprehension in his gray-green eyes.

"Journalist?" the man repeated, and chortled. "God forbid. I'm from the Antiquities Authority, the unit for the prevention of antiquities theft . . . Never mind, it's a little complicated, in any event . . ."

"You're going to Othniel?" Omer asked.

"How did you know?" asked the man.

"Well, have you brought him the coins at last?"

The man appeared confused. "Do you know Mr. Assis? How do you know about the coins?"

"He just went by, in the Renault Express, you didn't see him?"

The man shook his head. "I don't know him."

"Come," Captain Omer said, and rose from his crouch, while the driver tightened the wheel nuts. "We'll take you to him."

The David jeep roared up the incline, passed Ma'aleh Hermesh A., and turned onto the dirt road that had been prepped meanwhile for tarring by God knows who, who had flattened and leveled it and made it far more travel-friendly. The driver stopped at the guard post at the entrance to C., and Omer extended a hand to shake Yoni's. He sensed a kind of pre-longing, a feeling that always arose before the discharge of a soldier with whom he had spent a long time and who would soon leave, never to return.

"Call your soldiers," the company commander said, "we'll go post these things up."

"These things" were new demolition orders he'd received from the Civil Administration's Inspection Unit. They were similar to the orders that were posted on the same walls the year before, but this time they came with final authorization from the High Court of Justice. The defense minister's decision, from that fateful meeting at the end of the summer, to evacuate the outpost without delay, suffered delays in the form of legal petitions, appeals, government and cabinet debates, and other time-wasting actions, which included lengthy commentaries and analyses of the meaning of the word "Scram!" But according to the new orders, the residents of Ma'aleh Hermesh C. would now truly and seriously be required to evacuate the hilltop within ten days.

Omer and his team, along with Yoni and his soldiers, went in thick army coats from trailer to trailer, from house to house, silently sticking up the sheets of paper with a special adhesive, like workers hanging posters to advertise shows on a municipal notice board. The wind howled and no one disturbed them; everyone was tucked away indoors next to their heaters. Only when they approached Gabi's cabin did he open the door to receive them, but didn't say a word. Just stood there, his beard sparse and unruly, his broad skullcap motionless despite the wind, and looked into the eyes of the officer. Omer looked over the cabin and, after a few seconds, said, "Leave this, it's a different procedure. An order to suspend work will be issued against this." He turned and walked back to the jeep, sensing Gabi's stare on his back.

The Sponge

He stood at week's end on the looted linoleum floor, his hands in the sink, and began washing the pile of dishes that had accumulated. The average family washed this number of dishes after every meal, but the thought didn't comfort him while he checked the temperature of the water, which in the winter was never hot enough and in the summer never cold enough, and got to work. He looked for a moment at the dish scrub sponge. It was heavy and soaked through with stale water, the once-coarse scouring pad worn down to almost nothing; all that remained was a strip of faded green that within days would fray and tear and leak bits of sponge and disintegrate among the simple tableware he had amassed from here and there, three plates and a mismatched collection of cutlery and a mug that read THE BEST DADDY IN THE WORLD. He focused on the green remnants that had been scoured to oblivion on nameless frying pans and the remains of egg, toast crumbs, and baked bean sauce from a can, and wondered, Which of them causes the most wear and tear? Does the sponge prefer to clean a specific food? A specific dish? And on the other side of things—particularly loathsome food remains, prickly, painful? What kind of grip does it prefer or hate? Does it enjoy being held lightly between two fingers or when you smother it with your entire hand?

He suddenly realized what he was doing. It was a moment of clarity in which he gazed at himself from the outside and saw the lonely man, the bachelor, in a dilapidated trailer seeped in a sour, manly, odor, standing alongside a pile of dishes and contemplating a sponge. And he realized he was debating a dish sponge like his brother and his friends debated Jacob and Joseph and Esau and the Holy One, blessed be He. So much babble, so many interpretations and commentaries on some stories from the Bible, and a year later the cycle is repeated and they reinterpret the very same stories anew—in pamphlets and in synagogues and in homes. How much bullshit can you feed people about what to drink and how to eat and what to wear and what to say when and which button to push with which finger, all the questions and the answers. At first he even admired it, thought it might help people keep life in check, save one from the endless considerations of the secular world, the questions that relentlessly buzz in one's thoughts—What color? At what time? What should I eat now? But eventually he realized he preferred the secular considerations, despite the agonizing. He couldn't live according to a random interpretation of a few old books.

Roni let out a chuckle. He hated the smell of the sponge and its worn-out feel. He hated the fact that he had learned from his brother and his sheep to quibble over nonsense. Enough. He had to get out of here. He'd go to Tel Aviv the next morning, that was final. He had been avoiding it for a full year. Initially he feared the Israelis whose money he lost in New York. After that he was deterred by the thought of running into former colleagues and schoolmates. After a while he began toying with the idea, but always found excuses not to go. At some stage he grew so accustomed to the hilltop that he stopped thinking about it.

After Gabi sent him packing from his home, and Musa politely declined his request to sleep in the oil press, not to mention to earn a living with him by marketing Palestinian olive oil to the yuppies in Tel Aviv, he was so crippled, at such a dead end and so out of options, that he simply stayed. He couldn't begin to imagine returning to one of the former stations in his life, let alone beginning a new life elsewhere. The quiet, the negligible living expenses, the opportunity to remain cut off overcame the sense of being unwanted. Moreover, he understood later, it wasn't a matter of being unwanted. Musa did the right thing, from his perspective. Gabi, too, was right—living together was intolerable. Gabi had changed since then. Started showing concern for Roni. Come to visit. Already a reason to stay. After months of viewing his little brother only as a sanctuary and questioning his way of life, his choices, beliefs, Roni realized just how hypocritical he had been. Now he wanted to remain close and try to understand and give something back to his brother, who accepted him despite the patronizing and scorn, who gave up his trip to Uman for the failed venture. He wanted to make it up to him.

He moved into the Gotliebs' abandoned trailer. They had returned to Shilo, more balanced, more bourgeois, more suited to their level of tolerance. At first Roni simply squatted, without asking, without requesting, without paying. It proved effective—establishing facts on the ground, and later, acquiring the official stamp of approval. The Absorption Committee, which sought to redeem itself for its failure to select a suitable family the last time, agreed he could remain there temporarily until a family was selected from the waiting list—something that could happen only after Herzl Weizmann renovated and made the place livable for use by a family, and that would happen only after he completed the renovation of the synagogue and set up the prefab day-care structure.

To make a long story short, Roni remained on temporary-resident status that stretched on and on, and in the meantime paid the modest rent from money he scrounged up here and there, and did his share of guard duty and kept a low profile. He didn't bother anyone, and from the point of view of the outpost, any settler was a blessing—Roni even agreed from time to time to make up a minyan when he was asked.

But he withdrew into himself. The solitude weighed heavy on him. In Gabi's trailer there were arguments, tension, the feeling of claustrophobia, but at least there was interaction. Now Roni went days without going out, without saying a word, filling the small space with the stifling cigarette smoke and the rancid air of his guts, listening to the winds whistling and the muezzins wailing and Beilin and Condi performing their duet, and the current affairs programs on the transistor he got from

Gabi. The money started running out, to the point where he found himself subsisting on slices of bread, or resorting to the tactic of calling and hanging up so that people would call back at their expense, which caused his conversations with Ariel and Musa to trickle down to just a single drop here and there, and brought an end to the activity he could still term "work": his futile efforts to salvage something from the venture or at least repay Ariel and Gabi a portion of their investment.

Something wonderful, meanwhile, happened to Gavriel, practically a miracle: following a number of delays—the heavy rains of the start of winter, a cash-flow crisis that held up delivery of the roof tiles—he finally completed construction of his cabin, and with a single-coil electric heater and a single mattress moved into his new home on the edge of the cliff above the Hermesh Stream riverbed. The house was tiny, and the bathroom, sink, and refrigerator were outside, and the winter winds in the afternoons and evenings shook and rattled, and the power and water sometimes failed to materialize, and he slept curled up under a comforter and in four layers of clothing, and so on and so on—but all that was nothing. The place was his corner of the world, the humble abode he had built from scratch with his own two hands. It was his pride and joy, his great achievement, and he thanked God for it every day.

He didn't make an effort to conceal his disappointment and anger over giving up on the trip to Uman at Rosh Hashanah because he lent Roni thousands of shekels to purchase an electric motor for Musa's oil press, which in the end was never used. But after Roni left his trailer, Gabi was filled with compassion. He felt a little guilty for preferring to be alone. And from a distance it was easier for him to see the true extent of his brother's precarious situation, and to come to realize that this was the life of the Kupper-Nehushtan brothers. They were bound to each other, they protected each other, they were each other's family—every attempt by anyone else to join them was a resounding failure. So Gabi went to visit almost every day, dragged Roni out for a walk along the ring road, spoke to him, forcibly yanked him from total isolation.

The Foot-Dragging

R ain slammed down on the exposed hilltop. When they arrived home, Othniel and his two eldest children ran toward the house, trying unsuccessfully to fend off the rain with their hands. Gitit made tea for the three of them after Othniel said he wouldn't be going out to work in the fields in such weather, and tried to get hold of Moran the distributor on the phone.

"Look!" Gitit suddenly called from the kitchen. "Come, Yakir, come see how your friends from the army are protecting us."

Othniel and Yakir moved closer and peered out the kitchen window at Omer's soldiers posting notices on the trailers.

"Buffoons," Gitit said.

"How do you know what it is?" Yakir countered angrily. Othniel chuckled into his beard. He could no longer recall how many times he had seen soldiers posting orders and notices on the settlement's homes. He turned around and went to the bathroom.

Gitit and Yakir, shoulder to shoulder, continued to watch the soldiers. They saw Neta Hirschson come outside in a colorful head scarf and a long denim skirt and yell at them.

Yakir smiled. "So predictable."

"What do you want her to do? She's right. A righteous woman," his sister responded.

They couldn't hear her but didn't need to. The motioning of her hands and head and the occasional sounds that penetrated the weather and the window told of Hirschson's rage. The pair's attention then shifted together to the roar of Herzl Weizmann's engine, as he skidded to a halt on the gravel outside the synagogue.

"It's like watching a movie," Yakir said, "one incident after another, one character appearing on screen after another, until the arrival of the man who will change the course of the plot."

"Herzl Weizmann?" Gitit questioned, and her voice expressed just what she thought about the possibility that the energetic handyman would play such an important role. She was right: a second vehicle moved slowly down the road and passed the military jeep and Herzl Weizmann's four-by-four. A clean car, dark, cautiously driven, like the cars of visiting dignitaries who showed up from time to time. The car drove by the playground and approached in their direction. Now it had their undivided attention. The vehicle stopped outside their trailer, the door opened, and a hand appeared, and the hand opened a broad black umbrella. Following the hand out of the car was a suit. A tall silver-haired man was wrapped in it, he walked through the gate and up the path. Gitit said, "Dad?" And Othniel joined his children, who looked at him in silence, and then opened the door even before the man had a chance to knock, and a moment after the man uttered the words, "Everything okay, Mr. Assis?" Othniel realized who he was, and the purpose of his visit, and in a few charged seconds he was overcome with feelings of relief, excitement, and apprehension, feelings that intensified the longer he studied the eyes of the visitor, as he reached out his hand to meet his hand, as the visitor smiled and folded his umbrella, apprehension that meant No, everything was not okay, sir.

The issue of the coins had dragged on since the summer. Duvid, the antiquities expert, Othniel's friend, hadn't come to the hilltop in a long time. Othniel pestered him on the phone. Eventually, at some point in the fall, Duvid called to say that most of the coins had returned from abroad. The tests revealed that most of them were made in all likelihood during the time of the rebellion. They were ordinary bronze coins, and probably not worth much. A question mark still hung over two coins, and they hadn't come back yet. They might be silver shekels from the time of the Bar Kokhba Revolt, but he was waiting to receive the complete findings.

Othniel continued to pester, and his friend the coin expert continued to put him off for various reasons—more tests, waiting for a shipment, another expert who needed to weigh in. Othniel's frustration was driving him insane. Almost six months had gone by since Dvora discovered the coins. Why was it so difficult to get an answer? Until one day, some two weeks earlier, the phone rang, and Duvid was on the line.

"Do you want the good news first or the bad news?"

"The bad, of course," Othniel replied worriedly.

"Leave it, we'll start with the good. There's a final answer about the last two coins. They are indeed silver shekels from the time of the Bar Kokhba Revolt. One from the second year, which is worth up to ten thousand dollars, and one—take note—the fourth year, forty thousand greenbacks, Othni, you got that?"

"And the bad?"

There was silence for a few seconds, after which Duvid cleared his throat and said, "Ah . . . look. There was a small screwup. A misunderstanding. One of the calls I made was to a friend of mine, an expert in numismatics, the history of currency, and when he got back to me, he mistakenly called a different David, from the Antiquities Authority, and left him a message. And thus the Authority got wind of your collection." Duvid stopped there.

"What does that mean, that the Authority got wind of my collection? Why should that concern me?"

"Essentially, it shouldn't be a worry. Look, in principle, anyone who finds coins is supposed to inform them, although they know that no one ever does. But when there's a leak or a rumor, they have to come check it out. They're concerned primarily with documentation—photographing, cataloging, recording, marking. Things like that. They won't take the coins from you, I believe."

"You believe?"

"I've spoken with my people at the Antiquities Authority. Everything will be okay." It sounded to Othniel like Duvid didn't believe himself.

"So what happens now?"

"Someone from the Authority will come to visit you. They'll ask questions. They'll sniff around the cave. Give them what they want and I'll make sure from here that it all goes smoothly."

"A cup of tea?" Othniel offered to the man in the suit, who said he was from the Antiquities Authority, the unit for the prevention of antiquities theft.

"Thank you." The man sat on the sofa and opened his folder of documents. He rummaged through it, retrieved several pages, and handed them to Othniel.

"What's this?" Othniel asked.

"I need to complete these forms with you, regarding the trove of coins you discovered in the Hermesh Cave. Afterward we'll go to the cave and look around. We'll call in the unit's team and detectives, we'll check to see if there are more antiquities at the site, we'll document the location, and if need be, we'll preserve the site. After that we'll conduct precise tests on the coins that were found."

"They've already done tests. You can get the results from Duv—"

"We like to conduct the tests ourselves, at the forensic crime laboratory," the man interjected, and smiled closemouthed.

"And then you'll return the coins to me?"

The man laid the forms on the table and looked again at Othniel. "There's a good chance we will," he replied. "It depends on a few things. We'll definitely be in touch about the matter. And now"—he pointed at the papers with a thin pen—"let's start filling out the forms."

The Recognition

Herzl Weizmann had turned in recent months into Ma'aleh Hermesh C.'s resident contractor, a multitalented jack-of-all-trades, combination welder, handyman, floor layer, plumber, and various other tradesmen who always complained and raised prices because of the drive to the isolated—and *dangerous*, they claimed—hilltop.

The hilltop was experiencing a construction boom, insofar as that was possible in the framework of the freeze imposed by the irresolute government under pressure from the gentiles since the middle of November. Gabi finished building the cabin, Herzl constructed an extension for Hilik Yisraeli's caravilla, a pre-cast concrete structure was brought over in pieces from Ma'aleh Hermesh A. to serve as a day care and free up the synagogue for sacred work—and the synagogue itself underwent a comprehensive refurbishment that included a new roof, stone walls, tiles, colorful stained-glass windows adorned with images of the Temple, and an air conditioner.

On that day, Herzl Weizmann's laborers couldn't get there. Both were sick at home with high fevers and in sweats. And when you insisted on Jewish labor, it was hard to find replacements on short notice, certainly on a day like today. Herzl called en route and explained the problem to Hilik, who was overseeing the renovations on behalf of the settlement. Hilik wasn't even aware that Herzl was coming that day, but Herzl explained he had a little more work to do on the synagogue before the Sabbath, and on the day care, too. Hilik called Jehu, who didn't answer—he never answered; and then Josh, who was running errands in Jerusalem; and then Gavriel, who said he'd be happy to help at the synagogue, no problem, he'd be there in five minutes, it was impossible anyway to work in the fields in such rain, and no, no need to pay him, it's sacred work.

Hilik was pleased. He was a good guy, that Nehushtan. Hardly any like him left, who are willing to give and don't expect anything in return. If there were any at all, then they existed only here, on the hilltops. He walked over in his slippers to flip the switch on the kettle. Coffee, that's what he needed now. To sit inside with the heat on as the storm raged outside, and enjoy a coffee and a cookie and a Gershwin CD. He browsed through his CD rack, pulled out *Rhapsody in Blue*, and slipped the disc into the player. He thought about going to the university to work on his doctorate, but who'd be crazy enough to go out in weather like this? How many opportunities were there for a relaxing day? Thank God for such weather.

The phone rang. The display identified the caller as Othniel. Do I answer or drink the coffee in peace? Hilik agonized, adjusted his skullcap, stroked his mustache. "Well . . . ," he muttered. Curiosity got the better of him. Othniel didn't pester for nothing. He pressed the button to take the call. "Yes, Othni."

"Did you see they've posted new orders?" A small poisoned arrow shot out from the device straight into the coffee, cookie, Gershwin plans.

* * *

Gabi met Herzl at the synagogue. "Bless you," the handyman said. "Good for you, coming to help."

"Sure thing," Gabi replied, and removed the hood of his coat. The skullcap, broad and white on his head, with a pom-pom on the top, and that wide smile. "It's sacred work, and you're a good man for coming all this way for our Sabbath. A truly righteous man." While the two of them worked in the same field, and at the same settlement, they had never had a chance to work together. Herzl always had laborers, Gabi was always busy with Othniel or the cabin. Aside from "Hello—Hello" and once or twice when they borrowed tools or sugar for coffee, not a word was exchanged between them.

Not much was said when they first began working that morning, either. The work was simple. Herzl climbed a ladder, used a screwdriver and adjustable wrench to go over all the new fixtures, and attached a few final ones. Gabi handed him large bolts and nuts and in the interim cleared the synagogue's spacious hall of materials and tools, which he amassed in a corner and moved outside after the rain stopped. Together they fitted the uppermost wooden beams, which added a rustic and eye-pleasing dimension to the ceiling, as well as support.

During their first break, Herzl said, "You work well, I have to say. I wish I always had workers like you."

Gabi smiled and sipped the tea. "There's plenty of work to do, praise the Lord. But thanks. If I'm free, I'll be happy to."

Silence ensued. Steam rose from the tea. The rain continued to tap lightly on the roof without a break. Herzl said, "You know, the first time I saw you here, you looked so familiar to me." Gabi raised his eyes. They looked at each other for a long moment, brown eyes crossing in cold air.

"Really?" Gabi said.

"Ever live in Mevasseret, or thereabouts?"

Gabi shook his head. Why was there tension in the air? Perhaps the eyes registered before the brain, and sent signals into the air. "I grew up in the Upper Galilee. On a kibbutz. Were you perhaps . . ." Herzl's head shook from side to side. A half-smile gathered in the corner of his mouth. He lifted the mug and sipped with a noise caused by the meeting of tongue, lips, liquid, and air designed to cool the hot liquid on its way to the throat. When Gabi was living in the United States, an Asian donor once told him about the art of soup-drinking in the Far East. He took him to an authentic Chinese restaurant and said, "Listen." Gabi listened. He was surrounded by the sound of slurping, and when he looked around, he observed the technique, the pursing of the lips, the forming of the narrow tunnel, the inhaling of the air, and the sucking in of the soup. In a Western restaurant it would be perceived as ill-mannered, vulgar. Yet when Gabi took out a tissue and loudly blew his nose, the Chinese fixed him with a look of disgust. Every culture has its own definition of vulgarity.

"Where were you in the army?" Herzl asked, and immediately afterward, Gabi's pupils widened, a film covered his eyes, a few drops of coffee went down the wrong way; he coughed violently and hung his head. Yes. He recognized him. Of course. Oh my God. Oh. My. God. The eye sees and the ear hears and all your deeds are inscribed in the book. He closed his eyes and said to himself, God, Man, you are testing me, you sent him to me, what am I supposed to do, Man. The coughing fit passed and he opened his eyes, and Herzl Weizmann looked at him with a smile and tilted his head, and asked, "What?" and took out a box of L&M Lights and pulled out a cigarette from it and lit up, and from within the smoke and the squinting of his eyes and the blackness of his hair continued, "Everything okay, my bro?"

I couldn't sleep. I opened Mishali's footlocker and from it removed two stun grenades, large and smooth and purplish-brown in color, like eggplants. The cooks were animals, not human beings. I identified the room and dragged over a large, heavy wooden bench to serve as a barrier against the door. I walked around, found the window, and managed to open it. I pulled out the pins, reached in with both hands, released the grenades, closed the window, and fled from there to my warm bed, hearing on the way the huge booms . . .

Gabi signaled that all's well, just a sudden coughing fit, the wrong pipe. Weizmann sucked on the cigarette and looked and asked, "So where were you in the army?" And Gabi quickly answered, "Golani," but felt, knew, that Herzl would soon recall. He waited, told the God in his head that he was ready, let the man give him what he deserves, turned his gaze to the window, felt Herzl's eyes on him. How hadn't he remembered immediately? Herzl. One of the cooks who refused to prepare a late dinner. Who laughed in the face of his commander and beat him. Who were sleeping soundly in their warm room when the stun grenades blew them into the realms of trauma, horror, the hospital. Gabi waited in surrender to his fate, but Herzl only said, "Come, my bro, let's get back to work."

The rain eased off, and they went outside to check the synagogue's stonework. In addition to the yellowish and masoned Jerusalem stone, Herzl had added a layer of wooden boards between the stone and the drywall, for better insulation. Herzl took a step back and gazed with pride.

"It used to look like two trailers, huh?" He was right. The synagogue looked for all intents and purposes like a stone structure, with strong walls and a large and impressive roof.

"You're a righteous man," Gabi said, and believed it with all his heart—building and beautifying the hall of worship is sacred work—but inside of him a storm was raging and he was conducting a fierce debate with his God about what he should do.

They prepared cement in the manual mixer and completed the final wall. Gabi carried the stones and mixed the cement, Herzl applied and plastered and cleaned and banged with the wooden hammer. Little by little their conversation deepened. Herzl told Gabi about his life. He was twice divorced. The second time his wife behaved "really badly. I don't want to go into details, you're a religious man, you don't need to hear such things, but really badly." When Herzl discovered how she was behaving, he took a suitcase, got into the car, drove to the junior school where his son was in third grade, waited for recess, found his son, told him to get his bag, we're going on a drive. Drove off.

"Bro, I didn't have a chance," Herzl said. Chance of what? Gabi wondered. The rain came down again and Herzl said, "Let's get back inside."

Herzl boiled more water on the gas burner. "What terrible weather, my God." He smiled and extended a mug of tea to Gabi. "What about you? A reborn?" Gabi nodded and Herzl said, "It shows on you," and Gabi wanted to know what showed on him but there was a knock on the door and the two men turned their heads and saw a tall, blond, large-breasted woman enter the synagogue.

"I see you two work whole day in hard rain. People with gold heart. Deserves something to eat, yes?" Jenia Freud was carrying a tray bearing two sandwiches and two triangular pieces of baked apple pie and had an apologetic smile on her face.

"Jenia, thanks! You're a saint, you, believe me," Herzl said, and placed the tray on the concrete block that was serving as a coffee table. "I was just thinking about popping over to the grocery store in A to get something."

"No, what you mean driving, in rain like this . . . Eat, eat. Meat okay?"

A thin smile rose on Gabi's lips and he said, "Thank you, good woman."

She left, and Gabi recited the blessing over the food, and they ate the sandwiches with the pastrami, and Gabi recounted how Jenia had regained the trust of the hilltop residents following her exposure as a Shin Bet mole. Herzl thought she had acted wisely, plucking at heartstrings by means of a house-to-house campaign of apologies, tears, and supplication; rolling over the blame to the Shin Bet, who deceived her and exploited her naïveté; and drumming up sympathy through acts of generosity like this one. "Who's going to say a bad word to her when she does such nice things?"

"There are enough people here who'd say something nasty, don't worry," Gabi said. "They said she needs to go. That they'd always suspected her. That she's probably a shiksa, you know, because of the height and the hair . . ."

"Yes, and the . . . So how did she manage to stay?"

"Othniel. His decision. And I think also because Elazar Freud, her husband, forgave her, so the people here went along with it. They didn't want confrontation. So she made a mistake, so what."

"Tell me, you know what they call a mistake by someone whose name is Freud, right?" A foolish grin spread across his face as he glanced over at Gabi with his albino eyelashes. "A Freudian slip!" Herzl exclaimed, pleased with himself.

Gabi could still feel his heart fluttering in his throat. He finished the sandwich and said to Herzl while still chewing the last bite, "Back to work?"

"Just a moment, no rush, bro. We'll smoke a cigarette. Take a piss. Say the afternoon prayers, if you like."

Only that evening, in his cabin, before going to sleep, while chewing on a pickled cucumber from a can, would Gabi replay things in his mind and understand that Herzl had guided him, Herzl the righteous man, the good-hearted man, who came there in the heavy rain so that the outpost residents would be able to pray in an orderly and clean and comfortable synagogue on the Sabbath, come in the rain to make Gabi a better person, to help him conquer the sins of the past, praise the Lord, thanks, Man, for sending him to me, with Your wisdom watching over me and saving me, though I walk through the valley of the shadow of death I will fear no evil for Thou art always with me.

Herzl went out for quite a while and Gabi remained alone in the synagogue and prayed. He asked the Holy One blessed be He what he should do about a man who has suddenly recognized him as a criminal who once threw a stun grenade into his room while he was sleeping, and caused him hearing loss and anxiety and loss of control over his bowel movements; and now he's a righteous man and is helping to build the settlement, a day care for the toddlers and a roof for the families and the renovation of the house of worship. The Holy One, blessed be He, gave him the harsh but right answer, and Gabi finished praying and thanked Him and kissed the Torah scroll. He continued to work, his body weak but his faith burning strong, until Herzl returned and trumpeted, "Okay, my bro, one last push and we'll have you a beautiful little synagogue for the Sabbath!" Gabi remained silent. Herzl asked in surprise, "What's happened, your face has gone green. Gavriel?"

As was the case every afternoon in winter, the winds started whistling loudly. Pre-cast concrete structures, containers, and trailers swayed, straps and ropes lashed against the walls. Even a synagogue clad in rough Jerusalem stone felt it. Herzl and Gabi worked in silence on the final beams until Herzl said, "I'd get a small radio or something, but perhaps it's not appropriate in the house of God." He spoke about the day care he had built, which he called "nice work." Silence ensued again, and Gabi tried to address his proprietor, feeble, fainthearted, knowing what he has to do but incapable.

Several minutes went by and then Herzl said, "That's it." And then: "Come to the day care. The children have gone by now. I want to take care of a few things that Nehama asked me to do."

They walked between the large pools of mud that adorned the hilltop. The Civil Administration orders were visible on the trailers. It was bitterly cold, not a soul was outdoors. Gabi wondered if this was the right time, and decided it was, this was the moment, he opened his mouth, and then the Nokia tune rang out. Natan Eliav, the secretary of A., had a number of jobs for Herzl. "Sure, my bro, speak to Dr. Hilik about freeing me up for you next week." He turned to Gabi. "I swear, I should come live here, with all the work you're giving me."

At the pre-cast day care they dealt with the doors and the electrical sockets and filled a hole that had opened up under the steel stairs. "I owe you the end of the story," Herzl suddenly said, "where were we?"

"Your wife behaved badly," Gabi said. "You took your son from school. But you didn't have a chance."

"Wow, you were listening, huh? So, yes, I didn't have a chance. My wife's brothers caught me that evening. I have no idea how they knew where I had gone. I didn't even know where I was going, I simply drove north, I got to Galilee, God knows, I saw a sign for a bed-and-breakfast and went in. Two hours later they were there. Took the boy, and then came back with clubs and smashed my arms. Know what I mean, smashed? Crushed to bits. They said so I wouldn't think about stealing children or beating their sister, like I beat her. I never touched her. She was the one who behaved badly. Anyway, they took the boy, he cried, 'Daddy, Daddy,' but those guys were heartless, left me on the floor, poured acid on me that made holes in my clothes and bleached my right eyelash and eyebrow—here, here, you see?" As if he had to show. "Luckily I kept my eye shut tight and the stuff didn't get in, I would've gone blind. I barely remember how I got to the hospital, barely remember anything at all, but the plaster, permanent, probably." He looked at his arms, held them up on display, and his eyes wandered to the large watch wrapped around his wrist precisely at the edge of the plaster. "Wow, wow, it's already four. I need to get moving before dark, c'mon, dude." He pulled out a thick wad of notes from his pocket and started counting hundreds.

"No," Gabi said in a feeble voice, and placed a hand over the hand with the banknotes. "For work on the synagogue I don't want money. It's sacred work."

Outside in their coats they stood opposite each other. The pompom on Gabi's white Rabbi Nachman skullcap was standing upright because of the wind. Herzl embraced him, and Gabi embraced him hesitantly in return. "You're a good guy," Herzl said, and Gabi, the words got stuck in his throat. Now Herzl gripped his shoulders and fixed him with a stare. Two men on a rain-swept hilltop. Gabi couldn't, he just couldn't, I'm letting You down, Man, he whispered to his God from his faint heart, I'm letting You down, forgive me, guide me, and Herzl moved his face closer, Gabi felt the vapor from Herzl's mouth fluttering against the skin of his face and the hairs of his beard when he said in a quiet and stern voice, "I swore to get revenge, dude. But you really are a good guy. You found God, truly found God, you have faith. You've repented for your deeds. I did things, too, bless the Lord." Herzl held Gabi's face between his rough hands, felt the sparse beard, the pale skin. He kissed both his cheeks and embraced him again.

"I sinned," Gabi said. "There's no redemption for me."

"There's always redemption. I sinned, too, Gavriel, my bro. I didn't make food for you."

"Forgive me."

"Forgiven, righteous man, forgiven."

And with that Herzl concluded his embrace, got into his four-by-four, turned the key, and revved the engine a few times. Gabi remained motionless, his hands in his pockets. He was cold but a fire burned in his heart. The pickup drove off and Gabi turned and walked slowly to his cabin. It would be dark soon. He'd make tea. Something to eat. Evening prayers. Thanks, Man, You helped me, You watched over me. Thanks for sending Herzl Weizmann the righteous man to me. I am Your son.

The tears came, washed over him. He was happy.

The *Marranos*

While Gabi floated home on the waves of his absolution, Yoni was conducting a routine patrol along the ring road. He was being discharged next week. He had no idea what he was going to do. He thought about learning a trade through one of the courses the Welfare Ministry offered to discharged soldiers—he had heard an infomercial on Army Radio, and one of the options mentioned sounded appealing, but as he huddled in his padded coverall with the fur-trimmed hood that covered his small head, he couldn't recall which it was. His Ray-Bans lay folded in the front pocket of the coverall, one arm poking out.

He'd miss this quiet when he was sitting above a busy street in Netanya with his good friend Ababa Cohen. Both the quiet and also the chaos. And also the Arabs, and the settlers. And also the ones who shouted at him—Othniel, and Neta Hirschson. And also Gitit, of course. He was missing her already, ever since she was sent to the all-girls' high school in Samaria. He gazed at her parents' trailer. Yes, in Netanya he would miss Ma'aleh Ha-Hermesh, as he mistakenly called the place for the first six months he was there.

He recalled the strange incident that morning involving Neta Hirschson. "Leave us be, you brutes!" the beautician shouted at the soldiers. "Evil bastards! Shame on you! "

Company commander Omer's new driver fixed her with a frightened stare.

"Don't pay any attention," instructed Omer, who was in the middle of a call with headquarters while his and Yoni's soldiers posted the Civil Administration orders.

But Neta Hirschson recognized the soft spot and aimed her sharpened darts at it: "You! Is this how you were raised? To expel Jews from their homes? Families? Children? You appear to have been raised in a good home. Don't let them drag you into their crimes. Disobey the order!"

The driver tried not to look at the small woman who was shouting at him. Again Captain Omer said, "Don't pay any attention, she's always like that." The rain was falling and the orders got wet and tore and the wind was icy and Neta huddled into her coat, yelled one final "Traitors" and suddenly dropped to her knees in the mud and vomited. The terrified driver brought it to the attention of his commander. "Always like that?" he asked. Omer hurried over and laid a hand on her shoulder and asked if everything was okay, and when she failed to lash out at him in response, he realized she was not always like that, and escorted her to the nearest trailer.

Yoni considered stopping by Jean-Marc and Neta's now to ask how she was feeling, but decided it was too charged a day for a courtesy visit. There wasn't a soul outside, and twilight had fallen. Sasson's camel cow was enjoying some weeds, and Condi the dog joined Yoni on the patrol, wagged her tail, and gave in to the pleasure of his stroking. "I'll miss you, too," Yoni whispered to her, and then noticed a movement out of the corner of his eye, and lifted his head, and called out, "Hey! What are you doing? Come on, for real."

"Leave it, come on, you're getting discharged next week. Turn a blind eye," Josh requested.

"We didn't post these orders in the rain so you could come afterward and take them down, doesn't matter when I'm being discharged. These are signed orders of the State of Israel."

"Exactly," said Josh, smiling. "Merely orders of the State of Israel. There are more powerful orders, from a higher place."

"It's forbidden for you to do this," Yoni replied, unsure what the American had meant.

"Forbidden?" Josh chuckled scornfully. "What's forbidden is to expel people from their homes. Your army won't tell us that we can't live in our home. And certainly not you. I didn't come from Borough Park post-9/11 for the likes of you to tell me where to go. You got that? So scram . . ." Josh concluded with a rapid remark in English that was intended to sail over the head and fur-trimmed coat of the short Ethiopian soldier. But Yoni was familiar with the words used by the redhead.

Certainly the word "Scram," which had become trendy throughout the country ever since summer, when the defense minister spat it out on this very hilltop.

Yoni called Omer and told him about Josh. Yoni could read the silence on the other end of the line, was familiar with the slow-boiling rage of the commander. Mostly it was a pressure cooker that remained closed after coming to a boil and then cooled, but under the right conditions—if, for example, he had experienced an unsuccessful date, repaired a puncture in the rain, posted orders in the wind, heard that a disrespectful bully cursed and insulted a soldier who was there to protect him—Captain Omer Levkovich could perhaps explode.

When Yoni hung up, Josh taunted, "What's up, crybaby, did you call Daddy to come help? Daddy's busy and can't come?" Josh grabbed hold of another order, on the side of Shaulit Rivlin's trailer, and tore it off the wall. Yoni went on his way, ignoring Josh's cries of victory.

Omer arrived in a jeep with his team, and behind him came a command car with more soldiers and tools. Yoni was waiting with his soldiers at the entrance and hopped onto the wing of the command car and rode like that, standing, outside the vehicle, like a thin messiah in a thick military coat, with a Galil SAR diagonally across his back. The convoy drove slowly for dramatic effect, as if to declare, Attention, we are here, look what we're going to do. The vehicles stopped and spewed out the soldiers and equipment, their powerful front-mounted spotlights directed toward the cabin on the edge of the cliff, tunnels of lights that bore through the deepening darkness. Omer Levkovich assembled the troops for a quick briefing. After that, some lifted sharpened crowbars, and others five-kilo hammers. Omer approached and knocked on the cabin door, on which hung a small sign with the words "Enter Blessed." There was no answer—Gabi had gone to pray.

Josh appeared from somewhere, and from his mouth shot the words "What the hell . . ." which were answered almost instantly by a blow from Omer's crowbar that smashed the door of the cabin.

"Hey, hey, hey!" Josh yelled. "What are you doing? Hello?" The soldiers didn't respond. One by one they entered the cabin until they stood tightly packed inside. Josh tried to get in but there wasn't room.

no

He pressed the buttons on his phone in a panic. Inside, the mission was straightforward and clear, and the hammers slammed into the walls and the wooden roof, smashed them, broke them to pieces. Yoni swung the five-kilo hammer in his hands every which way, sweated from the work and the effort and the heat of the many bodies in a small room, though within minutes the space aired out because it was opened on all sides with the disappearance of the roof and the walls, and all that remained was the stone and concrete framework, which Yoni also went to work on in a fit of rage.

Omer looked on with a mixture of wonder and pride at this model soldier who was soon departing, with the bead of sweat on his smooth brow. That's the way to do it, how to show the young ones the meaning of conviction. Yoni vented the resentment of months. He'd defended these people with his life and force of arms, and they'd responded with complaints and sour faces. Yes, some of them, perhaps most, had invited him to Sabbath meals, brought cakes, and inquired into his well-being, but words like Josh's hurt, and he knew that others said them in private, particularly since the story with Gitit had emerged.

Josh screamed hysterically into his phone. Where's the swollen-headed peacock from earlier, thought Yoni, and suppressed the urge to smile at him. Josh tried to enter what used to be the cabin and grab the arm of one of the soldiers, but the soldier's elbow shot back into Josh's jaw and stunned him. He backed off, tried to yell something, but only managed a whimper.

Neta Hirschson turned up, screaming. "Who's in charge here? I demand to speak to the person in charge! What right do you have to destroy a Jewish home? What would you say if I were to come to your house and set about smashing it with hammers? Fascists! Traitors! Brutes! The Nazis would be proud of you!" The soldiers continued without responding. They were almost done—the cabin was so small, and although Gabi had needed over a full year to build it, Omer and his soldiers obliterated it in less than fifteen minutes.

Neta covered her face with her hands and shook her head from side to side. Next to her, Josh, limp and hurting in his coat, held on to an unidentified object he had salvaged from the cabin. Othniel and his children arrived on the scene, and Hilik and others stepped out into the cold from their heated trailers. The soldiers exited the remains of the cabin, the tools in their hands. An eerie silence befell the place. There was no protest, no shouting, only dark-uniformed soldiers on the one side, settlers on the other side, and the wreckage of the structure on the edge of the cliff.

"Omer," Othniel said.

"Yes?" replied the officer, and approached him.

"What was the good in that? What gave you the right to do it?"

"Othniel, don't be naïve. Here, by right of this." He removed an order from his pocket. "A Civil Administration injunction to suspend all construction work, which the dear home owners, who now act so surprised, were given in more than sufficient time, in a pleasant manner, along with a clear indication that the tolerance they had been shown would not last much longer. Not only did they build without permits and without asking and without proving ownership and all the rest of the things that every law-abiding citizen must do before starting to build a house, Othniel, it's also located in a nature reserve. Building houses in a nature reserve is forbidden. Half this settlement sits on Hermesh Stream Nature Reserve land. It's an initiative of the Nature and Parks Authority, throughout the country, by the way, to clean up the reserves. It's not political at all, it's to preserve our nature . . ."

"But why like this, a sneak attack?" Hilik said. "Isn't talking an option? Perhaps we would have come up with a nonviolent solution. Why do you come like thieves in the night? The home owner isn't even here." He turned to his fellow settlers. "Has anyone gone to look for Gabi? I saw him earlier in synagogue."

"Talking? Who are you going to talk to?" says Neta.

"Talking?" Omer responds. "You want to talk? Go to Beit El and talk to the administration. Why didn't you want to talk when we posted the orders this morning? You wanted to talk? You wanted to rip them, you wanted to laugh in our faces, and when"— Omer went red, sweated, the vein in his throat throbbed—"when a soldier who's protecting you asked that smart-ass what he's doing, he had the nerve to insult and curse him."

"Who cursed?" Othniel asked.

"Who cursed. Josh!" Omer pointed at the American, who was still rubbing his aching chin. "And don't go thinking he's the only one. That smart-ass woman called us Nazis two minutes ago, didn't she?" He turned his head toward Neta Hirschson. "You've all lost your minds!" The officer delivered the last sentence almost in a scream, his eyes bulging, his throat hoarse. Usually he tried to stay level-headed and maintain good relationships, but something had snapped in him, a dam burst. "*Who cursed*, he asks me," he said, almost to himself, "playing the innocent." The settlers looked at him, astonished. What's up with him? All because Josh called the nigger—a nigger? Or he'd been possessed by some left-wing bullshit? Or maybe his girlfriend dumped him, or his promotion's been held back? Thunder suddenly rolled in, and a heavenly voice rose and intensified and overshadowed the stormy voices debating who would give the IDF officer a dose of his own medicine—it was Josh, backed by tears and arm-waving and heightened emotions.

"You won't come to my house and tell me what to talk," he shouted in his still-modest Hebrew. "All I am doing is to protect our homes and to stop nonsense of your orders. I went to Aish HaTorah and came to Israel after 9/11 because to need to do something, it is time to not be silent anymore, and now army tells us to go and Arabs stay? You come and break house we built with our own hands for more than year? You tell me where to be? The land is ours like Torah says without the bullshit of telling me what to do, and here, too"—his voice rose and broke into the scream of a dog that's been kicked, a match for Omer's scream a moment ago—"I'm being told what to do? My family are anusim from Spain, you know what that is? Do you know history? You talk to me about a nature reserve? From Spain they expelled us, like dogs, and my ancestors traveled to New Mexico, converted to Christianity, were scared to be Jews. They became cowboys, but their traditions remained—one day I will tell you, if some senses returns to your head—and we became Jews again, I went to yeshiva, I studied Torah, I came to Israel, not afraid of anyone, and you say nonsense about a nature reserve?"

Three soldiers overpowered Josh and cuffed him. He continued to resist, and a few of his friends tried to intervene, but were met by the advance of other soldiers in their direction. "Anusim! Anusim! That's what we were, and that's what we are now, don't touch me, you piece of shit . . ."

"Smart-ass!" Omer yelled at the young American, who was put into the command car. "I won't accept talk like that about my soldiers and about the IDF and the state! There are laws here. Yes, we will tell you to obey them and you will listen. We're now going to post new orders in place of those you ripped, and I'm warning you. God forbid anyone dares to touch a single order. Because then I'll come and start taking houses to pieces, and I don't give a shit if the orders say it's to happen in ten days. I decide, and in a year or two, when there is nothing at all on this hilltop, it'll be simply a beautiful and peaceful nature reserve—who'll remember if the homes were razed ten days early?" Omer raised an angry fist. "I won't tolerate cursing and yelling. One by one we'll take you into custody for obstructing a soldier in the execution of his duty . . ."

The sound of a familiar clopping was suddenly heard in the distance, coming ever closer. The stamping of Killer's canter was well known to everyone on the hilltop, and now into view came the white diamond on the horse's brown forehead, and he slowed to a light trot before stopping with a tug on the rein. On his back sat Jehu and behind him Gabi, his eyes agape at the sight of the wreckage of the cabin, the soldiers, his fellow settlers, and a deep cry emerged and rose from his chest and from his rib cage and from the cradle of his heart, higher and higher it rose through his middle and into the throat and out the opening of his mouth—an intense scream of anguish that was answered by a desert echo and the wailing of jackals and the howling of dogs and the crying of children and women and a whinny and raised leg from Killer.

Omer was breathing heavily, the sweat glistened on his forehead and flushed cheeks. He hadn't finished all he intended to say, but Gabi's cry rooted him to the spot. Next to him stood Yoni, also covered in sweat and his heart pounding while the other soldiers returned to the vehicles, loaded the gear, retrieved new orders. One of them even plastered an order to the stone siding that had served as the backing for the cabin's wall. An icy gust of wind blew up papers from inside the cabin, knocked a tin coil heater onto its side, waved pieces of fabric.

Yoni remained fixed at his commander's side. If he wasn't being discharged next week, he'd probably have to leave. Remaining here would be impossible after this incident. He was confused and distraught, grateful for and moved by Omer's support, yes, they'd been pushed too far, but at the same time his heart weighed heavy for the stunned settlers; perhaps there had been another way? What would become of Gabi, who'd put his heart and soul into the cabin? Already he felt a sense of responsibility toward the settlers, and when his eyes wandered to them, he felt a pang of longing for Gitit, whose facial features and hair color he found in her younger sister Emunah, and a sentimental lump stuck in his throat.

The Informer

Every Friday Nir Rivlin made his way on foot from his new home in Ma'aleh Hermesh A. to visit his daughters and son at C. Ever since the separation from Shaulit, he had dropped the Friday-morning class at the Jerusalem School of Kosher Culinary Arts. In fact, he pretty much gave up on the school entirely—he no longer met the attendance quota, wouldn't pass the final exams, and wouldn't do an internship. With his guitar on his back, he crossed fields, descended along the Hermesh Stream riverbed, and climbed the dirt path to the settlement, among the puddles.

It was clear that morning. The heavy clouds had disappeared and left behind crisp and cool air that Nir liked to draw in between his teeth. Traffic on the road was abundant. He waved away offers of a ride. Thought about the Torah portion of the week, Shemot, about Moses and the Burning Bush, about the lesson from the rabbi he'd heard the day before yesterday. Ran a hand through the curly ginger hair he'd been growing of late, patted down his new skullcap, more colorful than its predecessor, stroked the beard he'd started trimming and grooming. He thought about the song he was going to sing to Amalia and Tchelet and little Zvuli; he was excited to see them. He tilted his head back and smiled up at the sky—life's good! If only Shaulit would agree to his coming home, it would be perfect, and he was sure she'd agree in the end. For the sake of the children. She was right to throw him out—he was drinking, was lazy, didn't help, was insensitive, lost control. But she'd see the change. The investment in the children. He hadn't had a drop of alcohol in more than a month, the pot he had stopped almost entirely. She'd break, she hadn't asked for a *get*, after all, and the rabbi was on his side, promised to appeal to her heart. Perhaps she'd forgive him today? A new Hebrew month was on the doorstep, a new Torah scroll, the sun in the sky—a perfect Sabbath for new beginnings. Or renewed. He reached the final steep ascent and tackled it with a burst of energy, navigating among the pools of mud, his calf muscles dragging his body upward, homeward.

Nir was shown the door after a night of rage when he drank one beer too many and swung a fist just centimeters from Shaulit's ear. The fist struck the wall of their bedroom and left behind an indentation that remained clearly visible. Shaulit looked at it every time Nir begged her to give him another chance. The indentation gave her the strength to withstand the onslaught. What was the punch for? Nir didn't remember, perhaps he no longer even knew he'd swung it, with all the alcohol swimming in his head, but Shaulit remembered well: Zvuli had been crying all that day, he was teething, probably, and perhaps his tummy was hurting, too. He clung to Shaulit. And then Tchelet and Amalia started fighting over a hairband in the other room. Shaulit yelled at them, but because she was breast-feeding Zvuli, she couldn't intervene. She could hear the discordant notes from the hammock in the yard and called to her husband again and again, and then yelled. Finally he came in with red eyes and slammed the door behind him. "What? What? What? Can't you hear I'm trying to work on a song?"

Shaulit ignored his Four Questions. "Go see what the problem is with the girls." The two girls were shouting and pulling at each other's hair, and Zvuli, perhaps in solidarity, had broken away from his mother's breast and joined in the general crying. Nir went to the girls and forcibly separated them. When he turned around, the battle resumed.

He turned back again, yelled "Enough!" and violently pulled Amalia off Tchelet. He pushed her forcefully to the one side of the room and her sister to the other.

The girls cried louder. Zvuli, too. "What are you doing?" Shaulit shouted. "Have you gone mad?"

"Quiet. Stay in the room, it's none of your business."

"What do you mean, none of my business?" Shaulit tried to approach Tchelet, who was howling louder still.

Nir blocked her path. "I said stay in the room!" he growled, and pushed her into the room, the look in his eyes wild and unforgettable. The girls' wailing continued, Zvuli was screaming, Shaulit tried again to approach, and Nir pushed her and she yelled and he pushed her up against the wall and slammed a fist centimeters from her ear. And then, bless the Lord, turned and left.

With every visit Nir begged forgiveness and said he'd made a mistake. Explained he was going through a stressful period. Mentioned Jenia Freud's exposure as the mole. "I did something for the hilltop when I uncovered the secret," he once said, "and in return they throw me out?" His estranged wife shot a glance at the indentation in the wall and didn't respond.

The night of the dent, he slept in the playground. In the middle of the night he opened his eyes suddenly and saw a shooting star and a frightening thought paralyzed him: Everything is so transient, everything can vanish in a second. Not only here. Everywhere in the world. But here especially. Everything you have can be lost. Our holy Rabbi Nachman of Breslov teaches us to go out into nature, to sit among the trees with the chirping of the birds, the wind on the air, to see the stars, the moon, to speak to God, to tell Him everything, to shout, to sing, to dance, to return home at ease and happy and loving. He fell asleep with a smile and in the morning came home filled with remorse. Shaulit said she wanted to separate. He promised he wouldn't drink. She said it made no difference what he was going to do, she didn't want him at home. When he insisted, she threatened to go to the rabbi, the neighbors, tell them what he'd done. He asked for one night's grace. Pack your things and leave, she said. He packed hurriedly and left, carrying a suitcase to his battered metallic-sky-blue Subaru.

He drove along the ring road, agitated and humiliated, and stopped outside the Assis family's home. Gitit was in the yard with one of her young brothers. Nir lowered the window and, with a curled finger, instructed her to come over. When she approached, he suggested she get into the car and join him for a drive. She didn't understand why the car all of a sudden, why a drive all of a sudden.

"Do you need my dad?" she asked.

"No, you." Nir Rivlin, his skullcap slipped forward on his head, looked up at her and smiled. And then said, "I know about you."

"What?"

"With the Ethiopian."

Her eyes widened. She tried to hide the panic. "What? What are you talking about?"

Minutes after failing with his wife, Nir again tried to impose his will: "If you don't want me to tell your dad, come with me for a drive."

"A drive? What are you talking about? Have you lost your mind?"

Perhaps he had lost his mind? Good God.

He drove off. Slept a few nights at his parents' house in Beit El. Called Shaulit every day. Eventually returned and found a room with a separate entrance in Ma'aleh Hermesh A. Promised the landlords that it was only temporary, "maybe a month." Had been living there for several months by then. One afternoon, after he again tried to persuade Shaulit, she fixed him with an alienated stare he wasn't familiar with and said in a cold, self-confident voice, "Nir, I don't want to live with you, why don't you get that?" He left the house and went to the neighbor's house and saw Gitit. He proposed that she marry him in exchange for his silence. She inquired into the possibility that he had fallen completely off the rails. When he declared that he was serious, she snickered. When he finished with "Well, what do you say?" she turned and walked away. He entered her father's home.

Gitit was sent to the Eshet Chayil all-girls' religious high school in Samaria.

Major General Giora received an urgent call from his friend and promised to punish the out-of-line soldier and remove him from the settlement. But Yoni's discharge date was drawing nearer anyway, and his commander, Omer Levkovich, convinced the battalion commander to leave Yoni at the settlement until then, and promised to prevent any chance of a relationship or contact between Gitit and Yoni: when she came home to the outpost for Sabbath vacations, Yoni would be sent home.

Gitit didn't tell her father about Nir's indecent proposals, but on one of the cold Sabbath nights on which she returned from the religious boarding school, the Vayigash Torah portion, Shaulit asked her outside the synagogue how she was doing. The "Okay" accompanied by a shrug and a sad smile left much room for interpretation. Shaulit placed her slender-fingered hand on Gitit's arm and asked, "Perhaps you'd like to come over after dinner?" Gitit smiled and didn't reply. Just the thought of the questions her father would ask, his suspicions. She preferred not to leave the house until the ride to Jerusalem on Monday morning. But later, when the house went quiet, after her brothers and sisters had fallen asleep, and her parents were also in bed and the stillness of the Sabbath had settled in; after the Sabbath timer had turned out the light in the living room and left her in darkness, she remembered Shaulit's invitation. She didn't feel like sleeping, too many thoughts and emotions swirled inside her. Silently she stepped out the house into the darkness of the hilltop. Beilin accompanied her a fair distance and then barked in farewell. The crisp air filled her with thoughts and memories and longing and passion, and she inhaled it. When she passed by Shaulit's home, she glanced over and saw her sitting outside on the bench swing.

"Good that you came," Shaulit said, "I've just made a pot of tea."

They hadn't spoken much during their years as neighbors, but something about their new circumstances made them bond. A covenant of the outcasts. The women who did the unthinkable—the one threw out her husband, the other guilty of forbidden relations. On that initial night Gitit told of her life after. It was hard for her at Eshet Chayil, but she felt she was moving closer to God and becoming more resolved in her faith and her opinions, was invigorated by the sense of togetherness of the girls when they sang Hasidic songs or danced Hasidic dances—lovely girls, Ethiopians, too. Shaulit nodded, noticed the young girl's gnawed fingernails.

The next time the religious schoolgirl was out for the Sabbath, she came again, and again they swung outside in thick sweaters and long skirts, and this time she spoke about Yoni. Before leaving, she said, "You're the first one I've told the whole truth," and Shaulit smiled and caressed her. It was raining the next time, and when Shaulit smiled at her in synagogue, Gitit couldn't wait for the moment her family would go to sleep. This time, clutching cups of tea in the cramped kitchen and taking care not to wake the children, she told Shaulit about Nir's bizarre marriage proposal.

Shaulit remained silent. She stood to pour water from the urn and then sliced a cake. Gitit kept her eyes on her in the kitchen. "Oy, I'm sorry, I was wrong," she said, "I shouldn't have told you. I think he was joking, he didn't mean . . ." Her voice died. Shaulit sat down again, slowly sipped the tea, stared blankly.

"I don't think he was joking," she said. "Maybe he didn't mean to actually get married, but he was after something. The fact is, the moment you said no, he went in and told your father." Zvuli mumbled something and then wailed and they both jumped to attention, but he went quiet. "Don't be sorry for telling me," Shaulit continued, "it's important that I know. He comes here asking for forgiveness. Sometimes I consider giving him another chance." She raised her eyes. "Okay, I'm terribly tired."

They hugged at the door and Gitit left. Shaulit turned and went to the bed and hugged the pillow and wept. Nir was a good father. He told her every time that he had changed, come to terms with the mistakes he made, stopped drinking, that for the sake of the children . . . Relentless pressure. She didn't want to go to the rabbi or to Othniel because she didn't want to hurt him anymore. She didn't want to distance him from the girls because they needed him and he them. She needed him, too. She had stood firm until now, and as she sobbed into the pillow in bed, she knew she'd continue to do so. It's hard alone but not impossible, her mother did it with six. And now she finally understood, Nir was not the man for her. She didn't want him to sleep in bed with her, didn't want to spend her life with him. He'd always be the father of her children, and with that he'd have to make do. She'd go to synagogue tomorrow without a head covering, she decided, publicly and openly announce her new status, for everyone to know, and herself, too, that it was final.

"Mommy," suddenly came the voice of Tchelet, her younger daughter, three and a half. She had gotten out of bed and now brought her head close to the head of her mother. "Why are you crying?"

Shaulit burst into another wave of tears and gathered the girl to her. "Oy, my sweet one."

"Why are you crying, Mommy?"

"I'll be fine," Shaulit answered, and sniffed, trying to smile.

"Are you sad 'cause Daddy's gone?"

"No, sweet Tchelet. I'm fine. Look, no more crying, okay? Give me a kiss and a hug." Tchelet spread her small, warm arms and wrapped them around her mother's neck, and then climbed back into her bed and fell asleep.

The Responses

Nir showed up that crisp and cold Friday morning, the guitar strap over his shoulder and in his head the songs he'd composed for the girls and the baby, and while he was still on his way over, he saw Shaulit out walking with the stroller and sweet Zvuli with his first two tiny teeth and light curly hair, with a piece of cucumber in his hand, smiling naturally and unconditionally at the sight of his father. Nir kissed his son excitedly, raised his eyes, and noticed the loose and beautiful hair of his estranged wife, and his heart soured within him because he realized he was no longer the only man who'd be able to enjoy the sight of it. And while he considered what to say and how to address the matter, he spotted the ruins of the cabin on the edge of the cliff and his jaw dropped and he asked, "What the hell?"

Musa Ibrahim asked the very same jaw-dropping question that morning. He rose shortly before sunrise, prayed, drank three spoons of olive oil and a cup of tea, ate something, and went on his way. The smell caught him first. What's burning? He reached his olive groves and stood fixed there for several seconds, couldn't comprehend what he was seeing, struggled to understand the change that had been made to the landscape of his life. Something finally clicked into place in his brain; he took out his cell phone and pressed the buttons and said to his sleepy son, "Nimer, come to the grove." He did nothing while he waited. Didn't want to go near. Those trees, he thought, were here for hundreds of years before him and were supposed to remain hundreds of years after him, the earth's trees, not Palestine's and not Israel's, trees that don't care who's there and who's in control and who builds above the earth. That's all nonsense to them, the real world is under the earth, and there they are deeply and widely rooted.

Nimer arrived in a gray sweatshirt bearing the words *Battalion 13— The Wild Ones*, and together they went down to the damaged trees. Twelve olive trees had been torched and chopped down. It emerged later that others had suffered damage, too: trees in other groves and plantations, the tires of cars were slashed, windows were smashed. Musa and Nimer worked in silence, cleaned up, cleared away branches, cooled still-smoldering trunks with water, fetched burlap sacks and wrapped the stumps in them. A burial ceremony.

When they had finished, Nimer said to his father, "Go home to rest, Dad. I'll saw the branches and finish cleaning here."

Musa asked his son, "Do you think it's Roni?" Nimer thought and replied, "Who could it be? Who'd want to get back at us?"

"But why now? A long time has passed since we went with the Japanese. The harvest was already a few months ago, many olives, a lot of money from the Japanese. Maybe he was angry. But the season was over a long time ago."

"God knows, we spoke about it, didn't we? He couldn't stop pestering us. Didn't stop calling. And came and shouted, clutching that contract and claiming you signed. They said he got depressed. The Jew's a snake, how can you trust him?"

Musa didn't say anything. Just sadly stroked one of the burlap sacks. Then walked slowly along the remains of a short stretch of asphalt that had been shredded down to gravel recently by the administration because it was paved without a permit. Musa believed that deep down Roni was a decent guy. He didn't say as much to his son when Nimer spoke about

Roni and the settlers and the need for a response, but he wasn't certain it was Roni. Musa was old enough to know that in this life, in this place, nothing was certain, and few things make sense.

Sackcloth was mentioned later in the morning, too, at an urgent meeting that convened on the new and gloriously sparkling porch that for the most part drew compliments of Hilik Yisraeli's caravilla. Someone suggested praying with sackcloth and ashes to mourn the destruction, which would maybe alert the attention of the Supreme Being to the injustices taking place under His nose, or at least the attention of residents and citizens. "Where did we go wrong?" was the question asked, and several possible answers were offered: There was no need to brazenly tear down the orders; Josh shouldn't have humiliated Yoni; it would have been best to take up the matter with friends in the Knesset, in the government, and in the army and deal with the orders in a diplomatic fashion.

Little by little, the wind changed direction. Self-doubts and remorse gave way to offense, and rebuke, and accusation. Yoni was always hostile, and Omer Levkovich was the devil, and the defense minister was a disaster, and even the leaders of the Yesha Council were leading them to ruin. All of them—the leftists, the administration, the government, the council, the media, the Americans, the Palestinians, the police, the army—they were all against us. Things had truly escalated this time, for the first time in the history of the settlement a home was destroyed, the army crossed a red line and upset the status quo. And why are they coming down only on us and not on the Arabs, who build freely without permits and scoff at everyone? Jean-Marc demanded they be taught a lesson—let the status quo be upset for the Arabs, too—"and inflict revenge upon His adversaries, and appease His land and His people." Those present exchanged looks, but then Othniel tapped his finger under his eye and said, "The eye sees, people," and not another word was said on the subject.

Othniel tried to call his friend the major general but couldn't reach him. Close associate MK Uriel Tsur had become far less accessible since his appointment to the post of deputy tourism minister. The meeting ended with a series of decisions: to organize a mass demonstration; to print a booklet that explained how several governments supported the outpost for years and thus it could not be illegal; to take up a collection and help Gabi rebuild the cabin to show that they were pressing on; and especially—to get in touch urgently with all required parties in order to quash the demolition and military demarcation decree, or at least delay it for some time in the wake of the crisis, and thereafter obtain new building permits for a cabin and additional urgently needed buildings.

After arranging the sawed-off branches in a heap and cleaning up around the wrapped trunks, Nimer Ibrahim sat down among the trees. They needed to complain. To call the army. Roni had taken revenge on their trees because they didn't go along with his plan. They needed to tell the army to arrest him. He probably got help from that village. Soon the army would come and they would tell them everything. The mukhtar needed to be told to talk to the army. Perhaps they should call someone. Or go to their village where the thin black soldier was stationed and tell him to tell the army. Or maybe to Roni himself and ask him what this was all about. He leaned against one of the burlap-wrapped stumps, looked around, waited for something to happen in response to the violent assault. But nothing happened. He huddled in the sweatshirt of BATTALION 13—THE WILD ONES against the cold wind. All that happened was the charred smell, and ants enjoying the loose earth, and the muezzin's call to the second prayer service of the day that brought him to his feet and led him to the mosque. He stopped by at home on the way to check on his father. He found him smoking a cigarette with a holder. "I called Roni," Musa said before Nimer opened his mouth. "He's been in Tel Aviv since yesterday. I heard the noise around him, the honking of cars. He's there, Nimer. I don't think he was the one who set the fire."

The day before at the outpost, Roni saw the soldiers arrive in their vehicles, the equipment they unloaded in the rain. When the demolition of the cabin started, he was in his trailer. He leaned over to the window and watched the commotion: searchlights and soldiers and the sounds of heavy metal implements crashing against wood. The longer the destruction of his brother's beautiful new home went on, the more resolved

Roni became regarding the decision he began forming while washing the dishes yesterday, to get the hell out of there. He needed a different vibe, alcohol, the sea. He wanted Tel Aviv.

Roni went out and walked with his head lowered, with his emotions running intensely high at the edge of the cliff. No one noticed him. It's now or never. He was wearing his coat, his wallet was in the coat, a little cash in the wallet. He didn't need a bag. Moran, the distributor and marketer for Othniel's farm, pulled up alongside him in his pickup. "You I haven't seen in a long time," he said to Roni. "Jerusalem?"

"Even better," Roni said, and got in.

"Finally the army's doing something," Moran said as he pulled off, and shot a cautious glance at Roni. He knew he was Gabi's brother, but wasn't familiar with his views.

"I don't . . . It doesn't really interest me . . ." Roni said.

"Me, neither. I come to work. Arrive, load crates, leave. Hardly exchange a word. Tell me . . ." Here was the question Roni knew was coming. "What happened in the end with the olive oil? Like, I know the Japanese set up that factory, but back then you spoke to me about something small, a boutique, like, did that work? Did you give up? Are you going now to that friend of yours?"

Roni didn't want to talk about it. "Forget about it, the Japanese . . . The Japanese took . . ." he said blankly, and turned his head to the side of the road. He thought, Shame I didn't shower before I left. When did I last shower? Shit.

"Too bad," Moran said, "it could have been a nice project. You had a nice idea . . . Cooperation. Traditional oil of a high quality. A small niche but . . ." Moran went on talking but Roni didn't listen. They drove through Jerusalem, where he hadn't been in many months. It's so simple, he thought. You get into a car and drive. He hadn't managed to do that for a year. Unbelievable. It was so easy to get stuck. He felt dizzy from the number of cars, from the green fields alongside the highway, from the new interchanges and railway lines under construction. Rain started to fall, and the wipers screeched with every movement. The prickles on his skin, the deep breaths, the pressure in his gut, they all signaled his excitement.

"Tell me," Moran said after an aggressive blast on his horn to a driver who cut in front of him at the Latrun Junction. "I've always been curious. The women settlers there, there are . . . like, there are some good-looking ones, huh? Othni's eldest daughter, and also, you know . . ."

Roni didn't help Moran. He was still a little mad because Moran hadn't allowed him to smoke a cigarette a few minutes ago.

"I mean, you're secular, right? Gabi is a reborn, but you're not, right? Gabi's a good guy, by the way. Works well, quiet, I've often had a chance . . . Anyway, so, is there any action? If you understand what I mean."

Roni felt tired. "Nothing, believe me." Roni had almost stopped thinking about sex recently, surprisingly. He wondered why. Maybe the depression, maybe something on the hilltop stifled the urge. At first he wandered about within the same familiar horniness, dropped signals, and waited for a response. There was the sexy left-wing demonstrator, there was Shaulit Rivlin, whom he had eyed and for a brief moment thought there was a chance with when she threw her husband out of the house, and of course, the beautiful Gitit Assis, who had a thing with the Ethiopian. Bottom line, it's just another barren secular fantasy—that smoldering below the surface of a conservative and modest community are intense passions, all you need to do is scratch the surface to get to them. Roni succumbed eventually to the doused mood, and only from time to time did he feel a flicker of yearning for a specific feminine body part—a curved and pristine calf, the smooth valley of an armpit.

"What do you mean? Nothing? C'mon, bro, give me *something*."

It was strange. Roni knew exactly what Moran wanted to know. But for the first time in his life he was looking at things from the other side, the side that doesn't understand the childish fascination with secrets, with the need to discover a different truth from the one apparent. With knowing that people have urges and give in to them.

An upbeat tune rang out in the space of the car and startled Roni.

"Hey, sweetie," Moran said.

"Daddy," came the sound of a small and cute voice. "I'm here. I'm at home."

"Good, Mai, sweetie. What did you do today?"

How long, Roni returned to his previous train of thought, it's 2010 already, holy shit. So long ago that he barely recalled the feeling and didn't even feel sorry for himself any longer. Roni Kupper a monk, who'd have believed it. Religion—Roni went on talking to himself while Moran spoke to his eight-year-old daughter—was an interesting social attempt to deal with the fact that all men are addicted to sex and violence. He had learned in the last year that when it comes to sex, at least, it manages to suppress the urge.

He noticed that the further away from it he drifted, the more his mind was consumed by a new pattern of thinking, or perhaps an old one. The simplicity of life at the outpost, the distinct guidelines and order it dictated—he was enchanted by it. But on his way to Tel Aviv, with his body thrilled by expectation, with his musings about sex taking him by surprise from within the darkness of the cellar in which they had been imprisoned all this time as if to prove the point, he realized: It's not for me.

Mai told her father something about her teacher and then played a song on the piano that Roni struggled to recognize. Then Moran's wife came on the line. Moran said he'd be back soon and blew kisses into the air. They hung up and Moran said to Roni, "Well, what about that daughter of Othni, nothing there? She looks like one who's about to explode under those long denim skirts. She looks hot to me, hot!"

The Kindergarten Teacher

Dressed in festive white, wrapped in a prayer shawl, eyes closed, Gavriel Nehushtan swayed purposefully beside the window that overlooked the Hermesh Stream riverbed. Sabbath evenings are always good, but this one was special, the synagogue was more beautiful than ever, inviting—with the rustic wooden beams and the roof impervious to the fine rain that hadn't let up for an instant. The love and support and offers of help he received from everyone moved him. He won all-around praise, too, of course, for the renovation of the synagogue, and although he tried to deflect it onto Herzl Weizmann, he was the star of the show and would be one of the first in line to be called up to recite the blessing over the Torah the following day.

There are Sabbaths on which the sense of sanctity intensifies, and this was one of them: a new book, the Shemot Torah portion, the Burning Bush. The mood in the settlement was bleak, the trauma of the demolished cabin hung in the wet air, tears welled in the eyes of the people as they prayed. Visitors came from A. and B. and farther afield to express solidarity and support, the synagogue was full and warm. Contradictory feelings flooded Gabi's soft heart, profound pain mixed with elation, and he swayed intensely, clapped his hands, his eyes closed, his face aglow, exalted be the living God and praised, the First, and nothing precedes His precedence. And also, he suddenly realized: a Sabbath without Roni. Without his sour, grouchy presence. It took him a while to admit to himself that it was a big relief, to notice that his praying felt freer and more profound.

In the middle of the service, he went out and walked the few dozen meters to the edge of the cliff and sat on the wet rock face. A fine rain fell pleasantly on the back of his neck, moistened his beard, the tears flowed from his eyes. You're the real deal, Man, You're the righteous One, You took me, small me, and placed me before this huge desert, and showed me the way, You're such a sweetie. And if You took my home, like You took my son, You had good reason. He stood for the Amidah prayer. You're a Hero to the world, the Provider of the wind and the rain, You are holy and Your name is holy. Gabi recited the Seven-Faceted Blessing and "A song of David. The Lord is my shepherd; I shall not want," and returned to the synagogue for Aleinu L'Shabeach, the last prayer of the service.

After the service and more slaps on the back and kisses on the hand and a good Sabbath, he left the synagogue and walked along the path. Yesterday, after he was left homeless, more or less everyone invited him to sleep over at their place, and he spent the night in Josh and Jehu's trailer. Now he was thinking about the fact that Roni wasn't in his old trailer and considered for a moment sleeping there, and while he was still weighing his next move and had raised his head to the sky and drizzling rain, he heard someone sniff and stopped in his tracks and turned his head to listen. The soft and black night air enveloped him. Another sniff. And the tiniest of giggles. And then: *"Shalom alechem malache ha-sharet malache elyon . . ."* He frowned. It wasn't surprising, it was the right time to hear the traditional Friday-night song, the families were sitting at the table and welcoming the Sabbath. But the voice sounded clear, nearby. It wasn't coming from inside a house but from a yard. Someone was sitting in a yard and singing the song in a clear and hypnotic voice. Gabi stopped and listened. He wasn't supposed to and didn't want to do it, didn't want to secretly eavesdrop on his neighbors, didn't want to listen to the woman, didn't want to disrupt his time alone with his God and his own plans to welcome in the Sabbath. But something about the voice rooted his feet to the spot and pricked up his ears. She hadn't meant her voice to be heard in public, hadn't sinned, she was singing in a small and sweet voice, like to a baby. He looked around him in the thick darkness and sang along with her in his heart.

It's the Rivlins' home, and it's Shaulit, singing probably to Zvuli. He had noticed in synagogue that she looked different but didn't register that it was the loose hair, the forgoing of the obligatory head covering of the married woman. Enough, he said to himself, go home now, and just then the sound of a scream came from inside the house and then a "Mommmmy! Mommmmy!" And another scream joined the first one, "Mommmmy, help! Where are you!"

Shaulit's daughters were crying, screaming, and their mother yelled, "Amalia? Tchelet? What happened? What happened? Come here, I'm outside!"

"Mommy, come here, help!" Sobbing voices.

"What happened? I can't, I'm nursing Zvuli outside, just a moment. Calm down and explain to me what happened."

"Mommmmy," came the sobbing duet from inside again, and was then boosted by another scream, high-pitched.

"Oy," Shaulit said, Zvuli started crying, Shaulit soothed him, "Shhh . . . Shhh . . ." The screaming continued. Gabi looked around at the peaceful settlement that was sleepily welcoming in the Sabbath. He walked through the gate into the yard. "Shhh . . . Zvuli, just a moment . . ." Shaulit calmed her son. She heard a noise and raised her head, surprised. Gabi mumbled "Good Sabbath" and quickly headed to the screaming girls inside.

The second time Gavriel heard *"Shalom alechem malache ha-sharet"* that evening, Shaulit's voice didn't hide in the shadows, but was powerful and moving and backed by the voices of her smiling daughters and his own voice. He closed his eyes to focus his senses on the beautiful voices that continued to sing about the Supreme King of Kings and His angels, and noticed when he opened them just how pretty Tchelet and Amalia were, how they had the same eyes as their mother, and when they went on to sing "A woman of valor who can find, for her price is beyond pearls," he couldn't hold back and looked straight into those eyes. She insisted he stay. Said there was an empty seat at the head of the table and someone had to recite the blessings over the wine and the bread, and if he didn't have other plans, if no one was expecting him, the girls were still in a state about the creepy-crawly and would happily welcome his calming presence.

The creepy-crawly: a hairy multilegged creature the length of a finger and a phosphoric shade of yellow. The hilltop was full of weird creatures, every child knew that, but this one was truly out of the ordinary—Gavriel had never encountered one like it during all his years on the hilltop, and even he, at the pinnacle of his manhood, flinched. The creepy-crawly had taken cover in the corner of the room, too close to Shoshana the doll, who was leaning up against the wall and appeared to have been taken hostage by it. Its antennae groped in panic and every now and then it made as if to make a run for it and was answered by a volley of screams from the sisters on the bed, pillows in their arms and tears in their eyes. Gavriel brought his shoe down onto the creature and squashed it—*pikuach nefesh,* he sighed to himself—and was now moved by the humble and warm sense of family. He had been invited in the past to families on the hilltop, had eaten with Hilik and Nehama Yisraeli and with Othniel and Rachel Assis and with other families, some who were no longer on the hilltop, but ever since Roni arrived, Gabi was no longer thought of as a lonely bachelor who needed to be invited over, and truth be told, he preferred it like that. Shaulit apologized for leaving the fish in the oven for too long, and Gabi said the fish was wonderful and praised Amalia for the salad she'd chopped.

All thanks to a hairy bug and a soft angelic voice. Cake after the food, and after the cake, coffee; the girls disappeared to play in their room, and the conversation flowed, and when Zvuli asked to be nursed, Gavriel turned his back and focused on *The Master and Margarita*, on Etgar Keret, and on *The Kosher Chinese Gourmet* by Yisrael Aharoni—bookshelves are always alike in terms of religious literature and differ when it comes to secular books. Shaulit lay Zvuli down in his crib and asked, "Want to sit outside?" And they returned to the bench swing. She hadn't planned it; the evening, like her life of late, rolled from one incident to the next, from putting out a fire to solving a problem, an exhausting, endless chain of events. But later, before she fell asleep, she thought that the decision to free her hair from its shackles had freed her in more ways than one.

Gabi and Shaulit spoke reservedly. They had never exchanged more than a sentence or two. She commended him for the synagogue renovation. "Finally there's no leak in the women's section." She smiled. "And the day care. Good for you. You must be very proud."

"It wasn't me," he said. "Herzl Weizmann and his laborers are the ones who did most of the work. The praise should go to him, and to whoever entrusted the tasks to him and financed them, which is the council, the committee, I don't know . . ."

"What are you talking about? Building that place with your own two hands must be a huge source of pride." And after those words, both thought immediately about his cabin, and Shaulit placed two fingers on his arm and withdrew them and whispered, "Oy, I'm sorry."

"Nothing to be sorry for," he said to her, moved by the gesture.

"God have mercy . . ."

A moment of silence in memory of the cabin. They weighed beginning a political discussion: gripes about the army, the government, the situation, the ongoing discrimination against the settlers. The silence appeared to suffice and they skipped over the idea.

"You know," Shaulit said, "you don't have to spend Sabbath eves alone. You can come here whenever you want."

"Thank you, you're a righteous woman, Shaulit," he said, and raised hesitant eyes to a reddish curl that fell down her forehead, remained there for two seconds, then was slipped behind her ear with a slender finger, still encircled by a ring, and well groomed following a Neta Hirschson manicure.

"Usually I'm not alone. My brother's here." A crack formed in his voice. "It's just that he went away today. Or yesterday . . ."

Yesterday. Moran went out of his way en route to his moshav in the Sharon region to drive him into the city. Roni got out on a busy corner and looked around in wonder, letting his senses spin his head: the excitement, the strangeness, the size, the noise; good God, the liberated breasts! Bouncing before his eyes, crying out for attention, perked up under wool and cotton fabrics. He headed toward the sea, thinking and not thinking.

The ring of a bicycle bell snapped him from the fantasy, and then came a shout, "Muthafucka, watch where you're going, you asshole!"

"Shut your mouth," Roni responded instinctively with claws bared, but the rider moved into the distance, the red light at the back of his bike blinking with ever-decreasing hysteria.

"Oh my God, these cyclists are a danger to life and limb, you all right?" a woman's voice asked, and Roni half turned and saw an angel. Okay, a little chubby, but the hair so brown and smooth and glossy, the lips so full. Okay, the schnozzle a little big, but eyes that could melt, a light shade of brown, which for him contained sadness and hope and flirtation. He imagined her on all fours, her ass in the air in expectation.

"Piece of shit," he agreed with her, and tried to take in the rest of her body in his look. On the drive here, he had been thinking about just how sexually uninspired he was on the hilltop, and look, Tel Aviv and its female residents required less than ten minutes to wake the beast from its slumber.

"As long as everything's okay," she said, and he, "Tell me something, want to have a coffee somewhere, to calm down?" his gaze wandering already in search of a place, "Where exactly are we? Ah, Ben-Gurion . . ." But she moved on hurriedly, not before fixing her light eyes on him, awash with scorn.

Oh well, too chubby, Roni consoled himself, and the nose—come on! Such snobs, these Tel Aviv girls. As he gathered himself and continued toward the sea, he thought, God, I used to do it differently. I managed at least to talk to them for a few minutes. I can't remember anymore how it's done. I'm all rusty. At the Sheraton, he sat on a beach chair he rented for ten shekels and watched the waves. The girls were few and far between, and taken, but the distinct contours of their breasts were a surprise, almost a stunning blow. For months he hadn't seen a sight remotely like it, and now he couldn't tear his eyes away. The sea raged.

Perhaps it was good to be rusty, he reasoned. The rust protects you, encases you. Rust is not only dirt but an ongoing moment of reconciliation. He fell asleep, and when the cold woke him, the people who were at the beach earlier had disappeared and left behind darkness. He went to Bar-BaraBush. Sat at the bar. Didn't recognize anyone. He looked the place over, lingering on the changes—new chairs, a bottle rack, German draft beer on tap. What a big chunk of my life I spent here, he thought, and after a while—I'm missing the quiet a little. Maybe I'm done with cities. Maybe I'm missing my trailer, the most fucked-up trailer in the territories.

He met a kindergarten teacher, Rina, at the bar. She started talking to him. And went on talking. For hours. Outside it was raining and inside no one was in a hurry to go anywhere. She wasn't his type, not in looks, not in line of work, and not in personality. But he enjoyed their conversation. She told him about various kinds of tea. Forms of yoga. Children's songs. She analyzed the Tel Aviv housing market. He drank beer and moved on to coffee and made do with tepid water from the faucet. She waited inside for him every time he went out to smoke a cigarette, until the rain came down harder and he stopped smoking and remained with her stories, about fathers of children at the kindergarten who had come on to her, the new organic produce store at the Gan Ha'ir mall, a simply divine ice-cream parlor he had to try.

He told her he had nowhere to sleep, and she didn't invite him to her place, but offered to allow him to sleep at her kindergarten, if he promised to be out of there by six. And thus, in the middle of a kindergarten

on Shlomo HaMelech Street between Ben-Gurion and Arlozorov, Roni
spent his first Tel Aviv night in ages, a sweet sleep on a clump of children's
mattresses. Her call woke him at six in the morning, her groggy and cute
voice said, "Good morning, time to get moving," and he kept his promise and tidied up and left, and spent Friday walking around, on benches
along the avenues, by the sea, in astonishment—where was the feverish
activity ahead of the Sabbath? Where were the odors of the cooking and
the dipping of the tableware into the mikveh? Where were the cars that
kicked up dust at the last minute? Where was the quiet that rolls in and
prevails over everything? The darkness, the white clothes, the smiles in
the synagogue?

He knew exactly where. He'd go back on Sunday, after two more
Tel Aviv nights. On Friday night there was another date with Rina,
unplanned despite the mutual exchange of telephone numbers the night
before. This time they began from a different starting point, no longer
a man and a woman meeting by chance at a bar and chatting for a few
hours and perhaps going on to who knows what. They spoke this time
in a broader context, they spoke about the past this time, and about the
present, but went beyond efforts to impress such as "I live in a trailer on
a hilltop in the territories" or "I'm a kindergarten teacher on Shlomo
HaMelech Street." This time they confessed the truth: "My trailer is the
most fucked-up trailer in the territories, and I have no idea what I am
doing there," and "The municipality is squeezing me and I don't know if
at the end of this year I'll have money or the energy to carry on." The time
passed quickly, the beer flowed, even a few long-serving Bar-BaraBush
customers who remembered Roni showed up; one of them told him that
Ariel was working on a new venture, something to do with frozen drinks
in a combination of sweet-and-sour flavors. It reminded Roni that he
hadn't spoken to Ariel in a long time.

At the end of the date, the kindergarten teacher sent him off to sleep
soundly in her closed kindergarten on Shlomo HaMelech until the late
hours of Saturday morning. On Saturday night the date was an arranged
affair, and they dared to speak a little about the future, too.

The Skullcap

Ever since blowing up the mosque in Second Life and his spectacular vomiting, Yakir hadn't gone back. Both from fear of being exposed by the game's internal police, and out of a sense of remorse and disgust for the actions and words of King Meir and his Jewish underground comrades, and also due to a lack of time, because he was managing the farm's orders website, conducting archaeological research, and was in the middle of the school year. Not to mention prayers, occasional work in the fields, and helping to look after his younger siblings. But despite his numerous activities, he was nevertheless a fifteen-and-a-half-year-old with the world at his fingertips and intensely curious and always questioning and thrilled by discoveries, possibilities, opinions, and new, different ideas. He knew that what had happened with Second Life—the aggression, the invasion of privacy and humiliation of others, the sense of superiority that gave license to hooliganism—made him feel uncomfortable. That wasn't him. What was, he didn't know. But when you're fifteen years old and that's your starting point, and your fingers lead you through the dark corners of the Internet for hours on end, there are many things you can discover, and change about yourself.

He started with music. From Eviatar Banai to black rappers to clips on YouTube to blogs to Internet radio stations with earphones because Mom complained about "that noise," and he went on to a Yom Kippur filled with thoughts about a million things aside from Kol Nidre. To conversations with Moran about "What do you secular people think about us?" And then to an organic vegetables forum and forums of green movements and yoga forums and liberal religious websites. More talks with Moran about secular people and left-wingers, and thoughts about what am I doing on this hilltop without friends my own age, and from there it wasn't a long walk to buying a smaller skullcap in Jerusalem to replace the broad woolen skullcap like Dad's. Dad didn't notice; Gitit did, snickered, and asked if he had lost his mind, if he was one of those watered-down religious guys whose skullcaps are barely visible, if he was ashamed. Ashamed—no way. But he continued to read a lot of interesting things. He observed Gitit when she returned from the religious school and it all suddenly seemed strange to him, the ease of knowing what's right, the difficulty of questioning.

Naturally, most of the things Moran told him sounded way out of his reach, a world beyond an abyss, a world where not only did he believe he couldn't get by, but one that also appeared to him unreal, odd, in many ways. By and large he loved his life, his family, the synagogue and the prayer services. But he also loved to ask questions. One evening, Yakir went into a forum for formerly religious people, and when he raised his head from the screen, it was two in the morning and his brain was fizzing. Afterward he started playing a game with himself in which he would find small, insignificant ways of desecrating the Sabbath: writing in a notebook, turning on a heater for a couple of minutes, listening to a song through earphones . . . Gitit continued to return from the school energized with belief, new confidence. Sometimes, from within the agonies of his doubts, he envied her. Thought that maybe he, too, should seek a self-assured education, which would take care of any doubts.

Yakir read an official report on the Antiquities Authority's website about two valuable coins from the time of the Bar Kokhba Revolt that were found in a cave in the Hermesh Stream riverbed. He informed his father, and Othniel quickly called Duvid. "Yes, that's right," the antiquities expert confirmed, "those are your coins. Those last two."

"Well," Othniel said excitedly, "so we can sell?"

"Sell what?"

"The coins, what do you think I mean?"

"Where are they, with you?"

"No, the guy from the Antiquities Authority said they wanted to conduct their own tests, but according to this report, I understand they've done so. So now I get the coins?"

Othniel heard a slow chuckle on the other end of the line. "Yes, I believe you'll get the coins. Let me try to speak to someone there."

Othniel closed his eyes tight. He was furious with everyone—with the

Antiquities Authority, with Duvid, with himself for approaching Duvid at all. "So when will they return them to me?"

"How am I supposed to know? Wait. You've waited this long, no?"

Othniel opened his eyes and looked at Yakir. He spoke into the device in a soft voice, but under it a tense tone clearly lurked. "I don't understand why you let those idiots find out about our coins. First you hold on to them for months. Now they take them, and are telling us what we already knew."

"I didn't let them, I told you, it was a mistake . . ."

Othniel hung up, retrieved the suited gentleman's business card from the drawer, and dialed. There was no answer. He tried again and reached the secretary. She put him through to another secretary who didn't know what he was talking about and passed him on to another one, who knew what he was talking about but said the gentleman wasn't in his office at the moment and no one else could assist him. "Try tomorrow," she suggested, "or better still, next week."

Othniel hung up and fixed his son with a long stare. Eventually he stood up and said, "Come, son, we're going to Jerusalem."

They searched in windswept Jerusalem for the offices of the Antiquities Authority on Sokolov Street, just off Keren Hayesod, because Othniel remembered the building from his youth. They went from building to building—no sign of it.

"Dad, why didn't you tell me you don't know where it is, I would have found it on the Internet in one second."

"But I do know where it is. It's here. Somewhere."

They made inquiries at the adjacent street and then returned to Sokolov and asked passersby, until they found a resident of the neighborhood who told them that the Israel Coins and Medals Corp. was once located there, many years ago.

"See?" Othniel said.

"What exactly am I supposed to see?" his son replied.

The neighborhood resident didn't know the current address, not of the Medals Corp. and not of the Antiquities Authority. Following several phone calls, they drove to the new Mamilla complex. They sat outside the office for close to twenty minutes, until Othniel created a scene. It

helped. They were told they needed to take the matter up with the unit
for the prevention of antiquities theft, which was dealing with the coins
from the Hermesh Cave. But the unit doesn't have an office, there's the
Antiquities Museum, which has offices, but it's not clear . . . Othniel created another scene.

If there's a plus side to the look of the settler with the broad skullcap
and beard and tzitzit and muddy work shoes, it's that when he creates a
scene, he's taken seriously.

Eventually they got to the gentleman who'd visited the settlement. He
was dressed again in a suit, remained bespectacled, and courteous, and
graying. "Ah, hello, gentlemen," he said, "Ma'aleh Hermesh C., right?"

Othniel nodded. His expression showed no congeniality, only expectation. He said, "I need my coins."

"The coins aren't here," the man said.

"What do you mean they aren't here?"

"We don't have them. They were at the Antiquities Authority. They
conducted the final tests, and were supposed to pass them over to us, and
we in turn back to Mr. . . . ." He paged through the papers on his desk. "To
Duvid . . . to you. But we have yet to receive them from the Authority."

"What do you mean, yet to receive them from the Authority? Where's
the Authority? Tell me and I'll go get them. What's this foot-dragging
all about? They're my coins. You said you completed the tests, you confirmed authenticity and age, you published an announcement on the
website. Now return them to their owners. What's all this bullshit?"

It didn't help.

On the way home, at the exit from Jerusalem, they spotted Roni Kupper
with his thumb out and took him along with them.

"Thanks, righteous men," he said, biting into a bagel with hyssop.

"Honored, honored, good man. Hallowed be His name."

From the junction they began the descent toward the desert and the
yellowing hills, passed by a new neighborhood under construction that
resembled a huge octopus, and then beyond to more yellowing hills dotted with olive trees and the homes of a nonhostile, or formerly hostile,
Arab village, and several kilometers later the military checkpoint that

declared territories from here on, and there the air was colored grayish, and the taxis were colored yellowish, and the license plates of the trucks were colored whitish, and the landscape started moving into the distance, and Othniel asked Roni, "So tell me, dude, what was the story in the end with the olive oil?" And Roni, like always, provided, almost subconsciously, the answer that best suited the time and place and, primarily, the listener. Information is modeling clay: the material is the material, but the way in which it is presented can alter it, knead it, flatten it, or inflate it.

"What could the story be?" Roni replied. "The story is that the Arabs can't be trusted, that's what."

Othniel glanced cautiously in the rearview mirror. Was he making fun?

Roni continued. "The story is that I had a great proposal for the Arab, I took his oil press that hadn't been in use for years, and said to him come let's start producing here again, bring your olives, your neighbors' olives, we'll make real, old, traditional oil with the dust and the hookah smoke like in the past, the Tel Avivians love it, we'll make a little money together. Initially he kissed my feet, said his grandfather would be spinning in his grave with joy, that I'm a saint. Everything was arranged, stores in Tel Aviv, an investment, marketing, the design of labels for the bottles with the symbol of the millstones like in Italy, so that people would know how pure and tasty the oil they're buying is . . ."

"Nice idea," Othniel said. "I'm not crazy about the fact that you do business with Arabs and help them to support themselves, yes? But the idea's nice."

"And then those Japanese showed up, we have signed agreements and all . . ."

Othniel blew out air through his teeth and pressed his tongue to his palate: "Tssssss . . ."

"And the son of a bitch pissed all over me and went with them. Without batting an eye. Why, because they're Japanese? They've got money? But what do they know about olive oil, tell me, the Japanese? What do they know about how to market and sell? I had all those pretentious Tel Aviv yuppies in my hands, they used to come to drink my beer when they were in their twenties-thirties and they would have come to drink my olive oil in their forties-fifties. But no, the Japanese came along with big machines, and his head was turned, how could it not have been turned, an Arab . . ."

Roni's thoughts meandered. The third night at Rina's closed kindergarten, how he had felt almost at home, and in the morning tidied the mattresses and sheets and ducked out at six, as she had requested, onto Shlomo HaMelech Street, and even the sun peeked between the branches and led him to a café along the avenue; how surprised he was by the speed at which he had readjusted to Tel Aviv, but went to the Central Bus Station and boarded a bus to Jerusalem, his head filled with thoughts about Rina and the nights in her closed kindergarten; how the idea took root in his mind.

"Pshhhh . . ." said Othniel. And Yakir thought, What would *you* do if a global Japanese company were to build an oil press and offer to buy olives from you—would you stick with some crackpot who is promising you the yuppies of Tel Aviv?

"Couldn't you sue him?" Othniel asked. "Find other growers? Listen, I want to plant olives at some point. It'll take them a few years to yield fruit, with the grace of God, but . . ."

"With the grace of God," Roni echoed. "I don't know. I've had the wind knocked out of my sails."

"Tsssss . . ." Othniel concluded, and thought, Just look how the gentiles and Arabs take everything that the Holy One, blessed be He, promised us, and the world remains silent. He said, "With the grace of God, it'll be okay. Don't worry. Like you said, what do the Japanese know about olive oil?" And in the silence that ensued, Yakir recalled the article about Matsumata that he had read on the financial website, he couldn't remember all the details, but recalled that the Japanese know pretty well what they do.

The Pregnancy

The sun came out after long days of heavy rain, and like a sunflower, the hilltop folk turned toward it and basked in its light and in its warmth, but the days were still the days of winter and chill, and Purim would soon be on the doorstep. Yoni stretched that morning at the entrance to his trailer, and his army shirt fastened up to two buttons from his neck exposed a slim, tan chest, as smooth as the surface of a fish pond, and the rows of white teeth moved apart in a wide morning yawn. The last week of his service at Ma'aleh Hermesh C. had begun, though the anger of the residents had yet to subside following the events of the previous week, and he longed for one more look at his girl before he left. Today he'd start packing his meager belongings, he thought, and reminded himself to retrieve from the settlers the flak jacket he'd promised to his good friend Ababa Cohen, who was facing a court-martial for equipment he lost.

The kindergarten kids came out for their first walk outside after the rain. The older kids Amalia and Boaz helped Nehama, the kindergarten teacher, push the crib on wheels containing the toddlers Yemima-Me'ara and Zvuli, and the others trailed along around them. The children have grown so much, Yoni thought, I remember Shuv-el Assis, that little one with the ponytail on the push car, bald in his baby carriage, as if it were yesterday; and Nefesh Freud pressed tight in a baby carrier to his mother's voluptuous chest, not too long ago, too. The older children were at school, the fathers and mothers at work, and Herzl Weizmann was finishing up something small on the porch of Hilik Yisraeli, who was drinking his mug of coffee in the glimmering sun at the window and thinking, Maybe I'll go to the Hebrew University, I finally have to write the chapter on the indulgent attitude toward the kibbutzim on the part of the pre-state leadership, and then perhaps I'll manage by then to get to the movement's break from its ideological and concrete assets. Beyond the large window, Sasson's camel cow was grazing on the soft shoots of a common desert plant, and a little farther below, Gabi Nehushtan was amassing from somewhere new wooden planks and sacks of mortar and gravel and all the other materials required to rebuild the cabin that the Israel Defense Forces had demolished the week before.

Condi and Beilin wagged their tails as a car drove by along the road, and Elazar Freud was speaking on the telephone in his modest yard, into which sneaked the sounds of Radio Breslov from inside the trailer. The water tanker arrived almost surreptitiously and hooked up to the white tank with the sloppily scribbled Star of David at the entrance to the settlement, practically opposite Yoni's front door, where he stood with hand on forehead and looked into the sun at the experienced driver and thought, Without the clear liquid that is now flowing to the top of the tower, there'd be no life here. The children reached the Sheldon Mamelstein playground and dispersed joyfully. The desert hills yellowed on the horizon, and the settlement of Yeshua rose up beyond the riverbed, and the olive trees of Kharmish stood silent in the saddle between the settlements. And then a scream rose and burst forth from one of the trailers, seeped in alarm and surprise and urgency and compassion and love and gratitude to the Creator of the world and all-encompassing faith: the scream of Neta Hirschson, who had squatted to pass water onto a Super-Pharm test stick, which now voicelessly said to her freckled face: Yes!

And to Othniel they said no. After the fuss he kicked up in Jerusalem, the matter was reviewed and the official response arrived: The coins that were found were the property of the State of Israel and would remain in its possession until further notice. As stipulated in the documents Othniel signed, the land, along with its natural resources and archaeological finds—both fixed and portable—were owned by the state. Responsibility for any verbal declaration made concerning alleged private ownership of the cache of coins rested solely with the declarer and did not constitute an official or valid obligation on the part of the state. The Authority thanked the citizen for his discovery and would do all it could to provide him with a few coins as a souvenir, and to help him obtain digging permits in the future.

Othniel opened the door to his home and sat down on an easy chair facing the beautiful mid-January sunshine, and blinked his eyes, and closed them, and gripped his beard, and remained frozen in place for several long minutes.

Gabi couldn't remember the dream he dreamed that morning, he hardly ever remembered his dreams, and if he did, only a handful of surreal disconnected details. But he thought that Shaulit had appeared in the dream, and that the dream was sort of stormy, and his body felt the ancient remnants of wild and fresh excitement, and so when he rose late and hurried to synagogue for the reading of the Shema and the morning prayer service, he added the Tikkun HaKlali, the set of ten Psalms that serve as repentance for all sins, just to be sure.

Shaulit, with her auburn hair in all its glory, was walking right toward him when he left the synagogue. Not exactly an unusual coincidence: Shaulit's home was the closest one to the synagogue, and Gavriel attended morning prayers at the synagogue almost without fail. Similar encounters had occurred in the past without leaving an impression. This time both their faces lit up with surprise and a small smile of recognition, and in a fraction of the second before the "Hi," Gabi knew that the previous Sabbath evening went through Shaulit's mind, too.

He asked her about the creepy-crawly situation at home. She asked him about his work. The remnants of the dream unsettled him a little, and she, too, felt a little off-balance without the children there to divert attention and allay tensions. She invited him over for a cup of tea, and made Turkish coffee for herself in a glass cup, and blew on the granules that floated to the top in a whirlpool of bubbles, sipping cautiously. She asked if he also didn't have hot water that morning. She couldn't wake up like that: without hot water, she couldn't brush her teeth, and without brushing, the day didn't begin. That was the hardest thing about life here for her, the hot water. He said he needed freezing water in the morning. If his face wasn't drenched in cold water, he couldn't shake off sleep, even in the winter, and it bothered him when, in the summer, the water wasn't cold and invigorating enough. He went inside to check the boiler, didn't find a fault, the water was hot. Sometimes after a cold night it took a little time for it to come through the pipes, he explained.

He tried afterward to reconstruct how they got onto the subject of Mickey. He was astounded by himself, by her—just like that on a wintry weekday with tea on a bench swing in the yard of Shaulit Rivlin's home. She asked why he hadn't been at some wedding that took place at Ma'aleh Hermesh A. The fact that she had noticed his absence warmed his heart, and he explained to her that he felt uneasy at weddings. The dancing, the circles, the songs, the seemingly unbridled joy—he felt sometimes, from the sidelines, that it was very bridled, almost forced, and noticed that for the most part he didn't feel a part of it. From weddings they moved on somehow to talk about birthdays. She told him that her late father, bless his memory, would have celebrated his birthday that coming week. She said that the pain seemed to be more intense on his birthday. On his birthday, of all days, not on the day he was taken by the terrorists, may they rot in hell. Well, said Gabi, the day of his death marks the end, the beginning of life without him. In fact, it's a remembrance day that reminds you of yourself. But his birthday marks the time that should have been; marks his life, which is no more. His birthday reminds you of him.

"How do you know that?" she asked him, like someone whose stream of hot water has suddenly appeared.

"I know," he replied. His own birthday was approaching, he told her. He smiled, and the smile exposed his large teeth, narrowed his pleasant eyes, tugged at the bachelor's beard that needed grooming.

"But how do you know the difference between the birthday and the day of the death?" she insisted. And he told her about Mickey. Mind you, not dead, thank God, but every year Gabi marked the day of the separation, the day after which he never saw his son again, a like-death day. He didn't explain why he couldn't see or talk to him, laid the blame on his ex-wife and said she'd fled to the other side of the world, that she was a little strange, and that she didn't allow him any contact. And he recounted how, every year as Mickey's birthday approached at the end of the fall, with the world gloomy and the days growing darker, he felt terrible. Mickey will be eight this year, he told Shaulit, and she listened with sparkling eyes, the first of the hilltop residents who heard about Mickey from Gabi himself. There was something liberating about Shaulit; she

414 · ASSAF GAVRON

drew you into relating the most intimate stories. He spoke about Mickey, and a pain paralyzed him, but he didn't stop: it was impossible to escape the pain of a child. The pining. The remorse for every argument, for every refusal. That void is so unfathomable, never-ending. He tried not to blame Anna. She didn't have the faith in God Almighty to give her the strength to cope.

"During a lesson I once attended," Shaulit said, "the rabbi said that longing is the engine of the world. The beginning and the end. Longing comes with so much pain that can break you. Whatever we do, we're broken vessels. Rabbi Nachman brought music out of longing. The heart beats and lets up. Longing—touches and leaves."

The phone rang in the house and Shaulit disappeared inside. Gabi heard "Yes, Hedva" and "What an insane day, right?" and silence the length of three sentences, and then "Just fine, Hedva, sure, I'll be there."

Gabi got up and walked to the pathway and saw Yoni carrying something. A wave of rage passed through him; he had been told of the fervor with which Yoni had led the demolition of the cabin. Gabi turned around and saw Shaulit emerge from the house, a tray in her hands, and on it a pot of tea and halvah cookies. She said she had a team meeting at the school in the afternoon—did he discern disappointment in her voice? Did the disappointment stem from the cutting short of their conversation? The tea and cookies said to him, We have a little more time together.

She sat down beside him again, and told of her longing for her father, of the pain. She poured more tea. Offered another cookie, made a face that said "I just can't be bothered" when the phone rang again. After every interruption she remembered the point at which he had stopped, heard every word. And understood. They felt like members of the same tribe.

"I always think about the choices we make," he said. "The bottom line is, nothing is incidental, there has to be some kind of design, otherwise how do things turn out the way they do? All the choices that led me and Anna to turn up on the same subway platform in New York at the same time—and all that has happened since: being together, returning to Israel, having a child . . ." He always returned to those thoughts, played with them, wondered if a different chain of events, one that stemmed from different choices, would have turned his life out differently.

"You can't agonize over choices you made. We are so insignificant. We don't have the ability to influence things. Rabbi Nachman also lost sons in his lifetime. That's God's design. He'll come back to you one day, you'll see."

He nodded. "That's true. I realized that there is someone who directs things," he said, "otherwise it couldn't happen, otherwise living would be impossible. And the moment I realized that, suddenly everything fell into place. I looked back on my life and I saw the providence everywhere . . . Though I walk through the valley of the shadow of death I will fear no evil for Thou art always with me. The pain doesn't let up, but you understand that it's part of something logical. And thus you overcome. Because I am not here for nothing. I have a mission in the world. Not for nothing did God Almighty put me through this test . . ."

"That's so right," Shaulit said as Neta Hirschson stepped onto the pathway leading up to the house and approached them, and from the look on her face, it was clear she didn't give any thought to the situation she was walking into, to the intimacy, to the grief, to the encounter that indeed isn't secretive or inappropriate, yet isn't exactly common, and could raise an eyebrow—Neta didn't raise an eyebrow, but instead said, "Friends, a party!" And to their blank faces, from within the shattered moment, she continued, "Enough crying and agonizing and mourning. It's Purim soon, and I'm organizing a party. We'll celebrate the festival at our hilltop, and also the fifth anniversary of breaking ground. And to unite against the deportations and the demolitions and the orders. And to show everyone that we are happy and together. And also"—a smile spread across her face and her gaze wandered between her two listeners and then she closed her eyes and tilted her head to the sky—"I'm pregnant, bless the dear and good Lord."

"Congratulations! Mazel tov and good wishes. Bless the Lord!" Shaulit said. "Just say when, we'll be there!" She looked at the time and got up hastily to collect Zvuli. Gabi stood and said to Neta, "Congratulations, hallowed be His name," and on the way home felt a mixture of relief, and wonder, and excitement, and the pangs of a longing for Shaulit that had already taken root, for her auburn hair and understanding eyes and unrivaled attentiveness, and wondered if, when she said, "We'll be there," she had meant only her family or was including him, too.

The Outage

The darkness sneaked in from below. Among thorns and rock crevices, from the depths of the east, from the chasms of the salt, from the fissures of the sickle, it crept in and stung the poor sputtering generator. The green rectangular box, the provider of light and heat and cold, the lifeblood of the computers, the telephones, the heaters and television sets, which was born in China and had survived years of afflictions and neglect and types of fuel that weren't diesel because it ran out, which had made it through heat waves and snowfalls and even taken hits from a few rocks—this time it went kaput, as they say.

Ma'aleh Hermesh C. sank into the heart of the darkness. Most of its residents were asleep. Reciting the Tikkun Chatzot prayer before the Holy One blessed be He, his eyes closed, Gavriel Nehushtan heard the silence, the final sputtering, and opened his eyes to find nothing, and above the nothing a few stars and a wisp of moon and the twinkling lights of Yeshua beyond the riverbed. He went down and pressed the switch, and checked it over, and waited and added more diesel and pressed again. Despite his anger, he went to Yoni and knocked on his door, and the soldier slipped into the leggings of his coverall and, gritting his teeth and without complaining, huddled up against the wind and tagged along and came and pressed the switch and checked it over and waited and added more diesel and pressed again. Then said: "Maybe this time it's done for good."

The chill seeped in slowly among the blankets, the refrigerators fell silent, the coiled lightbulbs of the cute night lamps in the children's rooms went out, and from here and there came the sounds of the chirping of babies and cries of alarm and soothing words and the whistling of the wind. More blankets were spread and hugs were exchanged and the future generations crawled into the beds of the previous generations, and men fumbled about in the darkness, put on socks and shoes from the corners of rooms and coats from hangers, and went out into the great blackness and felt their way to the generator and grumbled to themselves that this was impossible, how many years had they waited to be hooked up to the electric grid, how come power lines had yet to be laid from A., and the bastards at the Civil Administration's electricity division hadn't given the green light, and the fucking army, and the motherfucking wind . . . They pressed the switch and checked it over and waited and added more diesel and pressed again. Then said: "Maybe this time it's done for good." Returned, undressed, slipped under, pressed up close, caressed, and closed their eyes.

Roni was freezing. Of course he didn't get out from under his comforter. It was too cold, and he assumed there'd be enough volunteers, what did he know about generators. What am I doing here? he wondered. Over the past year that same question had flashed through his mind thousands of times, and with more intent the last few days, since he'd returned from Tel Aviv. He had slept there on children's mattresses in a closed kindergarten, wrapped himself in blankets that weren't warm enough, met someone nice, almost pretty, just a kindergarten teacher. Not the high point of his life, but he felt at home. Rediscovered his old self. Tel Aviv awoke in him the ability to see for a moment from the outside what he was doing on the hilltop: lazing about idly, without the energy to work. He's too cold. He's too hot. Freaking out. Frustrated, listening to the transistor, sinking into a depression. There was a period when he tried to convince himself that he was better off there. Why work hard if you don't have to, if you could sit on a hilltop and look out at a beautiful view, close your eyes, and simply be. But now sleep escaped him into a new clarity, an unfamiliar one, and he opened his eyes wide without seeing a thing and thought, It's too heavy, this world of Ma'aleh Hermesh C., too dark. If he wanted to stay, he'd have to step inside and become a part of it. And he couldn't. He had heard sermons, commentaries, lessons—he didn't get it. He had observed his brother, his sparkling eyes. Saw that he'd moved, seen the light, but he saw only what he saw now: nothing.

He recalled how, during one of his random encounters in Tel Aviv, someone had given him iPod earphones and said, "Listen." Some acoustic song. The strumming of a guitar. A nice melody. It sent shivers through his entire body. This place, after all, also had the strumming of guitars and nice melodies, but when the sounds diffused from the white earphones into his brain, he felt different. That's the solace. In the city, you could be a member of the flock, even if you were alone within the flock, that was the best he could do, and that was good enough, if it was his flock. He smiled a bright smile and felt the pressure rising in his bowels and squeezing out a loud, rolling fart, which he hoped would warm him a little. He remembered an expression from his youth and asked out loud, into the darkness, "Who cut the cheese?" and answered himself with a hollow smile in the silence of the befouled trailer.

Meanwhile, a tale of love and darkness. After all efforts to deal with the venerable generator had failed, and after the freezing wind had died down a little, Gavriel Nehushtan left the scene and decided to walk back the long way, in order to pass by Shaulit's trailer. He didn't plan to go in, only to check from afar, with a glance, that everything there was quiet, that the power outage hadn't ruffled the fabric of life in the Rivlin home. As his feet crunched over the gravel along the descent by the gate, he heard the door open and close and footsteps in the dark.

"Ah, it's you," Shaulit said in a broken voice. "What happened?"

"Nothing. There's a power outage. The generator died and they weren't able to fix it, it'll be like this all night. I just wanted . . . Will you be okay? The children? You have enough blankets?"

She smiled a smile he didn't see and giggled a giggle he heard, and whispered, "Thank you. Yes, I think so. If I can find them in the dark . . ." He laughed with her. And came with her to look for the blankets in the closet. And smelled her hair, drowsy and warm from an interrupted winter slumber. And heard the breathing of her children: tender, regular, soothing. And bumped into her leg and heard her stifle an uncontrollable stream of laughter that turned into a series of rapid, choked breaths.

Candles she didn't find; matches, yes. She made tea on the gas burner. He sat on the sofa and she on the armchair in the light of a blue, docile flame, under the kettle. They spoke in the darkness about the darkness: pitch darkness; the darkness falling on the world outside, and the light igniting inside; the ongoing conflict between inside and out; the plague of darkness that brought down death on all the land. And the darkness would become darker—you can feel the darkness. Following a series of invisible but clearly sensed yawns, Gavriel said, "Don't you want to go to sleep?"

"Dying to sleep . . . Too cold here in the kitchen . . . But I want to continue talking, too . . . Want to come to the other room?"

The pulse from one sentence to the next. The cold air that warmed with every word, every breath. The pulse in Gabi's wrist, in the vein. Of course he wanted to join her. She got under the comforter and he sat on the edge of the bed, excited and sheepish. They spoke quietly, took care not to wake the children, whose marathon of rhythmic breathing didn't cease for an instant.

"Okay, this isn't right," she finally said.

"What's not right? You feel uncomfortable, you want me to leave. Of course, sorry . . ." He got up from the edge of the bed.

"No, silly, it's not right that you aren't covered. Get under the blanket. The bed's big enough. Each on his own side. Do you think it's allowed? Maybe we should send a question to Rabbi Aviner's cellular Q&A service? Send a text message: 'Is a divorced man allowed to share a bed with a divorced woman, at two separate ends, without touching, without seeing one another?' . . ." Her words were broken up by her laughter, rattling and joyful, Gabi could only imagine her teeth and eyes, and perhaps because she wasn't able to quiet herself this time, Zvuli woke with a high-pitched wail. Shaulit fed him and hummed to him until he fell asleep again.

"If you carry on humming like that, I'll fall asleep in the end, too."

"Go ahead."

But he didn't fall asleep because she said something, and he replied, and they went on like that for who knows how long—an hour? More? And Gabi felt a tenderness come over his body under the comforter, and the heat of the air between them, and there were moments of silence and maybe dozing off, and awakening, without talking, only breathing. And then fingers touched his hand. His body atremble. She caressed the back of his hand with her fingers, so pleasing and forbidden, but some things are permissible even when forbidden, when the intentions are pure and faith is sound.

And after one of the times his eyes opened, the light was starting to faintly rise, and now it no longer seemed right, so he got up cautiously and set out.

The Operation

The winter brought such beautiful days that even the coldest nights were thawed and almost forgotten. A glorious sun smiled on the hilltop, almost a taunt of the night's tribulations—the forecast heralded an approaching cold front, but the sun was having none of it, the air stood still and the temperatures climbed. Roni Kupper sat in the doorway of his home, his feet on an iron stair sullied with dried mud, between his fingers the first cigarette of the morning, a cup of coffee beside him, and his already narrowed eyes on account of the light narrowed even more at the sound of the Nokia ringtone that came from the edge of the bed.

"Hello?"

"It's Rina."

"Rina!"

And already by early afternoon he was on his way to Tel Aviv.

Captain Omer Levkovich invited himself over for a look around the place, bearing a summons for Josh to appear before the Jerusalem Magistrate's Court for a hearing on charges of disturbing the peace and obstructing a soldier in the execution of his duty. Omer knew that Josh wouldn't respond to the summons, and that no one would insist on enforcing his appearance, due to time and staffing constraints, but he pretended to be looking for him, went down to the demolished cabin, noticed the new girders and the beginnings of renewed construction, paid no attention—because what was he going to do, anyway?—and then went to Yoni and handed him the summons and said, "If you have time, find him and give it to him. Holy shit, I can't believe you're leaving, makes me want to cry."

Yoni didn't have time to find Josh. He was supposed to report to the induction center in seventy-two hours, and the thing that concerned him most right then was that, due to a miscalculation, he was short on underwear, and it was too late to do laundry. So he wore long johns without underpants, and for the next two days aired out two pairs that were in relatively good condition. He was troubled next by thoughts about Gitit and the question of whether he'd have a chance to say good-bye to her. He knew Purim was approaching, and wondered if she'd be coming home. Third on the list of things that occupied Yoni's mind were the feelings of his commander, Omer, who had mumbled repeatedly that he couldn't believe he was leaving, and what was he going to do without him, and why didn't he sign up for longer, even if only for a few months, and he felt like crying. The fourth thing, and last for now, that weighed on the mind of the young Ethiopian soldier was Operation Bigthan and Teresh, about which Omer his commander had started briefing him.

Operation Bigthan and Teresh was the secret operation to empty the outpost of Ma'aleh Hermesh C. of its residents and homes. The target date was two days from now, Yoni's last day in the army. It had been scheduled, in fact, for the next day, but the head of Central Command announced a one-day postponement due to a communication issue with the riot police. Operation Bigthan and Teresh, Omer explained, would include the deployment of a massive number of army, police, and riot police forces in Humvees and armored personnel carriers, an engineering crew with D-9s to demolish the structures, a team of psychologists, two military ambulances, and a helicopter in which the head of Central Command and the defense minister would hover over the scene. Following the successful demolition of the cabin, the sentiment was *Enough with the nonsense*. The harsh response had proved itself. Move in quickly, demolish, evacuate, move out. No discussion, no bullshit. They've been feeding us shit for years, and everyone's had enough: the court, the command major-general, the defense minister, the U.S. president. The outpost was still making headlines, continued to be a thorn in everyone's side, proof of the ineffectual command of the defense minister vis-à-vis the army, and of the government vis-à-vis the settlers, and of the American administration vis-à-vis the Israelis, and of whomever you like vis-à-vis whomever else you don't like. Enough. Everyone was sick and tired of it.

A flush rose to Omer's cheeks when he got worked up. He explained to Yoni why he'd had enough: the place, the people, the fun they made of him. Once, when he first arrived in the area, he thought that watching out for the interests of the settlers and joining in the mutual back-scratching would help him get ahead in the army, but he was no longer convinced of it. He needed to be a commander, not a politician. To execute a mission: a vigorous and successful evacuation. Yoni couldn't understand how a complex military operation had fallen on his final day of service, why couldn't they have postponed it for one more day and allowed him to go home in peace. But he remained loyal to his army and his commander. He promised to carry out the necessary preparations, which didn't amount to very much, because the forces would show up by surprise.

"True, it may not be a surprise, because they've received demolition orders for that date. On the other hand, they've received numerous orders in the past, so they surely don't believe it's really going to happen."

While they were talking in Yoni's trailer, leaning up against the wall and sitting on the steel-framed bed, they heard the backup beeps of a large truck outside.

"What's that?" the officer asked. The sergeant shrugged.

"What's that, Herzliko?" Omer tried a minute later to aim the question at Herzl Weizmann, who was standing outside and using his plaster-casted arms to direct a truck bearing a huge crane. Written along the side of the truck were the words *Israel Electric Corporation*.

Omer didn't get a response and tried again. "What's this supposed to be?"

Herzl spun around. "Ah, honorable officer." He smiled. "How are you?"

Omer tried to ask a third time, this time in mime.

"The Electric Corporation," Herzl replied with the obvious.

"I noticed," Omer said, "but what are they doing?"

"I think they're finally hooking up the settlement to the electricity grid. It's about time, isn't it?"

"But . . ." Omer didn't want to and couldn't disclose the fact that the settlement would imminently be in no further need of electricity, and anyway, Herzl Weizmann wasn't the appropriate person to confront with that truth. "Where did it come from? I mean, who—"

"Listen," Herzl said, "I only know what I know."

"And what do you know?" Omer asked.

"That Natan Eliav called and asked me to come here this morning to help the guys from the Electric Corporation and build the infrastructure for them."

Omer turned and walked away while he punched numbers into his cell phone. A small crowd formed around the truck and expressions of joy rang out. "How fitting, on Purim!" said Neta Hirschson, rolled-up posters under her arms. "The Jews had light and joy! Tell me, why shouldn't the Bezeq phone company lay down cables here while we're about it, too? Cellcom's cellular service is terrible, and the Palestinians with their Paltel are always hogging the reception, not to mention the price . . ."

The battalion commander, the brigade commander, the division commander, and the head of Central Command were all surprised. The defense minister had been unaware. Malka, his aide, thought he had heard something about electricity at some outpost, but wasn't sure. The head of the Shin Bet security service was in the dark. A quick round of calls provided Omer with the following information: Deputy Tourism Minister Uriel Tsur had leaned as heavily as he could on his fellow party member—who attended the same Jerusalem neighborhood synagogue, and with whom he had studied at yeshiva years ago—the energy minister, who just that morning had spoken with the infrastructure minister on a similar yet different matter, and persuaded him to sign a temporary permit to lay a power line from the settlement of Ma'aleh Hermesh A. to the Ma'aleh Hermesh C. outpost, which had lost its generator.

"And all those people know that the outpost is being razed in two days?" Omer asked his brigade commander.

"Sure," replied the brigade commander. "But a cold front is expected over the coming days. They didn't want to leave them without electricity. Israeli citizens can't be left exposed to the forces of nature like that. We're human, after all, aren't we? It's easier to lay a cable from A. than to bring in a new generator. No one's got the money for a generator. And the permits needed to set up a generator now, with the construction freeze, you won't believe it. Besides, it'll give them a false sense of security. They won't be expecting an evacuation two days after being hooked up to the grid, now, will they?"

"But do the ministers and the command major-general know?" Omer tried nevertheless.

"Yes, yes, everyone knows. I mean, whoever needs to know . . ."

Omer hung up and turned to again face the gathering. Yoni beside him said, "Now they remember to hook up electricity? Dammit." Neta Hirschson walked over to the notice board on the playground. Omer followed her with his gaze, squinting. "Come, Yoni, let's go see what she's doing there."

She posted a large notice alongside the demolition order, which was holding up well. She noticed that Omer and Yoni were looking over her shoulder, and ignored them, but then she asked Yoni to lend a finger so she could insert a tack.

"What's an Adloyada?" asked the soldier. Neta ignored the question, but Yoni went on reading the notice. "Ah! It's on my last day here. You're throwing a farewell party for me?"

Neta continued to busy herself with the tacks and didn't answer, but then decided to cease the excommunication and addressed Yoni. "Sure, come, why not, perhaps you'll dress up as a human being, too." Then she addressed Omer. "And maybe you'll dress up as an IDF soldier who defends the citizens of his state from the Arabs instead of expelling them? Shame on you, it's the Sabbath of the Zachor Torah portion this week— you shall remember what Amalek did to Israel. The hatred of Amalek."

Omer, who cast a quick glance over the invitation, chuckled. "You're doing it here on the playground? In the middle of winter? Have you gone crazy? Haven't you heard a cold front is expected?"

"Look who's asking if I've gone crazy. I heard. It doesn't scare me. The warmth in our hearts will keep us warm. Come, have a good time, there'll be surprises. It'll be fun. Rejoice a little with your people, what's wrong with that?"

Neta had managed to secure a modest budget from Natan Eliav and Othniel. She sent Jenia Freud off to prepare hamantaschen and other snacks, called a Jerusalem company that specialized in providing DJs and sound equipment, and found an available car and a driver to take her to Jerusalem to buy prizes for the costume competition and rattles for the reading of the Scroll of Esther. Then she moved on to deal with the entertainment: She called Coco, second place at a Eurovision song contest for France in the '70s, who had found religion, immigrated to Israel, settled in Ma'aleh Hermesh A., and sometimes appeared as a country singer with an American neighbor who was a wonderful banjo player. But Coco had been struck ill with cancer, God have mercy, and was undergoing treatment at Hadassah Medical Center, she'd return to the stage, God willing in a few months, so Neta booked the Settlers, a wedding band from A. that promised a joyful occasion and gave a discount "in honor of C.'s birthday."

Omer looked at the large notice with a sense of astonishment mixed with admiration. "Adloyada!" it announced. "To make them days of feasting and joy! A big Purim party! Ma'alch Hermesh C.'s fifth birthday! United we'll stand against Haman the evil and the expulsion decree! The Jews will have light and joy in the Land of Israel! Costume competition! Music by the Settlers!" He shifted his gaze a few centimeters to the left, from the invitation to the demolition order: the date was the same date, 2.28.2010, and the Hebrew one, too, Adar 14, 5770, to avoid any misunderstanding; the message was a little different. Schizophrenia, he thought. He shook his head in wonder.

"Come, come." Neta softened her tone. "We'll celebrate the electricity grid, too, and Yoni's farewell if you like. And also . . ." She caressed her stomach with pride. It would still be some time before it showed, but the entire hilltop already knew about the pregnancy, about how the Holy One, blessed be He, had answered her prayers, about the acupuncturist's quince diet, about the recommendation from the rabbi's wife to change her husband's name to Yisrael and add the name, Bracha, to hers, about the blessing she gave her with water from the Jordan River. Neta mumbled, "Praise the Lord," and looked up at the skies, and the two soldiers instinctively followed her gaze. Then she straightened the hood on her head and walked away.

The Party

Achill settled on the hilltop during the course of the night and sparkled when morning broke in millions of refractions of frost from among clods of earth, gardening tools, cacti, upturned push cars, and on the windshields of vehicles. The day opened its eyes with a wide yawn, and hours would go by before it would shake off the cold. Neta Hirschson, after a bout of morning sickness, cut up a few small pieces of pear for herself, sipped cautiously on apple juice, and before going out made a few sewing alterations to her Purim costume and even managed to send off an annoyed talk-back response into the far-too-left expanse of the Internet. Her husband, Jean-Marc, mentioned the miracle of Purim when he recited the version of the blessing over the meal that opens with "For the miracles," and then devoured a breakfast of eggs and French toast, followed up with a croissant with butter and jam, and he still had a little room left for cornflakes with milk.

"I thought I was the one who's supposed to be on an eating frenzy," Neta said.

"I'm still wiped out from the Fast of Esther," Jean-Marc offered.

The synagogue was full and the mood festive. Hilik served as the cantor and recited the blessing to give thanks to God and continued with "In the days of Mordechai and Esther" and went on to the reading of the Ve'yavo Amalek Torah portion, and then the various blessings for the reading of the Scroll of Esther, and then the Scroll was read, and the rattles shook the heads of the worshippers and struck down Haman and his ten sons, the lips mumbled in unison, the tightly packed bodies thawed the freezing air that infiltrated from outside. And then came the final blessing over the Scroll and joyous singing of Purim songs.

Othniel huddled in quiet conversation with Hilik on the way out of synagogue. Not a word from the army in recent days. Othniel was his usual concerned self; Hilik was uncharacteristically upbeat.

"They wouldn't dare do anything on Purim, and certainly not without informing us first," Hilik said.

"Look at the date that appears here," Othniel said, and pointed to the demolition order posted on the synagogue wall. It stipulated Adar 14—March 5—as the very last and final day for the residents to vacate their homes. "That's today. This silence on their part, I don't know. I tried calling Giora yesterday, to wish him a happy holiday, to sniff around. He hasn't called me back. It's not like him."

"They wouldn't dare," Hilik determined. "They didn't realize it's Purim because they're fools, it's not the first time. And if they dare, Purim is a day of miracles, of the abolishing of decrees."

"I don't think so." Othniel twirled his beard with his left hand, and placed his right affectionately on the back of the neck of a teenager dressed in a PEACE NOW shirt, wearing a rubber baldness-wig on his head, adorned with round-rimmed glasses, boasting one of his mother's clip-on earrings, and puffing on a peace pipe that rested in the corner of his mouth. His son Yakir, dressed up as a left-winger. He was holding a menu that Moran had brought him from a café in Tel Aviv. Among the dishes were shrimp and other seafood. Children and adults asked to see and browsed eagerly through the menu, amused and stunned. "They dared to destroy Gabi's cabin," Othniel noted, "then, too, you said they wouldn't dare, didn't you?" They couldn't simply trust the status quo or rely on reason, he believed, because they'd already been violated.

"That was a different story. A nature reserve. The Nature and Parks Authority. Besides, why would they be hooking up electricity before an evacuation?" Hilik said. Othniel wasn't swayed. "I'm telling you, they're cooking up something." He had known the authorities for too long, knew they couldn't be relied on, they couldn't allow themselves to drop their guard.

An idea took root in his mind. He recalled an unusual incident that had occurred in Samaria a few years back. Out of the corner of his eye, he spotted Roni, wearing a curly wig and round plastic glasses, and approached him. Without any preamble, he sounded him out. Roni chuckled as if he had just heard an amusing story for Purim, and sipped on a bottle of beer. Othniel said he was serious. Roni took another sip and thought. Othniel's idea sounded over-the-top, but it could be an opportunity. It was his last day, and he wanted to bid farewell to everyone in good spirits, so why shouldn't he say a nice good-bye to Musa Ibrahim, too? After all, they had been through several months of shared work, shared hopes, a friendship of sorts, you could say. True, he was disappointed with the ugly end to his venture, and felt betrayed, but come now, it's Purim.

"But I'm not going alone," he said to Othniel.

"Maybe your brother?" Othniel suggested.

"No way," Roni replied.

Othniel thought, and then saw the answer standing right before his eyes—"Here, take this peacenik. Perfect!" He rested a hand on Yakir, his son.

"Your son?" Roni raised a Harry Potter–like eyebrow. "Seriously, you're not worried about him?"

"The area is crawling with army personnel. You'll be fine. Besides, just to be extra sure, take this with you." Othniel lifted the edge of his shirt to reveal the Desert Eagle Mark VII tucked into his pants.

The contrasting attitudes of Othniel Assis and Hilik Yisraeli more or less represented the split mind of each and every one of the hilltop residents: fear of the power, blindness, obsequiousness or perhaps guile of the defense minister and his army, on the one hand, and faith in the justness of their cause and the Holy One, blessed be He, who will save us from their hands on a festive day, certainly after the fast, the prayers for forgiveness, the Aneinu and Avinu Malkeinu prayers of atonement and the customary giving of gifts to the needy yesterday, on the other hand. Thus, every time the hum of an engine was heard from beyond the sentry post at the gate, all eyes turned worriedly in that direction, waited for the appearance of the vehicles and the news heralded by their identity.

The first to ascend and arrive in his large vehicle was Herzl Weizmann, who, along with two workers immediately began arranging the playground and readying it for the party: a stage, stands for lighting and speakers, electricity, the temporary dismantling of removable playground equipment, a partition to separate the men and women that was stretched down the middle of the playground.

The next in line were four nimble dairy goats, new additions to Othniel's farm. With so many worries on his mind, he almost forgot about the delivery, and here they were in all their glory, all several dozen kilograms of them, with their unkempt wool and their udders filled with goodness. And not only that, but out from the cabin of the truck stepped a beautiful Dutch girl, wooden clogs on her feet, a shiny blond wig on her head, heavily made up, sporting false eyelashes, her dress doll-like and European. The eyes needed a moment to adjust and focus, a gentle balancing of the mind between the recollection of facial features and recognition that it's Purim—Gitit!

Yoni's heart almost stopped at the sight of the beautiful smooth-skinned Dutch girl, and at the same time he was troubled. The forces were supposed to be here first thing in the morning, and Omer wasn't answering his phone, and everyone was here with their costumes and celebrations, and the cold was eating into his bones despite the coverall and dog-eared hat and a double layer of undershirts and long johns. The hum of another engine was heard, and Yoni raised his eyes and, from his lofty height of five feet and five inches, spotted the vehicle of the Jerusalem sound system company, whose crew quickly began unpacking crates and setting up speakers and lighting and hooking up electricity and sound. After them came the Settlers, four bespectacled settlers with matching crocheted skullcaps in different colors, cheap black jackets, and thin piano ties from the '80s, who conducted a quick sound check and went off to get something to drink.

Music came from the speakers positioned in the corners of the playground, a traditional Purim song from some festival collection or other. Silvery clouds were gathering in the sky. Omer finally answered Yoni and updated him. They were waiting for the final go-ahead. An urgent discussion was under way with the chief of staff—do they evacuate on the festival or not, do they deploy a helicopter or not. Like they hadn't been planning the operation for days. Like they hadn't known it was a festival and that the orders issued by the High Court of Justice of the State of Israel were about to expire. Omer asked Yoni not to worry. "I'm not worried, my bro," Yoni said, gritting his teeth. "I'll be at the induction center tomorrow, whether the operation moves forward or not."

"What's moving forward?" a large penguin asked him. It was Shaulit

Rivlin, who had come to the army's trailer in the company of an orange-ponytailed and freckled Pippi Longstocking, her elder daughter, Amalia, to deliver a colorful plate of treats.

"It's nothing. I'm just wondering if I should go ahead and buy myself a stereo system as a gift for my discharge." Yoni's hesitant smile revealed his white teeth.

"Why aren't you dressed up in costume yet?" Amalia scolded him, and he replied, "Ahh . . . I'll be dressing up soon . . ."

"As what?" pressed the girl.

"Amalia, it's a secret!" the penguin responded, and winked from inside her furry head. They left the plate of treats and walked off hand in hand back to the playground, from which another Purim song was now coming.

The playground gradually filled up. Bottles of wine and beer stood on a table in the corner alongside plates of crisps and crackers, because, as the rabbis of the Talmud said, a person is obligated to drink on Purim until he does not know the difference between "cursed be Haman" and "blessed be Mordechai."

The Settlers took to the stage and opened with "Shoshanat Yaakov." With the aid of lots of cardboard and aluminum foil, eleven-and-a-half-year-old Hananiya Assis had become a pointy space shuttle. To his disappointment, he'd go on to claim just third place in the costume competition. Bigfoot the Abominable Snowman, five-year-old Boaz Yisraeli, who was wrapped in a sheet with eyeholes and sewn-on bits of cotton wool, would be satisfied with fourth place. Gavriel Nehushtan was Kareem Abdul-Jabbar in long socks and high-top basketball shoes, a greenish tracksuit, sweatbands around his forehead and wrists, and under his arm a punctured basketball that once belonged to Shimi Gotlieb. His brother, Roni, responded "Harry Potter" to the children who asked what he was dressed up as, and Elazar Freud was Herzl in a black suit and black beard—up until shortly before leaving home, he thought he was King David, but couldn't find a harp or a red beard. Jean-Marc Hirschson was an IDF officer—he'd retrieved his reserve duty uniform from the closet and pinned an array of colorfully striped war veteran decorations and silver-plated commando unit foxes and wings to his chest.

Another vehicle hummed and drove up and everyone turned their heads. It was merely Nir Rivlin's Subaru—"So righteous is the Lord," Neta Hirschson whispered every time she saw no sign of the enemy troops—but not Nir Rivlin behind the wheel: it is but Rambo, complete with bleeding scars and bloated muscles and torn clothing and a plastic machine gun and chains of bullets. Two three-year-olds were his backup in the armed forces: Nefesh-Freud-the-policeman, and Shuv-el-Assis-the-cowboy, armed to the teeth with cap guns and munching on Bamba under a painted mustache. The same list could include Josh, as an Arab terrorist with a kaffiyeh covering most of his red hair and a large plastic mustache fixed above his lip. The Settlers moved on to a joyful Hasidic melody, and then a rock version of a traditional Purim song.

Gabi-Kareem-Abdul-Jabbar kept a tense eye on the encounter between Nir-Rambo and Shaulit-the-penguin. He felt like a kid in the corner at a party who follows the every move of his crush, waiting nervously for a slow dance. What's happening to me? he asked himself. When the penguin walked by or flashed him a half-smile, he went weak at the knees.

Rachel Assis was Snow White and Othniel, her husband—with the aid of an errant curl and a black hat that could have belonged to a rabbi and a sparkling red suit and eye makeup—Michael Jackson. And aside from their daughter the Dutch girl, and their sons—the left-winger, the space shuttle, and the cowboy—their family also included a fourteen-year-old archaeologist in a khaki outfit and carrying a magnifying glass—Dvora—and a red pepper, wrapped in a special soft rubber material that had been sewn to size and shape and painted a bold red, which won six-year-old Emunah second place in the competition.

Yoni found a brown-and-white-striped shirt and retrieved a pair of real metal handcuffs from the box of security equipment and cuffed one of his wrists—a prisoner. Jehu was Queen Esther complete with makeup and thick sidelocks, and his horse, Killer, wore a Santa Claus hood from Bethlehem. Jenia Freud was dressed as a supermarket cashier in a white robe and thick glasses and a lavish hairdo and repeating the slogan "Do you have a customer card?" Hilik, Nehama, and Shneor Yisraeli dressed up in a group as brides. The infants Zvuli Rivlin and Yemima-Me'ara received tiny pairs of sunglasses and toy guitars and were labeled a rock band. And Neta Hirschson brought along a professional makeup kit from home and helped to make up the children, and then went up on stage to preside over the ceremony. She welcomed the arrivals and badmouthed the government and invited everyone to eat and drink and thanked everyone who was helping out—she herself was dressed as an orange tigress, furry and sharp-clawed.

In first place: three-year-old Tchelet Rivlin, dressed up as corn on the cob, draped in row upon row of kernels sewn by Shaulit's patient hand for weeks, a pale yellowish corn dress made from the real thing. The idea was Tchelet's and the work a combined effort of hers and her mother's, including a hood made from warm fleece that was sewn in the right shape and the right size, with precise holes for eyes, nostrils, ears, and mouth. Perfect, as Neta Hirschson admitted when awarding the prize—a Torah, a festive assortment of treats and candies, and two tickets to the central Purim celebrations at the Convention Center in Jerusalem that evening, with performances by Avraham Fried and Mordechai Ben David.

Of all things not to hear, Omer's jeep. At that point the party was in full swing, the band was back to playing at full volume after the costume competition and speeches. Empty wine bottles piled up on the side, clouds darkened the sky, the biting cold was almost forgotten, thanks to the steam coming off the bodies packed tightly together in two small groups, women and men. Roni-Harry-Potter told his brother Gabi-Kareem-Abdul-Jabbar that he'd decided to leave the settlement, but Kareem was more focused on congratulating Shaulit-penguin on her daughter's victory in the costume competition, and the penguin thanked him and whispered that Nir-Rambo would be taking Tchelet-corn to the show at the Convention Center in the evening, so maybe Gabi-Kareem would like to come over to see her? Alongside the sheet that served as the partition, Jehu-Queen-Esther huddled together with Josh-Arab-terrorist, Yoni-prisoner fired glances at Gitit-luscious-Dutch-girl under the stern and watchful eye of Othniel-Michael-Jackson, and Elazar-Freud-Herzl huddled with Jean-Marc-IDF-officer, congratulated him on the pregnancy of Neta-the-tigress, and picked up Nefesh-the-policeman, who was sobbing bitterly. Tears were also choking Hananiya-Assis-Silvery-space-shuttle, who was sure he would win first place, and he was being comforted by Rachel-Snow-White. The spirit of Purim at its finest. And then the soldiers showed up.

The Gunfire

A helicopter hovered in the sky. Eyes turned toward it and toward Captain Omer Levkovich's David jeep and worried glances were exchanged. Othniel located Roni and said to him, "It's time. Get going." Harry Potter stared blankly at the Michael Jackson talking to him, his hand clutching his umpteenth bottle of beer. Then he remembered. "Ah! Right! You were serious, yes?"

"Yes," Othniel replied.

"No, because it's Purim, and all, and who knows . . ."

"Serious," ruled Othniel.

Roni found Yakir the peacenik and said to him, "Come on, let's move."

Yakir, who had also had a few drinks, replied, "Ten-four."

"While I'm thinking about it, take the Arab with you, too," Othniel said. He pointed at a masked man wearing a kaffiyeh.

"Josh?" Yakir replied.

The three headed out.

Omer's David jeep was followed by the arrival of Humvees. And armored personnel carriers. And D-9s. A noisy and heavy-duty convoy. The audio system of the Jerusalem sound company carried another traditional Purim tune from the instruments of the Settlers, with the song flowing somewhat surprisingly into a Mashina rock number.

Michael Jackson asked how can this be. And a bride in her wedding dress said it's incomprehensible. And a tigress screamed oppression. And Snow White cried, "Like so? On a festival? Have you no shame?" Michael Jackson whipped out his phone and called his friend the major general. No answer, not a word. The Settlers sang "He rode to Palestine on a two-humped camel." Rambo said, "What a mess," and it wasn't clear if he was enjoying the wine or concerned about the developments. Kareem Abdul-Jabbar looked for his penguin, and the prisoner was summoned to his commander but he, too, had been drinking a little, fuck it, it's his last day in the army, he's allowed to celebrate. The dogs barked, and the convoy came to a halt, and soldiers and blank-faced riot police emerged from the vehicles.

Approaching the Arab village were Harry Potter, a red-haired Arab, and a peacenik. They carried a festive assortment of Purim treats, a rustling cellophane bag with chewy candies, four mini chocolate bars, Jenia Freud's coconut-chocolate cookies, and more sweets for the people of the village. Yakir and Josh spoke in low voices about some technology issue and Roni walked ahead of them in silence, smoked, wondered about Rina the kindergarten teacher and the closed kindergarten where he had spent his Tel Aviv nights. A desert lark that suddenly took to the sky above the barren hilltops caught his eye—is he flying to warmer lands?—and he recalled his last conversation with Musa, when he called to say someone had set fire to trees in his grove. Roni sensed he suspected him, called to find out where he was, but he was in Tel Aviv. He promised Musa he'd look into it. And tried he did, but ran into a wall of silence that reminded him of the kibbutz—everyone seemed to know who did what, but God forbid someone should talk about it on the outside. And Roni was on the outside. Even Gabi gave him this answer: Forget it, don't poke your nose in, let us manage our own affairs. Roni wondered just how much his brother himself was a part of the inner circle on the hilltop, what did he know. He tossed his cigarette butt onto the soft earth and smiled a bitter smile. He was no fool. He'd been living here for a year, knew all the players. It wasn't hard to work out who served as the hilltop's go-to man for special missions, whether acting on his own discretion or on behalf of the community. The quiet kid on the horse called Killer, Jehu.

But Roni guessed only part of the truth—Jehu hadn't been there alone.

In the village of Kharmish it was a wintry and sleepy day that had been disturbed by the Jews' loud music. Someone looked out her kitchen window and saw the approaching trio and called to her brother, and the brother looked out the kitchen window and phoned a friend, and within minutes, despite the cold, a group of onlookers had gathered and were watching, with a mixture of curiosity, bewilderment, amusement, and agitation, the three Jews, or two Jews and one Arab, who were approaching them.

On the Sheldon Mamelstein playground at Ma'aleh Hermesh C., someone said, "Ooh-ah, look at that," referring to the riot dispersal equipment—helmets and clubs and large see-through plastic shields. Following orders, the soldiers and police positioned themselves in front of the collection of costumed characters. Nefesh Freud tugged on his father's sleeve and asked, "Who are those people who also dressed up as policemen?" Captain Omer went up onto the stage and requested the microphone. Only then did the band cease playing a slow waltz version of yet another traditional Purim song.

Silence fell while Omer cleared his throat and said, "Hello . . . Good evening, everyone. Sorry to disturb your Purim party. But the government of Israel has decided to evacuate this illegal outpost. Demolition orders were posted here ten days ago, and you were given the chance to leave quietly and without confrontation. This morning we received an order to come help anyone who has yet to leave. I'm asking for your cooperation and help in carrying out a peaceful and dignified evacuation. If you choose not to cooperate, we will respond accordingly. And I'm telling you now, so that you won't be able to say I didn't tell you. We're stronger, we're prepared, and we'll succeed. Thank you."

The silence ensued for a few seconds. And then the yelling began. And spitting. And people took off in every direction. The sheet that separated the women and men was pulled down and trampled. Urgent phone calls. And tears. And what the hell. And why right now. And what insensitivity. And what ugly provocation. And how come we're the ones who are singled out while the Arabs are free to build as they please.

The helicopter hovered in the sky, observed. A D-9 made its way slowly down the hilltop, beyond the playground, and approached the first trailer to its right. "Wait, wait, wait, why can't we talk for a moment?" For Hilik Yisraeli, with rouge on his cheeks and mascara on his eyelashes, it finally hit him. Stumbling in his high heels and bridal dress, a bouquet of flowers still in his hand, he chased after the large bulldozer. But the bulldozer didn't listen. Neta-tigress and Rachel-Snow-White each clasped a hand over a gaping mouth, in disbelief, as the D-9's blade slammed into the ceiling of the trailer and with a jarring, huge, heartrending noise, shattered the roof.

"What the hell?" roared the tigress, stunned to the core. "Disobey the order! Criminals!" Jehu-Queen-Esther galloped up on his horse, Santa-Killer, and tried to circle and approach the bulldozer from the front, but the D-9 went about its business. Captain Omer stood with his arms folded and observed the scene.

"Don't you have a heart? You're Haman!" a woman within a costume yelled at him. No, he answered to himself, I don't have a heart. I don't pity. I've had enough. The driver of the D-9 caught his eye for a second, and with a gesture of his hand, he instructed him, go on, go on. And he went on and demolished the trailer, contents and all. It sounded like the intense groans of agony of an elephant.

The prisoner grabbed the hand of the Dutch girl and pulled her forcefully, and she, her knees failing her, her mind in turmoil, went along with him. Her father was busy trying to get hold of the head of Central Command, who was overseeing the operation from the helicopter in the sky, and her mother was focused on maintaining eye contact with her younger brothers and sisters. She followed the prisoner. He reached the guard tower and climbed the stairs, and she behind him, her hand still in his. At the top, in the tower, he turned and held her and kissed her lips and said, "I've been going crazy, crazy, crazy without you." And she didn't answer, just kissed him back, and with a slender finger traced a line along his neck. He moved a hand to the buxom Dutch chest. She froze, didn't stop him, couldn't. Was in a dream. She was pure—that morning, at the boarding school, she had been to the mikveh, had even checked to make sure her period was over. For no special reason, she thought. Down below, screaming, rioting, straining engines, shattering fiberglass, tear gas, but she's a buxom Dutch lass who's been abducted to a high tower by a prisoner. And his small head with its thick curls was nestling between her breasts, and he moved aside her bra and panted, "Crazy, crazy," and she didn't stop him, she didn't stop.

* * *

Yakir Assis was the first to notice the welcome party for the trio heading for Kharmish, and quickly brought it to the attention of his fellow walkers. Roni tried to signal he was coming in peace by raising and waving his hand with a smile, and then by raising a second hand. But when the villagers recognized Roni under the curly wig and behind the toy glasses, and alongside him another Jew dressed as an Arab, and another one that looked odd, tensions rose. "It's Roni," someone said, "what does that scumbag think he's doing, what's he coming here for? And bringing along someone who's dressed up for the hajj? Has he gone crazy?"

Roni Kupper hadn't been a popular man in Kharmish ever since the attack on the olive groves in the village. He was the immediate suspect because of his link to the olives, his venture that had failed. The investigation conducted by the Shin Bet's Counter-Subversion Department made do with a solitary visit to the damaged groves and a brief questioning of Musa Ibrahim, and the people of Kharmish couldn't find any reason to suspect anyone other than Roni. Musa had indeed called him, and he had claimed to be in Tel Aviv. But maybe that was an alibi? Maybe he went there to shake off suspicion? Maybe he sent mercenaries on his behalf? After all, it was well known that the failed deal had left him frustrated and depressed.

"We don't need Jews here," Nimer said. Like many others in the village, he didn't buy into Roni's alibi. He wanted to respond to the settlers' aggression. His father, Musa, who was standing next to him, thought they could wait for Roni and hear what he had to say. Roni promised him, after all, that he'd find out who damaged the trees, maybe he's here now with the answer?

"We don't need Jews who are dressed up for the hajj," another youth said, and hurled a stone along a lengthy ballistic trajectory that culminated about a meter behind Josh and startled the Israeli delegation.

"Take it easy!" ordered Roni, the head of the delegation. "It's okay. They'll realize in a moment that we've come with good intentions. As soon as they recognize me, everything will be fine. Show them, show them the Purim gift." He waved his arms. "Musa! Musa!" he yelled. "It's me, Roni! Don't throw sto—" Another stone landed some two meters to their left. "No! Salaam!"

"Should I get the gun out?" Yakir asked. His heart was beating so intensely that he could feel it in his throat.

"No! Don't be crazy!" Roni shouted. But Josh picked up a stone and threw it back.

"Fuck you, sons of bitches," he yelled. "Go fuck off, Arabs! Afterward you don't wonder why we fuck you."

"Josh, take it easy. It's a mistake to, don't throw . . ." A barrage of stones rained down around them in response to Josh's stone, and in the cries in Arabic that were heard, Roni recognized the words "Go" and "Jew." Josh picked up another stone and threw it hard. A sudden gust of wind carried from behind them the sound of a loud blast, and a snippet from a song, and also a few—what are those—stray snowflakes?

Jehu gives me a saw. He pours gasoline. So it shall be done to a man. Dude, you're testing us. Want to see what we're made of. Sending soldiers to destroy my home, the fruits of my labors. There, take that, you bastards. You'll learn who we are. I can smell the wood from the cabin I built with my own two hands for a full year and they came and dare to . . . I close my eyes and saw. Take that. Jehu kneels with his Zippo. Josh went to smash windshields and slash tires. Nir kept watch to make sure no one was coming. Jehu organized us in secret, on the ruins of the cabin. Othniel saw us getting together and must have known what we were discussing. So shall it be done. Take that, treacherous Arabs, we come to you with good intentions and you stab us in the back. Roni gave you money—my money—and you screwed him over. You threw the money into the trash, Roni into the trash, my trip to Uman into the trash. How dare you. And next thing it's my home that gets destroyed? Sawing and sawing with eyes closed, vigorously. The bush is burning. You are holy and Your name is holy. I touch my sweaty neck, my wet shirt, wood chippings. Us you don't hurt. Us you don't screw over. Because You chose us and exalted us. I touch my face and smell the burning trees.

The stone that Josh hurled struck a young boy who was standing on the edge of the gathering, and the growl that rose from the Arab congregation did not bode well. More youths emerged from the homes, armed with sticks. Stones rained down from every direction. Roni looked back in bewilderment at the hilltop, where he could hear the indistinct sounds of creaking metal and random bangs. "Fuck," he said, and ducked down. The Purim gift wasn't going to happen. "Let's go back before they start going crazy. Josh, stop throwing!"

There was so much noise on the hilltop that no one was aware of the drama unfolding in nearby Kharmish. Even Othniel, who minutes earlier had followed the progress of the three figures who disappeared down the slope, was now entirely focused on screaming at Omer and at the D-9. Not that they heard him. This time there was no one to jump onto the D-9—Neta was pregnant, bent over on the sideline, nauseated, Roni was on a mission behind enemy lines, and Musa was at home. Beilin and Condi barked viciously at the soldiers.

Pippi ran this way, and space shuttle that way, and Bigfoot another way, and the dressed-up IDF officer wanted to but felt strange about taking on the real IDF soldiers, and Herzl shook his head in disbelief over the shattering of the dream, and the infant rock band burst into a coordinated symphony of howls, and drunk Rambo couldn't decide whether to help his family or forcefully oppose the soldiers, so, in the meantime, as a compromise, he stood next to the table with the wine and went on sipping from the plastic cup and moved his head to the rap music that the DJ suddenly decided to play. The wind blew cold and the tigress rose from her nausea to scream in a hoarse voice, "No! No! No! How can you feel no shame? Evil bastards!" Kareem asked the penguin if she was okay, and the prisoner who went crazy sucked on the breasts of the Dutch girl in the tower, and Rambo suddenly sat down in the middle of everything and strummed sad notes on a guitar. More tear gas was fired, startling the little ones and stifling the big ones, and the D-9 completed the crushing of its first trailer, flattened it, cleared it away, and prepared to move on to its next target, moving slowly along its tracks, and the crowd behind it. Tchelet-Rivlin-corn-on-the-cob cried woefully by the playground, because she had lost her parents and dropped the Torah she'd won, and the gift box of treats and candies lay scattered everywhere and no one was paying any attention to the costume champion.

Something shook the guard tower. Maybe the large bulldozer that was making the earth shudder, or a stray rock, but it was enough to startle the

Dutch girl out of her dream. No, it's not right. Not with a soldier in the deportation army, and certainly not while that army is demolishing the homes of Jews. She pushed away the prisoner's small, thick-curled head, fastened the bra and shirt buttons, descended from the guard tower still sensing his small agile tongue on her nipples, the moistness of his saliva, the arousal of her body, but she placed all that under lock and key, to remain thus for a long time, and ended the story without even a final glance to bring down the curtain.

Tchelet-corn-on-the-cob found her mother and her father. Her small hands warmed in theirs and she smiled up at the sky. Soft and slender flakes landed on her pretty face.

The residents of Kharmish, incensed and increasingly self-assured, took off in pursuit of the uninvited. The blasts and smoke coming from the hilltop told them something was happening, and when something happens, that means the Arabs are going to get it, even if the settlers get it first. They neared the trio. Someone next to Nimer fired two flares into the air to frighten them. Nimer himself drew a pistol and fired twice into the air. Why is the one dressed for the hajj? And why does that one have a rubber bald wig and Roni a curly wig and glasses without lenses? They're making fun of us? They're drunk?

They were drunk. They stumbled and tried to flee. They were so afraid. Yakir wept in fear and rage at his father. Roni was no longer trying to convince anyone of his peaceful intentions. Josh continued to throw stones and curse. They ran toward the outpost. When Yakir heard the shooting and blasts, he threw down the Purim gift, pulled out the Desert Eagle, released the safety, and fired into the air. The thunderous blast startled Roni, who screamed, "What are you doing, jackass!" The pursuers scattered—like Jenia's cookies from the torn packet—but then renewed the chase with increased vigor. Roni was sweating, but somehow it didn't occur to him to remove the wig and glasses. Josh, too, stuck with the kaffiyeh and Yakir with his leftist paraphernalia—you don't think about such things when you're running for your life. Yakir fired into the air again, and again the shot momentarily deterred the chasing Palestinians, but then more shots and blasts came from them, too.

"Enough, enough with the shooting," said Roni, his throat hoarse and out of breath, "we're almost there," and Josh turned and hurled a fistful of stones. The Arabs gathered with renewed strength and increased adrenaline. Tires appeared from somewhere and were set alight, and black smoke rose and befouled the cold air. Josh yelled, "Shoot them in the head," and Roni responded, "Have you lost your mind?" And Yakir took aim and fired one last shot into the sky, and thought with a quivering heart: It's not worth it, I don't want to die for this nonsense.

And then the snow stopped hesitating and really began to fall—in thick, slow, soft, regal chunks.

Soldiers, police, and settlers turned their heads toward the shots heard from the south, and saw a Palestinian mob storming toward them from the direction of Kharmish and black smoke rising into the air. "What the fuck?" mumbled Omer Levkovich just as the D-9 struck an electricity pole, the music stopped and the lights went out, a series of pops rang out and sparks flew from power cables, cries of panic and oh-my-God filled the air, and everyone scattered in all directions, and screamed, and cried, and only the mild-mannered snow continued its quiet descent, like Mordechai's raiment.

The End

The snow lay on Ma'aleh Hermesh C. for three whole days, covering, silencing. The quiet froze, and the peacefulness slowed, and the surrounding hills winked in their whiteness, and the distant landscapes, the desert landscapes, the lower-lying ones, joined in the mood with a lighter than usual beige, which was reflected in the sky, which whitened and blinded the sun, which finally appeared somewhat feebly, hanging its head in humility.

And from within the silence came nothing but the sound of a small hammer, banging, knock-knock-knock: Gabi resurrecting the cabin. And the joyful cries of the children making snowballs in the Mamelstein playground and sliding down the hilltop slope on their bottoms on plastic bags.

Roni Kupper spent the first night after the Purim party in Josh and Jehu's bachelor trailer, which was also Gabi's temporary residence. He was consumed with thoughts and emotions from the events of the past days, from the phone calls with Rina and the quick visit to Tel Aviv, from the smashed trailer that had been his home in recent months, from the peace delegation he had led to Kharmish that went utterly awry—but in the end, he realized, achieved precisely the objective that Othniel had envisioned.

Despite the adrenaline and racing thoughts, he fell asleep the moment his head hit the mattress, and woke in the morning to the white hilltop, marveling at its pristine beauty. Rina rang, and they spent the snowy days on one endless heart-to-heart call, and the moment cars could set out from the hilltop, he went to Tel Aviv. They shared a clumsy embrace when they met, and a hesitant kiss on the cheek. Over lunch they continued to develop the idea: a bar-nightclub that they'd call Kindergarten After Hours, which would operate during the night hours out of Rina's kindergarten on Shlomo HaMelech Street. Rina stressed over and over—as if trying to convince herself—that the partnership between them was strictly business. She desperately needed money, because the municipality was bleeding her dry and children had left the kindergarten and the costs weren't coming down and she was spiraling into debt but didn't want to shut down. She loved the work, that's what she knew how to do, and she did it well. Roni was sure Kindergarten After Hours was going to be a hit. The customers would love the kindergarten décor because it wasn't décor but the natural setting of the place. People like authenticity. He'd set up a small bar in the one corner. He'd make sure that at the close of every night the place would be clean of cigarette butts and beer stains, fragrant and tidy. He even thought that by pulling a few strings from his pub days, he'd manage to get a semi-official permit from the municipality. He was excited, because he wanted it. Because it suited him. Yes, he promised Rina, it's strictly business, that's clear. But they parted with a long stare and a lengthy embrace, and when Roni wandered through the streets of the city afterward, he knew he was excited not only by the business and the return home but also, and perhaps mostly, by the warmth of her body and her brown eyes.

On his next and last visit to Ma'aleh Hermesh C.—after the snow, after the winds had died down, after the final decision to return to Tel Aviv—he'll show up with a small black puppy, from a litter birthed by the dog of Rina's best friend. A charming puppy, quiet, tiny, and furry, that Roni decides will make a great roommate and friend for his brother. A farewell gift. It'll bring a smile to Gabi's face. He'll tickle the puppy under its chin and lay down a bowl with water and another with cottage cheese, which the dog will lick with its small and sturdy tongue. Amalia and Tchelet will go crazy for it, Gabi will think. He knew his brother thought he needed a friend to relieve the loneliness. Okay, let him think so, good luck to him. If he hasn't understood by now that I am never alone with the Master of the universe, he'll never understand it. The dog's cute, seriously cute. It'll have a good life here. We need to find him a name, we'll think about one with the girls. Gabi will tell Roni that it's tailor-made for him, Kindergarten After Hours. He'll wish him only well. And his brother will reply, "You know what? This Breslov thing, with the pompom at the top, is tailor-made for you, too. This time you'll manage to hold on, and the new cabin, too, may it be built quickly. Honestly, my bro." They'll share a long embrace, and Gabi will feel light, light, light as a feather.

Roni will make do with a visit to his little brother. On his way out he'll stop and rest his eyes on Musa Ibrahim's olive groves. What's done is done. His gaze will wander to whatever remains are left of the trailer, the mobile home where the Gotlieb family got burned, the one that turned up one day by mistake, and stayed, and was nationalized, and looted, and populated, and deserted, and populated again, and again deserted, and finally demolished by the teeth of the heavy-duty engineering machinery of the Israel Defense Forces. Bad karma it had, that trailer. Perhaps its fate was for the best.

The guy from the Electricity Corporation will explain that there was an electrical short. It probably started in the trailer that was destroyed, which was full of patchwork electrical jobs. The electrician won't understand the manner in which they were hooked up to the grid, it was completely amateurish, and dangerous, and fortunately nothing worse happened. He'll install a new control panel and a spanking-new fuse box, a new world of three-phase electrical power on the hilltop: without power outages and voltage drops and thinking twice about water boilers and geysers and air conditioners and heaters and losing material on the computer. "Just tell the guy from the demolished trailer," the man requested of Othniel Assis and Hilik Yisraeli, who were escorting him, "to take it easy with exposed cables and improvised electrical connections, and not to leave the coil heater on all the time."

"We'll tell him, we'll tell him," Othniel will say, and slap the technician on the shoulder. They won't say a thing to Roni Kupper, of course, because Roni will no longer be using electricity on the hilltop. If they were to say anything at all to Roni, Othniel thought, it would be a huge and massive thank-you with all their hearts: once for the exposed cables, the electrical patchwork jobs, and burning coil heater that led to the installation of an excellent power supply system; and a second time for the naïve quest to deliver a Purim gift basket to Kharmish, which led to the mother of all Arab riots, with stones and burning tires and shots in the air, the redirecting of the military resources from the outpost to Kharmish, and the postponement of the evacuation to an as-yet-undetermined date, which would be set, or so they were assured, "next week."

But that same "next week" will see the government fall in a no-confidence vote initiated by the centrist and left-wing parties in the wake of a corruption scandal. The defense minister will devote all his attention to the race for the party leadership and other internal battles (in which the popular slogan aimed at him will be "Scram!"). When Malka, his trusted adviser on settlement affairs, nonchalantly hands him a document for signature that approves the paving of an asphalt road between Ma'aleh Hermesh B. and C. to make things easier for the security forces to move around in the area, he'll sign and won't bother to ask what it's all about.

Major General Giora will be part of the next round of high-ranking appointments and land a senior post with military intelligence, and take along with him Omer Levkovich, who made a good impression on him during the course of the events, and promote him to the rank of major, and they'll spend their days in a quiet office in a well-kept neighborhood somewhere in the heart of middle-class Israel, the center of consensus, with air-conditioned vehicles and comfortable work hours. In the United

States the time for congressional elections will also approach, and the polls will predict a heavy defeat for the president's party, and once the elections pass—with a heavy defeat, indeed—the ground in California will shake violently, and by the time everyone emerges from the rubble and shakes the dust off their clothes, no one will remember Ma'aleh Hermesh C. any longer or the *Washington Post* article, and even the newspaper's editor, who was planning on sending Jeff McKinley to write a "One Year Later" article, will drop the idea due to budget cuts on the foreign desk and instructions from the top to focus on domestic news, and anyway, McKinley himself will be coming to the end of his mission in the Holy Land, will go on a long trip to Burma, fall in love with a young local married woman, get into a messy situation, and quit his job.

No one will have the time to deal with a small, insignificant outpost.

The thirty-eight bronze coins from the period of the Revolt that were found in a cave in the Hermesh Stream riverbed will rot in the warehouses of the Antiquities Authority, and of the two more valuable silver shekels, one will be given to the Israel Museum and the second will be sold at a public auction in New York for $42,000. Othniel will rue the fact that he lost that money, but bless the Lord, he was still in possession of five more coins. Well, of course he kept them. He's too wily a fox, wily enough to know that you never part with all your treasure. When he went to the cave with Dvora, before Duvid's first visit, he swiped several of the coins and kept a few on which he identified Jewish symbols and the words *Sacred Jerusalem*. When Duvid failed to deliver on his promise as an expert, Othniel decided not to tell him about the additional coins. Luckily so. He'll put other connections to work, this time extra carefully, and get to the right person, an antiquities dealer who knows what he's doing. Three of the five coins were silver shekels from the time of the Bar Kokhba Revolt: two from the second year and one from the fourth year. The fortune they bring him will come at just the right time.

The heavy snow on Purim will cause devastation at the organic farm. The frost will destroy the asparagus, mushroom, arugula, and cherry tomato crops. In addition, Moran (on the ground) and Yakir (from the website) will report a radical increase in demand for organic goat-milk products. And as if to round things off, Gabi will decide that he's sick of serving as a jack-of-all-trades. He'll ask Othniel for clarification regarding his position, salary, and professional focus. At the end of a meeting the four will hold at Othniel's home over crackers and tea, a few weeks after Purim, a decision will be made to focus on developing the goat farm and dairy, and they'll even draft a multistage five-year plan that will be aided by the profits from the coins, with the objective of increasing the size of the pen to two hundred head and more. Othniel will handle the downsizing of the crop fields and afterward their sale or abandonment (although he will continue to cultivate for self-consumption so as to provide arugula and cherry tomatoes for Rachel's refreshing salads). Gabi will be sent to take a training course on a goat and sheep farm, which will also provide Othniel with new goats. Yakir will reduce the scope of the Internet operations and Moran will switch to direct marketing to stores, particularly in the central region of the country. Gabi will be responsible for the jewel in the crown—the upgrading of the dairy, the acquisition of new machinery, and the creation of a new line of high-quality cheeses: fresh, matured-soft, matured-semi-hard, yogurt, yogurt cheese, with herbs and spices, with microbes and various molds. He will oversee all stages of the preparation—from the pasteurization and the curdling and through to the packaging. His wages will increase significantly, including benefits, terms of employment, and advanced training.

Gitit's Cheesery will flourish thanks to the "Listeria Hysteria" that will strike Israel later in the year. Following an inconclusive case involving a miscarriage that may or may not have been related to the listeria bacteria, Health Ministry inspectors will conduct raids on dairies large and small throughout the land and discover at many of them frightening concentrations of the listeria bacteria. Tons of cheeses will be tossed from store shelves, which will lead initially to the public flocking to buy organic cheeses from private farms, but in the wake of an investigative report by one of the large newspapers, which will warn against unpasteurized organic cheeses that haven't been properly matured, the public would remain confused and hungry. Into the vacuum will slip the cheeses of Gitit's Cheesery—a small, organic, boutique dairy, which indeed uses pasteurized milk, because of a decision Othniel made at the outset, before self-identified experts determined that pasteurization kills the good enzymes and destroys the flavor. Othniel, after all, kept his distance from those opinionated connoisseurs like he did from the plague, already from way back in the days of his run-in over the plot of land with that patronizing vintner from Ma'aleh Hermesh A.—the run-in that, for all intents and purposes, gave rise to Ma'aleh Hermesh C. Either way, demand will rise by thousands of percent, and Gitit's cheeses will become renowned throughout the country, even after the listeria hysteria subsides.

When he feels too closed in by the developing pen and dairy and longs for the open expanses, Gabi will go out to tend the herd. Once, long ago, he got bored, out with the goats, but now he'll enjoy every moment with them. He'll love stepping out of the physical and into the spiritual, to feel light-footed and not to be enslaved to the place; perhaps he'll feel it's time to broaden his horizons. Like Abel, like our forefather Abraham, like our King David, like our teacher Moses. Out in the pasture, in the company of the veteran goats and young kids and the nameless herding dog—Amalia suggested "Darkie" and Shaulit "Cosby," but Gabi felt neither was appropriate—he'll find peace, sense the providence, seclude himself and chat with his God, pray and sing and be joyful, for through joy your prayer will enter into the palace of the King. Always through joy? Maybe not always, because longing is infinite, but the agonies are for the good, because the intent of God, blessed be He, is surely there only for the good. Every day he'll walk among the hills and the fields and the wilderness, rest in the shade and chew on the sweet bulbs of the desert storkbill plant, love his beasts and they him, and late in the evening, with the grace of God, he'll hold Shaulit in his arms, and the nameless dog will blow air from his little nose and curl up at their feet with his eyes closed, and she'll sing to him in her charming voice, and her auburn hair will tickle the tip of his nose, and his heart will swell in his chest.

Winds will change, and days will end, and life will go on. The children will grow, the worshippers will pray, the Roman olive trees, the vast majority, at least, will survive just as they have for thousands of years—long before and long after every one of the individuals who pass through here for a fixed period of time. The elderly Arabs who've seen it all will begin their day like always, with two spoons of natural honey and three spoons of olive oil (mild and too clear, suited to the Japanese palate), and the soldiers will continue to come and go, to climb and descend, to be replaced and return, and eyes will open in the morning and the sun will rise over the desert and set in the evening behind the mountain, and eyes will close, and in between work, and prayer, and rest, and love.

A final inconsequential picture, then, from the days after the snow. Winter on the hilltop, chilly and quiet outside, a few children riding bicycles, Beilin barking out of boredom, and a solitary monotonous sound can be heard over and again: knock-knock-knock, the sound of Gabi's hammer, leisurely knocking nails into planks of wood, which will be assembled one on top of the other, and become walls, and thus resurrect his cabin, which once was, and is no more, and will return. He hammers and hammers with infinite patience. And with the knocking as his backdrop, the thoughts come rushing back, the memories rise to the surface—of people who were and are no longer, who've come and gone their own way, who've played out their roles. Of one immense and powerful and holy God, who sees and knows everything. Of a small hilltop, in the middle of nowhere, in the middle of everywhere, bedecked by rocks, and some thorns, and a handful of souls.